# DYING TO SEA

# Dying to Sea

Frank Heavey

iUniverse, Inc.
New York  Lincoln  Shanghai

# Dying to Sea

iUniverse books may be ordered through booksellers or by contacting:

iUniverse
2021 Pine Lake Road, Suite 100
Lincoln, NE 68512
www.iuniverse.com
1-800-Authors (1-800-288-4677)

ISBN-13: 978-0-595-34815-2 (pbk)
ISBN-13: 978-0-595-79544-4 (ebk)
ISBN-10: 0-595-34815-7 (pbk)
ISBN-10: 0-595-79544-7 (ebk)

Printed in the United States of America

# Dedication

I dedicate this book to my beautiful wife, Whitney, who has supported my dreams, kept me grounded, and never stopped believing in me. I fall in love with you again every day. Thank you for all your love and encouragement. Chatham is a special place because I can share it with you.

# Acknowledgements

The writing of this book was a labor of love. I want to extend my gratitude to those who have helped me in my journey. First and foremost, I thank my wife, Whitney, for being so patient and supportive; I could never have finished this without your advice, wisdom, and love. You are the greatest. Thank you for painting the cover of this book. To my wonderful girls, Grace and Maddie: thank you for being such an inspiration to me; your love and laughter fill our lives with boundless happiness. I thank Mary Ulbrich, the greatest teacher I ever met, for her thoughtful insights and encouragement in editing my manuscript. To Ellie and Joe Wymard: thank you for your support and introduction to the world of publishing. To Cam Hemmerdinger, Julia and Bob Abbott: thank you for reading my manuscript and giving me sound advice and resolution. I thank Judy Hansen, who worked as my agent for two years and helped me polish the manuscript. To Mary and Michael McQueeney, Bobby Heavey, Jack and Terry Heavey, Lisa and Pete Evans, Chris Lacey, Ellen Furlong and Dave Halligan, Susie and Joe Alex: thank you for your enthusiasm and consistent inquiries; you helped motivate me. I thank Judith Kimble-Iversen for sharing the dream, being a valued reader, and offering encouragement when I needed it; best of luck with your book, Judy. To the Doggetts: thanks for sharing your fishing adventures with me. To John, Nancy and Scott Alexanderson: thank you for being so supportive and loving; I cherish our times in Chatham with you. To my Dad: thank you for instilling in me the benefits of perseverance; I am proud to be your son. Lastly, I thank my Mom for her love, wisdom and support that more than anything has shaped my person today; I miss you every day, Mom.

# PROLOGUE

———————— ▼ ————————

# AUGUST, 1863
# OFF THE COAST OF CAPE COD

"Hold on!" Captain John Barnett screamed to his crew as the avalanche of water surged over his ship. Seconds later, he breathed a sigh of relief when he realized they were still afloat, still moving.

Barnett looked out at the madness engulfing his ship and felt a fear he had never before experienced in his twenty-two years at sea. The beleaguered steamer tossed about in the twenty-foot swells like a toy boat. All around the ship, the ocean looked like a raging battlefield. Atop the rolling swells, the wind-driven white-capped waves fought an endless war against themselves. Torrential rains poured down on the ship in every direction as if it were under a waterfall. The winds, which had started as periodic cannon blasts hours earlier in the late afternoon, now slammed into the ship in a constant bombardment that brought on an orchestra of straining cries from the ship's wood.

Built in 1860 in Liverpool, England, and christened the *Argo*, the double side-wheeler steamer had been purchased in 1862 by the Confederate States of America. Measuring two hundred thirty feet long, with a beam just over twenty feet and a draft of less than eight feet, its designers had built her for the sole purpose of running the Union blockade of the South. With the exception of its wheelhouse, situated five feet off the deck and between the two side wheels, the schooner-rigged fore and aft masts and two telescoping funnels, which could be lowered almost to its deck, the *Argo* had a low silhouette. This, coupled with its slate gray hull, made the steamer less visible on the open seas. Its narrow shape and two 180 horse-power, double-oscillating, Watt steam engines, which burned smokeless anthracite coal, gave the steamer the ability to knife through calm water at top speeds of sixteen knots. But in hurricane, the steamer was almost as helpless as a rowboat.

"Roller on the starboard!" Billy Randall, the First Mate, yelled.

Barnett turned the wheel into the wave and bent his legs as the steamer heaved over the hill of water.

The longer the war continued, the greater the strain had become on the Southern economy. By itself, the C.S.A. could not economically nor militarily outlast the might of the richer, more populous Union states. To survive and maintain any hope of winning the war for its independence, the Confederacy desperately needed to sell its cotton abroad to sympathetic and capitalistic Europeans, and return with the necessary money and war supplies to keep its struggling troops in the field. The meager output of munitions by the few Southern factories not under Union control could not provide General Robert E. Lee and his armies with the amounts of powder and guns they needed to fight off the onslaught of Union drives into the South.

To strangle the Confederate economy, the Union Navy had created a massive blockade of the southern coast and critical ports, thus pinning the Confederacy's hopes of survival squarely on the backs of the adventurous blockade runners.

After almost three dozen trips, each time delivering 800 to 900 bales of cotton to Bermuda, the Bahamas or Havana, and returning with munitions under the cover of darkness on moonless nights through a gauntlet of Union blockading ships, Barnett's reputation as one of the best blockade runner captains was well known throughout certain circles in the Confederacy. The tighter the Union made the blockade, the more John Barnett rose to the challenge of breaking it. But now he was on an entirely different mission in unfamiliar Northern waters, not under the cover of darkness, against a new enemy—Mother Nature.

The *Argo* had started its current mission two days earlier with a crew of just fourteen sailors, a third of its normal crew. Two men had already been washed overboard by the mountainous waves that had crashed over the ship's five-foot-high gunwales. None of the remaining dozen men could manage to stand upright without placing a death grip on a railing or rigging.

A searing coldness permeated Barnett's bones as he desperately struggled to keep his ship afloat and on course. He blinked his bleary gray eyes in an attempt to wipe away the sweat that poured off his bald head. At just a few inches taller than five feet, with a broad chest, Barnett was built like a blunt nose cannon.

With his short, powerful fingers he gripped the wheel tightly and stuck out his square, unshaven jaw as if to challenge the storm.

In the wheelhouse with Barnett were Joseph McDonald, the ship's Navigator, Billy Randall, and the only non-sailor on board, William Douglass, a representative from the Davis Administration. Douglass looked like the negative of Barnett; he had a tall, lanky frame, a small head, and wore wire-rimmed glasses perched on the end of his narrow nose that helped draw greater attention to the bags under his narrow, blue eyes. Never before had Barnett had a member of the government travel with him. He hoped it would be the last. Douglass had personally delivered the confidential orders for the mission to Barnett and had him swear an oath of secrecy regarding the ship's destination. At their departure from Wilmington, North Carolina, when the ship had not been filled to the brim with cotton bales, but instead with five dozen wooden coffins, Barnett had known he was not going on a typical blockade run.

Barnett looked off the starboard side as a dark, foamy mass poured over the ship's gunwale. In the last hour, conditions on the sea had turned dramatically worse. The wind no longer just gusted against the wheelhouse; now, it slammed into it with such constancy that it felt to Barnett like the hand of God was trying to knock the steamer over. He knew it wouldn't be long before the twenty-foot waves would grow larger and wash over the narrow ship and capsize it.

Barnett looked at Douglass and saw the expression of a man who was beyond exhaustion and worry. He was not surprised. Douglass did not have sea legs.

"How are you feeling, Mr. Douglass?" Barnett said loudly above howling wind and thunderous surf.

Douglass held one hand to his ear, while he gripped a railing with the other. His face was pale and his eyes bulged from sickness caused by the salt air and the ship's constant rocking motion, but he did not answer the baited question. "Where are we, Captain?"

"Off the coast of Cape Cod, nearing…"

"Captain! There's a ship off the starboard," Randall yelled, the telescope still pressed against his eye.

"Can you make its class and heading?"

Randall struggled in vain to keep track of the ship as the *Argo* slammed down in a trough. As the steamer rose on the next wave, he regained his target. "It's a frigate, all sails full. It came out of nowhere and is now running parallel to us. They just doused all but their bridge lights, sir."

Barnett kept his emotions in check. He had slipped in and out of Wilmington past scores of Federal ships many times before and had learned to trust his skills and his luck. "Keep track of her and let me know if she turns."

The door flung open as a drenched sailor stepped into the wheelhouse; a look of despair covered his face.

"Captain, we're taking on water through the stressed planks. The pumps aren't making a difference. I don't know how long the hull will hold."

Barnett clenched his teeth. He knew he never should had allowed Douglass to force him to embark from Wilmington before he had fully inspected the hasty repairs that had been done on the steamer's hull after they had hit a sandbar on their last run into Wilmington.

"How deep?"

"It's approaching the base of the engines, sir. If it rises any more, we'll lose…"

"Use more coal," Barnett cut off the sailor. "Keep the engines running as hot as the boilers can take it. Do whatever it takes to keep them powered! Do you understand?"

"Aye, aye, Captain," the sailor responded and then quickly exited the wheel-house.

"What's our position, Mr. McDonald?" Barnett quickly asked.

The navigator looked at his compass, and then used his dividers on the chart he had pinned down to the lone table in the wheelhouse. "Five miles northeast of Nantucket Island, sir. Heading north by northeast."

Barnett looked at Douglass, who stared blankly out at the whitewashed deck of the *Argo*. "Keep our present heading."

Though the storm had darkened the evening sky, and the wind-driven rain blew against the wheelhouse windows in sheets that temporarily blinded them, there was still enough light for them to see each approaching wave. For a few minutes, they stood silently in the wheelhouse, rolling with the swells and bracing themselves as the surface waves pounded into the steamer.

"Mr. Randall, what's the position of that ship? Can you make out if it's a merchant class or not?" Barnett called out.

"It's difficult to see, Captain, but I believe it's a two hundred foot frigate with full battery, all sails full," Randall replied then swore. "Captain, she's tacking to port! Looks like she's setting a course to intercept us!"

"How long?"

Randall paused for a few seconds as he studied the ship. "If we maneuver, she'll have to keep tacking, but it won't take them more than an hour, sir."

Suddenly, the steamer violently convulsed, then lost half its speed. Seconds later, the wheelhouse door opened just as a wave slammed into the steamer sending seawater and a sailor pouring into the wheelhouse. After a second of panic, Randall reached the door and slammed it closed, but not before the wheelhouse had been filled with four inches of water.

The sailor who had opened the door scrambled to his feet and swept the salt water from his eyes. "Captain, the port engine's dead! It's swamped, but still blowing off steam, but not enough to turn the wheel. If it takes on any more water, it may explode."

Barnett grabbed the sailor by the arm. "Open all the valves on the port engine. That should buy us more time," he yelled.

The sailor nodded his head, said, "Aye, aye, Captain," and left the wheelhouse.

"Mr. McDonald, set a course for the nearest harbor."

Douglass erupted from his trance of fear. "You cannot do that, Captain! My orders specifically prohibit you from entering any Federal port."

"Douglass, I'm in command here! I said harbor, not port."

Douglass moved closer to Barnett. "Regardless, *Captain*, I forbid you from entering any…this is a vessel of the Confederate States of America and you are under direct orders from President Davis himself. You *will not* waiver from our instructed course."

"Captain!" Randall interrupted, "that frigate is gaining on us and I think they're readying their guns."

Barnett stared coldly up at Douglass. "President Davis is not in charge of this ship. I am! We'll never make Halifax in these seas. We won't even make it around Cape Cod. Do you understand what's happening here? Do you?" Barnett's face bulged from yelling. "This ship's not made to travel in a hurricane. If that engine explodes, we go down. If it doesn't explode, we'll never escape that frigate. If we make it to a harbor before they reach us, they won't follow because they'll run aground."

"Then what? They'll just wait until we leave the harbor?"

"Right now, we have no choice but to find shallow waters."

"Why would that frigate want to stop us? They have no cause."

Barnett shook his bald head, then pounded the wheel with his fist. "Because *only* a Rebel ship would not be at port in this storm."

Douglass shook his head. "Still, the President has ordered…"

"Do you want to die?" Barnett shouted.

Douglass looked at Barnett for a few seconds, then blinked.

"Mr. McDonald, find us the nearest harbor."

"Aye, aye, Captain." McDonald gazed at the chart for a few seconds, then looked up. "Head five degrees port, sir. Chatham Harbor is our best option. It's surrounded by outer banks on its north and south so it must have low waters just like Wilmington, sir. The first lighthouse will be on the port side. Then there'll be two more off starboard."

Barnett changed the ship's course accordingly and immediately had to grip the wheel with greater strength to keep it from spinning out of his control. To maintain the new course, he forced the steamer to ride the waves at an angle, which he knew was dangerous. All it took was one rogue wave much larger than the rest to capsize the ship. They would have little chance to see such a wave approaching because of their new direction. Barnett said a silent prayer.

The raging wind howled through the less than airtight wheelhouse as the *Argo* rocked violently from side to side, bow to stern. An echoing thunderclap erupted from the hull each time the steamer pounded down the trough of a wave. With increasing frequency, it could not power out of a trough before another wave inexorably rushed over the struggling ship. When they finally reached the crest of a wave, the sailors felt as if the bottom were about to drop out from under them.

"Light off the port!" McDonald pointed.

"Where?" Douglass asked.

"Wait for the rise of the ship."

"There's two more over there," Randall said. "We've made it!"

Suddenly, they heard a deep, slow, twisting sound that vibrated and wrenched the wooden ship. In an instant, the *Argo's* forward momentum stopped and they were thrown forward against the front of the wheelhouse.

"Jesus, what was that?" Douglass cried, picking himself up off the wet floor.

"Reverse engines!" Barnett yelled.

Randall struggled to his feet and threw the engine order telegraph in reverse. The *Argo's* lone engine made a loud, deep grinding sound, while the hull vibrated under the increasing strain.

"Come on, come on!" Barnett pleaded.

As the waves crashed against the *Argo*, the prow of the ship pounded deeper into the sandbar despite the efforts of the engine to back away the crippled ship.

"She's turning broadside, give her more power!"

"She's at full steam, there's nothing left to give, sir," Randall lashed back.

"If we stay like this we'll be crushed," Douglass screamed.

Suddenly, the darkness flashed into light as a flare erupted in the sky above the *Argo*.

"Launch the counter flare," Barnett yelled.

Randall quickly retrieved the flare gun from its mount on the wall, stepped out of the wheelhouse and fired the gun into the air. It was a time-tested counter-measure used by blockade runners to deceive a Federal ship as to the runner's true position. If timed correctly, the approaching ship would follow the path made by the second flare and not know the difference.

When another huge wave slammed into the grounded steamer, the *Argo* listed precariously forty-five degrees to its port side, making it impossible for the men to stand upright in the wheelhouse.

"She's grounded!" Barnett screamed over the roar of the violent surf. "McDonald, go below and tell the crew to board the life boats."

McDonald scrambled out of the wheelhouse in a panic.

"We must take four coffins with us, Captain," Douglass pleaded.

Barnett looked at Douglass in complete disbelief.

"The Federals cannot get their hands on the contents. It's too valuable. We cannot leave them!"

Immediately, Barnett realized the true nature of the desperate mission. The Confederacy was trying to launch another Fifth Column from Canada.

"The four are the only ones marked with a cross. We can deliver them to Halifax by land."

"No! We save the lives of these sailors first," Barnett screamed back.

Douglass grabbed the Captain by the arm. "You don't understand. Those coffins contain the means to secure the aid of a thousand Canadians willing to launch an invasion of the North. It is our country's only hope to win this war and our freedom. We must not fail our country, Captain!"

Barnett pulled his arm free and turned to Randall. "Go prepare the lifeboats!"

Randall threw open the wheelhouse door as walls of seawater poured over the crippled *Argo*. He held onto both door jams to resist being washed to the other side of the wheelhouse, and pulled himself onto the open deck. The thunderous roar of the wind and the piercing cold water slamming into his body temporarily disoriented him. He lunged for the railing with his right hand and used his left arm to shield his face from the stinging wind. Suddenly, the *Argo* tilted farther to port and Randall lost his footing, but managed to keep his hold on the railing. He scrambled to his feet and pulled his way along the railing for ten feet until he reached the first lifeboat. Looking up at the rigging securing the lifeboat, he gasped at the sight of a monstrous rogue wave towering above him. He threw himself into the lifeboat just as the sixty-foot wave crashed down on the *Argo*.

# CHAPTER 1

▼

# JUNE 2005

The flame orange Trans Am hit every pothole in the dusty, country dirt road while it sped at sixty miles per hour. After each bump, Rick Kellerman swore, what he called dropping the f-bomb. Each time he cursed, his passenger, Buster Sykes, laughed aloud.

"Wow, Kellerman, your car's taking a beating," Sykes jested.

"Shut the fuck up," Kellerman dropped another f-bomb.

For another five miles they rode in silence, save Kellerman's swearing and Sykes's laughing. Because the car had no air conditioning, they traveled with the windows open to battle the Virginia summer heat, but at the cost of dust gathering in their eyes and throughout the car. At the end of the road, the car slowed at a rusty, dented mailbox with a twisted door that hung lifeless from being shot dozens of times with an air rifle by the local teens. They turned into the driveway.

"Can't believe we had to drive half way across the fuckin' state to pick this guy up. This is bullshit, man. What kinda guy doesn't have wheels?" Kellerman didn't try to hide his contempt. He was a two-time loser with a chip the size of Montana on his shoulder. Maybe it was his constant rancorous look, or the military buzz cut hair and stubble goatee, but people instantly marked the twenty-nine-year-old as having a bad attitude as if it was stamped on his wrinkled, sunburned forehead. He had never finished high school, never held a job for more than a year, was a convicted felon, and still, for some reason, thought that society owed him something.

"Hey, watch what you say about Carson," Sykes warned. "He said his Lexus was in the shop getting fixed. And don't forget, before we met him, the best we did was trailer parks and shitty used cars not worth a crap."

Buster Sykes was a wide-framed man with short legs and even shorter arms; by any standard, except maybe his mother's, he was an ugly man. His gut stuck out over his belt, making him look much shorter than five foot six. Only pads of hair above his ears and a few strands across the top prevented him from being totally bald. He intentionally grew the sides long to make up for the lack of hair on the top. But Buster Sykes had more than enough hair on the rest of his body; his five o'clock shadow began at noontime right below his eye sockets and connected with a sweater of chest hair that always stuck out of his shirt. A sallow complexion made him always look ill. Most people immediately thought of him as ignorant because he spoke with a wiry smile on his face and his lazy left eye always looked at his nose. He tried his hardest to prove to people he was not dumb, but most people, especially Rick Kellerman, believed otherwise.

The Trans Am stopped at the end of the dirt driveway in front of a two-story farmhouse that had been neglected for some time; paint no longer covered most of the siding, shingles dangled from a patchwork roof of plywood boards, two windows were boarded up. The shell of a car sat up on blocks in the dirt and weed front lawn.

Carson Ridder sat in a rocking chair on the rotting front porch with his black rattlesnake boots propped up on the Birch log railing. He folded his massive arms across his chest to reveal a black dragon and barbed wire tattoo on his imposing biceps. His furrowed brow and pock-marked skin always made him look pissed off, and now was no exception. He stood up, took a monstrous last drag from the filterless cigarette hanging from his lower lip, then spit the butt off the edge of the porch onto the weed-choked lawn that was littered with dozens of other spent cigarettes.

Sykes got out of the car with a smile on his round face. "Howdy, Carson."

Ridder strutted to the car. "You're late, asshole," he said in a deep, rough voice. He tilted the passenger seat forward to indicate Sykes would ride in the back.

For five miles no one spoke. Kellerman kept his eyes on the road and acted like there was no one in his passenger seat. When they reached the county highway, his control finally gave way.

"We gonna find out where we're going tonight, or we just gonna drive around? Gas ain't free ya know."

Ridder shot an angry glare at Kellerman. Two black eyes, deeply accented by an aquiline nose, glared at the driver. "Take a left, head toward Charlottesville," Ridder said in a deep voice.

"So Carson, what ya got lined up for us tonight?" Sykes eagerly asked, leaning forward between the two front bucket seats.

Ridder didn't answer immediately. He reached into the breast pocket of his black tee shirt and took out a crumpled half pack of Marlboros to continue his dissolute habit. He methodically went through the same ritual each time to light the cigarette. He bit off the filter and spat it out the window—filters were for those not manly enough to handle a full load of nicotine and tar. Screw the Surgeon General. He dexterously lit the match with one hand, ignited the filterless cigarette and took a deep pull.

Satisfied he had made them wait long enough, Ridder said in a measured tone, "Gotta real fancy place up in Charlottesville. Real rich, old guy. Should be easy. Lives by himself."

They drove for twenty more minutes until Ridder said, "Take a right down this side street."

Kellerman brought the car to a stop. "What now? I don't see no big house?"

"Christ are you stupid. Drivin' into a wealthy neighborhood in this orange piece of shit? Now that's a real good idea. We'll be takin' somethin' that won't stand out and we can dump later."

Sykes looked behind him, across the main street. "Good idea, Carson. Like one of them cable vans over there."

"So quick, Einstein. You're comin' with me." He turned to Kellerman. "There's a supermarket down the road on the left. Meet me behind it." He looked at his watch. It was eight o'clock.

As Ridder and Sykes approached the parking lot in front of the CableVA store, Sykes looked around nervously. Though he tried real hard to play the cool, calm, experienced thief, his hands shook and his chest trembled as his lungs convulsed to get more air.

"Just act like you're supposed to be here." Ridder went to the driver side of one of the vans while Sykes looked around the lot in quick bursts. In a few seconds, the passenger door sprang open and he quickly jumped in.

"Jesus, Carson, you're fast."

In less than thirty seconds, the motor was running and Ridder pulled the van out of the lot onto the road toward the pick up point. It was four minutes past eight.

"Wow, Carson, how'd ya hot wire it so fast? And in one try."

Ridder grinned at Sykes and shook his head. He made it a practice not to discuss what he considered the art of stealing cars because he was determined never to return to jail where his loose lips and arrogance had once landed him. Three years before, he had gotten drunk at a roadside dive one night and had bragged how he could steal any car regardless of the alarm in less than thirty seconds. A couple of tough guys had bet him a thousand dollars he couldn't steal the car of their choice in that little time. After having searched for an hour for a target, they had found a brand new Jaguar parked at a hotel, which Ridder stole in fifteen seconds and collected the thousand dollars at gun point. Being sore losers, they called the cops on him and he spent a year in the Albemarle County jailhouse.

After picking up Kellerman, Ridder drove the van for another fifteen minutes before stopping behind an abandoned gas station.

"Now what?" Kellerman asked.

"We wait for the call." Ridder tilted back the driver's seat, put his hands behind his head and tried to stretch out his six-foot-four body.

For the past few months he had been paying maitre d's and hostesses at various high end Charlottesville restaurants to tip him off when a rich patron was eating at their restaurant. Ridder would receive three calls in the set up. The first call would tell him when the client, as he called them, had a reservation, after which Ridder would case their home. The maitre d' placed the next call when the client arrived at the restaurant. When the client left the restaurant, Ridder received the final call. The system worked like clockwork and reaped a huge profit with little risk compared to the alternatives of pushing drugs or holding up banks.

He made sure never to use one restaurant connection for too long. The last connection had been very profitable for Ridder, until the two men working for him had screwed up and tripped a silent alarm in a house. Ridder had escaped, but the local police grabbed his two accomplices. Though the police had known there was a third culprit, neither of the men ratted on Ridder—his reputation for dealing with rats was well known by the local low lives. He had once pinned a former co-worker against a wall with his car for setting up a meeting with the police. The man lost a leg because of Ridder's legendary temper, but he didn't talk. Ridder thought seriously of doing the work alone because of the constant threat of loose lips, but he liked how six hands could grab more than two.

When the phone call came in, Ridder said nothing but a series of deep-throated "yeah's" to the caller. Things were all set; the prospective client was at the restaurant and would be for awhile. He was a talker and he had company.

They each got out of the van and put on green one-piece work suits with a large, blank oval patch on the back. Ridder told them to keep their bags inside their suits until they were inside the house. When Kellerman got back into the van he reached into the small duffel bag he had brought and pulled out a Beretta handgun. He looked at Ridder in the driver's seat, then at Sykes in the passenger seat. Neither of them paid any attention to him as he stuffed the gun in his jump suit.

The 1776 was packed as usual. Known for its mouth-watering, traditional menu and delicious daily specials, plus a legendary wine list people claimed included bottles from Monticello, the restaurant had a conservative atmosphere that appealed to those who believed that spending less than thirty-five dollars on an entree was paramount to going through the drive-thru at the local burger joint. Antique muskets from the colonial era and portraits of leading Virginians hung on dark green walls above cherry-stained wainscoting, while copper lanterns shed warm light on the diners. It was a favorite among Charlottesville's upper class—even on a Wednesday night there was a line to get a table for those patrons without reservations.

Professor Walter Hutchinson never had to wait. He was able to get his small table in the back corner, where it was quieter, any time he wanted. He had frequented the restaurant since he had married fifty years ago and had been friends with the previous owner. And though his wife had passed on eight years ago, the professor still came to the 1776 because he liked the food and it made him happy to think of his wife. He was a man of habit. He ate at the same restaurant, at the same table, and always wore a blue blazer, white shirt, and bow tie, regardless of the season or occasion.

Professor Hutchinson was seventy-three years old with white hair and a neatly trimmed white beard. Though his face bore evidence of his years, making him look tired in the eyes, the corners of his mouth still turned up to make him appear to be smiling all the time. He was a warm soul who believed in hard work, honesty, respect, and pride in the accomplishments of his great nation.

"Good evening, gentlemen, may I get a drink for you before you order?" the young, clean-cut waiter asked with a sincere smile.

"I'll have a Jim Bean with a dash of water. Garland?"

The professor looked over at his dinner companion, Garland Triste, a fellow professor at the University of Virginia. He had begun his teaching career at the University of Virginia under the tutelage of Hutchinson, and the collegiality grew into an enduring friendship, especially after Hutchinson retired in 1994. At half the age of Hutchinson, Triste appeared more like a son than a colleague. His thick brown hair looked unkempt from his habit of running his hand through it when he sat thinking. The forest green turtleneck he wore under a khaki sport coat and his round glasses made him look like the intellectual he was.

"Martini, dry, please," Triste said with a smile.

As soon as the waiter left their table, Hutchinson leaned across the table and said, "I hardly get to see you any more, you know, with all this research. How's your family? Well, I take it?"

Triste smiled. The professor always answered his own questions. "Doing quite well, thank you. Margaret still complains I spend too much time doing research."

"I remember those days. My Sarah used to tell me the same things. But she understood my need to do my work. Just try to be around the house as much as you can, she used to say. Very understanding. But if I ever missed…"

The professor started to cough until his face turned red. His shoulders hunched as his chest heaved from the struggle to control the fit. When he caught his breath, he continued. "Never missed a dinner date with my Sarah." He coughed again.

"You mentioned on the phone how excited you are about your research progress. How's it going?" Triste asked.

Hutchinson held his fist to his mouth to cough, but managed to talk through the deep hack. "I had the big breakthrough the other day. Could say I found the Rosetta Stone. Oh, it is wonderful, Garland. Truly authentic. Should prove all my skeptics wrong. It will solve the mystery of…" He began to cough more violently while beads of sweat appeared on his forehead. Triste held out a glass of water for him.

"Excuse me, Garland, I need to use the rest room," Hutchinson coughed out in fragments.

Hutchinson walked slowly in the direction of the men's room, all the while coughing. A few minutes later, he returned to their table, his face red and his eyes watery from the attack.

"Are you okay, Walter?" Triste asked as he stood, a look of concern covering his face.

"I am very sorry, Garland. We're going to have to postpone this merry engagement. It appears I am not feeling well. Getting old, you know. Just need to get some rest." He tried to smile to hide his discomfort.

"Not a problem, Walter. Do you need me to drive you home?" Triste said as he reached out and touched Hutchinson's elbow.

"No, thank you." Hutchinson waved an arthritic hand in front of his face. "You get home to that beautiful wife of yours. I'll be just fine. I live only a few miles from here and I have my neighbor's car because the old Dodge," he coughed, "is back in the shop. Don't worry, I'll manage."

Before they left, Hutchinson flagged down the waiter and paid for the drinks despite Triste's objections. They walked together through the crowd of people standing at the bar. At the foyer, they walked behind the maitre d' as he politely argued with a woman who claimed she had a reservation for five people not two. Without being noticed, the two professors walked out of the restaurant.

"I hope you feel better. Let me know if there's anything I can do for you. And let's try to do this again soon. I can't wait to hear about your research."

"Thank you, Garland. Why don't we try this again in a few days? I'm sure to be feeling well then." Hutchinson started to walk slowly to his car, then stopped and turned. "Give Margaret and the boys my best."

Triste smiled and waved goodbye.

Ridder drove the van to a very wealthy section of Charlottesville and parked out front of twenty-five Londonderry Avenue. The house was located in an old neighborhood comprised of homes built right after the War of 1812 that typified Federalist architecture, which to people like Ridder and his crew meant one thing—money. Most of the houses on the street, including number twenty-five, sat back a distance from the road, with dense woods separating them, characteristics that offered more privacy to the owner, and thief.

Before they emerged from the van, Ridder looked at his watch again. It was nine o'clock and almost completely dark.

"Remember, act like we belong here. You know the routine once I get us inside. Don't fuck around. Stay focused. Gold and silver only. Cash if you find it. I'll take the top floor; you two take the downstairs. We go when I get back down."

They left the van and followed Ridder around to a side door off a small flag-stone patio. Tall pine trees provided a dense canopy overhead, making the side of the house even more dark than the front.

Ridder quickly looked around as he approached the door, and after sensing nothing in the area around them was out of the ordinary, he cupped his hands to his eyes while leaning close to the glass window. Without saying anything, he reached into his jump suit and pulled out a small glass cutter. He quickly cut the glass, used a small suction cup to pull out the cut piece, reached his hand inside and unlocked the door. Immediately, Sykes and Kellerman saw why Ridder had chosen this door. An alarm mounted on the wall next to the door flashed in green lights and beeped. Without hesitating, Ridder stepped inside, popped open the alarm box casing and snipped three wires. He pulled out a black wire from his suit and connected it to two of the alarm's wires. Instantly, the alarm's off button flashed red. Sykes let out a deep, audible breath.

They stood at the end of a short hallway that led to the main foyer, staircase, and living room. Off the hallway were the dining room and a study. They saw in the dimness of the few lights left on that Ridder had picked a good target. Everything in the house said old money. The high walls were decorated with stately molding, mirrors and art work. Classic shaped silver candlesticks of different sizes adorned tables and antique stands.

"The higher the ceiling, the more the money," Sykes said with a smile as Ridder disappeared up the staircase.

"You take that one," Kellerman looked at Sykes and pointed to the study. "I got the dining room."

Sykes walked through the open doorway of the study into a room with walls lined with books and immediately became distracted despite Ridder's stern warning. Books and other signs of intelligence always amazed him. He looked up at the books, his mouth open, as he walked over to a side table next to a chair and picked up a sterling silver ashtray that had never been used. He stuck it in his bag without looking, then walked over to the large mahogany desk, which had papers spread out over it. As he picked up a round gold paperweight with the initials W.L.H. on it, he glanced down at the papers and books on the desk. A small, open book with handwritten pages caught his eye. He picked up the old leather journal and began to read the open page.

Three minutes later, Kellerman popped his head through the doorway. "Hey, asshole, cut that shit out and get to work!"

Sykes quickly looked up from the book. "Kellerman, come here. Check this out. This is unbelievable!"

"Forget that shit. We ain't got all night."

"Relax, it ain't like the guy's coming home any time soon."

The cool air from the car's air conditioner made Professor Hutchinson's lungs feel slightly less on fire with each onslaught of coughing. He silently asked for pardon from his wife for not listening to her pleas to give up the 1972 Dodge Dart and buy a modern car. She had been right.

How he missed her and the way she lovingly helped coordinate his life in her own bossy, yet adoring way. She had always let him know that his belt did not match his shoes, or that his nose hairs were getting too long. Despite his outward appearance of stability and expected good humor, he felt utterly lost without her. It was as if he were an empty shell acting the way he did because he knew no other life. But when he stopped and thought about what his life meant without his dearest Sarah, he felt a sense of despair and loneliness he knew eventually would snuff out the modicum of desire he had to live. He felt the familiar throb begin deep in his throat as tears welled up in his tired eyes. If he could just fall asleep before his thoughts drove him over the edge, the new day would make things easier—it always did.

He took a deep breath and realized for the first time during the ten-minute ride that he had not exploded in a coughing fit. A smile emerged on his face as he pulled onto Londonderry Avenue and waved to Molly Alt, the nine-year-old girl who lived in the house on the corner of the Londonderry and Freemont, as she dragged a trash barrel to the street. He had wished he and Sarah had been able to have children. By now, he would have been a grandfather. The thought made him sigh as he drove past a van parked on the side of the road.

He drove past his house and pulled into the driveway of the house next door. His neighbor, Nathan Gradison IV, a widower like himself, was too crippled to drive his Town Car, but never hesitated to loan it to his lifelong friend when he needed it, as long as it was returned safely to his garage.

After parking the Town Car in the garage, Hutchinson walked through the small grove of trees that separated the two properties. Half way through the grove he stopped as he pondered whether he should have knocked on Nathan's door to check on his old friend instead of just leaving the key to the Town Car under the driver's visor as he always did. He turned and looked at Nathan's dark windows then decided it was better not to disturb him.

When he reached his front door, he sighed, and stumbled with the key in the lock. He could never get use to entering his house and not hearing the sweet voice of his Sarah welcome him home.

He opened the door, stepped inside and flicked on the light in the foyer.

Kellerman's heart jumped when he heard the door open. When the light burst into the dining room, he drew his gun and quickly stepped to the protection of the wall next to the open doorway to the foyer.

"Hey, Kellerman, kill that light, you trying to get us caught?" Sykes said from the study.

Kellerman spun around the corner and pointed the gun at a trembling, elderly man holding a phone.

"Put it down. Now!"

The old man turned and froze; he held the phone to his ear and his right pointer finger shook inches from the keypad.

"I mean it. Put the phone down!"

The old man didn't move.

Sykes came around the corner at the same time Ridder bounded down the stairs. The slight distraction caused Kellerman to take his eyes off the old man for a second. When he looked back, the man's finger was on the number 9. Kellerman pulled the trigger. The old man let out a choking gasp, clutched his chest as his eyes rolled white, then collapsed onto the floor. Crimson blood flowed though his hand and poured down onto the hardwood.

"What the hell are you doin'?" shouted Ridder.

Kellerman lowered the gun. Sykes was instantly at his side.

"Holy shit, Kellerman, what the hell happened?"

Kellerman didn't answer.

Sykes gasped. "You killed him!"

"He was calling the fuckin' cops. You saw him," Kellerman screamed back.

"Shut up!" Ridder looked around. "Shit. Grab your bags and get to the van. We need to get the fuck outta here—*now!*"

# CHAPTER 2

▼

The ambulance screamed past them as they turned onto Londonderry Avenue, causing Detective John Ditchman's stomach to twinge. The memory of the shooting and his ambulance ride was still very vivid to him. He shook his head and scratched the thick, gray mustache that hid his upper lip. The combination of a square jaw, defined cheekbones and wiry black hair made Ditchman look as if he belonged on a cigarette magazine advertisement. He had deep blue eyes with a twinkle of life in them that always made him look like he was deep in some positive thought. Most of the single, female cops in the city, as well as dozens of other eligible women, all who found his aloofness irresistibly sexy in some way, had courted Ditchman over the years. At age forty, he had served on the Charlottesville police force for twenty-one years, and never thought twice about diverting any of his attention away from his work. It wouldn't be fair to her, he always said to those who tried to set him up. Having been shot reinforced his belief that his work would only bring heartache to anyone he let get close to him.

Five police cruisers lit up the neighborhood with their flashing strobes of blue and white. The sudden energy of the street brought Ditchman back to focus. The first case back would be another measuring stick.

"Twenty-five Londonderry. Here we are. Looks like a bit of a circus, eh, Ditch?" Rusty Hammond, Ditchman's younger partner, said as he parked the car behind a cruiser.

At age thirty, Hammond had been a detective for just under a year, but a cop in some form or another since high school. He stood six-foot-three and weighed one hundred and sixty pounds with his clothes on, a stark contrast to Ditchman's linebacker-like frame of an even six feet and two hundred and ten pounds. A former high school basketball star, Hammond still maintained the boyish look of a teenager. His strawberry blond hair, smooth skin and natural inclination to smile made it difficult for him to look like a tough cop, a characteristic that bothered him, though he never verbalized it.

"Time to play ball. Stay focused and alert." Ditchman's usual short pep talk made Hammond smile.

As they got out of their car, the detectives immediately adopted their game faces, as Ditchman called it. Latex gloves were donned; hair nets and shoe nets would be put on once inside the house, if necessary. No mistakes, Ditchman thought. Take in everything. Shooters always leave a clue. He felt a rush of adrenaline from being back on the job.

As they approached the front of the house, a portly uniformed cop opened the large front door for them.

"Perimeter's sealed, Lieutenant. I was first on the scene. Nobody's been inside without nets on, 'cept me. Found the victim inside by the phone stand in the front hall. Walter Hutchinson, elderly guy in his early seventies, according to his neighbor. History professor at the university. Shot in the chest. He's on his way to the ER now. Doesn't look good. Activity upstairs and down. I called in Williams and his dust crew. Figured you'd want them. Looks like a possible, well, you know what you're doing, you'll see. I also saved you from having to run over to UVA." He produced a clear bag with a wallet in it. "Took it from the victim before the EMT's took him away. Nobody's touched it." He handed Ditchman the bag. "Good to have you back, Ditch."

The uniforms knew the routine with Ditchman. No time was wasted and everyone did his job. Clockwork, Ditchman called it.

"Thanks, Pete. Who called it in?"

"Next door neighbor. Jonathan Schone. Lives in the house to the right."

"Where's he now?"

"Sitting on a bench just inside. He's a wreck."

Ditchman and Hammond entered the house and began surveying the scene. Immediately, they saw Schone slumped against a wall in the foyer, his head tilted down and shaking back and forth as he listened to a female uniformed cop who was trying to comfort him. To their right was a doorway to a formal dining room. On the left side of the foyer was a large, marble staircase leading to the second floor. Ditchman looked up and noted a large chandelier hanging from the fifteen foot-high ceiling.

"Rusty, why don't you take upstairs and have the crew take pictures of every room, from every angle. Keep your eyes open. When you're done, photograph the downstairs. I'll talk to Schone after I check out down here."

As Hammond climbed the stairs, Ditchman walked over to a bathmat-size pool of fresh, dark red blood that covered the spot where Hutchinson had fallen. He knelt down and looked at the pool for a few seconds, then stood and looked in each direction, noting that the spot was visible from a number of areas.

At the end of the hallway off the foyer, Ditchman found where the assailants had entered the house. He slowly examined the side door that was partially open and had a circle cut from the window next to the doorknob. Just inside the door on the wall, an alarm box with a spliced wire hanging from its open casing told him why the side door had been chosen as the point of entry, clearly the work of no amateur.

In the dining room, he found a very large, empty mahogany table occupying the center of the room, a matching serving table against one wall, and an ornate China cabinet, its glass doors open, against the adjacent wall. Ditchman could see faint dust marks of objects that had previously occupied the two shelves inside the cabinet and made a note in his book. He then opened each drawer in the bottom half of the cabinet and found nothing of worth until he reached the lowest drawer. Inside, in plain sight, were sterling flatware and a candlesnuffer.

When Ditchman finished inspecting the cabinet, he walked across to the study, which looked more used than the dining room. In the corner was a worn, brown leather chair, with a navy blue cardigan sweater draped across the left arm and on the seat, the day's copy of the Charlottesville-Albemarle Tribune, folded so page three faced up. The books on the shelves surrounding the room told Ditchman the victim was a Civil War historian.

After eyeing the perimeter of the room, he focused on the desk in the center of the room. A phone with blood on the receiver sat to one side. In the left corner was a framed photo of an elderly couple holding hands. Hutchinson and his wife, Ditchman concluded. Papers were scattered across the middle of the desktop. He took a closer look at the handwritten notes on legal paper, but made nothing of them.

"All set upstairs," Hammond said as he entered the study. "Looks like only the master bedroom got hit. Pillow cases aren't missing. The dresser has been rifled through. Strange thing though, Ditch, a jewelry box in the bottom drawer of a dresser was open and it looks like some of the jewelry is missing, but there's some left, including some nice pieces."

Ditchman raised an eyebrow. "I found the same thing down here—some valuables were left in the dining room. The perp came in through that door, cut the glass to get to the lock and bypassed the alarm system, one of those old models that the bad guys easily know how to fool." He paused and looked at Hammond. "So, what do you think?" Ditchman loved to test his younger partner.

"Well, we've got a man shot. He's by the door. The phone's on the floor. Valuables are taken, but not all of them. Could've been Hutchinson walked in on the perp. Looks like he was trying to use the phone when he was shot."

"What else?"

Hammond stared blankly while thinking. "Possibly made to look like a burglary to cover up another motive?"

"Maybe."

"But, Ditch, come on. Why would someone want to kill an old history professor?"

"Who knows, maybe he failed someone. You have to remember to never just assume the obvious. There's a lot of wackos out there. It's not clear-cut like it used to be. Why don't you finish shooting the downstairs." Ditchman turned as he saw Jake Williams' forensic team in the hallway, then he turned back. "And Rusty, make sure you get some good ones of the papers on the desk here."

He turned back to Williams in the hallway. "Usual job, Jake. Pay special attention to this doorway," he pointed to the side door, "the hallway, the dining room, this room, the master bedroom, and the banister. Who knows, we might get lucky. Let me know when you've got the results in from the vacuum tests."

"You got it, Ditch," Williams replied with a mock salute to Ditchman's control. Then he smiled. "Good to have you back."

Schone stood in the foyer in an undershirt, Bermuda shorts, and tennis shoes with his arms crossed, his hair unkempt from rubbing his head, his eyes extremely red from crying. He slowly rocked back and forth on his feet as if in a trance.

"Mr. Schone. I'm Detective John Ditchman of the Charlottesville homicide unit."

"Homicide? Oh, God, has Walter died?"

"No, sir. He is in critical condition. We were called in because it was a shooting." Ditchman left off that he was called in when a shooting would probably result in a death. "You were the first to find Professor Hutchinson?"

Schone nodded.

"Well, then can you give me as much detail as possible about what happened? Start with where you live and how you came over here."

Schone took a deep breath. "We live next door, my wife and I and our three daughters. I had just stepped out our back door to take our dog out when I heard what sounded like a fire cracker, only louder."

"What time was that?"

"Well, let's see." He paused. "I had just told our youngest to go to bed because it was past her bedtime which is nine o'clock."

"Good. What did you do next? Did you hear or see anything?" Ditchman asked.

"I pulled the dog back inside and ran over here. I didn't see anything because it was dark. But I did hear a car's wheels squeal."

"Did you get a look at the vehicle?"

"No, I was running through the woods. Our girls used to visit Mrs. Hutchinson so much when she was alive they wore a path through the woods. It's just quicker. Would have taken me just as long to get to the end of our driveway."

"Then what?"

Schone wiped his forehead with his hand and took a deep breath. He looked flushed. "When I got to the side door, I found it wide open and went inside calling for Walter. That's when I found him." He hesitated and looked at the blood stains on his hands and shirt. "I immediately called 911. I used the phone in Walter's den."

"Before you tended to Mr. Hutchinson?" Ditchman looked at Schone's hands.

"Of course not. I went right to Walter. He was bleeding profusely. I tried to stop the bleeding. But I realized he needed an ambulance. The phone was pulled out of the wall jack, so I left him to go call 911 from the den," Schone said defensively.

"You did the right thing." Ditchman retreated a bit. "Did Professor Hutchinson say anything to you? Was he at all conscious?"

"He muttered something I couldn't understand so I put my ear closer to his mouth. I don't know, I think he kept saying, 'my work, my work.' Then he lost consciousness."

Ditchman raised his right eyebrow. "What do you make of that? What work?"

Schone shook his head in despair. "I don't know. Walter was a professor emeritus at UVA. He was always researching something. God, how could this have happened? Walter wouldn't hurt anyone. He was a kind, old fellow."

Tears flowed heavily from Schone's eyes.

Ditchman patted him on the back. "Thanks, Mr. Schone. You've been very helpful. One of my men will need to fingerprint you. Routine, you understand.

We need to rule out your prints in the house. If you think of anything else, please call me." Ditchman handed him his card. He added, "Is there anyone you should call? Children?"

"Walter and Sarah didn't have any children. That's why they were so fond of our girls." He began to choke up again. "Why did this happen, Detective? Who would want to shoot Walter?"

Ditchman shook his head. "That's what we need to find out."

"What am I supposed to tell my girls?"

"Tell them the truth."

Members of the forensic team were busy doing their job of dusting for latent prints and vacuuming up possible trace evidence without giving much attention to the detectives standing by them. Ditchman extracted the wallet from the evidence bag. The brown leather looked like a road map because of its spider web cracks formed from age and stuffing too many pieces of paper into an insufficient space. Ditchman emptied the contents of the wallet, two twenties and a bunch of wrinkled papers, onto an antique table under a large mirror in the foyer. He looked through the papers and found a half dozen store and ATM receipts and handwritten notes with phone numbers.

"Rusty, take a look at this." Ditchman held out a piece of paper.

After quickly studying it, Hammond said, "A credit card receipt from that restaurant the 1776. Dated today at 8:43 p.m." He looked up at Ditchman. "He must have been there just before the shooting."

"Good. What else do you see?"

"He paid sixteen-fifty, including tip. You can't buy a meal at that place for less than thirty bucks, so it must have been drinks."

"And I doubt the good Professor had two drinks by himself. We need to find out who was with him. It may shed a little light on Hutchinson's background if this was anything more than a routine burglary gone bad." Ditchman looked around and found the officer who had met them at the front door. "Hey, Pete, I want you to take your boys and canvas the neighborhood. See if anyone saw anything. Hit all the pawnshops. See if anyone's itching to make some quick cash."

"What now, Ditch?" Hammond asked, his eyebrows raised high.

"I'm heading to the hospital to see if Hutchinson can talk if he's alive. You go to the restaurant. Find out who he was with. Let me know what you get." Ditchman shook his head slowly as he stroked his mustache. "This just doesn't feel right."

"You're thinking a possible burglary cover to mask the shooting?"

"I don't want to rule out anything just yet."

After dumping the CableVA van behind the supermarket where Kellerman's car had been left, they drove fifteen miles west of the city to where the state of Virginia became rural, rolling hills again and people minded their own business. After several miles on an unnamed road, they pulled up to an old, dirty white ranch house which looked like its heydays had passed along with the Great Depression. Overgrown, neglected fields of brown corn stocks surrounded the house on three sides. The only building within sight of the house, a burnt-red barn twice the size of the house with a partially collapsed roof, left no doubt that the neighborhood was not in any jeopardy of being overrun by potential house-buyers in search of the trendy place to live.

"What the hell we doin' here?" Kellerman demanded.

Ridder said nothing, just retrieved the bags from the trunk and went up the steps to the front porch door. He felt around the clapboards on the left side of the doorjamb, then pried back one board. A silver key dropped onto the deck.

"This place safe?" Sykes asked.

"Relax, buddy of mine owns it. Let's me use it whenever. Ain't nobody comin' way out here." Ridder flicked on a light inside the door.

The inside of the house was in no better condition than the outside. A cloud of dust floated into the air as they stepped into what had been the front parlor. A ripped drapery fluttered in front of the two broken panes in the window to the left of a paisley patterned Victorian era sofa that looked as no one had sat in it for a few decades.

Sykes violently sneezed four times in succession.

Ridder carefully dumped the stolen goods onto a large table across from the sofa. "Ah, this is bullshit! Wasn't even worth all the trouble." He stared at Kellerman who returned the glare.

"What are you looking at?" Kellerman challenged.

Ridder pounded the table with his fist. The tattoo dragon on his arm swelled. "Man, you fucked up tonight, big time. First you waste the old man at the house. You know what that means? I'll tell you, asshole. It means the cops are goin' to be all over that house lookin' to nail our asses!" Veins bulged out of Ridder's forehead and neck as he unconsciously flexed his hands into fists.

"What the hell do you want from me, Ridder? The guy was calling the cops. What was I supposed to do? Let him just I.D. us? What the hell's your problem?"

Ridder paced around the room. "And you screwed up in the van, takin' your gloves off before we finished the job! What are you, fuckin' stupid or something?"

"What did you call me?" Kellerman took in a deep breath that enlarged his upper body. Though six inches shorter than Ridder, he was not going to back down.

"Hey, whoa, whoa, fellahs. Come on, settle down." Sykes stepped between them, a look of pure fear in his eyes. "The old man was a mistake. And don't worry Carson, I wiped down the van real good. No need to get in a fight. Tonight wasn't a complete bust. Take a look at what I got." Sykes pulled out the small leather journal from under the pile of jewelry, silverware and candlesticks on the table.

"What the hell's that?" Ridder asked, his eyes not leaving Kellerman.

"Have you ever heard of the legend of the *CSS Argo*? That ship during the Civil War that was loaded with gold but sank?"

"What the fuck do you know, you never even graduated from high school," Kellerman said as he stepped back.

"Neither did you, Rick. But when I was doing time, I got to reading. Nothin' else to do in a cell. All they'd give you was magazines. Civil War, mainly. There was an article about this ship called the *Argo* carrying gold and some guy found most of it, but not all of it."

"So what?" Ridder said.

Sykes held up the small journal. "This thing tells where the rest of the gold's at. Look here." He opened up the book and flipped through a few pages. "Says 'On September 15, during a hurricane, the *CSS Argo* ran aground.'" He flipped a few pages. "Then it says, 'After waiting on the beach for the storm to die, I returned to the half sunk *Argo*, destroyed the quarterboard, but could only retrieve a portion of the gold before the waves completely destroyed the *Argo*.'"

Ridder grabbed the journal out of his hands and threw it down on the table. "Christ, Buster, I don't wanna hear any more of that crap. Gold, my ass," he said with teeth clenched. He turned to Kellerman. "Give me your piece."

"*What*? Why?"

"Because I don't trust your stupid ass to get rid of it to save my ass."

"Fuck you, Ridder."

Ridder quickly reached behind his back into his waistline and pulled out a .44 Magnum. He pointed it at Kellerman and pulled back the hammer. "I'll say it one last time. Give me your gun." Ridder's black eyes bore into Kellerman.

"Just do it, Rick," Sykes pleaded.

Kellerman slowly reached under his shirt and pulled out the Beretta by the barrel and handed it to Ridder while staring into his eyes.

"Good, now get the fuck outta here and lay low for a couple of days. And if I find you…"

"What about our share?" Kellerman demanded. "I ain't leaving unless…"

"I *said* get the fuck outta here!" Ridder screamed louder while extending his gun toward Kellerman's head.

"Hey, hey, Carson, keep cool." Sykes took a step closer to Ridder while raising his hands. "We're going, we're going. Be cool." He paused and swallowed hard. "You can call us after you sell the stuff. Okay, Carson?" Sykes padded Ridder on the shoulder, and then quickly retracted it when Ridder glared at him.

"Come on, Rick, do what Carson says. Everything's cool." Sykes turned and guided Kellerman out by the arm.

# CHAPTER 3

▼

A lone couple holding hands sat at one of the dining tables of the 1776 while employees hustled about in preparation for closing so they could get home. Hammond walked up to the man behind the maitre d' desk who was busy tidying menus.

"Excuse me."

The maitre d' looked up, startled as Hammond flashed his badge.

"I'm Detective Hammond, Charlottesville homicide. I need to speak with your manager."

The maitre d' hesitated, and swallowed. "Yes, of course." He looked around. "I'll get him for you."

Within a minute, a tall, skinny, white-haired man appeared dressed in an Armani suit and wearing half-glasses at the end of his narrow nose. "I'm Nicholas Stoneham, the manager, how may we help you, Detective?" He shook Hammond's hand.

"We're investigating a shooting that took place tonight. The victim was at your restaurant right before he was shot." Hammond pulled out the receipt. "We would like to know if he was with anyone. His name's Walter Hutchinson."

"No! Professor Hutchinson?" Stoneham's head sprang back. "He's one of our most frequent and loyal patrons. My lord, he was shot? Is he okay?"

"I'd like to talk to whoever served him."

Stoneham looked at the receipt. "Server 56 is Robby Orsen. Hold on, I believe he's still here. Just a minute, please."

A minute later Stoneham walked out of the kitchen with a young man dressed in his waiter garb of a starched white Oxford shirt and black pants. He looked college-aged with neatly trimmed sandy hair parted to one side.

"You waited on a Professor Hutchinson tonight?"

The young man hesitated.

Stoneham said, "He is the older gentleman who always sits in the back corner."

"Oh, yes, I did. I'm sorry. It's been a busy night. Sure, they ordered drinks and that's it. No meal."

"They? Do you know who he was with?"

"Some man, I don't know who he is. He looked kinda familiar."

"We get a lot of the professors in here from the university," Stoneham interjected.

"Do you think you could identify him in a picture?"

Orsen shrugged his shoulders. "Maybe. Yeah. What's going on?"

Hammond looked him in the eye. "Professor Hutchinson was shot tonight, just after he was here, so we need to speak to the gentleman he was with."

"Jesus! Shot? Why?" Orsen's face stretched in shock.

"Excuse me a second, please." Hammond stepped away and pulled out his cell phone. His speed button dialed Ditchman.

"What's the latest, Rusty?"

"How'd you know it was me?"

"You're quicker than the rest."

"I've got the waiter here. Says he might be able to I.D. Hutchinson's dinner partner. Could be a university colleague."

"Good. Get over to campus. Get photos of all the professors. And, Rusty, I don't care if you have to wake up their damn president, keep this trail hot. I'm just about at the hospital. Call me later."

Hammond turned to the two men. "How late were you planning on being here?"

"How late do you need us to be here?" Stoneham replied.

"Maybe about two hours more. I'll be back in a while. Thanks for the cooperation," Hammond said as he started to walk for the exit.

The distinctive medicinal smell of the UVA Medical Center brought back memories for Ditchman he had hoped he had forgotten. The last time he was there, he was on a gurney in an emergency room having a bullet removed from his forty-year-old body.

A stressed out receptionist with hair pinned up in a bun and a pencil in her mouth hustled around the reception desk of the emergency ward. She stopped in her tracks when she saw the badge.

"Detective Ditchman, Charlottesville homicide. I need to speak with the doctor who worked on Professor Walter Hutchinson."

"Yeah, honey, just a minute," she said with a touch of rudeness as she picked up the phone.

She looked back up at Ditchman a few seconds later. "Dr. Bradley is still in surgery with Mr. Hutchinson. You can wait down there." She looked at a waiting room down the hall before returning her attention to her paper work.

"Thanks. Where can I get some coffee?"

"There's a vending machine in the waiting room," she said curtly without looking up.

Half of the twenty seats in the small, sterile waiting room were occupied. Some people waited to see a doctor; others waited to visit a patient. None of them made eye contact with Ditchman, few talked to each other, each looked unhappy to be there. Two children played tag around the center row of seats while their mother sat with a bereaved looked on her face, her chin resting on one palm. Ditchman sat against the back wall a seat away from a young man who held a white bandage against his forearm.

As he drank what he thought was decent coffee considering it came from a vending machine, he ran through in his mind the night he was shot. He did this often to test himself and to make sure he realized all the mistakes he had made, and the options he had not taken, so that he would never again end up in an emergency room.

He closed his eyes, took two deep, cleansing breaths, and he was back in the apartment building with Hammond. The smell of urine and stale cigarette smoke filled his nose.

After a month of investigating dead-end leads to solve the murder of the owner of a mom and pop corner store, Ditchman had serendipitously received a tip of the whereabouts of the shooter, Rodney Santos, from an unlikely source. The disgruntled ex-girlfriend was making sure she had been beaten up for the last time.

But Ditchman wondered if the girlfriend had set him up because all hell had broken loose when he and Hammond stepped out of the stairwell onto the fourth floor of Santos's apartment building. A man at the far end of the two hundred-foot hallway had shot at them then fled around the corner.

With Hammond a step ahead, they had run down the hallway, guns drawn. Just before reaching the corner, Ditchman had alerted the uniformed cops stationed at the front and back of the building that the suspect was on the run. They had then stopped at the corner with their backs pinned against the wall. Ditchman could feel his heart race again.

When they had heard a door open and looked behind him, Ditchman had realized in an instant that Santos must have doubled back through the corner apartment's second door just as a nine-millimeter bullet slammed into his chest.

Ditchman instinctively grimaced from the thought and opened his eyes. Never assume a corner apartment only has one door, he reminded himself.

"Detective Ditchman?" a blurry-eyed doctor dressed in stained surgical wear asked as he came into the waiting room.

Ditchman sprang up and followed the doctor to a more private area of the corridor. "How's the Professor?"

The doctor took in a breath then spoke in a deliberate tone. "We were able to remove the bullet from his chest, but he had already lost a lot of blood. The bullet clipped a major artery to the heart and at his age, it was too much. He didn't make it." Bradley handed Ditchman a clear bag with a nine-millimeter bullet in it.

"Did he say anything before he died?

"He was unconscious the whole time. Is there any thing else, Detective? I don't mean to rush, but I've got others to see."

"Just one more thing. In your judgement, how close was the shooter?"

"Well, judging from the extensive damage to the chest cavity, I'd say rather close."

"Thanks, doc."

As Ditchman walked out of the hospital, he quickly called Hammond. "Rusty, Hutchinson didn't make it. The doctor said it was probably a close range shot. Any luck finding out Hutchinson's dinner partner?"

"I went to campus, got a photo book after some arm twisting and wake up calls. I'm at the restaurant. The waiter just identified the guy as a Professor Garland Triste. Lives at 165 Moreland Street."

Ditchman pumped his fist in the air as he reached his car. "I'll meet you there in fifteen minutes. Good work, Rusty."

Hammond was leaning against his car as Ditchman pulled up to the house on Moreland Street. Neither of them said a word as Ditchman stepped out of his car. They knew what they were about to do was the worst thing about being a cop, but something they had to do. Ditchman hoped the wife would not answer the door. It was always worst when the wife answered the door.

It took a number of knocks before the door finally opened. Garland Triste stood in the doorway in a bathrobe, the expression on his face revealing he immediately knew something was wrong. Police visits late at night were never innocuous.

"Mr. Garland A. Triste?" Ditchman asked.

"Yes?" he said hesitantly.

"I'm Detective Ditchman, this is my partner Detective Hammond. Were you at the 1776 restaurant tonight with Professor Walter Hutchinson?"

"Yes. Oh, God. Is Walter all right? He wasn't feeling well. He..."

Ditchman interrupted to get it over with. "There's been a homicide. Professor Hutchinson was shot by an intruder in his home. He died a short while ago at the UVA Medical Center. I'm very sorry."

Triste leaned against the doorframe as the blood drained from his face. Immediately, his eyes became teary and he opened his mouth to say something but no words came out.

"What is it, honey?" Triste's wife said with concerned anticipation as she reached the door and put a hand on his shoulder.

Triste turned to his wife, and as he hugged her, repeated what Ditchman had just told him. Mary Triste immediately began to cry on her husband's shoulder. Triste cradled her head then looked up at the detectives. "Please, come in."

He led them to the living room where a baby grand piano, adorned with photos of family and friends, sat in the far corner. Hammond sat down on a floral chintz couch. In front of him was an antique cherry coffee table with magazines neatly placed on it.

After taking his wife back upstairs to lie down, Triste returned looking more composed, but still red in the eyes.

"Can I offer you some coffee?"

"Thanks, black, please," Ditchman replied. Hammond nodded his head. Triste retreated to the kitchen.

"Seems like they were close. Both of them are taking this pretty badly," Hammond whispered.

Ditchman looked at the photos on the piano, then picked up one in a silver frame and identified a younger Triste standing with a man who Ditchman instantly recognized as Hutchinson from the photo he had seen in the professor's study.

"You have a good eye," Triste said, returning with the coffee. "That was taken fifteen years ago, when I first joined the university faculty. Walter and I shared an office until they could find me one." Triste looked closely at the photo. "Always was altruistic." His nostalgia quickly ended when he looked at Ditchman. "When did this happen? *What* happened?"

"He was shot when he arrived home from the restaurant based on the time scenario we've put together. We believe he may have walked in on a burglary." Ditchman tried to look Triste in the eye, but it was hard for him. Hammond sat with his hands in his lap and looked at the floor.

"What do you mean 'may have'?"

"To be honest with you, Professor, I believe this was a burglary. But because we just launched the investigation I don't want to jump to conclusions."

"What then? In god's name, who would want to kill Walter?"

Hammond sat forward in the couch. "Was Professor Hutchinson a wealthy man?"

"Walter's wife had family money. But they were not in any way ostentatious. You'd never know they had money, except that they lived in a nice neighborhood."

Ditchman took a long, slow sip of his coffee then sat down in a wing backed chair. "As far as you know, would any one have reason to harm Professor Hutchinson?"

"Like what?" Triste asked in disbelief.

"Gambling, maybe..."

Triste shook his head. "No, no, none of that. Walter was as good hearted and straight as they came. The only bad thing he probably ever did was not returning a book to the library on time. So you're on the wrong track there, Detective."

Ditchman rubbed his mustache. "Thought so. Sorry, I had to ask. Let's get back to the restaurant. Did you eat with Professor Hutchinson routinely?"

"We used to. Lately, it was whenever he called. He called me a day ago very excited and said he wanted to have dinner with me."

"Why the excitement?" asked Hammond.

"Walter said he had made a huge breakthrough in the research he was working on."

"And what was that?"

"I don't know. He never told me. I assumed it was the ostensible discovery of the missing clue, if you will. But, again, I'm only speculating. Walter never got around to telling me what it was because he wasn't feeling well and so left the restaurant shortly after we arrived."

"What was his research about?" Ditchman asked.

Triste took a drink of his coffee then rubbed his eyes. "I can't see how that's relevant."

"Maybe. Maybe not. We'd still like to know."

Triste raised his eyebrows then nodded his head once. "Though Walter was a wonderful classroom teacher, his true love was field research. He had become somewhat famous for his research of a lost Confederate ship, the *Argo*, which was en route to Canada in 1863 to deliver a shipment of gold to buy much needed aid for the Confederacy."

"They'd just lost Gettysburg and Vicksburg, I assume?" Ditchman asked.

"Very good, Detective. You learned your history. Yes, the South was in dire straits. Walter had claimed the ship and its small crew never made it to Canada because a hurricane hit the East Coast and she sank, gold and all. Now, we have no documentation of this ship from the Confederate government. What we knew comes from folklore. However, back in 1982, Walter's research led to his discovery of the remains of the ship near Monomoy Island, off the coast of Cape Cod."

"Did he find the gold?" Hammond asked.

Triste smiled briefly. "Over two million dollars worth."

Ditchman shifted forward in his chair. "I remember reading about it in the papers. Did he get to keep the gold?"

"No, it went to the university because it had funded the grant for his research."

"So what was Professor Hutchinson working on recently?" Ditchman asked.

"Well, Walter contended that the *Argo* had been carrying more gold than he found, but could never prove it."

"Do you think the Professor was going to tell you tonight that he solved the mystery?" Hammond asked.

"Maybe. But again, Detectives, I don't see how this is in any way related to Walter being shot." He stood up and walked to the piano.

"Did any one know of Professor Hutchinson's research?"

"Sure, he was the leading historian on the matter. But it's like being the leading historian on the Fountain of Youth. Do you understand?"

"Certainly." Ditchman thanked Triste, handed him his card and walked to the door.

"I pray you find whoever is responsible for this. Walter was a prominent and much loved member of this community. And not just because he was a brilliant historian. He was a Lee, from his mother's side."

# CHAPTER 4

▼

Ditchman sat on the edge of a desk on the second floor of the new station house in downtown Charlottesville. Though most of the veteran cops disliked all the newness, "Takes away the spirit of the place," they claimed, Ditchman appreciated the lack of clutter. But that was just how his mind worked—clutter distracted the vision—it was all about the case, nothing else. And he knew that was why he would never marry.

Rusty Hammond arrived three minutes early with two cups of coffee, one black. He handed it to Ditchman. Like his partner, he had been up most of the night working the case, yet looked worse than he felt. Finally, Pete Wilcox arrived looking haggard just from taking the stairs to the second floor.

"Williams will be here shortly," Ditchman said as he looked at his watch and noted it was nine o'clock. "Let's go over what we know. The clock's ticking and we need some solid leads. The way I see it, we're dealing with at least two suspects, probably three."

"How so?" Hammond asked.

"By the pattern of things taken in each of the rooms. The bedroom was cleaned out, except some jewelry, and some silver pieces were left behind downstairs. If it were just one person, wouldn't he have cleaned out a room before moving on to the next?"

Hammond nodded his head. "I called the alarm company. They said they had a slight interruption in their connection to the house at 8:52. But no alarm was tripped. The neighbor said he heard the shot shortly after nine. In that short amount of time, yeah, there had to be more than one guy to be able to work that many rooms and to carry the stuff out in probably one trip."

Ditchman raised his eyebrows, then stroked his mustache. "What did you find out, Pete?"

Wilcox tried to sit up in the chair. "Nothing so far at the pawn shops. It's been quiet, but we'll keep an eye out."

"What about the neighbors?"

"Two sisters across the street were out collecting fireflies in their driveway last night, and one of them claims to have seen a light colored van with writing on it."

"How reliable?"

"Well, I checked out the stolen vehicle report, and this morning a CableVA van was reported missing. We found it behind a supermarket on Sycamore and it fits the girl's description. We're impounding it right now to have it dusted for prints."

Ditchman took a long drink of his coffee. "Good. What about the neighbor, Schone, the guy who found him?" He turned to Hammond.

"He's clean, Ditch. His family was very close to the Hutchinsons."

"What about finances?"

Hammond shrugged. "Again, straight arrow. I made some calls. Guy was wealthy, but did nothing with it. Mainly fixed income stocks and bonds. Retirement stuff."

Jake Williams sat down next to Wilcox and nodded to Ditchman.

"So what did your all-stars find this time, Jake?"

Williams smiled. "Sorry, Ditch. No prints, just a bunch of hair. Judging by the lack of evidence, I'd say it wasn't an amateur job. The bullet is nine millimeter, good markings."

"Okay, thanks guys. Let me know if you find anything else." He turned to his partner who was wiping sleep out of his eyes. "Let's do a run through of all the burglaries we have on file for the past, say, three months. See if any resemble this one." Ditchman drained his coffee. "Did you have any breakfast yet?"

"Just liquid." Hammond held up his cup of coffee.

After an hour of reading old case files, some solved, fewer unsolved, Hammond sat back in his chair and stretched his arms in the air. "Nothing. That's it for my share."

"Bingo!" Ditchman held up a manila folder. "Here's one from two months ago. The house was robbed while the family was out for dinner."

Hammond sprang forward in his chair. "Jesus, I missed that connection. I think I have one like that, too." He dug through the stack of folders and pulled out one with the name Sorrenson on it. "Same thing here." He opened the file.

"Guy is out at dinner with his girlfriend, comes home to find his place cleaned out and the case was never solved."

"I think we could have a restaurant ring going here, Rusty." Ditchman smiled. "Alright, who at a restaurant knows when people will be eating?"

"The hostess or maitre d'."

"That's who we're going to start with then."

The first restaurant they checked out was a bust. Of the two maitre d's employed during the possibly connected burglary two months before, one had quit, the other had been fired for getting caught with his hand in the tip jar. Though the lead did not result in anything concrete, the firing of the one increased Ditchman's suspicions of a possible burglary ring. Just because you worked at a classy restaurant didn't automatically make you a law-abiding citizen, he told Hammond. The second restaurant was not open for business until dinnertime. The third on the list was the 1776.

Since the restaurant had just opened, only a few people ate an early lunch at the 1776. The manager greeted them kindly again, said how terribly sorry he was that Professor Hutchinson had died, and asked what could he do to help the detectives. Without tipping his hand, Ditchman asked for the names of all employees who worked the reservation stand. Though the manager raised an eyebrow, he produced the list without question. Ditchman called in each name to be run through the computer back at the station house. The two males on the list had criminal records. One of them, Vincent Cummings, worked the previous night.

"When could we speak with Vincent Cummings?" Ditchman asked the manager.

"Let me see," he looked through his schedule book. "He's due in at noon to help with the lunch crowd, but he usually arrives early. You're welcome to stay, maybe have a bite to eat?"

Ditchman checked his watch; it was 11:30. "Thanks, just a couple of coffees."

Right on schedule, Vincent Cummings walked through the double glass doors at 11:50. He was a short, sharp-dressed man with thinning hair. Ditchman and Hammond got off their bar stools and walked toward him. Cummings recognized them instantly, flushed, stopped in his tracks, and then turned to retreat out the door.

"Whoa, whoa, Mr. Cummings." Hammond got to him first and grabbed him by the elbow. "Why in such a big rush? Your shift is about to start."

Ditchman led them outside to save the restaurant any embarrassment. "I'm Detective Ditchman, this is my partner Detective Hammond. We need to ask you a few questions, Mr. Cummings."

Sweat droplets suddenly developed on his large forehead and he refused to make eye contact while he kept licking his dried lips.

Ditchman could smell the fear. This should be easy, he thought. Guy's incriminating himself without saying anything.

"We're investigating the homicide of a gentleman who ate here last night. When he got home, someone was in his house and shot him."

Sweat stains appeared under Cummings' arms. "I don't know anything about that."

"We think you do, Mr. Cummings. You see, there's been a number of burglaries lately. Each time, the person ripped off was eating at a restaurant. Now don't you think that's a bit of a coincidence?"

"I told you, I don't know what you're talking about."

"Mr. Cummings, you can make this real easy. Don't make us subpoena all the restaurant's phone records, then go through every call last night and find the guy you called to let him know that Professor Walter Hutchinson was at the restaurant so the coast was clear to rip him off and kill him!" Hammond raised his voice intentionally.

Ditchman sensed Cummings was about to break so he said in a more calm voice, "Think about that, Mr. Cummings. Professor Hutchinson was a 73 year old man. And now he's dead. I know that's not what was supposed to happen, but it did, and now if you choose not to cooperate, things are going to be…"

"All right, all right!" Cummings cried, shaking his hands violently like he was trying to bat away demons. "Jesus, I never thought anyone would get killed. I'm not that kind of person, you know. It was supposed to be just robberies, small stuff."

"Who were you working with?"

"Christ, I don't know. Some guy called the restaurant one night while I was working and tells me if I don't help him he'll tell my manager I spent time in jail and I'll lose my job. This is the best job I've ever had, but it doesn't pay all the bills. This guy said I would get a percentage of the money."

"What's the guy's name?" Hammond asked.

Cummings shook his head. "I don't know, I swear."

"What's the number you used?"

"God, I can't remember. He'd call and give it to me. He used three different numbers."

"How'd he pay you?"

"He said some kid would deliver my share to me. I don't know anything more, I swear it. Damn! Why'd I get involved in this?" He stared at the ground and shook his head.

The morning sun streaming into the living room of the ranch house made him wince from the pain in his blurry eyes. His back ached from sleeping on the sofa that had more grease on it than a short order cook's apron. A mostly empty bottle of Jack Daniel's lay on the floor at the head of the sofa. Carson Ridder rubbed his temples to ease the pounding of his head while he swished the last remnants of the whiskey in his mouth to try to get rid of the feeling that a rat had died in his mouth.

Sitting on the edge of the sofa, he looked across the room at the table with the stolen goods on it. Suddenly, he remembered the events of last night, specifically the shooting. He stood and let out a grunt as he fought his body's desire to collapse in a heap back onto the sofa.

On the floor next to his black boots, his cellular phone rang with ear-piercing force to someone with a hangover. "Yeah?" he said with a gravelly voice, the effort to bend over making his head swell with blinding pressure.

"Hey, Carson, its Buster. I gotta tell you…"

"Sykes, what the hell time is it?"

"It's almost eleven. Listen, I just got back from the library and…"

"Thought I told you to lay low for a couple of days!" Ridder was beginning to slip out of his daze.

"I know, but I had to find something out. Just listen. I looked up that story I was telling you about. The one about the legend of the *CSS Argo*. Remember? The ship with the gold? The one I read in jail? Well, I found it at the library. It was written by a guy named Walter Hutchinson." He deliberately pronounced the name. "Know who he is, Carson?"

"No." Ridder grumbled tersely, being in no mood for guessing games.

"I found other stories on the *Argo*. All of them say Hutchinson's the expert. And, I saw the Tribune today, the cover story. He's the guy we robbed last night. The old man Kellerman waxed."

Ridder lay back on the couch. "So we know the stiff's name. Who gives a shit?"

"Well, back in 1982 when he discovered the ship, he found millions in gold."

"Yeah, so what?"

"Well, that's just it. He claimed there was *more* gold than he found."

Ridder clenched his teeth. "Buster, I ain't in no mood for this crap."

"Wait, Carson, let me explain. One of the stories said that this Hutchinson guy found a letter written by some Civil War soldier named Randall, right? The guy was dying and he wrote to his wife about being on a ship carrying gold."

"Get to the fuckin' point, Buster."

"Sorry, Carson. Anyway, that letter helped Hutchinson find the ship and the gold. And, he claimed there was more gold, but he didn't find it because it wasn't on the ship, right?"

"Buster!"

"Hold on, Carson. Here's the good part. That journal I took last night was written by the same soldier, this guy, Randall, the guy who wrote the letter to his wife. It had his name on the first page. I swear I saw it. And the journal says where the rest of the gold is buried, I swear it does, Carson. I read it, I swear."

"Oh, yeah, where's that, dumbass?"

"Hutchinson found the gold off some island on Cape Cod, and that journal tells where the rest is buried. I had to stop reading it because the old man walked in and all. Go grab the thing off the table. Read it yourself. You'll see. I'm telling you, all these magazines say the lost gold is worth millions and that tons of treasure hunters have been looking for it for years 'cause it's finders keepers."

Ridder struggled over to the table and sifted through the loot. "Ain't here."

"What? Look again."

"I said it ain't here!"

"Shit! What could have happened to it? I left it right on that table. Has anyone else been there?"

"Just you two assholes last night." Suddenly Ridder's mind cleared. "Where's Kellerman?"

"I don't know. Probably over at his slutty girlfriend's dump."

"Call him, then call me back." Ridder hung up the phone and went looking for a drink to kill his hangover.

Within minutes Sykes called back. "He left last night. She said he looked like he was going some place. I asked her if he said where he was going and she said he was mumbling about Cape Cod and being a rich man."

"That bastard! Never did trust that asshole. If what you're tellin' me is true, Buster, and Kellerman's crossed me, he'll pay. Pack a bag, and get on over here. We're goin' on a little vacation to tie up a loose end. I can't have Kellerman or any fuckin' journal linkin' me to the old man's house. And bring those stories with you, I wanna read 'em. Try to remember what you read in that journal. And don't tell no one where you're goin'." He was about to hang up, but said, "Buster, what's that fake name Kellerman uses?"

"I think it's Leo Reynolds."

Ridder slammed the cell phone on the table. He felt his muscles tense as he thought of Kellerman and his hangover instantly abated. Without giving it any thought, he made a fist with his right hand and punched the tabletop.

The Charlottesville Albemarle Airport was crowded with tourists on their way to see one of America's greatest architectural wonders, the home of Thomas Jefferson. With school vacation in full swing, families flooded the historic area to visit *Monticello* and the surrounding colonial tourist traps. Kellerman was glad it was so busy. He walked through the airport trying to act as inconspicuous as possible. The sneakers, jeans, blue polyester shirt and leather jacket made him look like the average Joe, which he wanted. He had even shaved off his goatee. He couldn't remember the last time he was completely clean shaven and he barely recognized himself in the reflection of the airport store windows. The few cops he saw didn't give him any notice, as he had hoped.

The woman at the gate took his ticket from him and smiled that fake 'I'm smiling, but I hate this job' smile. She wore a blue uniform with a scarf tied around her neck that accented her round breasts, which Kellerman stared at with admiration.

"Have a nice trip to Boston, Mr. Reynolds," she said with a slight Virginian drawl. "Thank you for flying US Air."

After boarding, Kellerman sat in a window seat on the Boeing 737. An empty middle seat separated him from an elderly woman reading a romance novel that commanded her full attention. Kellerman felt his body melt into the soft back of the seat. He knew he'd be home free once off the ground and the thought of Ridder and Sykes sweating out the police investigation pleased him. They deserved it, the assholes.

Staring out the window as the plane taxied to the runway, he pondered whether he should buy a BMW or Lexus after he found the gold. Hell, he'd have enough money to buy both cars. He reached in his bag under the seat, took out the small leather journal and flipped through the pages as the plane began to position itself for takeoff. Then he read the lead article in the Tribune again. As US Airways flight 3416 lifted off, Kellerman drifted off to sleep trying to calculate the value of the gold he would soon find.

*        *        *        *

While Rick Kellerman flew across northern Virginia, Sykes and Ridder drove Sykes' black Monte Carlo into a long term parking space at Dulles International Airport. With only a bag each, they quickly made it through the busy airport corridors to gate 35, and onto their plane.

Within minutes of sitting down in their assigned seats, a female voice came over the intercom. "Welcome aboard US Airways flight 1684, nonstop service to Boston. We should be arriving in Boston at our scheduled time of 2:50."

Sykes looked around at the nearby passengers, each still scurrying to shove oversized carry-on bags into the remaining spaces in the overhead compartments. The air in the cabin was heavy and getting hotter, but it didn't bother Sykes. He leaned closer to Ridder to his right and smiled.

"So tell me how you found out where Kellerman was going."

Ridder looked at Sykes and couldn't tell if he was looking straight at him or out the window because of Sykes' lazy eye. He rolled his eyes and laughed a breath. "I called all the airlines that fly from Charlottesville to Boston. I made sure I was talkin' to some bimbo. Took a bunch of calls 'til I found one. Then I told her that Leo Reynolds was my brother and was on one of their flights and I was supposed to pick him up in Boston. Except I couldn't remember the flight information and it was his wedding day and all. Most of 'em wouldn't tell me jack, but this idiot almost started to cry 'cause a similar thing happened on her pathetic wedding day, and sure enough, that was the airline he was usin'. Stupid bitch."

Sykes nodded his head, amazed with Ridder's conning ability.

"That asshole's got a stopover in Philadelphia so he'll arrive in Boston after us. I can't wait to see the look on his face when he gets a load of us!"

# CHAPTER 5

▼

The police station hummed with the well-tuned precision of a marching band, though it seemed overly frenetic, chaotic. Ringing phones and constant talking, accented by frequently raised voices, permeated the room.

The phone on Ditchman's desk rang. "Ditchman."

"Ditch, Henry Joseph. Good news, we lifted a nice clean print out of the van. We're running it through our files right now. Seems like this could be your lucky day, my friend."

Ditchman smiled as he hung up the phone. He turned to his partner. "They lifted a print from the van."

Hammond looked up from a stack of reports on his desk and nodded. "Good. I finished going through all the burglary reports. No more restaurant connections."

Captain Jack Conrad walked over to them and sat on the edge of Hammond's desk. "Okay, whatta ya got?" he asked. He was a tall, burly man with strapping arms and a leathery, bald head, who had a reputation for being imperturbable. Ditchman admired that in him. For seven years, Conrad had been Ditchman's superior; not once did Ditchman second-guess the fifty-five year old Captain's leadership or instinct. He had seen his share of criminal activity during his thirty-three years on the force, and had grown wise by following a simple motto which he constantly told his rookies: The best detective knows what to ask and when to shut his trap and listen. God gave you two ears and one mouth—use them in that proportion. Ditchman had been schooled in the same philosophy.

"We have the maitre d' from the 1776 in a cell. He confirmed our restaurant ring conspiracy theory, but doesn't know the guy running it. No prints from the house, but Williams found some hair. It'll be good enough to put them at the scene. Joseph's running a print lifted from a stolen van we think was used to do the job last night. A kid from the neighborhood believes that was the van she saw."

Conrad nodded his head a few times, but said nothing. Hammond looked at Ditchman and raised his eyebrows.

"Good, keep me up to speed. The faster you wrap this up, the sooner I get the press off my tail. This Hutchinson's like a celebrity around here because of being a Lee and finding that Civil War ship," Conrad said, then went back to his office.

Ditchman's phone rang.

"Ditch, Henry Joseph. Bingo. Print belongs to one Richard P. Kellerman. We picked him up a few years ago for B and E and possession of cocaine. He's also got a prior for A and B."

"Good work, Henry. Any address?"

"Sorry. No luck there, Ditch. Last known is for a downtown apartment building that's been demolished."

Ditchman hung up the phone and repeated the information to Hammond.

"Well, then let's take his mug shot and find out what the street knows. Who knows, maybe our luck will continue," Hammond said.

"When are you going to learn that a good detective makes his own luck," Ditchman smiled.


Ridder and Sykes stood in the crowded waiting area next to Gate 8 so they would not be in the direct line of view of the passengers coming through the adjacent Gate 6. Despite their efforts to be inconspicuous, people still looked at them. Ridder wore stone washed jeans, his usual rattlesnake boots, and a long sleeved black shirt that had big Harley Davidson logos on the front and back. His long, black hair was oily and in need of a washing. Sykes wore brown Dickies work pants and an armpit-stained, white polyester blend collared shirt, which, because he wore it tucked into his Dickies, gave him some relief from the Confederate flag belt buckle sticking into his belly. He had not shaven for a few days so a scraggly beard was taking shape on his bulbous face.

Ridder looked at his watch. "Any minute now. Remember what I said, Buster. We grab him without makin' a scene."

Sykes finished the hot dog he was eating. "Yeah, I got it. No problem, Carson. Look, here they come."

They stretched their necks and stared intently at the mass of people exiting Gate 6. A family of five, lead by a father who looked like he was about to lose his temper, made a big commotion as they argued about whether to get something to eat now or later. Despite having a tall blonde with a low cut shirt distract his attention for more than a second, Ridder tried to scan the entire crowd in order not to miss one person. Soon, the number of people exiting the gate began to dwindle.

"Shit! He ain't on this flight!" Sykes cursed.

"There he is." Ridder said in almost a whisper after he recognized Kellerman's crewcut hairdo.

Kellerman walked right past them without even noticing because was checking the signs on the ceiling pointing out the various airport locations.

"Looks like he changed his looks," Sykes stated the obvious as they began to follow Kellerman, "Wonder why he shaved clean?"

Ridder glanced around and saw a good spot ahead with no authorities around. He poked Sykes with his elbow. They began to jog, then slowed their pace as they reached Kellerman. With Sykes on Kellerman's left side, Ridder grabbed him by the elbow and pulled him near a large concrete column away from the walking traffic.

"Hey, Kellerman," Ridder said in a sarcastic tone. "Fancy meetin' you here. Betcha didn't expect to see your ol' pals here, did ya, you little shit?" Ridder increased the pressure on Kellerman's arm.

"What the fuck do you think you're doing, Kellerman?" Sykes demanded, his one eye looking at Kellerman, the other looking at Ridder.

Kellerman tensed his face. "What the fuck do you think *you're* doing? I'm just going to see my grandmother in Boston. Remember, you told me to lay low." He glared at Ridder. There was no hiding the hate between them.

"Where's the journal, Kellerman?" Ridder demanded, his black eyes not blinking.

"What journal?"

"Bullshit! We know you took it. Now hand it over or I'll beat it out of you!" Ridder scowled as he grabbed Kellerman's arm again.

"Fuck off!" Kellerman yanked his arm free, then threw his duffel bag at Ridder and ran.

Ridder rifled through the bag. "Shit! He must have it on him."

They looked up and saw Kellerman thirty feet ahead of them trying to cut his way through the throng of people in the terminal.

As soon as there was enough room among the people walking, Kellerman began running down the long corridor. No one paid any attention to him as running through an airport was common for those late for a flight. He looked back and spotted Ridder and Sykes. They, too, began to run.

Sweat began to stain Kellerman's shirt as he frantically looked around for a place to hide.

As he turned a corner, he abruptly stopped and looked around, trying to figure out what to do. His breathing became heavy and short and his mind raced in confusion. With a trembling hand, he quickly pulled the journal from the inside pocket of his jacket.

Holding the journal by his leg, he walked right into a young man entering the Beantown Tavern and Grill. As the young man looked up in surprise, Kellerman dropped the journal into his open duffel bag without the young man noticing.

"Pardon me," Kellerman said without stopping, then looked back at the corner and saw Ridder and Sykes twenty feet away.

When he passed through the automated door to the outside, he sprinted across the road into the first row of a parking garage. He felt himself beginning to hyperventilate as his mind raced for a solution. He crawled under the third car, a green Chevy Suburban, in the first row and held his breath as he peered out from under the SUV. The smell of motor oil dazed him for a second, but he came to his senses when Ridder and Sykes ran by him. Using his arms to pull his body, Kellerman crawled on his belly from under the Chevy and crouched behind the back wheel while he tried to catch his breath and count to ten. When he hit ten he picked his head up and looked through the dirty, back windows of the Suburban. He squinted his eyes and moved his head slightly to find them, but saw nothing.

The feeling of swallowing his tongue returned. He stuck his head three inches out from the end of the Chevy and looked with one eye. For a moment he didn't see them, then he realized they were slowly checking under each car at the far end of the row, three hundred feet away, and working back toward him. Kellerman slowly pulled his head back and looked over his other shoulder. The Isuzu Trooper next to the Chevy had pulled into the space right up to the five-foot wall. He would have to climb on the bumper to get around it. He quickly glanced back around the corner of the Chevy. Ridder and Sykes were twenty feet closer. Kellerman realized he would have to make a run for it. Going over the wall would make him stick out and possible slow him down. All he had to do was make it around two cars and then across the street. Back on the terminal side of the street he could blend in with the people getting dropped off and picked up. Maybe he could even catch a taxi if one pulled up in time.

He took a deep breath, looked around the corner of the Chevy, saw Ridder and Sykes looking under cars at the same time, and realized he wouldn't have a better chance to escape. He took two quick steps from behind the Chevy, then lost his nerve. But it was too late—his body had frozen. He quickly looked down the row and met the enraged eyes of Carson Ridder.

"Kellerman!" Ridder yelled as he began running.

Kellerman ran back across the street and through the automatic doors. He opened the stairwell door immediately inside the terminal and raced up the concrete stairs.

A yellow taxi skidded to a halt as Ridder ran in front of it.

"Watch it, asshole," the driver yelled in a Boston accent. Ridder saluted him with his middle finger as he ran past the car.

"He's taking the stairs!" Sykes pointed as he ran around two businessmen pulling their suitcases on the sidewalk.

When they reached the enclosed stairwell, Ridder put his hand across Sykes' chest to stop him. Ridder listened.

Kellerman ran through the door at the top of the stairwell, stopped and took a deep breath to fill his burning lungs. The bright sun made him squint as the roaring thunder of jet engines and open air confused him for a second. With nothing but the open tarmac between the parking garage and Boston Harbor, the wind swept across the top level as if the garage stood on the edge of the water, not a half-mile away. Kellerman looked out at the Harbor, then at the Boston skyline, and then back at the full lot and immediately realized coming here was the worse thing he could have done. He had no options but to once again hide among the cars. He ran down the first row and ducked behind a white Toyota Camry parked five spaces from the stairway door. His head nervously twitched back and forth with growing paranoia, and then he saw it. Next to the door hung a large, silver metal box with a round speaker in the middle above a white button. Above the box an orange sign read "Emergency Assistance Intercom."

For a brief moment Kellerman let himself think he would be safe. He could easily make it back to the intercom. But what if they were coming up the stairs? He didn't know if they had followed him. Wouldn't they check the other floors first? What if he left his hiding spot and they opened the door while he was standing there completely exposed? The thought of Ridder's rage overcame his desperate desire to race to the intercom. But if they hadn't followed him up the stairs he could easily call for help. Hell, he could walk right out of here.

Just as he had convinced himself to stand up, the door crashed open. He quickly ducked and felt his heart begin to race again. Though the muscles all throughout his body shook uncontrollably, and he suddenly felt the contents of his stomach rising to his throat, he realized he couldn't just sit there and let them find him—he had to get moving. He crawled to the end of the row at the edge of the parking garage, crouched between a silver Honda and the four-foot cement wall and tried to look under the cars to see their feet. Suddenly, Kellerman felt like a cornered animal. Maybe they'll miss me, he thought as he slithered under the last car in the row, a Subaru Outback. Staying completely still, he strained his ears to hear any footsteps, but heard nothing but the wind blowing across the parking garage and a jet plane rumbling down the runway.

Kellerman tried to stay put, but not knowing where Ridder and Sykes were gnawed at him so much he crawled out from under the Outback to look around. Just as he looked up a giant black boot slammed into his face, splattering blood against the Subaru's door.

"Here's the bastard." Ridder leaned down and picked up Kellerman by his collar as blood poured out of his nose and his eyes rolled back into their sockets.

"Where's the journal, asshole?" Ridder shouted in his face, strings of saliva engulfing Kellerman's face like a spider's web.

"I don't know what you're talking about," Kellerman blurted as he struggled to breathe, his left eye looking like raw sirloin.

"Bullshit!"

Ridder's right fist smashed into Kellerman's stomach, forcing the remaining air in his lungs to burst from his mouth as if he were throwing up.

"Fuck you, Ridder," Kellerman wheezed.

Ridder's eyes grew large and intense as he took in a deep breath and gritted his teeth. He held Kellerman by his shirt collar and rammed him into the four-foot high concrete wall at the edge of the garage. All the air in his lungs blew out in one exhale.

"Search him!"

Sykes reached into Kellerman's jacket pockets and behind his waist.

"It ain't on him."

"Where is it, Kellerman?" Veins bulged in Ridder's forehead as he yelled.

"Fuck you!"

Ridder let out a deep groan and hoisted Kellerman over the wall so that he dangled five stories above the pavement below.

"Whoa, whoa, Carson! Take it easy," Sykes pleaded as he grabbed Ridder's left arm.

"Last time. Where's the journal? You got two seconds to talk or you die." Ridder shifted his grip and Kellerman's eyes bulged.

"Okay, okay. Just don't drop me. I dropped it in some kid's bag."

"What kid?" Ridder demanded.

"Fuck if I know. Some kid I bumped into back inside when you were chasing me. Tall kid with blond hair. Now pull me back up!"

Ridder shook his head. "Stupid asshole."

Kellerman looked straight into Ridder's black eyes, drew in a breath, and spat blood in his face.

Ridder slowly grinned, then released his grip.

"Jesus Christ, Carson!" Sykes quickly looked over the wall and saw Kellerman's motionless, twisted body sprawled on the concrete five stories below, a dark pool of blood encircling his head.

Ridder stepped back from the wall and pulled out a red bandanna from his back pocket to wipe Kellerman's blood off his sweaty face. "Fuckin' douchebag."

"We gotta get out of here, Carson! There's gonna be cops all over this place now!"

Ridder grabbed Sykes' sleeve. "Relax, it'll look like the asshole jumped."

Sykes ran his hand over his bald head and looked around the parking garage. "Come on, Carson, we gotta go before the cops…"

Ridder grabbed Sykes' shirt and yanked him closer. "Not until we get what we came for. We gotta find that journal. I ain't leavin' without it and neither are you. Unless you want the one link to two deaths just sittin' out there for the cops to find and nail your ass seein' that it has all three of our fingerprints all over the fuckin' thing?"

Sykes swallowed and shook his head.

They ran down the same staircase and then slowly walked back into the terminal. When they reached the intersection with the long corridor that led to the gates, Ridder stopped.

"We had him in our sights until he turned this corner." He looked around. "Then he bumped into that kid. You better pray he's still around."

Matt Gallagher took a long, full drink from the bottle of Sam Adams, then wiped his mouth with the back of his hand. The bar was empty except for the few patrons at the back waiting for him.

"Pressures on, Matt. Try not to choke, because we've spend too much time here already," his friend, Tucker, said.

Matt stood there in his khaki shorts, green polo shirt and leather boat shoes. He dried his right hand on his shorts and ran his left hand through his thick, short blond hair while trying to ignore Tucker's heckling.

"Okay, let me get this straight." He stepped away from the white line. "If I throw any double, I win?"

His opponent, a fortyish man in a charcoal-gray pinstriped business suit, nodded and smiled. "Any one, doesn't matter which."

"All right." Matt stepped back to the line and held the blue and yellow tailed dart in front of his face. He breathed slowly as he stared at the board, then pulled his hand back and let the dart fly.

Tucker pumped his fist in the air. "Double ten! Finally, we can get out of here."

The man in the suit stretched out his hand. "Good game. You sure you never played darts before?"

Matt grinned and shook his hand. "Sorry, I hustled you. I minored in it in college, plus this is usually how I kill time instead of waiting for my luggage."

"Congratulations." The woman behind the bar handed Matt a white tee shirt with the word Boston printed in neon purple on the front.

"Thanks," he said, somewhat embarrassed by the prize, which he threw to Tucker.

"Here you go, Tuck. Welcome to Boston. Now you can throw away that rag you've been wearing."

Tucker McKinney looked at the shirt and winced. "Thanks, but this one is more my style." He tugged at his old, gray tee shirt that had dozens of small holes in it from being washed hundreds of times. Unlike his friend, Tucker rarely concerned himself with his appearance, as evident by his white shorts that had blue and brown dried paint on them, and the beat up, old running sneakers that had knots in the laces and could not be pulled tight.

With the exception of his cut physique, he was the negative of Matt. He was shorter, about five-nine with shoes on, had dark skin, curly black hair that was in need of a cut, and brown eyes that women always seemed to whisper about at parties.

"And also for winning five games in a row," the woman said with a smile, "you're also automatically entered into our sweepstakes for a home-installed replica of an English pub, including a mini bar, stools, and professional dart board." She handed Matt a pad of paper. "Just complete the entry form."

"Does the bar come fully stocked?"

"Oh, I forgot. It comes with a year's worth of top shelf liquor."

"No beer?"

The woman frowned, "I'm not really sure."

"Just fill it out, and let's get going," Tucker said. "We've waited long enough; our bags must be ready by now."

Matt quickly scribbled out the form and handed it back to the woman, who tore the form off the pad.

"Ready to rock and roll, my friend." Matt looked at his watch. "We've got plenty of time. I told Annie we'd be there by six. With no traffic at the bridge, we should have smooth sailing."

The two young men walked out of the bar into the noisy corridor filled with frantic parents trying to keep track of their excited children, befuddled tourists looking for some clue as to how to get out of the large airport, and stern-faced businessmen who showed nothing but contempt for less experienced travelers who slowed them down as they raced through the airport with only minutes to spare to catch the next commuter flight.

Tucker looked at Matt. "Where do we get our bags?"

"Downstairs."

They found the carousel that carried their flight's luggage and stood together watching bag after bag go around as the baggage pickup area became overly crowded with more travelers doing the same. While people pushed to get a better view of the luggage, Matt and Tucker held their ground until, without warning, a large man in a black Harley Davidson shirt bumped into Matt's left shoulder.

Matt stumbled but did not let go of his carry-on bag.

"Excuse me!" Matt said sarcastically.

The large man turned and glared at Matt, then walked away.

"What a jerk," Matt said loudly to make sure the man heard him.

"Matt, come on, let it go. Here's our last bag." Tucker quickly grabbed a large duffel bag from the carousel. "Where to now?"

"My car's in the garage across the street. God, I hope it's still there. I still haven't got the locks fixed. But then again, new locks would probably cost more than the shitbox's worth, right?" Matt grabbed his two bags and led the way down the corridor. They did not see the man in the Harley tee shirt and another man walking twenty feet behind them.

"Hey, thanks again for flying down to see me play. I really appreciated that." Tucker looked at his friend to make sure he knew he was sincere.

"The NCAA lacrosse all-star game at Hopkins? The mac-daddy, the grand Pooh-Bah of lacrosse games? Are you kidding? I wouldn't have missed it for anything. But the only reason you got to play was because I got injured in the Amherst game." Matt grinned.

"Yeah, right. You just keep telling yourself that," Tucker poked back.

"Seriously, I had a good time in Annapolis. It was good to meet your Dad, even if it was just for a second."

"Yeah, he's a real pal, especially when he's around, which is never," Tucker said.

"You complain your father is not enough in your life, and I want my old man to get the hell out of mine." Matt shook his head in disbelief.

Within a few minutes, they were in the parking garage. Neither noticed that the two men had followed them up the two flights and out onto the parking deck. Matt's black Volkswagen GTI was parked three rows away.

"This ought to cost you a pretty penny parking here." Tucker laughed knowing money was not a problem for Matt.

When Matt dropped his bags to open the car door, the two men rushed them and the big one grabbed Matt's carry-on bag. Being quick enough, Matt grabbed one handle of the bag and was brought chest to chest with the man in the Harley shirt.

"Hey, man, what the hell?" Matt yelled.

The smaller man grabbed Tucker by the left arm to pull him away, but Tucker rolled his right hand into a fist and swung at the man's face, hitting him square in the left eye socket. A popping sound echoed in the garage as the man collapsed to the cement.

"Give me the bag, asshole," the big man demanded, but Matt wouldn't let go despite being shoved around.

Tucker ran over to Matt's side, gritted his teeth, and let fly a punch to the big man's nose. The man stumbled back, and let go of the bag. He quickly regained his balance, and took a deep breath which enflamed his eyes. But as he was about to charge forward a siren echoed throughout the garage.

The smaller man grabbed the big man's arm and pulled him away. "Come on, Carson, let's get out of here."

As the big man struggled to pull his arm free, Matt and Tucker jumped into the Volkswagen. Matt started the car in an instant, slammed the gears into reverse, and gunned the accelerator just as the big man slammed his fist into the hood of the Volkswagen.

"Come back here, you fuckin' little puke!"

Though he was tempted to shift into first gear and ram the man in the Harley shirt, Matt's instincts told him to just keep going in reverse. Within a few seconds, he was at the end of the row of cars and far enough away to put the car in forward gear. As he pulled away, he looked back at the two men and flipped them the bird.

Neither said a word as they left Logan Airport, each trying to catch his breath and understand what had just happened.

Tucker finally broke the silence. "Welcome to Boston! Man, my first time to the city you've been bragging is the greatest in the world and we get mugged in the parking lot. Hellava place, Matt! What else do I have to look forward to?"

"Jesus, what was that guy's problem? I think that was the same guy who bumped into me at the baggage claim. Why'd he want my bag so badly? There's nothing valuable in it, just a bunch of crap that wouldn't fit in my other bag. And where the heck did you learn to fight like that?"

Tucker looked at his left hand and stretched it a few times. The knuckles were red. "Let's stop and get a six pack to split on the ride down. I need to calm down; I got adrenaline pumping through me like you wouldn't believe. And maybe we should also stop and buy a gun."

"Real funny, Tuck. Seriously, let's keep this between us. If we tell Annie, she'll just freak out and I really don't want to start the summer having to deal with that."

# CHAPTER 6

▼

Chatham was the eastern-most town of the Commonwealth of Massachusetts. Located at the elbow of Cape Cod, it had the distinction of being surrounded by water on three sides. To the south were the warmer waters of Nantucket Sound. Due east were the cold ocean waters of the Atlantic. To the north of Chatham was beautiful Pleasant Bay, a large body of water protected by a barrier beach.

With a population of close to seven thousand year round residents, mainly fisherman, local merchants, and retirees, Chatham's population increased four fold in the summer. Though the town was still a fishing village by nature—locals jested it was a drinking village with a fishing problem—those with commercial interests were increasingly populating Chatham. But regardless of the recent onslaught of real estate development and new stores, Chatham maintained its genuine look and feel of an old New England fishing village. Its residents were proud of their town's juxtaposition of modernization with antiquated beauty and style that maintained the town's seaside historical character. New homes took on the look of the older houses—weathered shingles and the traditional white trim remained the norm throughout the town.

The residents, both year-round and seasonal, understood why Chatham was so unique. It was this love of their special place and the mutual respect and admiration for the sea that allowed the locals and summer residents to coincide peacefully for the three summer months. For everyone who spent any time walking along Main Street in downtown Chatham, strolled along any of the seventeen miles of shoreline, caught a striped bass in the bay, or stood at the Chatham Lighthouse as the sun majestically glowed on the waters of what they called "The

Cut," they immediately knew there was no other place like Chatham. No one understood this love more than Annie Hopewell did.

But as she drove past familiar landmarks, she did not know how to feel. The demons of pain and abject emptiness she had anticipated were not there in full force yet. She remembered her summers here and wasn't devastated from the memories, though she felt herself trying to suppress her feelings. For four years that is what she had done; it was a natural reaction now.

She drove around the rotary onto Main Street, and tried to relax. The town seemed more crowded with tourists and vacationers than she remembered, especially for a beach day. When she was young, Main Street had always been barren on sunny days. She looked over at the Ben Franklin store, where her father used to buy her beach toys, and sighed. Further down Main Street, she noticed a new complex of shops and wrinkled her nose in disapproval.

She stopped at a crosswalk to allow a family on their way to the beach to cross and smiled when she heard the father said to his young son, "And you'll get to see all the fishing boats going out to sea." The memories began to flood back to her. She looked to the left and smiled when she saw the familiar pink awning with the brown bow atop the entrance to the Candy Manor, its screen door allowing the delicious smell of the chocolate and fudge to entice the weak of will to enter the store. She took a deep breath through her nose and smelled the sinful samples, as her mother had called them.

She looked to her right as she slowly drove past her favorite restaurant in Chatham, the Squire. With its weathered shingles and familiar sign of a seagull dressed as a fisherman, it was a local landmark of well-deserved fame. No other place kept a beat on the town's pulse much like the Squire. It served the best food on the lower Cape and the bar was *the* place to go at night.

A few buildings down from the Squire was her favorite store, the Mayflower, the treasure chest of goodies for children. She smiled as she thought of the first time she had gone by herself into the white store with green and white striped awnings and inviting front display windows. With money in hand, and too small to look over the counter, she had bought a coloring book of Cape Cod lighthouses, which she still had.

She drove along Main Street very slowly so she could detect any more change to her special place and was happy to see that everything seemed to be the way she remembered it. When she approached the Chatham Lighthouse, she took a deep breath into her lungs and felt her soul stir. Being back in Chatham made Annie wistful, yet the smell and taste of the salt air instinctively made her smile.

Clearing the last of the houses on the shoreline, she reached the parking lot in front of the white, eighty-foot Chatham Lighthouse. She looked at the Lighthouse and the adjoining Coast Guard station and nostalgia burst her face into a full smile. No other landmark meant the wonders of a Chatham summer and all its enchantments for a child more than the Lighthouse overlooking The Cut.

Annie got out of her Cherokee, walked over to the fence protecting the unstable bluff above the beach, and gazed at The Cut. A slight ocean breeze rippled her khaki shorts and white tee shirt. When she took the barrette out of her hair, the breeze caught her shoulder-length light brown hair and made a familiar humming sound in her ears.

At just under five-foot-seven, with broad yet delicate shoulders, Annie had the combined look of someone being both tender and strong. The taut muscles in her arms and slender legs, developed from years of diligent jogging, spoke of her athleticism, while the gentle curve of her cheekbones gave her face an innocent look. By anyone's standard, she was more than pretty, though she never really took the time to notice.

A few fisherman and a hundred or so sunbathers enjoyed the beach today. Directly in front of Annie, a group of three boys flew kites high into the air above the channel, while a local fishing boat tenaciously labored its way out of The Cut against the incoming tide under the late afternoon sun.

The scene was the same as it had been when she was last at the lighthouse, with the exception that the breach between North Beach and South Beach looked less tumultuous than four years earlier. South Beach even looked as if it had grown. But the smell of the saltwater and the sounds of the crashing waves and playful seagulls were the same, and so was the feeling she was enjoying.

Annie pulled herself away from the intoxicating vista and drove the long way to the house so she could wind around Stage Harbor. As she drove slowly over the wooden drawbridge on Bridge Street, the timbers made a familiar rumbling noise. A young boy, with fishing rod in hand, stared intently over the railing of the bridge. Annie remembered how her father had taught her to fish at the very spot and how proud he had been when she caught a Snapper Blue on her first cast.

She took a deep breath and was filled with the salty smell of the marshes as she looked over to her left at Stage Harbor. The masts of the many sailboats rocked back and forth with the sea breeze and guiding tide. Life was slower in the harbor than at The Cut.

After she passed the yacht club, she saw the cut to Nantucket Sound. Harding's Lighthouse stood out as a silent beacon of welcome. No longer an operational lighthouse, it was still widely photographed. She had a framed picture of the white lighthouse at sunset that had once hung in her mother's kitchen.

Annie had not anticipated the euphoria she felt when she pulled into the driveway of the Lockwood's house. After four lonely years, she was back in Chatham. She did not realize a smile had occupied her tanned faced since taking exit eleven off the Mid-Cape highway.

The Lockwood's house, a typical four bedroom Cape house that had weathered shingles and white trim, stood overlooking Oyster Pond. Behind it was the guest cottage, which the Lockwoods rented out each summer. It too was a Cape, with weathered shingles and white trim, but was much smaller than the main house. Three green Adirondack chairs sat on the porch that extended from the front of the cottage. To the right of the porch, set back a few feet, was a small garage which had two barn-like, gray doors that did not completely close together. Annie noted that nothing had changed in four years, and smiled.

As she parked the Cherokee on the white clamshell driveway, the Lockwoods came out of the main house to greet her.

"Annie Hopewell, you're here! Oh, welcome back, Annie!"

As Mrs. Lockwood hugged Annie, her delicate perfume made Annie feel overwhelmingly nostalgic.

Mrs. Lockwood was grayer than the last time Annie had seen her and her face was even more accented by a patina of fine lines, which she called her smile wrinkles. But she was as peppy as ever. She wore a flowered sundress and a pink sweater with little white sneakers. Her maternal look had always made Annie feel secure.

Annie turned to Mr. Lockwood, who wore a short-sleeve white collared shirt. He still kept his eyeglass case in his front pocket, though Annie had never seen him take off his half-glasses—they just always sat on the end of his nose with the black string draped around his neck.

"So what time are we going fishing, little lady?" He gave her a bear hug.

"Hi, Mr. Lockwood." Annie blushed. "I was hoping you'd ask me that."

"Now, Charlie," Mrs. Lockwood interrupted, "the dear child just arrived. She needs to unpack and relax. She can't be running off with you to go fishing just yet." She ended with a slight huff, which made Mr. Lockwood wink at Annie.

"Maybe tomorrow, hey kid?"

"Sure. I bet Matt and Tucker will want to go, too."

"Oh, that's right. When should we expect the boys?" Mrs. Lockwood asked.

Annie looked at her black runner's watch. It was just after five. "Within the hour."

Mr. Lockwood peered at Annie over his glasses. "So how do you know these boys that will be staying in the cottage with you?"

She smiled, understanding Mr. Lockwood's protective nature. "Matt and I met one summer at the fish pier. His family used to rent here."

"Oh, I remember when you worked there. Didn't you and Matt date for awhile?" Mrs. Lockwood asked.

Annie blushed. "For a short while."

"Where's Matt from?" Mr. Lockwood asked.

"Cambridge."

"And Tucker is a friend of Matt's?"

"They went to Connecticut College together. I can't tell you much more than that. I've never met Tucker."

"So what are your plans for summer, dear?" Mrs. Lockwood asked.

"I'm volunteering at the Cape Cod Retardation Center."

"Oh, you've got a heart of gold, Annie."

Annie walked around the Cherokee and opened the back hatch and a beautiful yellow lab jumped out.

"And this must be Fenway. I haven't seen her since she was a pup. Hey, girl, you wanna go fishing with Uncle Charlie?" Mr. Lockwood rubbed Fenway under her chin.

As Mr. Lockwood played with Fenway, Mrs. Lockwood gently touched Annie's elbow and looked her in the eye. "We are so glad you decided to come, dear." She hugged her again.

Annie pressed her lips into a smile. She didn't want to get choked up after such a wonderful day. "Thanks, Mrs. Lockwood. I'm glad I'm here, too."

Ditchman had a love-hate feeling towards those on the street that gave out information. He loved when they gave him information he could use, but he loathed having to turn to would-be criminals for information he used to think a good cop should discover for himself. But that idealism had been lost long ago. Now he knew it didn't matter what the source was as long as it helped solve the case.

They stopped in the south side of the city across the street from an old, seven-story apartment building that had dozens of broken windows and crumbling cement patches desperately holding together the façade where red bricks were missing. Hammond got out while Ditchman stayed in the car. A group of five young, truculent white men sat on the cracked concrete steps smoking cigarettes and drinking beer. When Hammond reached the curb, two of them quickly went inside the building.

"What brings you to our fine neighborhood, Detective?" said the scrawny one in a dirty white tank top. "We ain't done nothin' wrong. Least not as far as you know." He laughed.

Larsen "Lube" Dualty was a career criminal, and proud of it. He organized drug rings, money laundering, and racketeering operations. Though small scale compared to the activities of the big city criminals, Lube was good at what he did. The cops usually knew what he was up to, but could never put him away. Three times he had been arrested, three times he had been acquitted. The cops gave him the epithet Lube, not because he was good with cars, but because he was too slick to put away. The first case Hammond had worked on as a detective had ended with Lube going free.

"Got a minute? I need to talk to ya, Lube…alone." Hammond looked at the other two men.

Lube smirked. "Maybe, maybe not. Depends."

Hammond walked up two steps, causing the other two men to stand.

"Hey, be cool." Lube put his arms up to the side.

Hammond leaned closer and said calmly, "Depends, Lube? Depends? Depends, nothing. How about I pull out the search warrant I've got in the car and fill your name on it so I can take a look at what's going on inside?" He nodded at the building. "Judge Miner gave me a nice blank one and told me I could use it any time to bust drug pushing scum, I think is the way he put it. Now, I bet all you're doing in there is filling out your voter registration cards, right?" He paused for effect. "So how about we just talk? I just need some information about a guy."

After a few minutes, Hammond returned to the car with a grin on his face.

"Get anything?" Ditchman asked.

"Yup. Idiots should learn the law if they plan on breaking it. They fell for the old blank warrant routine. The only thing Lube knew was that Kellerman had a girlfriend who lives in the City View Trailer Park just outside the city. He thinks her name is Rene."

City View Trailer Park looked like a parking lot of abandoned aluminum rectangular boxes. With only a few feet between neighbors, the lucky ones had a small patch of burnt grass in front with a rusted, white garden wire fence. Older model cars and beat up children's toys, tricycles and plastic motorcycles littered the roads in the park. Two shirtless boys with dirty faces playing catch with a tennis ball on the side of the main road watched as they drove by. Hammond stopped the car at a trailer that had in front of it a manager sign dangling by one screw from a wooden post.

Ditchman knocked on the screen door and a bald, middle-aged man without a shirt on opened the door. His hairy gut jiggled as he swayed back and forth on his feet. "What can I do for ya?"

Ditchman showed the man his badge and explained they were looking for a woman named Rene who lived in the park. The manager excused himself for a short while, then returned with a cluttered black notebook.

"Yeah, Rene Campenol's only Rene we got based on what they tell me. But who the hell knows who's living here." He held up the tattered notebook. "She lives in number 79. Take your next left, halfway down on the right." He scratched his left armpit then closed the door.

Number 79 was a long way from being the most sordid home in the complex. A little garden with freshly planted flowers attempted to brighten the brick walk-way to the steps of the trailer. Ditchman looked at the welcome sign made out of small pine cones that was nailed next to the door.

After the third knock, a woman in her early thirties wearing a waitress outfit, an inch long ash precariously hanging from the cigarette in the side of her mouth, answered the door.

"Rene Campenol?"

"Yeah? Who are you?"

"I'm Detective Ditchman. This is Detective Hammond." He showed her his badge. "We have some questions for you about Richard Kellerman."

"Christ, everybody wants to know about Rick. Well, whatta ya want? He's done something stupid again, right? Sonofabitch." She took a long drag of the cigarette and savored the smoke as if it were medicinal.

"We just need to talk with him. Do you know where he is?"

"Came by late last night. Packed a bag, then left." She pursed her lips.

"Did he say where he was going?"

"Never does. He was talking nonsense about getting rich, or somethin'. Jerk was probably drunk again." She took another long drag of the cigarette then flicked the ash to the side of the door.

"You said, 'Everybody wants to know about Rick.' What do you mean?" Hammond asked.

"This morning, this guy, Sykes, calls me looking for Rick. Asked the same questions you did."

"Do you know this Sykes' first name?"

"I think it's Buster. Rick runs with him occasionally." She took another drag of her cigarette.

"What did you tell him?"

"Said he packed a bag and was talking about being rich."

Ditchman exchanged looks with Hammond. "Did he say where he was going?"

"I don't know. Was talking nonsense about some place, Cape Cod or something." She blew the smoke out. "Listen, you tell that prick when you find him to stop comin' 'round here late at night wakin' up my kids. Payin' me no respect." She shook her head.

"Can you describe this Sykes guy?" Hammond asked.

"I only met him once. Real winner. Short, stocky, and…oh, yeah, bald." She began to laugh. "Guy's got a forehead the size of the moon. A real loser, if ya ask me."

"Anything else?"

She sucked on the cigarette and shook her head.

"Thank you ma'am."

Back in their car, Ditchman looked at his partner. "Well, now we've got something. Call the station to do some fishing with the name Buster Sykes."

The Volkswagen pulled around the circular clamshell driveway and stopped behind the Cherokee. Matt and Tucker got out of the car and simultaneously stretched their arms and legs. A green sticker on the bumper of the Cherokee caught Tucker's eye: "Women belong in the House AND the Senate." He chuckled. Fenway ran around the house and cheerily greeted them by wagging her tail furiously and barking. They looked up and saw Annie standing on the front porch.

"Hey, Annie!" Matt walked over and gave her a big hug and kiss. "This is Tucker. Tucker, Annie."

Tucker looked at Annie's brown eyes and stuck out his hand. "Hi, Annie."

"Hi, Tucker." Annie shook his hand and smiled back.

"What a great dog. Matt didn't tell me you had a dog. What's her name?" Tucker rubbed Fenway's belly as she lay on her back in the grass.

"Fenway."

"As in Fenway Park?"

"My Dad was a big Red Sox fan."

"I'm an Orioles fan myself."

"That's okay. We won't hold it against you. Now, if you were a Yankees fan, you couldn't stay here." Annie kept a straight face until Tucker realized she was only joking and the two chuckled, knowing how much the Yankees were hated in Boston and Baltimore.

"Hey, sports fans," Matt chimed in, "let's get unloaded so we can get down to the Squire."

Annie laughed incredulously. "You don't want to waste any time, do you, Matt?"

As they stepped inside the front door with their bags, Matt and Tucker stood and looked around the inside of the cottage that would be their home for the summer. With hardwood floors made of wide, wooden barn boards, and the walls and classic trim tastefully painted white, the downstairs typified the classic Cape cottage.

"Wow, this place is great," Tucker said.

In the living room was a green and white striped couch and lobster trap coffee table in front of it and a wicker rocking chair to the side. Built-in bookshelves, full of well-read paperbacks and photos of Chatham scenes, lined two walls of the living room. A three-foot high built-in bookcase separated the living room from a small dining room, which contained a square harvest table, four wooden chairs, and a hutch that was built into the far corner. Off the living room was a small kitchen big enough just for the cutting board table that stood below a lone window next to the back door.

While Matt took his bags up the creaky wooden staircase to the first of the two bedrooms, Tucker followed Annie to the kitchen sink and poured himself a glass of water. He looked at Annie as she finished putting some of the canned foods she had brought with her into the cabinets and admired her toned body.

"So how did you meet Matt?" he asked even though he already knew the answer.

Annie stopped putting things away and looked at Tucker, admiring his curly, dark hair, chiseled cheekbones and the way his tee shirt hung nicely off his broad shoulders. He was taller than she was, but not too tall.

"We worked together down here before college. How'd did you guys meet?"

He took a big gulp of the water. "We played lacrosse together at Conn. Where'd you go to school?"

"Skidmore."

"Any plans for next year?" Tucker began to wash his glass out.

"I'm going on a cross-country trip before I decide on what I want to do." She looked down at her feet and unknowingly tucked her hair behind her ears. "I've been planning the trip for a while now. What about you?"

"I'll be teaching history at a boarding school in Maryland."

Annie looked up and smiled. "Really? Teaching? I've thought about that. I'd love to work with children with special needs. After I took a class on special ed., I worked for a semester at a local school for children with learning disabilities. I loved it."

"Well, there you go. You should do something you love."

Matt walked into the kitchen holding a small leather book, a look of puzzlement on his face. "Hey, Tuck, check this out."

"What's that?"

"It's an old diary or something. I found it in my bag. It's not yours, is it?"

Tucker shook his head. "Nope. Never seen it before. It's not yours?"

"I've never seen it before either."

Tucker took the journal and flipped though it. "Do you think that's what those two guys were after when they jumped us?"

"Two guys jumped you? Where? Are you okay?" Annie asked as she stepped toward Matt.

"Oh, it wasn't a big deal. We were going to my car in the parking garage at Logan and two jerks grabbed us. One of them tried to take my bag away from me."

"Did you call the police?"

Matt shook his head. "Annie, it was no big deal, really."

"How'd the diary get into your bag if it's not yours and it's not mine?" Tucker asked. "Maybe that's what they were after."

Annie walked over to Matt. "Why don't you read it and see what it says."

As Matt opened the small leather book he was interrupted by a knock and a "yoo-hoo" at the front door.

Annie walked to the living room. "Hi, Mrs. and Mr. Lockwood. Come on in."

The Lockwoods walked in carrying two large trays covered with dishtowels.

"Hi, boys. I'm Trudy and this is my husband, Charlie." The four shook hands. Mr. Lockwood had yet to smile. He stared at Matt and Tucker as if measuring them up.

After a few minutes of small talk about traffic and the weather, Mr. Lockwood changed the subject.

"So, how will you be spending your summer?"

Matt and Tucker looked at each other. Matt spoke first. "I'll be working at the Squire as a chef again. I start next week."

"And I'll be working at the fish pier."

Mr. Lockwood puckered his lips and looked at them over his glasses. "Good. Sounds like honest jobs. I was worried that you were planning on throwing wild parties all summer long." He smiled for the first time. "Now, more importantly, do either of you fish?"

Matt and Tucker let out a collective gasp of relief, then explained how much they loved to fish, but didn't have any gear.

Mr. Lockwood rubbed his hands. "Well, I'm sure we've got plenty. How about we go tomorrow morning? Annie?"

"Great. Yeah, let's do it," Matt said, then looked at Annie.

Annie smiled politely. "Thanks, Mr. Lockwood, but I think I'll pass this time."

"That's okay, young lady." He turned to the boys. "Boat leaves at five A.M. out front of our house. If you're late, I'll leave without you. That's the rule."

Tucker looked at Matt and mouthed "five A.M.?"

"I was hoping you two were fisherman so Charlie would have someone to talk fishing with. But for now, boys, no more talk about fishing. I just get bored after a while." Mrs. Lockwood giggled like a young schoolgirl, then walked over to the counter and took the towels off the trays. A cloud of steam and the aroma of corn and fish wafted through the room. "I knew you'd be hungry so we brought over dinner. We've got corn on the cob, and Striped Bass Charlie caught this morning." Mr. Lockwood nodded his head in pride.

Matt looked at Annie, realizing the Squire would have to wait.

"Thanks, but you didn't have to go to any trouble," Annie said.

"Oh, nonsense. Now boys, why don't you set the dining room table? And if you must talk about fishing, Charlie, do it in a whisper."

Matt put the journal down on the coffee table and took a place mat from Mrs. Lockwood.

The forensic tests on the hairs found at the Hutchinson house and the stolen van were in. There was a match between two sets of hairs found at both scenes. Hammond looked at Ditchman and raised his eyebrows. "Simple arithmetic, Ditch. Kellerman must have been in Hutchinson's house."

Ditchman looked at the report. "Not necessarily. You're assuming there was only Kellerman and one other person. What if there were more than two people? The hairs could be from two people other than Kellerman."

"But we've linked the van to the house. So Kellerman's linked to the house. We've just got to find out who's linked to Kellerman. Maybe it was this Sykes guy."

With the exception of a few hours of sleep, they had been working on the Hutchinson case for twenty hours. Hammond's eyes were red and watery and he kept stretching his hands above his head to shake off the effects of sleep deprivation.

Though Ditchman was just starting to catch his second wind, he, too, kept rubbing his eyes. He always told his younger partner that the highest probability of solving a homicide was within the first forty-eight hours. Thereafter, the odds were increasingly against you. They were almost halfway there.

"So, let's go pay a visit to Mr. Sykes' last known address," Ditchman said as he took the report back from Hammond.

William "Buster" Sykes was a convicted felon. Three years ago, a jury had sent him to Greenville for five years for breaking and entering and grand larceny, but he had been released for good behavior after having served half his sentence. His rap sheet certainly matched the present situation, with the exception of murder.

After driving for fifteen minutes, they found the address in a blue-collar neighborhood in South Charlottesville. Identical triple-decker houses, separated only by narrow driveways between them, and distinguishable only by the amount of brown, tan or mildewed white paint peeling from its siding, lined both sides of the two hundred-yard street.

It was trash pick-up day in the neighborhood so Ditchman and Hammond had to navigate around huge heaps of garbage bags, rusty bed springs, old kitchen appliances and cardboard boxes in the gutter and on the curb to reach a set of rotten wooden stairs that led to the address on Sykes's rap sheet.

As Ditchman knocked on the door, Hammond looked up and down the street at the garbage, much of which lay in the street from when the collectors failed to completely haul away the previous week's refuse.

"How can people generate so much garbage?"

After rapping on the door for a minute without a response, Ditchman gave up the effort.

As they were retreating back down the stairs, a screen door on the neighbor's house burst open with a clang as a woman dressed in a dirty pink bathrobe, curlers in her hair, and a cigarette dangling from her bottom lip stormed out on the porch.

"And don't think I won't divorce your fat ass, you good-for-nothin' sonofabitch," she yelled back through the door.

"Excuse me, do you know if this is where Buster Sykes lives?" Ditchman asked the woman as she sat down on the front step.

The woman looked up without showing any discomfort about her appearance. "Yeah, I think. What's it to ya?"

"Have you seen him lately?"

"What do I look like, mister, the neighborhood social planner?" the woman said then stood, flicked her cigarette off the porch and went back inside her house.

"Now what, Ditch? That was our last lead," Hammond said.

"No, we're still waiting for the restaurant's phone records to find the number that called the maitre d' last night."

"Yeah, but that's gonna take a while. What are we supposed to do in the meantime?"

"Pursue this Buster Sykes character."

When they arrived back at the station house, Hammond slumped down in his chair just as his phone rang. In a few seconds he was off and gave his partner a disappointing look. "Phone lead's dead. They traced the call to a stolen cell phone. Figures."

"Hey, Ditch, this just came in over the fax. Conrad said you should look at it," Pete Wilcox handed the paper to Ditchman.

Ditchman looked at the piece of paper as Hammond jumped to his feet to do the same.

"Boston police found the body of Richard P. Kellerman at Logan airport."

Hammond frowned. "There goes our only suspect."

"Maybe, but it might be a lead to who was with Kellerman in the van, and thus in the house."

Ditchman grabbed his phone and dialed the number on the fax, waited a few seconds then said, "This is Charlottesville Homicide Detective John Ditchman. Detective Marty O'Donahue, please." He stroked his mustache while waiting a minute. "Yes. Thanks, I got the fax…no, that was good thinking. We were looking for him…did anyone see anyone else at the scene with Kellerman? We're looking for another guy. Yes, but I can't get there tonight. There's no way my boss is going to okay that. I'll be there tomorrow as early as possible. I'll call you once our plans are set. Thanks."

Ditchman hung up the phone and looked at his partner. "Pack a bag, Rusty. We're going to Boston. The Boston detective I just spoke with thinks Kellerman was murdered."

Hammond grinned. "And you're thinking that where Kellerman was, we'll find Sykes?"

Ditchman rubbed his mustache then patted his partner on the back. "You're learning, Rusty, you're learning."

# CHAPTER 7

▼

Tucker sat up in bed, stared at the small digital clock on the dresser at the far wall of the small bedroom, and blinked his eyes into focus.

"Shit! Get up, Matt! We've got five minutes to make it to the boat."

Matt rolled over and pulled the pillow over his head. "Give me a couple more minutes," he groaned.

"Seriously, Gallagher, if we blow this one, Mr. Lockwood will be pissed. We can't just blow him off and sleep in. Not to mention, I really want to go fishing. So get up or I'll kick your ass!"

Tucker's threat worked. In less than three minutes they threw on shorts and tee shirts, ate a breakfast of peanut butter on an untoasted English muffin, slugged down a Pepsi, and ran to the shore of Oyster Pond in front of the Lockwood's house. When they got there, Mr. Lockwood was quietly laughing and bobbing his head.

"Not used to getting up this early, eh boys?" He wore faded Nantucket red pants, a navy blue flannel shirt, and old brown leather boat shoes. A weathered, tan baseball hat with a striped bass embroidered on the front adorned his head. "Wait here, I'll just be a minute."

He rowed a six foot white pram out to his boat and within minutes was back at the edge of the water in the twenty-four foot Boston Whaler. Charlie Lockwood had gone fishing so many times, he could do the routine without thinking. It was his way of relaxing.

While Mr. Lockwood readied the boat, Matt stretched his arms and legs and looked around. Though the sun had not yet broken the horizon, enough light was splashed across Oyster Pond so they could see the beautiful seascape. A tear-drop-shaped body of water, measuring about a quarter mile at its greatest width, Oyster Pond was as still as an undisturbed bucket of water. At the far end of the pond to the left, a small public beach blanketed the shore. On the far side, large, old estates, carefully situated far from each other to maintain maximum privacy, stood like guardians of the pond. The eastern side of the pond narrowed into the Oyster River, which led to Stage Harbor and Nantucket Sound.

As was the case around most of Chatham's shoreline, boats of every type, reflecting the two passions of Chatham residents during the summer, work and play, were moored in the pond and river. Large, pristine white crafts with flying bridges, utilized by their owners for nothing more than cruising the waters of Nantucket Sound and the Atlantic; small skiffs with large outboards awkwardly hanging on their transoms, their props tipped up to prevent unnecessary corrosion from the saltwater; Cat boats with naked masts; old, stripped down runabouts used by clammers; and small, flat boats with a poling platform erected above the engine made the waters by the shore look like a crowded boat yard. It was obvious which boats the wealthy homeowners along the water's edge owned, and which the people who parked their cars at the town landing at the end of the Lockwood's road owned.

Once Mr. Lockwood brought the Whaler to the shore, they loaded the fishing gear into the boat and proceeded up the river toward Stage Harbor without a word, Matt and Tucker copying Mr. Lockwood's stoic silence.

A slight cold permeated from the dwindling morning darkness as they glided on a plane through the calm water. Only patches of the usually ubiquitous fog that engulfed Chatham were present. Except for the fishermen and clam diggers, Chatham was still asleep. The only sound heard above the perfect morning silence was the well-tuned hum of the Whaler's two hundred horse power Yamaha engine.

After they cruised through the cut at Harding's Beach into Nantucket Sound, the sun began to rise and warmed them for the first time in the morning, despite the increasing speed of the Whaler.

Two hundred yards out of the cut, Mr. Lockwood turned the Whaler to port in front of a huge sandbar sticking five feet out of the water.

"I don't remember that being there," Matt called out as he pointed at the sandbar.

"Fisherman call it Widow's Bar. Developed last winter and has been growing ever since. Almost like an outer beach at low tide. Even sticks out at high tide. Two channels pushing tons of water and sand are feeding it. Fishermen hate it because it's another obstacle to avoid. Tourists love it because it's a great beach at low tide," Mr. Lockwood said loudly.

They rode along the back side of Monomoy Island, a seven-mile-long dune island, a declared National Wildlife Refuge. Other than the few other recreational fishing boats which made their way out to the fishing grounds, and the clammers, some on their knees looking for their keep in the shallows, others using bull rakes from work skiffs, the early morning and pristine landscape were theirs.

"Where we going?" Matt finally asked.

"Fishing," Mr. Lockwood replied. He smiled and added, "Off the southern end of Monomoy." He pointed at the island to his left.

Suddenly, Mr. Lockwood killed the throttle. Like a hunting dog he straightened his neck out and stared straight ahead. "Get your rods, boys, we've got action ahead. See those swirls? Look closely and you'll see some tails out of the water."

Matt and Tucker strained to see any movement ahead. When finally a large fish slammed its tail down in the water, both of them started to get excited and yell.

Mr. Lockwood pinched his lips and furrowed his brow. "Now I've been doing this for a long time, and I've seen very calm, experienced fishermen completely lose their cool out here and forget how to even hold a rod in his hands. What you need to do is relax, don't panic, those fish will be here for a while. They're probably feeding on sand eels. You don't want to spend your whole time out here untangling your line, so take a deep breath, boys, and let's go catch us some fish. Matt, why don't you take the bow position."

By nine o'clock the sun was warming the air; Annie looked up at the sun over the Lockwood's house, then reached down and patted Fenway, who wagged her tail twice, but did not lift her head off the porch floor.

Annie sat in an Adirondack chair on the porch, her bare feet pulled up against her legs on the seat. Her hands reached around her tan legs and held the leather journal as she flipped through the pages again and again, rereading some sections. Occasionally, she looked up at the sun rising into the sky over the Lockwood's house and the beauty of the morning made her feel warm inside. She never had to wonder why her parents had loved Chatham so much.

A few minutes later, the fishermen proudly walked around the corner of the Lockwood's house. Matt held a fifteen-inch Bluefish by its gill.

"Looks like you guys had some success. That's a good looking Blue, Matt. Perfect size for eating. Any luck, Tucker?"

"Mr. Lockwood took us right to them. We all caught a bunch of great size Stripers and Bluefish. What an awesome morning. You should have come with us, Annie. The fishing was unbelievable. All top water action."

Annie nodded. She used to love fishing in the mornings off the rips of Monomoy. Nothing beat the feeling of being out on the ocean when the orange and red sun peaked above the horizon and lit up the waters with fire. She had gone many times with her father and Mr. Lockwood and had become quite skilled at landing even the largest of cows on ultra light tackle regardless of the time of day or movement of the tide. But she knew she wasn't ready to do again just yet.

"Maybe next time." She forced a smile.

"Thanks again, Mr. Lockwood. We had a great time," Tucker said, extending his hand in gratitude.

Mr. Lockwood pumped Tucker's hand and grinned. "You boys did pretty well out there. That was definitely one for the memory books. Where did you learn to handle a boat like that, Tucker? I took you for a landlubber, but I'll tell you, I was impressed with how you handled her when I had that keeper on and we were drifting towards Monomoy."

"Growing up in Annapolis I spent a lot of time out on the Chesapeake Bay." Tucker looked down at the groove his foot had been making in the ground.

"The sea's in his blood. Tuck's dad was in the Navy," Matt interjected.

"A naval man; I knew there was a reason I like you, son. What's your father do now?"

"He used to teach at the Naval Academy. Now he works with the State Department. They send him from ship to ship to do research work."

"Ship to ship, eh? Ever heard of the battleship *North Carolina*?"

Tucker paused and tilted his head in thought. "Sure, which one? The one built after the War of 1812? The Confederate ironclad? The one which was the first to launch an airplane while underway? Or the *North Carolina* that fought in the Second World War?" He smirked. "I wrote my senior thesis on Alfred Thayer Mahan's theories of naval power."

"And he loves to show off how smart he is," Matt jested.

Mr. Lockwood bobbed his head up and down and proudly smiled. "Well, I'm impressed, Tucker. But the one I'm talking about was the last one."

"Didn't it take part in the invasions of Iwo Jima and Okinawa?"

"That's right. I served on her for three years. But that's a story for another day." He patted Tucker on the shoulder then looked at Annie and Matt. "The man knows his history and his ships. Listen, I need to go see my beautiful, young bride before she never lets me go fishing ever again. Annie knows the waters around here and she's a great captain, and you've proved you know how to handle a boat. Take this key. I've got a spare." He tossed the red and white buoy key ring to Tucker. "You kids can take the Whaler out whenever you'd like as long as you let me know when you're taking her and fill up the gas. Just leave a note if you have to."

All three said thank you simultaneously in a tone of amazement. After Mr. Lockwood entered his house, Matt jumped up.

"Sweet! Mr. Lockwood just totally hooked us up for the summer because of you and your nautical savvy." He whacked Tucker on the shoulder. Tucker looked at Annie and smiled, which Annie returned.

"Hey, I was looking at this old journal you found in your bag, Matt." Annie held it up. "Have you read it yet?"

"I flipped through a couple of pages last night. Something about a ship and a big storm or something."

"There's a bit more to it than that. I read it while you guys were out on the boat. It's a pretty incredible story."

They each sat down in an Adirondack chair. Fenway got up and stuck her nose under Tucker's arm, prompting him for a pat.

"Hey, before you tell us, let me grab some beers," Matt said.

"Matt, it's not even noon yet!" Annie said, prompting Matt to roll his eyes.

"Give me a break, Annie. You're starting to sound like my old man."

"You don't think it's too early to start drinking?" Annie asked, a look of concern on her face.

Matt stopped and put his hands on his hips. "No, and I don't think it's anyone's place to tell me when I can or can't have a drink. I mean, come on Annie, live a little. I plan on living it up this summer. God knows if we'll ever get the chance again. Tuck?"

"No, I'll pass, thanks."

Matt returned with two bottles of Budweiser. "So what's the deal with this thing?"

Annie shook her head then sat forward and held the journal in front of her. "I think it's a diary of a Confederate sailor named William J. Randall, who was shipwrecked."

Matt grabbed the journal out of Annie's hands. "Let me see that."

"Go ahead, Matt, read it yourself." Annie sat back in the chair and crossed her arms. "Read aloud so Tucker can hear it. Skip the first half of it, it's just about how he became a sailor and the first part of the trip. Start with the entry of October 25."

Matt opened the small journal and flipped through until he found the spot.

"October 25, 1863. Back in Virginia after long travel through the North. Safe now to write account. On September 15, during a hurricane, the *CSS Argo* ran aground."

"*Argo?*" Tucker said. "That's a strange name for a Confederate ship. They used to name their ships after southern places, like the *Alabama*, the *Virginia*. The *Argo* was the name of the ship Jason and the Argonauts sailed in search of the Golden Fleece."

Matt cracked a second beer. "So what?"

"They were a bunch of heroes. Guys like Heracles, Orpheus. They sailed on the *Argo* to the edge of the world, a place called Colchis. They had to go through all these tough challenges to get there."

Annie sat forward and tucked her hair behind her left ear. "And what, you think the Confederates called this ship the *Argo* because it was looking for some golden fleece?"

Tucker threw up his hands. "I don't know. I was just telling you about the name."

"Yeah, right, you're just trying to impress Annie by showing off that brilliant mind of yours. You're so full of crap, McKinney."

Tucker flipped Matt the bird and smirked at him.

"Well let's find out more about this *Argo*." She walked into the living room and opened her laptop computer on the coffee table.

"Tucker, could you plug this in for me, please?"

Tucker plugged the cord into the phone jack and within seconds Annie was ready.

"Are you going to surf the Internet?" Matt asked.

Annie shook her head and tucked her hair behind her ears. "I tried getting a connection earlier, but it didn't work down here. But it doesn't matter. I'm going to a better source." She paused while setting up the right file. Matt and Tucker waited for the answer. The computer beeped again. "My Godfather, Albert Nylan. He's an English professor at Harvard."

Annie began to type.

Dear Albert,

I hope all is going well for you. I am in Chatham for the summer. Two friends and I rented a house near the water. It's been wonderful. I was wondering if you would settle a little argument we are having about a ship called the *Argo*. I know the myth about Jason and the Argonauts. Is there a ship in American history with the same name? If so, do you know anything about it? Also, how could I find out about a Confederate soldier named William J. Randall? Would you mind checking with some of your friends at Harvard? You can either email me or reach me at Orr, Williams, Cousy, Russell, Orr, Yaz, Yaz. Thanks!

Love, Annie.


Matt gave Annie a quizzical look. "What's with all the Orr, Williams, Yaz stuff?"

"When I was younger, my father and Albert used to throw out an athlete's name and the other would try to guess his jersey number. It got pretty competitive, but was always a lot of fun. And then we all just started using it whenever we had to remember a phone number. Pretty effective, actually." The nostalgia made her smile.

"Lynn." Matt grinned.

"Oh, real tough one, Matt. Fred Lynn, 1975 Rookie of the Year and MVP, first player every to do that, and he wore number 19." She smiled. "Why don't you finish the rest of the entry, smart guy."

Matt opened the journal and read. "Before the crew could abandon ship, the *Argo* was broadsided by a rogue wave. I was the only one to make it to the life boats. I found Captain Barnett in the water. He was badly hurt. Before he died, he told me what our mission was and that I had to remove the ship's quarterboard and retrieve the gold so neither would be found by the enemy."

Matt's head jerked up. "Holy shit, gold!"

"Just keep reading," Annie said as she pushed Matt's shoulder.

Matt continued. "After waiting on the beach for the storm to die, I returned to the half sunk *Argo*, destroyed the quarterboard, but could only retrieve a portion of the gold before the waves completely destroyed the *Argo*. I now doubt I can deliver the gold for it is too dangerous to return north. Once the war is over, I will return."

Matt looked up. "This is unbelievable."

"Keep going, Matt. What else does it say?" Tucker said.

"Then there's this poem." Matt continued.

"At the elbow,

An afternoon of sand.

See no life

Until the guiding hand.

Stand against it,

Facing first morn',

A year to uphold

The duty sworn."

"What the heck does that mean? Why didn't the guy just write it in plain English?" Matt scoffed.

"Let me see it." Tucker grabbed the journal from Matt. "The guy probably wanted an easy way to remember where he hid the gold without having to write it down, or he didn't want someone to figure it out in case he lost the journal. I say we figure it out. 'At the elbow.' That could mean anything."

"You're not reading it right." Annie took the journal from Tucker. "It says, 'At the elbow, an afternoon of sand.' You have to consider the entire sentence." She looked up from the journal and mouthed the words elbow and sand.

"Sand like in the beach?" Matt asked. "But what's an afternoon of sand. Bucket of sand, a patch of sand, a bathing suit full of sand. I've never heard of an afternoon of sand."

"Afternoon is a reference of time, four, five hours, right? So maybe it means walking on a beach for that long," Annie said.

"So what beach could you walk on without seeing life? I assume that means people, right?" Tucker asked.

No one answered him for a minute, then Annie said, "Monomoy. That's what it's talking about. Think about it. Monomoy is an island of sand that sits at the elbow of Cape Cod." She made the shape of Cape Cod with her arm as if she were showing off her biceps.

"No way." Matt waved his hand in the air as if to bat down Annie's answer. "First of all, Monomoy's actually two separate islands, North and South Monomoy. So you can't spend that long walking on it because you'll end up in the water that separates them. And there's no church on Monomoy."

Annie laughed. "A church?"

"Yeah, that's what 'guiding hand' means. Come on, Tuck, back me up here."

Tucker shrugged his shoulders.

"Matt, the 'guiding hand' is the lighthouse at the end of Monomoy, which used to be one not two islands. In fact, it used to be connected to…"

Before Annie finished her thought, the sound of a car driving on the broken clamshells interrupted her. Mrs. Lockwood stopped her La Baron in front of the cottage's porch.

"Could you kids be dearhearts and give me a hand bringing in my groceries?"

Annie put the journal on the porch under the Adirondack chair. "We'd love to help, Mrs. Lockwood."

# CHAPTER 8

▼

Buster Sykes stood in the doorway of the red brick North End apartment building with a clear view of both ends of the narrow street. With the exception of Carson Ridder sauntering toward him with a cigarette hanging from his lip, the street was empty. Sykes looked again in both directions, then casually nodded to Ridder.

Within thirty seconds, Ridder had the two-door, black Buick Regal open and running. Having stolen his first car at age thirteen, there were few cars he could not jack in under a minute. To be sure, he always went after older model cars, ones without alarms, like the Pontiac he had stolen the day before from the airport.

"You get the shields?" Ridder asked without taking his eye off the red Explorer in front of him as they entered the Callahan Tunnel heading into East Boston.

"Yeah, at some army navy store. They look fake if you look real closely."

"They'll do. How 'bout a piece?"

Sykes pulled a Glock .9mm from his waistband. "I asked some guys hanging out on some corner. They tell me to wait ten minutes. And sure enough, Carson, one of them returns with it. God, I can't believe they wanted a hundred bucks for the thing. Back home I could get me a piece for twenty-five if I wanted to. Right, Carson?"

"Shut up and give it to me and give me the rest of the cash. Where'd you dump the car?"

Sykes handed him the gun and a roll of bills. "Found a parking garage a few blocks away after I dropped you off. Looks like one of them long term places and there weren't anybody around that saw me." He grinned, then looked at his polyester blue button down shirt and gray rayon pants, then at Ridder, who wore a white tee shirt under a black sport jacket and jeans. "You sure we look okay?"

Ridder glared at Sykes. "Trust me. The cops probably shop at the same dumpy second hand store we got these from. Just relax."

After reaching the end of the tunnel, Ridder took the exit for Logan International Airport. At terminal B, he pulled up to the curb in the one space available and immediately frowned as a taxi double-parked to his left.

"Let me do all the talkin'. Just shut up."

"No problem, Carson."

The sidewalk was crowded with people hustling with their luggage to find the end of the long curbside check-in line. A black man in an airport uniform who was talking with an elderly woman looked over her shoulder at Ridder.

"Hey, buddy, you can't park there." He shook his hand back and forth. "Loading and unloading only. Your gonna have to…"

Ridder whipped out his wallet and quickly flashed the fake police badge attached to it.

"Police," he said like he had said it a thousand times.

The man nodded and went back to helping the woman.

The terminal was exceptionally crowded for the middle of the day and the Beantown Tavern and Grill was no different. It was packed with hungry, noontime travelers, most of who sat at tables eating their lunches. Ridder walked up to the bartender, a woman in her early thirties with big, frizzy, blonde hair and bright red lipstick, and checked out her tight designer jeans and clinging white oxford shirt with B.T.G. embroidered over her round, left breast.

She looked at Ridder and smiled, revealing big white teeth. "Hi. What can I get for you?"

Ridder adroitly flashed the badge. "I'm Detective Stevenson. This is Detective Gibbons. Boston Police."

Sykes nodded at the woman who nervously wrung a towel. The fake badge proved to be surprisingly efficacious.

"This about the suicide, murder, whatever it was, yesterday?"

"Were you workin' yesterday when it happened?" Ridder said with a straight face.

The woman nodded.

"We have just a few questions. We're lookin' for two young guys seen comin' out of here. One has blond, short hair, about six feet, big build. The other is slightly shorter, muscular, with curly black hair. Any chance you saw 'em?"

She scrunched her nose and forehead as she thought. "Yeah, actually I did. Two guys were in here yesterday like that. They were playing darts. You're looking for those guys?"

"We'll ask the questions," Ridder shot back. "They tell you anythin'? Where they're from? Where they're goin'? You get any names?"

Again, the woman paused to think. "God, I talk to so many people. I think they were talking about the Cape."

Sykes raised his eyebrows.

The woman looked at him. "You know, Cape Cod."

Ridder shot Sykes an angry look then turned back to the bartender. "You get what town?"

"I'm not sure. I get 'em all mixed up."

"How 'bout any names?"

"Listen, I can't keep track of all the names I hear. All I remember is it was something plain, ya know. Sorry." She paused for a second. "Actually, now that I think of it, the tall one won a dart game then filled out a sweepstakes form." She reached under the bar and pulled out a shoebox-size plastic container and placed it on the bar. "Gotta be near the top. Yeah, here it is. I remember the messy handwriting."

"We'll be needing that." Ridder shoved the paper into the inside pocket of his sports jacket.

"We 'preciate your help, ma'am," Sykes said just before they turned and quickly walked out the bar.

Ditchman leaned his head against the headrest and exhaled a deep breath. For a few hours he could get some rest. He stared out at the clouds and wondered if they'd arrive on time.

"So Ditch, how'd you convince Conrad to let us go to Boston?" Hammond asked.

"It wasn't that hard. He recognized the lead we're pursuing. Then it was just a matter of the bottom line."

"So this is coming out of our own pockets, right?" Hammond chuckled.

"I'm sure they'd like that, but no. I played up the whole Lee family connection thing and all the press the department will get when we bring in Hutchinson's killers."

For the next half hour, they tried to get some rest, but neither could fully relax. They tried to talked about anything but the case, but found it difficult to find a subject worth any amount of attention or interest. Finally, Hammond asked his partner about the shooting three months before. Ditchman answered all his questions, natural questions for a young cop who'd never been shot before. How did it happen? What was it like? Did you feel like you were going to die? Did you ever think you'd stop being a cop? Ditchman answered all the questions in order to help his partner learn, but also to help himself heal. Being single and living alone, he had not had someone to talk with about the shooting. Instead, he bottled up his feelings, and he knew it was time to let them out.

He explained how he had let his guard down for just a second in the apartment building. He had not expected the shooter to still be in the building. He should have called for more backup. It hurt like hell, but he never thought he was going to die. It wasn't until after he came through the surgery that he was told how close to death he had been. As for thinking about quitting the force, he couldn't see himself wearing some stiff suit, sitting at a desk, typing away at a computer and making phone calls and sucking up to people he probably hated. No way. Not to mention, he didn't know how to do anything but be a cop. He didn't need to mention he loved what he did.

Just after midday, they landed at Logan International Airport. They immediately went to the lower level to retrieve their bags and rent a car. Standing at the rental counter, Hammond said, "So where we supposed to meet this guy?"

"She said right here."

"Marty O'Donahue's a woman?"

Behind Hammond a gravelly, feminine voice said, "Any problem with that?"

Hammond spun around, his face red. He looked at a woman wearing a black ribbed silk knit pullover sweater and double-pleated gray pants that accentuated her narrow waist. A gold badge hung from a thin black belt. Hammond gulped. "No, I just thought…"

"No, Detective, you *assumed*." She paused, then smirked. "But don't sweat it. I'm not one of those radical feminists." She stuck out her hand and introduced herself to them.

Detective Martha O'Donahue was a native Bostonian. Her accent gave that fact away. She stood just under six feet tall, had a broad frame, and auburn hair that hung just over her square, slender shoulders, but the delicate features of her face and her slender legs didn't allow anyone to confuse her gender once they met her. She had joined the Massachusetts State Police as a cadet when she was just out of Northeastern University, where she had studied criminal justice. After serving in the force for nearly ten years, she was promoted to the rank of detective and assigned to Troop F, the unit of the state police in charge of law enforcement at Logan.

"Let's go to my office and I'll go over where we are in the case," she said.

As soon as she was out of earshot, Hammond glared at his partner and whispered, "Thanks, Ditch, for telling me she's a woman."

Ditchman grinned. "You never asked."

In the back corner of Troop F's headquarters was Detective O'Donahue's small office. It had pale white walls adorned with framed commendations and degrees and pictures of colleagues, friends and family. A lone window looked out onto the tarmac of terminal D. In one corner was O'Donahue's desk, tidy, yet full of evidence of her busy schedule and responsibilities. In the middle of the room was a small, square table with four chairs around it.

O'Donahue poured three cups of coffee from the pot in the hallway off her office and handed them to her guests. They sat down, and O'Donahue explained her side of the investigation.

At first, she believed the victim, Richard P. Kellerman, had committed suicide by jumping from the fifth level of the parking garage. But deep bruises to his upper body, especially around the neck area, suggested there was a struggle before he fell. No one had witnessed the fall. O'Donahue would be the only detective assigned to the case as the majority of Troop F that was not on standard detail was helping out in the investigation of the airline workers' drug ring at Logan and the overdose death of one of the baggage handlers while on the job.

Ditchman leaned forward in the wooden chair and rubbed his mustache. He explained how they had connected Kellerman to the burglary/homicide. He pulled out a photo. "We also know this guy, William 'Buster' Sykes, was looking for Kellerman early the day after the homicide. We'd like to see the parking garage, then show this around the airport. See if anyone recognizes him."

At the top of the terminal B parking garage, Ditchman and Hammond walked around with their heads turned down toward the asphalt inside the area that had been cordoned off by yellow police tape.

"We've been over the scene very meticulously, I assure you, Detective Ditchman," O'Donahue said.

Without looking up, Ditchman politely said, "I have no doubts about your team's diligence, Detective O'Donahue. We are simply trying to get a sense, a feel for the scene for ourselves. And I'd prefer you'd call me Ditch, everyone else does." He smiled then walked over to the edge of the garage where Hammond stood looking over the wall at the pavement below the five stories where a barricade of blue police sawhorses and yellow tape surrounded the lonely white outline of a body.

"Hey, Rusty, give me a quarter."

Hammond reached into his pocket, fished out a coin and handed it to Ditchman. "What do you need that for?"

"Watch." Ditchman stood against the four-foot concrete wall and stretched out his right arm straight in front of his chest, then let the quarter drop from his hand. All three of them leaned over the edge to watch the quarter land directly in the middle of the outlined body.

"He didn't jump, did he?" O'Donahue said.

"He may have, but don't most people push off when they jump? Helps them to overcome the fear that's anchoring them. But this guy went straight down like he was dropped."

"Or was hanging on over the edge and then fell."

Ditchman looked at O'Donahue and raised his right eyebrow. "Maybe."

Sykes drove the stolen Buick Regal into a parking lot off Route 1A, just north of the airport. A few cars, mostly older models, occupied the lot in front of the run-down, out-of-date strip mall made up of marginally profitable, anachronistic stores whose heyday had not survived the economic transition into the 1990s.

At the curb, Ridder got out and walked over to the lone phone booth, a half-booth model that the telephone company hadn't ever bothered to update. He pulled out the sweepstakes form from his pocket, unfolded it, then dialed the number, somewhat incredulous when a clear dial tone greeted him.

"Hello?" A young, brooding, female voice asked, as if agitated she had to answer the phone.

"Is Matt there?"

"No."

Ridder paused, expecting the young woman to then tell him where he was or when he would be back, but there was only silence on the other end. "Well, do you know when he'll be in?"

"I have no clue," she said tersely. "May I ask who's calling?"

Having anticipated such an inquiry, Ridder quickly and smoothly responded, "Mike, from college."

"Oh, hey Mike, it's Brooke, Matt's sister. I think I met you at the graduation party."

Ridder grinned; it was a stroke of luck getting the younger sister who, by the abrupt change in her attitude, was obviously smitten with college boys. "Sure, sure, I remember. How ya doing, Brooke?"

"Great. I'm pretty sure Matt's already gone to the Cape for the summer."

"Yeah, I was hopin' to hook up with him. He told me, but I can't remember where he's stayin'."

"He and some friends rented a place in Chatham, but I don't know exactly where." She paused for a second. "My mom would know, but she's away for a week at a conference with my dad. If you'd like, you can call when they get back. I won't be here 'cause I'm going to equestrian camp for two weeks with my friend, Kristin."

Ridder had to bite his tongue to prevent saying what he was thinking: how about I just come over now and pay you a visit? "No, I only have this week off, so I can't really wait. Can you think of any way I can get a hold of him?"

There was a brief pause.

"Actually, yeah. In past summers, he worked at a bar called the Squire. I can't remember if he's working there this summer. But I guarantee that if he's not working there, he's hanging out there. Everybody does. It's like the coolest place in Chatham."

Ridder smirked; he could picture the arrogant college kid and all his puke friends hanging around some bar trying to act like real men. Ridder unconsciously nodded his head in enjoyment as he envisioned the look on the kid's face when he looked up from his beer and found Carson Ridder staring down on him, knowing that he's about to get the ass-kicking of a lifetime.

"Great, thanks. Any chance you can tell me how to get there from Boston?"

After Brooke carefully gave Ridder general directions to Chatham and the location of the Squire, he thanked her, and hung up the phone.

"They breed 'em even more stupid up here," he said sardonically.

Back in the car, Ridder pulled out a Marlboro, bit the filter off, spat it out onto the curb, lit the butt, and took a deep pull.

"How'd it go?" Sykes asked patiently.

Ridder blew the remaining small amount of smoke that did not get absorbed into his lungs at Sykes. "Was talkin' to a broad. How'd you think it went?"

No airline had a record of a passenger named William Sykes and the terminal's gate workers who were on duty in the afternoon on the previous day couldn't remember seeing Sykes; "too many ugly, bald dudes," one worker reasoned. Ditchman highly doubted if any airport personnel, who see thousands of people every day, could identify Sykes, unless Sykes had done something to draw attention. Still, he wanted to question all the people who had worked at the gates that had serviced flights from the mid-Atlantic region, including Virginia, during the last few days. The shift supervisor of security suggested watching hours of video surveillance tapes to spot Sykes, and with Ditchman's blessing, O'Donahue ordered the video marathon to commence.

A mid-day lull in the influx of travelers brought about a relative calmness to terminal B which gave Ditchman and Hammond a much better chance to study the flow of people and the position and duties of the airport personnel. They spoke with cleaning crewmembers and sky cabbies, anyone whom they had not spoken to previously. None recognized Sykes from the picture.

"If the workers who saw hundreds of people yesterday can't remember seeing Sykes, maybe we should check in with some people who don't see as many. You know, like shop clerks."

"Or like a bartender," Ditchman smiled. "Is there a bar in this terminal?" He looked at O'Donahue.

"The Beantown Tavern and Grill, right down there," she pointed.

The last remains of the lunchtime crowd were in the bar. A waitress wiped down empty tables without looking up at them as they walked in. O'Donahue waited at the bar until she caught the bartender's eye.

"Excuse me, miss. I'm Detective O'Donahue with the State Police. We'd like to ask you a few questions."

The bartender put down a dishtowel and walked closer to the detectives. She stared at the badge pinned to O'Donahue's belt. "Wow, I'm attracting a lot of you guys today. What can I do for you?"

O'Donahue looked back at Ditchman, then back to the woman. "What do you mean by that? You've talked to other detectives?"

"Yeah, just a while ago, maybe couple hours. Two guys. What's the problem, you guys not sharing notes or something?" She smiled.

O'Donahue turned back to Ditchman. "I don't remember any of my men telling me they checked out this bar." She turned back to the bar and slid the photo of Sykes across to the bartender. "Have you seen this man?"

"Detective, you should know your own people. He's one of the guys that came in here."

Hammond looked at Ditchman. O'Donahue continued. "What did this *detective* ask you?"

The woman shrugged her shoulders. "Nothing. The other one did all the talking. Boy, was he rude, too. He asked me about two young guys in here yesterday. Some kinda connection to that guy dyin' here out at the garage and all, I guess."

O'Donahue leaned over the bar. "This is very important. Can you remember exactly what they asked you, and what you told them?"

She raised her eyebrows, tilted her head and bit her bottom lip. "Well, he asked the two guys' names and where they were from. I couldn't remember their names or anything, 'cept they were talking about Cape Cod."

Ditchman approached the bar with a small pad of paper. He asked the bartender to carefully describe the two young men and the man with Sykes. He wrote down all the details the woman could remember. The one who did all the talking was very tall, real big shoulders, had jet black hair in a pony tail tucked into the back of his shirt, and had really deep set, dark eyes, and never smiled. The woman remembered the eyes most vividly.

"I felt like the guy was looking through me. Wicked creepy, if you ask me. Does that make sense?"

"Yes, ma'am," Hammond said.

She looked up suddenly as if startled. "Hold on, you just reminded me of something else. The other guy, the short, bald one, called me ma'am. Nobody does that around here. And his accent—he twanged certain words—just like you do." She looked right at Hammond and smiled. "It only comes out with certain words. And he had funny eyes, too. Wouldn't look straight."

She couldn't remember much about the two young men, other than their build and hair color. "The blond was definitely taller than the one with the black, curly hair. They didn't seem like the type who'd kill someone, you know, just regular college kids."

Hammond stepped to the bar. "Did either of the two younger ones have any distinguishing marks you can remember?"

The barmaid smiled. "Other than being gorgeous, the taller one had a serious clef in his chin, like that guy in the movies, what's-his-name."

"Is there anything else you can think of that could help us contact any of these four men?" O'Donahue asked.

"Oh, that's right, the tall one, he filled out a sweepstakes form." She pointed to the sweepstakes advertisement behind her. "The evil looking guy with the pony tail took the form from me. Real jerk, if you ask me."

"May I see a blank form, please?" Ditchman asked.

She pulled out the pad and ripped off the top form.

He quickly examined it. "Standard stuff, including address and phone number. Any chance you got a look at his form after he filled it out?"

The woman shook her head. "I just remember he had real messy handwriting, sorry. That's what I told those other guys."

"Do you usually rip off the form before a person fills it out?" O'Donahue asked.

The woman shrugged her shoulders. "I don't know. Why?"

"Because if he filled out the form while it was still on the pad, there's a good chance his writing left an imprint on the next form, especially if he used a ball point pen," Ditchman answered.

The woman reached into the folded apron around her waist and pulled out four ballpoint pens with the bar's logo on it. "It's all we got here."

Hammond examined the entry form. "Ditch, they're numbered."

"Ma'am, could we see all the completed entry forms?" Ditchman asked, already understanding Hammond's logic.

The woman quickly searched the shelves under the bar and retrieved a plastic box. "Here's where we keep 'em. There's a bunch in there 'cause it doesn't cost anything to enter, you know. All you gotta do is win five games."

Within a minute, Ditchman had pulled out three forms. "There's three missing, and based on the numbers, these should be the forms that were after each one."

O'Donahue picked up each form, one at a time, and examined it by tilting it in the light. "Looks like pretty heavy stock, but I can see some imprints. Our lab technicians should be able to pull something off." She looked up at the bartender. "Have you given out many of these in the last few days?"

"Being free, yeah, loads, especially when there's a layover or delay. The bar fills up pretty quickly then."

"Did the two younger guys have any bags with them? Maybe you might have noticed as they left?" Hammond asked.

Again the woman shook her head. "I don't remember. I think so, but I can't be sure. Anything else? I got customers I gotta get to."

"No, but call this number if you think of anything else." O'Donahue passed her a card.

Ditchman didn't bother sitting down once back in O'Donahue's office. "Listen, Detective O'Donahue…"

"Call me Marty, please."

"Okay, Marty." He smiled. "Let's go over what we know." Ditchman started pacing the room, clicking off the points on his fingers. "We've got a dead man in Virginia, apparently the victim of a robbery gone bad. We've got some hair from the crime scene and one scared maitre d' who we believe was used as the informer for the burglary ring. The only contact he had was over the phone, but he might be able to identify the voice if he heard it; I'm sure he'll be willing to cooperate." He walked over to the lone window in the office that looked out on the busy runway. "We've got one fingerprint from a stolen van we believe was used in the felony as well as hair that matches the crime scene. The print belongs to Richard Kellerman, who has now been found dead here. Accident? Murder? And we know that Buster Sykes was calling on Kellerman the day after the murder. Now we know that Sykes was here, with another guy, posing as cops, and asking questions about two young guys. So what questions does this raise?"

Hammond looked at O'Donahue and she nodded for him to go first.

"Why are Sykes and this other guy looking for the two young guys? The bartender mentioned the young guys were talking about Cape Cod. The question is, were they coming back, or on their way there? I think if we can figure that out, and track them down, we might find Sykes and his partner. What else do we have to go on?"

"What I want to know is why Kellerman came here from Virginia. Was Sykes and the other guy with Kellerman? Neither name is on any airline passenger list, so they must have been traveling under aliases." O'Donahue leaned back in her chair. "And is Kellerman in any way connected to the two young guys who Sykes and his buddy were looking for?"

Ditchman began to pace as he always did while brainstorming out loud. "Well, if we put Kellerman at the scene of the burglary and murder in Charlottesville, and then here at the airport, can we assume at this point that Sykes and this big guy were with Kellerman in Professor Hutchinson's house?" He suddenly stopped. "If they were together at the burglary, and then one of them dies, not at his own hands, nor by accident, what would be the reason? What are the two main reasons people kill?"

"Money and revenge," Hammond answered quickly, having been asked the question by Ditchman during every homicide investigation they had worked on together.

O'Donahue smiled. "Payback."

"But for what?" Hammond asked. "If we assume these guys were together, maybe the college kids know something about Kellerman's death; maybe they saw something or maybe they had something to do with his death, and Sykes and the big guy are looking for revenge."

Ditchman rubbed his mustache a few times. "That could explain why they were looking for the college kids."

"But Kellerman was pretty well bruised, especially around the neck area. And his face looked like a pound of raw meat. Why would a bunch of college kids do that? Not to mention, the timing is off. Based on the time we discovered the body and the time the bartender placed the two college guys at the bar, why would they hang around the airport for a game of darts if they just killed someone? It doesn't make any sense." O'Donahue shook her head. "And why would Sykes and the big guy pose as cops? Maybe the two college kids did see something they weren't supposed to have seen."

Ditchman grinned. "What about the possibility that Kellerman took the stolen goods for himself? And his two former accomplices caught up to him. But when they go to teach him a lesson…"

"They're seen by two young guys making a human airplane out of Kellerman," Hammond finished Ditchman's thought. "Again, my bet is, if we find the two college kids, we find our two suspects."

O'Donahue picked up the three sweepstakes forms Ditchman had laid on her desk.

"What should we do while we're waiting for the lab?" Hammond asked.

"We'll make more copies of Sykes' photo and have some more of my men check the hot spots in Boston," O'Donahue said.

"Like where?" Hammond asked.

"Well, since we're monitoring all flights, and they have yet to be spotted, I think it's safe to assume they're still in the area. Now what are the chances they packed a bag? If in fact they were after Kellerman for being doublecrossed or to retrieve whatever he took from them—my guess would be the money they made off the stolen goods—then they probably didn't plan on staying around for very long. If they got what they came for then they're probably after the two college kids to cover their tracks."

"So they'll need transportation and a change of clothes," Ditchman said.

O'Donahue smiled at Ditchman. "Exactly. And I suggest we start with stolen car reports. It doesn't fit their M.O. to be renting a car. Not to mention it would take too many man-hours to reconcile a list of passengers on Mid-Atlantic flights to the rental car records, and then check out each person. I'll send some uniforms out to check with the local consignment shops. I highly doubt these guys are going shopping on Newbury Street."

# CHAPTER 9

▼

The evening in Chatham was pleasant. A cool breeze came off the ocean and filled the air with the medicinal smell of the salt water. Annie sat on the porch with Fenway at her feet and listened to the broadcast of the Red Sox and Yankees game on a small transistor radio she held in her left hand. Many times she and her parents had sat on the porch of the house they rented on Stage Harbor. While her father listened to his beloved Red Sox on the same transistor radio, she and her mother played a game of guessing the next type of boat that would come through the cut at Harding's beach. Annie always guessed a sailboat.

"Hey, Annie, your laptop just beeped," Matt yelled from the living room. "You've got an email."

Annie came into the living room and opened up her laptop and punched a couple of keys.

"It's from my Godfather. It's about the *Argo*."

Tucker came into the room and sat down next to Annie on the couch. Annie read the email out loud.

Dear Annie,

So good to hear from you. I hope you have a wonderful summer in Chatham. As to your inquiry about a ship named *Argo* in American history, I checked with a colleague who teaches history. For nearly a century after the Civil War, a legend existed about a Confederate blockade runner called the *C.S.S. Argo* that had been on a secret mission to deliver gold to

Canada. Most historians, including my colleague, had believed the story of the *Argo* was nothing more than a grand story, as much fictitious as the Greek myth, which I'm sure you know. The Confederate government had many times supported what is called a Fifth Column. These were paramilitary expeditions in which the hired northerners or Canadians would act essentially as terrorists with the aim of turning the northern populace against the Union war effort.

In 1972, Walter Hutchinson, a University of Virginia historian, discovered a letter written by a Confederate sailor who claimed to have been on board the *Argo*. A decade later, Professor Hutchinson led an expedition that found the remains of the sunken *Argo* and its gold off the coast of Chatham.

However, Hutchinson claimed that the *Argo* had been carrying more gold than he had found—which gave birth to a new legend. People just love to believe in legends!

So, just as Jason and the Argonauts, my colleague believes the story of the lost *Argo* gold is nothing more than a myth. He said unless authentic facts are discovered to support the claims, the legend of the lost gold will remain nothing more than a fun story to tell.

As for your inquiry about a William J. Randall—I called the Library of Congress and found two Rebels by that name. One died at Antietam in 1862; the other died in May of 1864 at the Battle of the Wilderness. If you'd like to know more, let me know.

I hope this information helps in settling the argument. Please keep in touch.

Much love,

Albert

Annie looked up at Tucker, then at Matt. "Well, what do you think?"

"Maybe the journal is the piece of evidence that substantiates the legend of the lost gold. Think about it. If the *Argo* sank, and only Randall survived, and he was only able to save some of the gold, maybe he buried it on Monomoy like the poem says? And if those goons who jumped us had read the journal and knew about the legend, wouldn't that explain why they tried to rip off my bag?" Matt asked.

Tucker tilted his head. "Yeah, but how would they have known it was in your bag?"

"Maybe someone mixed up their bag with mine at the airport. Who cares? I say we go look for the gold ourselves. We got the description of where it is. Think about it. If the Randall who buried the gold and wrote this journal was also the one killed in 1864, that would explain why he never came back to retrieve the gold, right? And, why else would those goons try to take my bag if they weren't looking for something valuable, like directions to a ton of gold? I mean, come on, guys. If you were going to mug someone at an airport, wouldn't you pick out some rich-looking dude in an Armani suit who drives a Jag, not a '86 Volkswagen?"

"I don't know. Sounds just too fishy to me," Tucker replied. "I mean, come on, Matt, get real. Gold?"

"Yeah, gold. I'm dying to see if it's buried out there. Think about it. What an awesome adventure. How could you not want to go looking for it? This is like a childhood dream come true. Tuck, tell me you don't want to at least check it out. Come on, what's the harm? It'll be fun. Aren't you at least a bid curious?"

"I think we should just send the journal to Albert, and let his colleague figure it out. I really don't want to spend my summer chasing fool's gold," Annie said.

Matt stood up; his face was serious. "But what about those goons at the airport?"

"Matt, those guys were just trying to mug us."

"Then how do you explain how the journal got in my bag, huh?"

Tucker shrugged his shoulders.

Annie typed on the computer. "I'm emailing Albert to let him know we are sending him the journal. Okay, Matt?"

Matt shook his head. "Okay, but I still say it would be awesome to find it ourselves instead of letting a bunch of stuffy, old academics get the credit."

Annie glared at Matt. He looked back at her, realizing he had hurt her.

"I'm sorry, Annie. I didn't mean that about your godfather."

"Let's drop the subject. The journal's being sent to Harvard. On to more important things, like what we're doing tonight," Tucker asked as he raised his palms and tilted his head as if to help others understand his line of thinking.

"Anyone up for going to the Squire?" Matt said in a conciliatory tone.

"I'm going for a run," Annie answered without her usually present smile. She looked at Matt, then looked away.

"I could go for a run. Mind if I join you?"

Annie shook her head and forced a smile.

Tucker turned to Matt. "How about we meet you at the Squire?"

"Sure, yeah, whatever."

Annie looked at him, disappointment painted over her face.

"Don't worry," Matt said in a more repentant tone, "I'll stop off at the Post Office on the way to the Squire, and then we'll be done with it."

Chris Shaughnessy leaned back in the office chair and stretched his arms high above his head. A string of crackles popped as he twisted the fatigue out of his backbone. For four hours he had been sitting hunched over a monitor, watching surveillance videos while holding a picture of Buster Sykes in his left hand.

Feeling minor relief from the atrophy, he picked up the piece of paper that had the description of the other man he was trying to spot.

Tall, black hair, pony tail. Jesus, he thought, do they know how many guys fit that description? He pressed play on the video machine and began watching the black and white screen again. Having watched tapes from seventeen different cameras, and with twenty more to review, he wondered if he was going to get home in time for the hot meal his wife always had ready for him when he returned from work. He hoped it was steak night as he imagined the sweet aroma of the sautéed onions, grilled to perfection medium rare filet mignon, and steaming hot baked beans and found his mouth beginning to water.

"Any luck, Shaughnessy?" The pessimistic voice of his usually indefatigable supervisor, Ed Hawthorne, startled him back to his work.

Without lifting his eyes from the screen, Shaughnessy, grunted. "You'd think in this day and age, we'd be using better cameras. This is pretty fuzzy. Is Bayon having any luck?"

Hawthorne sat down in the vacant chair next to him. "Nope and his eyes are about to pop. He said they all start to look the same after so many hours, so he's taking a break." He padded Shaughnessy on the shoulder. "Well, just keep trying." He paused. "Hell, I might as well join you."

For the next twenty minutes they sat in front of the monitor, their focus dancing between the hundreds of people to cross the screen, with the only sound to break the monotony coming from the Shaughnessy's self-imposed chiropractic therapy on his vertebrae.

"Whoa, stop it right there. Back it up a bit. Yeah, yeah, there." Hawthorne leaned forward and pointed at the still image. "Look, there's the bald guy, and there's the big guy with the pony tail." They stared incredulously at the discovery.

"Real slow, let the tape run." The frames slowly changed on the screen. "Freeze it!"

On the screen was the face of Carson Ridder, looking straight at the camera.

After enlarging the still frame and printing it, Hawthorne took the photo to O'Donahue's office where he found her just getting off the phone. Hammond sat at the table in the center of the room looking over his notes. Ditchman stood just to his right, cradling a fresh cup of coffee.

"It's not the best quality, but I think we found your man," Hawthorne said as he placed the photo on O'Donahue's desk. She hung up the phone, pick up the photo and examined it, then handed it to Ditchman who had walked over to her desk.

"That's definitely Sykes in the background, so I agree that's our man in the foreground. What do you think, Ditch?" She handed him the photo.

He looked at it closely and nodded. "Fits the description. Take a look, Rusty."

After Hammond looked at the photo and gave his agreement, and Hawthorne excused himself from the room, Hammond asked, "Now what? Who do we send this out to?"

O'Donahue rubbed her temples, the strain of the day's activity starting to show on her face. Her brown eyes, once crisp and bright, looked weary and watery. The control that had defined her at the beginning of the day was slowly eroding. "I think it would be premature to send this out to every cop in Massachusetts. There's no sense in extending our effort until we have narrowed down our search a bit more. We should have the bartender look at it first." She stood up and walked over to the window and looked out at a plane taxiing to a runway. She turned and looked back at them. "And I just got off the phone with one of my officers. No leads from the consignment shops."

"What about stolen cars?" Ditchman asked.

O'Donahue walked over to her desk and picked up the phone. After speaking briefly and jotting down some notes, she hung up the receiver and sat down in the chair.

"In the last three days, ten cars have been reported stolen from within the city limits. Two were reported stolen from Jamaica Plain, ten miles from here. One has been recovered in Charlestown, across the river. I doubt anyone would go that far from the airport to steal a car. Two other cars stolen from a parking garage near Fenway Park were recovered, one in Worcester, in the central part of the state, the other on the North Shore. The other four," she looked down at her notes, "a Ford Explorer, a BMW 535i, a Buick Regal, and a Honda Accord are not accounted for yet. Of course, these are just the ones reported missing. You know, someone could be on vacation for a week and never know their car had been stolen until they got back." She raised her eyebrows and tilted her head.

Hammond leaned back in his chair and folded his hands behind his head. "And what about the lab? Any way you can get them to move more quickly on the sweepstakes forms?"

O'Donahue shook her head and didn't try to hide her grimace. "They're just finishing a big job involving the homicide of a state senator's son. And because of all the press the case has received, the forensic lab's been in overdrive. But my contact there assures me he'll get to it as soon as things slow down over there, hopefully tomorrow."

Annie and Tucker ran past Oyster Pond on their way to what people called "the loop," a two mile course along lazy roads with inspiring views of classic Cape homes and magnificent water views. The evening was still and the air was pleasantly warm; no wind rippled the glassy waters where Annie had taken swimming lessons as a child. They took a right onto Cedar Street, which gradually climbed to a slight hill. The right side of the street was lined with ten-foot high shrubs that granted privacy to the large estates on the eastern side of Oyster River. An elderly couple on bikes leisurely rode past them in the opposite direction toward the village.

Though Tucker considered himself in good shape, having just finished his final season of college lacrosse and receiving All-American honors, he had to work hard to keep up with Annie. Many times he allowed himself to drift behind her when they came to a narrow spot on the sidewalk where mailboxes jutted out in their path. Each time, he examined Annie's slender body in her running shorts and white tee shirt. She was in excellent shape from running five miles a day.

As they turned a sharp corner on Champlain Road, they caught a full view of Stage Harbor. Moored sailboats and fishing boats dotted the harbor, paying homage in perfect alignment to the incoming tide. They ran past the Stage Harbor Yacht Club, the dirt parking lot filled with trucks and empty boat trailers, and onto Bridge Street. At the boat ramp, two crusty men in green rubber waders carrying wire buckets filled with clams crossed the street in front of them. On the bridge across the Mitchell River, two small boys and a girl leaned patiently against the railing while staring hypnotically at their fishing lines.

At the top of the hill, where Bridge Street met Main Street, they reached the Chatham Lighthouse. Annie led Tucker to the sidewalk of the vista overlooking South Beach. Despite its being a weekday, the parking lot was full with sightseers and vacationers taking in the breathtaking view of the cut to the Atlantic Ocean.

"Hey, Annie, can we stop for a minute," Tucker said, trying to hide his heavy breathing.

Annie stopped and turned to him. "You okay?"

Tucker laughed. "Well, I'll admit, I'm sucking some wind. But I also want to check out this view. This is amazing. What a beach!" He leaned against the fence and looked out at The Cut and South Beach. Despite being a spectacular mile-long stretch of pure, clean sand along the crystal clear waters of the mouth of Pleasant Bay, the lack of parking around the area of the lighthouse prevented hoards of sun-worshippers from overpopulating the beach. The few hundred people still there played in the surf, flew kites, threw Frisbees or just slept on their towels, and had plenty of room away from each other to enjoy their experience in peace. "What a view. Want to take a walk on the beach?"

Annie hesitated.

"Come on, it will be fun. If I bore you, we can run to the end of the beach and back." He smiled.

They walked down the steep, metal steps leading to the beach and immediately found it more difficult to walk in the sand compared to the hard pavement of the road. When they reached the crest of the beach, they stopped and watched the waves gingerly roll up on the sand. It was a warm evening and the wind barely blew. Tucker wiped sweat off his face.

Annie finally broke the silence. "So, tell me about Tucker McKinney."

"What do you want to know?"

"I don't know. Like where you grew up."

Tucker smiled. Since he had met Annie he had wanted to get to know her more. Now she wanted to know about him. "I moved around a lot with my father when he was in the Navy, so we never lived in one place for long. I guess I would call Annapolis my home because we lived there the longest. It's really the only place I identify with."

They began to walk along the waterline toward the point. "What about your mom? What does she do?" Annie asked without shifting her eyes from the sand in front of her.

"My mom died when I was born, so I never knew her."

Annie blushed. "Oh, God, I'm sorry, I didn't know that."

"That's okay. My dad raised me the best he could. But because he traveled so much with the Navy, as soon as I was old enough, he shipped me off to boarding school. To tell you the truth, I feel more like an orphan because I hardly saw my dad much. I can't remember the last time we talked, I mean really talked. I've stopped leaving messages with his secretary. He's always off doing work for the State Department. Hell, I don't think he's ever even seen me play lacrosse, now that I think of it. He didn't even come to the all-star game. He just swung by the house for a minute, said that was all he had, met Matt and was gone again. Poof."

There was an awkward paused until Annie spoke again. "Where did you go to boarding school?"

"I went to a junior boarding school until high school. Then I went to Saint James School in western Maryland. That's where I'm working starting in September."

"So when did you first meet Matt?"

"Well, I went to a local college for two years, then transferred to Connecticut College my junior year when I realized I wasn't getting much of an education. Funny, I was having such a great time partying and all, I didn't realize until it was almost too late that I wasn't learning anything other than how to shotgun a beer while standing on my head." He chuckled. "I guess one day I woke up and decided I was sick of being hungover and needed to go to a good school. And, of course, I wanted to go to a school that had a great lacrosse team. And that's how I got to Conn. Sorry, I'm babbling, aren't I?"

Annie smiled. "No, no, keep going."

"Anyway, I went to a keg party the first night I was at Conn and Matt was bartending and that's how we first met."

They strolled in silence for a minute and watched the fishing boats make their way through The Cut.

"Have you been friends with Matt since you met him?" Annie asked.

Tucker nodded his head. "Yeah, we hit it off right from the get go. I don't know why, to tell you the truth; we're kinda like Mutt and Jeff."

Annie stopped walking. "Do you think Matt's changed in the time you've known him? I mean, he seems to be pretty edgy right now."

Tucker picked up a smooth stone and tossed it in the water. "I don't know. He's under a lot of pressure right now from his old man. Did you catch any of his phone call with his father today?"

Annie shook her head.

"It got pretty heated, I guess. His father wants him to go work for him at his firm like his older brother, but Matt doesn't want anything to do with that. His father said he thought we were down here to enjoy 'voracious indolence.' Sounds like a hell of a guy."

Annie grimaced. "Poor Matt, no wonder why he's acting a bit indignant. So, what's he want to do?"

"He says he just wants to be a cook at his own restaurant. But his old man won't listen to any of his ideas about starting a restaurant. When we were down in Maryland, he called Matt. Really chewed his ass off on the phone for not being more goal-oriented and finding a real job."

"How'd Matt take it?"

"He took it from him, but, man, was he pissed when he got off the phone. Hell, I bet Matt just doesn't want to be like his father and brother. He says he is sick of following all their paths. Probably why he drives that piece of crap Volkswagen."

Annie nodded. "I remember when he decided to go to Connecticut College instead of going to Penn like his brother and father. His father didn't talk to him for a whole semester." Tucker shook his head in disgust.

"Maybe that's why he's still playing the role of the party animal. Maybe he doesn't want to face the reality that college is over and it's time to grow up and face the fact that he has to make tough decisions, like getting a job that maybe his father doesn't approve of."

They walked on the cool sand for a few more minutes, not talking, just admiring the water and watching the flyfishermen artistically cast their lines to waiting Striped Bass.

"What about you. Tell me about Annie Hopewell. How you met Matt and the Lockwoods, you know, the whole deal." He smiled.

They sat down next to each other in the cool sand and Annie tucked her hair behind her ears while looking down at the sand. Tucker tilted his head down so he could see her face as she spoke.

"I grew up in Concord. My parents used to rent a house in Chatham during the summer and they were at a party one night, years ago, and my dad and Mr. Lockwood found themselves holding up the same wall, both being the wallflower type. They soon started talking about fishing and thereafter were fishing buddies. The Lockwoods don't have any children, so they really took a shine to my parents and me. That was when I was pretty young. I don't really remember much other than going fishing with my dad and Mr. Lockwood, or walking on the beach with my Mom and Mrs. Lockwood. They've been a second family for me."

"How'd you meet Matt?" Tucker asked.

"We met working at the fish pier. He worked on one of the fishing boats and I worked helping offload and separate the catch. There were tons of high school kids working there, and everybody ends up knowing each other if you spend enough time here in the summers." She blushed. "We became friends and dated for a while. He's more like a brother to me now." Annie picked up a handful of sand and let it slowly sift through her delicate fingers. "So you'll be teaching history next year?"

"Yeah, I'm pretty excited, but a bit nervous, too. Hey, any chance I could talk to your godfather, professor…"

"Nylan. Sure, he's a wonderfully generous man, I bet he'd love talking to you about teaching."

"How does one go about getting a Harvard professor as a godfather?"

"You really want to know?"

Tucker looked straight at her. "Sure."

Annie smiled but didn't look up. "Shortly after my parents were married, my Dad started at the Harvard Law School. They rented this tiny apartment above a garage in Cambridge. They didn't have much, but it was real cute. My Mom worked fulltime at a gallery in the Square until a few weeks before I was born." Annie's eyes began to glisten as she talked of her parents. "Albert lived in the house next door. He took my parents under his wing after they met, which was great for my parents because they were new to the East coast and both sets of my grandparents were back in Oregon. I've always thought they served kind of like the children he never had."

"He never married?"

"He always said he would have made a fine priest, but instead he married academics. But my Mom said he had been married when he was real young and his wife died soon after they were married. He was so devastated, he never remarried." She paused. "He took a liking to my Dad immediately because they both were diehard Red Sox fans."

Tucker looked up from the sand suddenly. "I thought your dad was from Oregon?"

"But he lived in Massachusetts until he was nine. And as anyone who loves baseball knows, it's during those years that you pick your team." She giggled and tucked her hair that had blown into her face behind her ears. "Where was I before I was so rudely interrupted?" She smiled at him. "When I was born, my parents asked Albert to be my godfather."

"Are your parents still close to him?"

Annie looked down at the sand at her feet, picked up a handful and transferred it between her hands. "Matt didn't…?" She paused.

Tucker tilted his head. "Didn't what?"

"My parents died in a car accident four years ago."

Tucker reached out his right hand and gently touched Annie's shoulder. "I'm sorry, Annie, I didn't know. I can't believe Matt didn't tell me."

"I asked Matt not to because people always walk on eggshells when they find out. They end up treating me differently without even knowing they are. I didn't want to start the summer off with you acting that way."

"So why tell me now?"

Annie looked Tucker in the eyes. "Because I feel like I can trust you not to act that way."

"We don't have to talk about if you don't want to."

Annie leaned back on her hands. "That's okay." She took a deep breath. "It happened in October when I was a freshman at Skidmore. It was a rainy night, and some drunk crossed over the yellow line on Route 2 and hit them head on. When school was out, I stayed in Saratoga, and did until graduation three years later. This is the first time I've been back to Chatham." Annie looked around and out at the water. "Matt's been real good to me since my parents died. He called me each week to see how I was doing." Annie paused, then smiled. "He begged me to come to Chatham for the summer. I really didn't want to at first, but I felt like I at least owed him for being so kind to me. When I got here, I couldn't help but think that maybe I wasn't ready for this yet. But now I'm glad I came."

"I guess we have more in common than we thought."

Annie looked at Tucker and smiled.

Being the week before the Fourth of July, the Squire was more crowded than usual. The dining side, known for its nautical theme, friendly atmosphere and great food, was filled with gray-haired retirees and vacationing families with sunburned kids. An aroma of seafood filled the room. Pretty waitresses hustled about on the red Stuart plaid rug carrying large metal trays of shrimp scampi, broiled swordfish, and bright red lobsters. An orchestra of noises—clinking glasses, silverware, and dishes, and energetic conversations—made the Squire come alive. A line of people waiting to be seated for dinner ran from the crowded bar area to the door and onto the sidewalk.

The under-thirty crowd filled the tavern side of the restaurant where the walls of the bar were decorated with faded murals of old Chatham seascapes, beer company logos, and license plates from around the country. A juke box, standing next to a door labeled in large letters WC, blared "Thunder Road," by Bruce Springsteen. Two small rooms off the end of the bar were filled with college-aged patrons. In the first room, four young, intoxicated men played an enthusiastic game of foosball. A group of well-groomed women stood next to the table and whispered into each other's ears and laughed at the players.

In the end room, called the back bar, patrons stood like riders on a subway car, with just enough room to hold their drinks to their chests. An array of New England sports memorabilia and beer mirrors decorated the walls. An assortment of braziers hung on rafters above the bar.

Matt Gallagher sat at the little bar and looked up at the bras. In all the times he had been at the Squire, he had never seen a woman take off her bra and hang it like a trophy in the rafters. He took another drink from his beer and felt the warmth of an increasing buzz.

He looked at his watch. Where the hell are they, he thought. As much as he liked to think of himself as a partying kind of guy, he didn't like being alone at a bar. As he stood up to get a better view of the adjoining room to see if Annie and Tucker were in the bar yet, he noticed two familiar men talking to one of the waitresses. Suddenly, he recognized them as the two guys from the airport who had tried to mug him and a chill shot down his back. Matt quickly looked around and saw a tightly packed group of people blocking the back exit and felt a rush of panic come over his body.

When Matt looked back at the two men he saw them surveying the crowd as they pushed through the people toward the back bar. He looked back at the exit then at the men approaching. They would be on him well before he would be able to fight through the crowd to the door. He needed to buy some time. That was it, he thought, and reached into his pocket and took out his wallet.

A college student in a tie-dye shirt sat next to him, with his back towards Matt. Matt tapped the guy on the shoulder. "Hey, man, want to make an easy twenty bucks?" Matt flashed the bill in front of the guy.

"Yeah, sure," he said with a big smile.

"See those two guys over there coming this way?" Matt nodded with his head to the left.

"You mean that huge, ugly guy and that square, bald dude?"

"Yeah, that's them. I want you to go up to them and act like you know them, just pretend you haven't seen them in a long time and you're happy to see them. Make sure you're standing between them and the exit door. You know, just get in their way for a minute. Got it?"

"Dude, this is the easiest twenty bucks I'll ever make. No problem."

He took the bill from Matt and proceeded to push his way toward the two men while Matt did the same toward the exit. Just before he made it to them, Ridder pointed at Matt and began to push forward against the crowd.

As Matt reached the door, he looked back at Ridder and Sykes. He made eye contact with Ridder just as the college kid reached Ridder. The kid slapped Ridder on the shoulder and started to hug him. Come on, come on, Matt said to himself as he pushed.

"Get out of my way," he yelled at a couple standing in front of the door.

As he burst through the door, he looked back and saw Ridder and Sykes were ensnarled in a pack of people. Matt was almost across the parking lot behind the Squire, when he heard Ridder yell, "Go around front to the street."

Matt ran past the ice cream store at the far corner of the lot, down a flight of stairs, into a municipal parking lot. He ducked behind a minivan to catch his breath. Jesus, he thought, why didn't I take my car tonight?

He peeked from around the van and saw Ridder running from car to car, looking under each one. When Ridder looked under another, Matt sprinted toward Main Street. He hoped he was further down the road than Sykes so he could double back on the other side of Main Street.

Within seconds he was at Main Street. Though it was dark, Main Street was well lit from the store lights and car headlights. Matt hoped they wouldn't be able to see him in the throngs of people on the sidewalks. He praised his decision to wear a dark purple Polo shirt tonight. He had almost decided to wear the yellow one. Without looking, he dashed across the street in front of a car. A group of six people walked leisurely on the sidewalk. Matt stepped behind them to use them as a shield. He looked back across the street and saw Sykes, then Ridder. The two frantically looked up and down their side of the road, then to the other. Matt slumped down behind the group.

When he stood up to find Ridder and Sykes, he looked right at them: they were running toward him. Matt sprinted down the sidewalk, dodging pedestrians in his way. He ran past the Candy Manor, then crossed the road at the May-flower. He started to go down Mill Pond Road, then stopped in his tracks as he remember the road ended at a town landing.

"Shit!" He quickly turned into the driveway to his left. A Lexus was parked on the right side, ten feet from a six-foot high white fence, which connected to the house. Matt ran over to the fence and frantically searched for a door. Finally, he gave up the search and put his hands on the top to pull himself over, but then stopped when he realized there maybe no way out. Suddenly, he felt like a trapped animal. As he stood there, cursing his inaction and feeling waves of panic overcome his body, he saw the metal trash cans.

When Ridder and Sykes reached Mill Pond Road, they slowed to a stop. Sykes stood hunched over, clutched his knees and wheezed for air. "I think I'm gonna puke," he said in an oxygen-deprived voice.

Ridder put his hand on Sykes' shoulder. "Shut up, Buster. Listen." Ridder strained his head up and turned it from side to side. "If that fucker was still running, we'd still hear 'em. So he must…"

The sound of a garbage can being knocked over interrupted Ridder.

"He's behind that house. Come on, Buster."

They quickly raced into the first driveway and found the fence, but no door. Ridder swore and pounded the fence with his fists. Then he made Sykes drop to his hands and knees and sacrifice his backside so Ridder could boost himself over the fence.

With Ridder finally on the other side of the fence, Sykes slowly got up off the ground. He took a deep breath, still winded from running more than he had since high school gym class. His struggle to catch his breath preoccupied his attention enough so he didn't notice Matt slip out from beneath the car.

"He over there, Carson?" Sykes asked.

"Hey, douche bag!" Matt called out from behind Sykes.

Sykes turned in astonishment and Matt smashed him square in the face with the underside of the metal trash can lid. A loud crunch echoed off the fence wall right before Sykes' limp body slammed into it.

"What the hell was that? Buster? Buster?" Ridder's voice boomed.

Matt turned to his right and saw Ridder pulling himself over the fence. Without hesitating, Matt sprinted back to Main Street. He kept looking behind him, but could see little because it was too dark and there were few stores to illuminate the sidewalk at this end of Main Street.

After running for a few more minutes, Matt abruptly turned down the next street he came to, but immediately stopped when he realized he had never been down the street before and worried where it would end. Quickly surveying the area, he saw a thick canopy of leaves covered the street and a large row of hedges lined the left side of the street. With no other option, Matt ran behind the bushes, dove to the ground and held as still as possible. Within seconds, his heart rate accelerated as he heard footsteps turn from a running pace to a quick walk.

"Bastard's gotta be here somewhere."

While Matt kept his face to the ground he realized he was perched on a layer of dry leaves left from the previous Fall. If he made just the slightest movement, the leaves would give him away. The footsteps grew closer. He could feel his heart pounding in his chest. He tried to hold his breath. The footsteps stopped right in front of him. Matt closed his eyes.

"I don't see him, Carson. Must be up the road."

"Shut up and keep lookin'. He ain't got wings so he's gotta be here somewhere."

The footsteps started again. Matt let out an inaudible breath as he realized they were moving down the street. He waited a minute, then carefully crawled to the opening in the shrubs. Lying on the ground, he looked down the street. The canopy of trees and lack of any street or house lights made it almost impossible for Matt to see how far down the road his pursuers had gone, so he closed his eyes for twenty seconds. When he opened them, he could barely make out the outlines of Ridder and Sykes. They were at least fifty yards away, Matt figured, but he suddenly feared they might double back if they didn't find him down the road.

Praying they were looking in the other direction, Matt quickly dashed across the street into a driveway. Without looking back, he ran down the driveway, across the side lawn and into tall marsh grass. Ducking low, he silently ran through the grass to the edge of the Mill Pond.

With a fog bank rolling across Chatham, the moonlight was dampened. Matt slid into the water without a sound and began to swim. The water was warm, but refreshing. The scratches on his knees and hands he had received when scampering under the car now burned from contact with the salt water. Thirty feet out, he stopped behind a moored dinghy and caught his breath as he treaded water. He tried to hear if they had followed him, but only heard the echoing sounds of lines clinking against sail masts.

Within ten minutes, Matt reached the other shore and looked back across the water, but couldn't see anything because of the thick fog. Though he knew it was useless, he stared across to try to detect any movement on the far shore.

With the washed up eelgrass to dampen his movement, he began walking along the water line in the direction away from the village. Every fifty yards he stopped and looked around. At first, every sound made him freeze. Just as he grew used the sounds, his eyes started playing tricks on him and he kept thinking he saw movement out on the water. At one point, he stood still for five minutes because he kept thinking he saw a rowboat approaching him.

An hour after crossing the Mill Pond, Matt could see the lights on Bridge Street. He knew if he could make it to the road, he would be able to run the loop back to Oyster Pond and the cottage. He felt utterly exhausted and cold as his thoughts raced. Maybe he should have called the cops like Annie had wanted. But then he would have to deal with his father's wrath for having the family name tarnished in some police report. Maybe he shouldn't have mailed the journal. Maybe he should have held onto it and just given it to them. Then again, maybe there is a treasure buried in Chatham. Why else would they be so persistent? As much as Matt knew he'd love having a ton of money, and thus financial freedom from his father, he was too tired and worn out to care. All he wanted was to get home and go to sleep.

When he reached the edge of the marsh, a truck drove down Bridge Street and stopped on the bridge. Matt quickly came to his senses and dropped to his belly in the grass. The truck's headlights illuminated the marsh and the small boats moored in the cove, but Matt hugged a small embankment in the shadows, safe from detection.

Finally, the truck sped away. Matt scampered up the embankment and looked down Bridge Street. He could barely see the truck's taillights, but could tell it took a right, back toward the village.

The rest of the way back to the cottage, Matt ran on the side of the road and ducked into the woods each time he saw any headlights. He feared if they could find him, maybe they could find where he lived. Jesus, he thought, maybe they talked to someone at the Squire. He thought of Annie and Tucker and increased his speed.

When he reached the cottage, he found the door unlocked and the lights on. Matt rushed into the living room, out of breath. "Annie, Tucker?" He ran upstairs, but found no one. Bad thoughts began to race through his mind.

He ran back downstairs and found a note on the coffee table.

Matt,

We stopped by the Squire, but you weren't there. Where are you? We've gone with the Lockwoods to get ice cream. Be back soon.

A.

Matt breathed deeply and thought about what he should tell them, but decided Annie would just freak out and call the cops, and he didn't want to have to deal with that.

As Ridder drove the stolen pickup along Route 28, toward Harwich, he gripped the steering wheel tight with one hand and a half-empty Milwaukee's Best can in the other. He finished the beer, crushed the can and threw it out the window, then grabbed another beer out of the brown bag.

Sykes looked over at him. "What now, Carson?"

Ridder shot him a glare. "I'll tell you *what*, Buster. Tomorrow, we find where that fucker Gallagher lives and we wait for him and his little shit friend. Then we jump 'em and pound their skulls against a fuckin' wall until they give us that journal or bleed to death."

Sykes felt his eye and nose with his hand and winced. "Yeah, I can't wait to pay back both those assholes, 'specially the big one. I'll smash *his* face with a fucking garbage can. See how he likes it."

"Once we get the journal back, we burn the fuckin' thing and get the hell out of here."

"But what about the lost gold I told you about?"

Ridder pounded the steering wheel with his fists. "Christ, Buster, you should be worrying more about keepin' your fat ass outta jail. And, hell, you don't even know for sure there's any lost gold."

Sykes stared straight ahead. "I'm sorry, Carson. I told you, I only skimmed the pages." He swallowed hard. "I'm telling you, Carson, that guy we robbed claimed there was more gold than what he found, and the journal tells where. I swear. Alls I can remember is the *Argo* ran aground on some beach, or something."

Ridder laughed sarcastically. "Or somethin'? Buster, do you know how many fuckin' beaches there are here? What do you propose to do, dig up the whole fuckin' coastline? No, we're gonna find those bastards and get rid of that journal. Then you can think whatever the hell you want about some lost gold."

Matt was sprawled on the couch falling asleep when they walked in the cottage. He jolted up when the door closed.

"Hey, chief, why so jumpy? Man, you look awful." Tucker handed him a cup of black raspberry ice cream.

Matt rubbed his eyes and sat up. "Thanks." He looked at the ice cream and then at Annie. "Good memory, Annie." She smiled. When they had dated, he always ordered black raspberry.

"So where were you tonight? Tucker and I stopped at the Squire ready to 'throw a couple down,' as you like to say." She playfully shoved his leg. "Why are you all wet?"

Matt put the ice cream down on the table and rubbed his head. "Oh, I left because I didn't think you guys were going to show."

"So where've you been?" Annie asked.

"I went and sat in the life guard chair at Oyster Pond, then went for a swim. You know, being communal with nature and all." He forced a laugh that caused Annie to raise her eyebrows.

"Well, we've got some great news. Guess what?" Tucker said.

Matt threw up his hands, he was in no mood to play games, but he went along with it. "I don't know. What? You won the lottery."

"Better. The Lockwoods have invited us to go with them for two days to Nantucket on their boat. They leave tomorrow morning."

"All of us in that little Whaler? Yeah, right!"

Tucker laughed. "No, Mr. Lockwood's got a big cabin cruiser. Remember, that one moored near the Whaler?"

"Sounds great." Matt smiled. "Yeah, let's do it. It'll be good to get away for a while."

# CHAPTER 10

▼

The 1936, forty-foot, classic raised-deck, sedan cruiser with a flying bridge and rebuilt Ford four cylinder, diesel engine sat motionless in the still water of Oyster Pond. Charlie Lockwood had spent the last six years restoring the boat. When he had retired as CFO of a large Wall Street brokerage house, he and his wife had moved to their summer home in Chatham. Worried that he would be bored with so much time on his hands after having worked fifty hour weeks for forty-two years, Trudy Lockwood had encouraged him to take a boat building course at a local boat yard. Without taking the instructor's advice of starting off with a relatively easy project after completing the course, Charlie bought a run-down, engine-seized, rotting 1936 cruiser for a song. For years it sat in a cradle in his side yard while he meticulously worked on it. In order to do all the work himself, he bought and read countless books on how to restore antique wooden boats and rebuild car engines. With the exception of receiving some help from a local mechanic on the engine, Charlie did all the work by himself. He replaced the transom and a quarter of the hull's planking, re-caulked the hull, sanded down all the teak and mahogany, installed modern amenities, including a new galley and head, varnished and re-varnished the hardwood seven times, painted the hull white, replaced all the hardware and fittings, and painted in classic gold lettering the name *GERTY* on the stern. After six years of snail's pace meticulous work, Charlie Lockwood had finished his retirement project.

Annie could not believe it when she saw the *Gerty*; the once rotting, paint-peeling, eyesore was now a beautiful, head-turning masterpiece with its classic blend of rich mahogany decks and trim, brass fittings, and white hull, replete with all life's essential amenities. The last time she had seen the boat, it was in such poor shape, no one, including Mrs. Lockwood, believed Mr. Lockwood could ever finish it. And, yet, there she was, ready to take them to Nantucket.

After loading their supplies, gear, and luggage onto the *Gerty*, they left at precisely 8:00 A.M., as the captain had called for. Mr. Lockwood stood proudly at the helm as his passengers raved about the beauty of his boat and the fine work he had done on her.

Once through the Stage Harbor cut and into Nantucket Sound, Mr. Lockwood increased the throttle and the *Gerty* planed at a comfortable sixteen knots. The sun sparkled and danced on the calm waters of the Sound; the rhythmic slap of water against the hull and the sound of the cascading waves created by the boat had a medicinal effect on the passengers. Everyone wore a smile.

Annie lay against her elbows on the bow deck. Tortoiseshell sunglasses sat on top of her head. She wore a one-piece, white bathing suit; the high cut at the thigh accentuated her long legs. Though she had never been one to just sit out until the sun ruined her skin, she had a tan year round, the kind of tan that looked healthy and beautiful, not overdone and crispy. She believed it was because she had one Native American ancestor on her mother's side. While her friends used to waste hours lying out on the beach trying to get a tan, Annie swam and played football with the boys. She knew her girlfriends always held a grudge against her for never having to work at her tan.

Now she lay on the mahogany deck not intently to get a tan, but more to enjoy the experience of being on the open water on a beautiful, sunny day with as little clothing on as possible. Fenway lay to her right with her head resting between her paws. Annie felt completely relaxed. Nantucket Sound was a calm sheet of shimmering sparkles that hypnotized her. She slowly tilted her head back and closed her eyes and felt the warmth of the sun and coolness of the ocean air. God, I've missed this, she thought.

Once they had passed the southern end of Monomoy Island, Tucker came out on the bow deck. It was the first time Annie had seen him without a shirt on. Not bad, she thought, muscular and firm, but not bulky. She laughed to herself for doing what she hated most men for doing to women, although part of her hoped Tucker would notice her.

"Wow, this is a great spot," Tucker said with a smile.

Annie looked up at him as he laid his towel next to her and sat down. She smiled back. "I love being on the water. Makes me feel so free, so…"

"Relaxed?" he finished her thought.

"Yeah, relaxed," she nodded her head and smiled. "Where's Matt?"

Tucker laughed, looked back at the flying bridge, then at Annie and said in low voice, "Poor guy. We were up there and Mr. Lockwood cornered him. He's getting an earful of stories about naval life. I slipped out first chance I got."

Annie looked over at Tucker as he stared out at the water off the port side of the prow. She had not looked at a man like this since her parents had died. She recognized the feeling immediately and enjoyed it.

"Have you ever been to Nantucket?" she asked.

Tucker shook his head as he turned his attention to her. "No, this is actually my first time to Massachusetts. How about you?"

Annie sat up, crossed her legs under her and tucked her hair behind her ears. "Well, you're going love it. Nantucket's amazing. It's got the most beautiful beaches, tons of art galleries and antique shops, and great restaurants. And if you're into boats, you can walk along the piers for hours checking out all the million dollar yachts. The island's become quite the playground for the rich and famous. And everything's within walking distance so you don't need a car like you would on Martha's Vineyard. I used to come to Nantucket with my parents when I was younger. We used to take our sailboat over for a weekend each summer." She looked right in Tucker's eyes. "My Dad used to go fishing off the jetties while Mom and I would walk through the village and go shopping. We always brought my Dad back a novel and a cold beer." She smiled even more. "And every time, sure enough, he would finish the book before we left the island. I used to try to find the thickest one to see if he couldn't do it. Nobody loved to read like my Dad."

She looked out at the water as a school of baitfish jumped off the port side of the bow and suddenly realized she was freely talking about her memories of her parents and that guarded feeling that usually rose from her gut was not there. For years she had bottled up her emotions, remained reticent. She had repressed her memories for fear of feeling that pain again, the pain that ripped at her heart with every breath she took and sight she saw that reminded her of them and the way it used to be before the pain that had driven her to the edge and made her want to jump because she didn't know how else to end it. But something in her held on, for what she didn't know. She had vowed never to feel that much pain again in her life. Now, she had let her guard down without realizing it and the memories began to flood back to her.

She looked again at Tucker and waited till he looked back at her. Within seconds he looked into her eyes. "Do you realize you are the first person I've been able to talk to about my parents?" Tucker smiled with his mouth closed. "What is it about you, Tucker McKinney?"

Before Tucker could respond, Matt walked out on the deck, sat down and let out a deep breath. "Thanks, Tuck, thanks a lot. When we come home, one of you guys is riding with Mr. Lockwood. Man, I now know the entire history of naval operations in the Pacific Theater during the years 1942 to 1945."

As Matt continued to complain about having his ear talked off by Mr. Lockwood, Annie was lost in her own thoughts. She wondered if Matt would mind if she and Tucker became more than friends, though she wasn't sure yet if she truly wanted to be more than friends with him. The possibility of having her fragile emotions shattered again terrified her, yet she couldn't deny how attracted she was to him.

Annie's thoughts were interrupted when Tucker said, "Okay, smart guy, you know so much about World War Two naval history, what was the name of the ship the Japanese formally surrendered on?"

"Oh, oh, I know this one," Annie jumped to her knees.

"Matt? What's the call? Put up or shut up!" Tucker said with a grin.

Matt shook his head. Tucker looked at Annie.

"The Missouri!" she yelled.

"And we have a winner! Better go talk a little more with Mr. Lockwood, Matt."

"Real funny, McKinney. You're such a smart ass."

Within two hours they could see large homes along the shores of Nantucket and the majestic white steeple of a historic church rising above the village. After passing the Brant Point lighthouse, they sailed into beautiful Nantucket Harbor, which was teeming with activity as people cruised between multi-colored lobster pot buoys that dotted the clear blue water in every type of boat imaginable. A few hundred sailboats and motor yachts rocked lazily at their moorings while scores of tourists walked up and down the piers admiring the vessels and shopping at stores located in converted rustic fishing shacks.

Mr. Lockwood docked the *Gerty* at the slip he had reserved and gave out instructions for being back at the boat by six o'clock for dinner. He and Mrs. Lockwood headed into the village while Annie, Tucker and Matt grabbed their towels and headed for the beach. Fenway fell asleep on Annie's Skidmore sweatshirt lying in the shade of the main cabin.

At just before eleven o'clock, Jetties beach, located less than a mile from the village, was beginning to become crowded. The sun blazed overhead in a sky devoid of any clouds. The breeze they had enjoyed while cruising to the island could barely be felt. Being a rather hot day, there were almost as many people in the water as on the beach. Because the beach was on the Sound side of the island, the wave action was minimal. But people didn't come to Jetties beach to play in crashing surf; they came to enjoy the warm Sound water, take in views of the lighthouse, and watch the multitude of boats coming into the harbor.

After they had laid their blankets out on the white sand, Annie asked if anyone wanted to go swimming. Matt looked at Tucker and said, "We'll meet you in there."

Annie shrugged her shoulders, smiled and tilted her head slightly as if to question, but said nothing. She grabbed her tee shirt from the bottom and pulled it over her head, then took off her cut off jean shorts. Both Matt and Tucker tried to nonchalantly grab a long glance at her as she undressed.

After admiring her toned body as she walked to the water, Matt turned to Tucker and said, "Hey, Tuck, I have to tell you, I haven't seen Annie this happy since, well, for at least four years."

"You mean since her parents died. I know, Annie told me."

"I didn't know she had. She doesn't tell many people. Listen," Matt looked right at his friend, "I care a lot about Annie. I see how you two act around each other and I'm totally cool with that. If you two want to hook up, that's great by me. Just don't hurt her, Tuck. She's too special."

"Thanks, man. I was kind of worried about what you'd think. But don't worry. I can already tell Annie's not like other girls. I can't figure it out, but she's different. She's got this jazz about her." He looked at Matt for confirmation.

"Cool. Let's get in the water before she starts thinking we're talking about her."

They stripped off their shirts and ran down to the water. Annie was about twenty feet out in water to just below her chest. When they reached her, Annie said with a straight face, "So, how was your conversation about me?"

Matt and Tucker looked at each other with guilty expressions. "What? Come on, Annie. We were talking about what bars we're going to hit tonight and how many babes we're gonna bag," Matt said with a big smile but with a slight hesitation in his voice.

Annie looked at Tucker who tried to keep a straight face. "Yeah, right," she said with a grin.

Ditchman and Hammond were waiting in O'Donahue's office when she walked in triumphantly waving three forensic reports in the air. The state forensic lab had finished analyzing the sweepstakes forms; O'Donahue's connection had paid off. Despite not being finished with the senator's son's case, without telling his superiors, O'Donahue's friend had quickly finished the analysis on the papers.

The forensics reports on all three forms were incomplete because either a section of information asked for on the form was not completed by the signer, or the person had not pressed down hard enough to make an indentation deep enough to detect without spending more time sending it to a lab with more sophisticated and specialized technology.

Ditchman looked at each report then handed them to Hammond.

"One address, three names, three phone numbers," Ditchman said.

"But further down the report it says two of the forms were done with sloppy, cursive handwriting so the accuracy is questionable," O'Donahue added as she sat down behind her desk. "I'll make a call to find out the other two addresses based on the phone numbers."

"The bartender remembered the messy handwriting," Ditchman said with a smile as he took the papers from Hammond and handed them to O'Donahue. "Let's make a phone call to our lucky winner."

Within a few minutes, O'Donahue finished making the three calls and received no answer at any one of them. At the second and third numbers an answering machine answered the call. The second's message was that which would befit a group of college kids living together: "Hey, we're probably at a party, so leave a message." The third's voice message was much more like that of a family's. A mother's patient voice thanked the caller and stated they were unable to come to the phone at the moment, the safer response to a would-be burglar looking to find out if anyone was home.

O'Donahue waited a few minutes before making a second round of calls, during which time Hammond paced from the door to the window as if on a treadmill. Ditchman calmly sat at the center table drinking a cup of black coffee.

On a second attempt she connected with a person at the first number. She quickly explained who she was and why she was calling.

"I'm looking for Stew Hannaford."

"Stew's not in right now, officer," the woman on the other end said nervously. "This is his wife, is he okay? Is he in trouble or something?"

"Has he been at Logan airport within the last three days?"

"He's been on a business trip in New Orleans for the past week. He left from Logan. He comes back tomorrow. What's this about?"

"We were looking for some information regarding an incident at Logan the other day, but since you husband has been out of town, he won't be able to help. I'm sorry to have inconvenienced you."

O'Donahue hung up the phone, looked at Ditchman and Hammond and shook her head. "Nothing like getting a completely innocent person all riled up."

When O'Donahue tried the second and third numbers again, she was met again with the same voice mail messages. "Change of plans. I don't feel like waiting around for these people. I'll find out the addresses, they're both local, and we'll do a little on-site visitation."

Because the two mystery people, James Calbridge and Matt Gallagher, lived in towns relatively close to each other, O'Donahue decide not to send out separate cars. After a few minutes traveling west on the Mass Pike, they headed into Watertown, just outside the city's limits, to the first address.

Through Watertown Square, O'Donahue made a series of turns down side streets until they arrived at a brown, early twentieth century, two-family house. A collection of bicycles littered the sidewalk in front of the house.

While Ditchman stayed in the car to continuously call the other number, O'Donahue and Hammond made their way around the bikes to the front porch of the house. O'Donahue knocked on the door, and with no answer, knocked on the other apartment's door. Again, no one answered.

"May I help you?" a voice behind them asked.

They turned to see a small woman in her mid-thirties standing on the sidewalk with three bags of groceries in her arms and three small children, each with a bag, in a line behind her.

"I'm Detective O'Donahue with the State Police. Do you live here?" She pointed at the door to the right.

"No, we live to the left." The woman walked up the steps and Hammond helped her put the bags down. "What's the problem? Is Jim okay?"

"James Calbridge?"

The woman nodded.

"When have you seen him last?" O'Donahue asked.

"I'm pretty sure he's away on a shoot. He's a freelance photographer. I think he's doing a job now for some children's nature magazine. He's been away for a couple weeks now, Alaska, I think."

Without any explanation, they apologized to the woman for alarming her and then were back in the car heading to Waltham, just west of Watertown, and the address that matched the phone number of Matt Gallagher.

Within ten minutes they were in the downtown area of Waltham, which, like Watertown, was a town with an industrial history, due its location on the Charles River, and had a mix of hard-working, blue collar people and those of new affluence who commuted into Boston's financial district.

Two large, stone columns adorned with wrought iron lanterns framed the driveway entrance. Just outside the stonewall that ran parallel to the street and connected to the left column was a yellow "for sale" real estate sign. The house sat a good hundred yards from the road in classic Victorian style. The slightly inclined driveway circled in front of the house; a large porch rapped around the front side of the Victorian.

"Big bucks for this jumbo, I bet," Hammond said as they got out of the car.

While O'Donahue repeatedly rang the doorbell and knocked on the door, Ditchman went around to the back of the house. In no time he was back.

"Looks empty."

O'Donahue pulled out her cell phone and dialed the number she had seen on the real estate sign. She had a quick conversation with the broker, who confirmed that the house was vacant. The sellers had moved to the Chicago area two months prior.

When she got off the phone, O'Donahue looked at Ditchman and then at Hammond, who leaned against the porch railing. "This doesn't make sense. This is the right number, but the wrong house." She looked back at Ditchman who stroked his mustache.

"Could be the wrong number."

"How?"

"Didn't the lab technician say that with such a rush job and the messy handwriting there were no absolutes?" He walked over to Hammond and pulled out the small pad of paper and pen he always kept in his shirt's breast pocket. "Rusty, do me a favor and write down your phone number." Ditchman pulled off a piece and held it on the railing in front of Hammond.

Hammond briefly looked at Ditchman, raised his eyebrows, then quickly obliged. Ditchman lifted the paper up and looked at it, then handed it to O'Donahue. "What's Rusty's number, Detective?"

She quickly looked at the paper and said, "It's 732-5509."

Hammond smiled as he realized what Ditchman had figured out. "Good one, Ditch. How'd you think of that?"

"Wait a minute. Think of what?" O'Donahue said, a slight trace of annoyance mixed with eagerness in her voice.

"Rusty's number is 732-5504, not 09. Having made that call over and over again, and then thinking about what you said, this being the right number, I realized it had to be the wrong number. And I know that Rusty is one of those people that makes a four with a slant from the top."

O'Donahue smiled. "Which when written quickly or sloppily looks exactly like a nine. Great job, Ditch."

Within the twenty minutes it took them to drive back through Watertown, through Newton, and into Brookline, O'Donahue had been informed by her station that the number and the property belonged to Ridley Johnson Gallagher, III. Ditchman used her cell phone to call the number, but received no answer, not even an answering machine.

O'Donahue used her cruiser's radio to call Ramona, her administrative assistant back at the airport. She instructed Romona to do a quick check of the state's database for Ridley Johnson Gallagher, III, and to call her back immediately.

The house was on was a busy road in a wooded area of Brookline, near Boston College, about five miles outside of the Boston city limits. The vast majority of the houses in the area sat quite a distance from the road; privacy and estate-like living was the norm, whereas a house that could be seen from the road was a rare exception, or the servants' quarters.

A large, twelve-foot high iron gate sprawled across the entrance to the driveway impeded them from approaching the house so O'Donahue parked the car on the shoulder of the road and the three got out.

"There's an intercom on the gate," Hammond said as he walked toward it.

"Rusty, no. Don't touch it. We can't be sure Sykes and his partner aren't already here. We'll approach the house unannounced," Ditchman said as he pointed to the top of the ten-foot high brick wall that connected to the gate. "I believe we're covered by probable cause, wouldn't you Detective?"

O'Donahue shrugged her shoulders. "It's a stretch."

"You coming, Detective?"

O'Donahue looked at her shoes. "Not in these heels. Just make it quick. And, hold on." She reached into the car and pulled out two radios and handed one to Ditchman. "Call me if you need any back up."

After five minutes, Ditchman and Hammond scampered back over the wall to find O'Donahue standing outside the passenger side door of the car, talking into the radio. When she saw them she ended her conversation. "Anything?"

"Guy's got a five-car garage full of cars, but no one's home," Hammond replied.

"Well, we've got one more lead. My assistant looked Mr. Ridley Johnson Gallager up in the state database and came up with nothing. But then she decided to do a search on the Internet because the guy's name is so unique. Sure enough, the name comes up all over the place."

"What's his story?" Ditchman asked.

"He's the founder and CEO of RJG Asset Management. Mutual funds, hedge funds, bonds, real estate, you name it, this guy's doing it. Ever heard of the Aristotle Funds?"

"The one in all those commercials with the bull running through that Greek place?" Hammond asked.

"The Parthenon," Ditchman added.

"That's the one. We're talking assets larger than most small countries."

"So where can we find him?" Hammond asked.

"Financial district, downtown Boston."

As O'Donahue drove into Boston, she used her cell phone to call RJG Asset Management. A receptionist answered and connected her to Gallagher's office where she was greeted by a female voice mail recording which indicated Mr. Gallagher was unable to take the call at the moment, the typical brush-off phone message. Annoyed, O'Donahue hit zero on the phone to connect with a receptionist. She explained who she was and how it was extremely urgent that she speak with Gallagher. The woman calmly explained that all calls to Mr. Gallagher were routed through Mr. Gallagher's assistant and if the voice mail answered the call, then probably the assistant had already left the office for the day. O'Donahue tried the connection again, and when greeted by the same message, connected back to the receptionist.

"It is absolutely imperative I speak with Mr. Gallagher. Is there any one there who would know where I can reach him?"

"I'm sorry, officer, only his assistant knows his schedule."

"What's the assistant's name, home number, and address?" O'Donahue asked curtly.

There was a slight pause. "I'm sorry, it's against company policy..."

"Listen," O'Donahue cut her off, "I'm on my way to your office right now. In fact, I'll be there in about five minutes, and unless you tell me what I want to now right now, I'm going to arrest you for interfering with a police investigation. And we're going to park a dozen police cruisers with flashing lights right outside your building. Won't that make a great PR splash on Wall Street!"

Immediately the receptionist complied. Gallagher's administrative assistant was Gloria Maherski; she lived on Bowdoin Street, near the State House. Ditchman wrote down the phone number as O'Donahue repeated it.

After handing the phone to Ditchman for him to make the call to Gloria Maherski, O'Donahue checked her watch. It was just after five. If the traffic wasn't too bad through the city, they could be at Maherski's apartment building in ten minutes, maybe less. "Just keep calling until you get an answer," she said and then put the siren light on the roof and sped through a light that had just turned red.

She looked at herself in the full-length mirror and was amazed at what she saw. The tight-fitting, black mini-skit and low-cut, pearl color silk blouse made her look sexy, yet with an air of confidence and style. She had occasionally worn the four-inch high heels, but the thong was a whole new sensation; it made her feel sexy and decadent, and she liked it because she knew he would like it. She looked at her face. The red lipstick was more than she had ever dared to wear, but tonight she was going to shed her old self.

Tonight she was going to live for the moment. Carpe diem, she thought. She had done all the right things that a single, professional woman in her mid-thirties should do to meet an attractive man. But what had that gotten her? She had spent virtually every weekend night going to bars and clubs with her girlfriends in search of the man who would sweep her off her feet just as she had dreamed since adolescence. But after countless dejection and wasted hordes of money and borderline alcoholism from the routine of it all, one by one, all her girlfriends, the crowd, as they called themselves, had married and settled down, just as she had always hoped to do. She looked at her size four figure in the mirror and stuck out her firm, round breasts. No, she wouldn't spend any more nights in loud bars where she felt older than everyone there. She wouldn't go looking any more. She had found him. And it didn't matter anymore that he was married. He had spent the better part of the year hitting on her at work. He was a portfolio manager, a rising superstar in the eyes of everyone, so she thought he was only teasing her. But when she had found the note on her desk inviting her to meet him at a hotel, she knew that she could not longer pretend like she found his advances abhorrent. No, tonight, she was going to have her due. After all, she had put in her time and she heard the wife was a real bitch, and they didn't have any kids, so what was the harm?

She pursed her lips, then turned and strode out of the bedroom as if she were on a fashion show runway. Just as she reached the door, the phone rang. She hesitated, the ringing almost bringing her back to reality. Maybe it was one of her friends inviting her over for dinner with her husband and kids. The phone kept ringing. She turned to retreat into the room to pick up the phone, but as she did, she caught a glimpse of herself in the mirror on the far wall. She stopped. No, tonight was her turn to feel alive, to feel love.

Gloria Maherski turned, grabbed her overnight bag, opened the door, and left her apartment while the phone continued to ring.

After enjoying a dinner of steamed lobster, corn on the cob, and watermelon on board the *Gerty*, Matt, Tucker, and Annie profusely thanked the Lockwoods for the hundredth time for dinner and for watching after Fenway, then excused themselves from the boat to go into the village. Annie felt a sense of schoolgirl joy and excitement for the first time since she could remember. Then a slight feeling of hesitation emerged. Just enjoy it, she kept thinking.

The village streets near the piers were crowded with tourists wandering aimlessly at a casual pace while looking at the various shop windows and antique buildings. No one was in a rush to meet a deadline or get the latest stock quote or make it to a meeting on time. People were relaxed and enjoying themselves.

The three walked for a short while down Main Street, a beautiful street made of cobblestones lined by large brick buildings built back in the early nineteenth century. Annie enjoyed checking out the people, most of whom were young, good-looking professionals or college students. Suddenly, she realized Tucker had drifted over to walk next to her. She suppressed a giggle. Thoughts of being back in seventh grade with Tommy Wilshire at the movie theater sprang into her head. He had tried to put his arm around her by pretending to yawn and stretch his arms. They don't change much, she thought.

Annie couldn't remember the last time she had gone out with some friends. After her parents died, she stayed in her apartment on virtually every weekend night while she was at Skidmore. She had tried to enjoy her college experience, but felt overwhelmingly guilty for going to parties. People in mourning simply don't go to parties, she had reasoned. So, while most of the other students had romped from bar to bar, or went to some wild keg party on campus, Annie had stayed in her apartment reading, painting landscape scenes of Cape Cod, or playing her guitar. Many young men had courted her when she had arrived in Saratoga; she had a unique spark that attracted men. But when she shut herself in her apartment after her parents died the October of her freshman year, the spark had disappeared and the number of young suitors eventually had dwindled to none.

Annie was now beginning to feel that spark again. She felt alive and giddy, and the feeling made her almost want to skip along the cobblestones of Main Street.

Across from a popular bar called the Quahog, which the locals simply referred to as "the Hog," Matt stopped and turned to his friends. "Alright, enough walking. Whatta ya say we go in here and tie one on?"

Annie and Tucker looked at each other and hesitated. Matt looked over their shoulders and saw a stunning red head with long, shapely legs glance over at him then walk into the bar. "Oh, come on, it'll be fun," he pleaded.

Reluctantly, they agreed and stood in a long line to be carded by the bouncer. After waiting fifteen minutes, they reached the front and pushed their way into the bar where they immediately found it crowded and noisy. Annie followed Tucker and Matt through the tight spaces between people until they found a refuge of small space at the far end of the bar.

The Hog was a large room with multiple tiers that provided patrons with good vantage points for surveying the crowd of people. As was typical of most of the bars on the island, the decoration motif was nautical. Lobster pots hung from the ceiling; fishing nets adorned the walls. A jukebox in the corner blared a Jimmy Buffett song.

Though it was barely nine o'clock, the patrons at the Hog were in a gregarious mood. Annie felt like she was back at one of the few keg parties she had attended in college, and quickly remembered why she hadn't been to more.

Matt disappeared for a minute, and then returned with three beers. "Cheers. Here's to a great summer and great friends," he screamed over the noise.

They clinked their beer mugs together and took a drink. As they did, Annie caught Tucker looking at her. He initially turned away like a young teenager, but then looked back. Annie smiled at him and he returned the smile.

For about fifteen minutes they stood there in their tiny space trying to have a conversation by yelling in each other's ear. Annie could barely hear what Tucker was saying, something about parties at Connecticut College, but she smiled and nodded her head as if she heard every word. She noticed that Matt seemed distracted. He constantly kept lifting his head up to scan the room.

Despite being with her friends, Annie felt completely out of place and the rowdy atmosphere made if even more difficult for her to enjoy the night. As more people entered the bar it was getting louder and more difficult to maintain any personal space. Guys who obviously had too much to drink kept banging into her. Finally, she had enough.

Annie nodded her head at Tucker and he instinctively put his head closer to hers so his ear was near her mouth.

"This scene is getting old real fast," she said.

Tucker nodded his head in agreement. "Hey, Matt," he yelled while poking Matt in the ribs to get his attention. "Let's get out of here. It's too crowded."

Matt shook his head. "You guys can go. I'm going to stay for a bit."

Annie noticed Matt smile and flick his head in the direction of the redhead. Tucker smiled understandingly and patted him on the back.

"I'll see you back at the boat," Matt said before he pushed his way in the direction of the redhead.

After fighting to get out of the Hog, Annie and Tucker finally reached the street and clean, crisp air. They both took a deep breath. Annie felt a bit of awkwardness coming on until Tucker said, "Want to take a walk?"

"Sure. Where to?" she smiled.

"I don't know. Let's just walk and find out when we get there."

"I like that philosophy."

They walked to the end of Main Street and took a left. While Tucker talked about how excited he was to teach in the fall, Annie listened with a curiosity and openness she had not known before. She felt like she was in a trance; she was walking next to him, listening to his voice, nodding her head, and was particularly aware of the absence of that nagging, guarded feeling. Suddenly, thoughts of Tommy Wilshire again popped into her head. She chuckled and Tucker stopped his soliloquy on the high received from standing in front of a class of students and teaching them the history of the United States.

He turned and looked at her. She wore a parchment colored ribbed v-neck sweater that casually hugged her trim shoulders and chest. "What's so funny?" he said in a shocked tone.

Annie touched his arm. "Oh, no, Tucker, I wasn't laughing at what you were saying. I think what you're doing is great. I'm sorry."

Tucker smiled. "Okay, but since you interrupted my wonderful oration, you have to at least tell me what made you laugh. Right?"

Annie looked at him and smiled back. "You remind me of Tommy Wilshire."

Tucker laughed. "Who the hell is Tommy Wilshire?"

As they reached Jetties beach, Annie took off skipping down toward the water. "Wait, who's Tommy Wilshire?" Tucker smiled and jogged after her.

When he reached Annie, she finally stopped. She turned to him and said, "Let's sit here for a while, okay?"

They sat down on the cool sand about twenty feet from the edge of the water. Tucker sat as close to Annie as he could without touching her. She looked at him and could see his face in the moonlight. The lighting reminded her of candlelight. Even though there was a chill coming off the water, Annie felt very warm inside. The smell of the seawater was strong and the incoming tide rushing into the harbor sounded like a river. She looked around and didn't see anyone else on the beach.

"Okay, now tell me why I remind you of Tommy Willowmeter."

"Wilshire. Tommy Wilshire. He was my first boyfriend. We were in seventh grade. He use to talk a lot, especially," she paused, "when I wanted him to kiss me."

She looked up into Tucker's face. In the dim light she could see there was a genuine kindness in his eyes. She felt safe, secure, and uninhibited. He hesitated for a second, then leaned over and kissed her. At first they just touched at the lips, but as they kissed with more intention, she draped her arms around his shoulders and pulled him to the sand and straddled him. She had not felt this way for years and all the pent up sexual tension and desires began to overwhelm her. Her body was soon swimming in a sexual asphyxia. As she explored his mouth with her tongue, she felt his excitement grow. She hesitated for a second, a learned reaction, but then continued and allowed the moment to carry her. This time she wasn't going to deny herself pleasure for fear of being hurt again.

She sat up, still straddling his hips, and without a word while looking into his eyes to watch his reaction, Annie pulled off her shirt, and unhooked her bra from behind in a quick, fluid motion. Tucker reached up and gently squeezed her full breasts. She arched her back then collapsed onto his chest and gently whispered in his ear, "Make love to me."

# CHAPTER 11

▼

At nine o'clock the Squire had yet to become overly crowded. A few college-aged people were in the bar early, but the majority were those who couldn't wait the expected hour for a table on the restaurant side. With most people busy eating or talking, no one gave notice to them as they strolled into the bar. Sykes sat at the bar and ordered a beer while Ridder surveyed the room until he saw a prime target, a young woman wearing a turquoise short sleeve shirt with the Squire logo over her right breast who stood behind the bar washing glasses and placing them on a plastic rack. Her auburn hair, which had streaks of blonde in it from spending too much time on the beach, made her look much younger than the rest of the women working in the bar, especially because she had it pulled back in a ponytail.

"Hi, what can I get for you?" she asked with a smile.

Ridder didn't return the smile. If you only knew, he thought while looking at her young body. He showed her the badge and explained he was a Boston detective investigating the mugging and rape of an elderly woman and that he was looking for a key witness, a young man who reportedly came to Chatham and has been seen in the Squire.

The young bartender's mouth opened. Good, she's buying the story, he thought. Stupid broad.

"God, that's horrible. Is she gonna be okay?"

"She's in intensive care in pretty rough shape." Ridder forced a scowl and shook his head as he feigned disgust. "We sure wanna stick the guy who did this to poor Mrs. Kellerman."

Her face grew determined. "So what can I do to help? Who you looking for?"

"Matt Gallagher. He's tall, blond, has a clef chin."

"Sure, Matt's one of the chefs here. He's not working tonight, I don't think. Is he in some kinda trouble, or something?"

Ridder shook his head. Not until I find the little shit, he thought. "No, no, not at all. We believe he may have had accidental contact with our prime suspect right before the crime took place. He probably doesn't even know it. So do you know where I can find him?"

"Hold on." She walked over to a male bartender, a man in his mid-thirties. He nodded his head and looked over at Ridder as they talked for a less than a minute, then she returned.

"I think he's renting a place down on Oyster Pond. Take Main Street to twenty-eight and hang a left at the stoplight. I think he's on the road next to the supermarket there. I sure hope you find whoever did this."

Ridder grinned. "Oh, we will now."

A few minutes later, Ridder and Sykes were driving the Oldsmobile Cutlass Supreme they had stolen from the Nantucket ferry parking lot in Harwich down the heart of Chatham. At the traffic light, Ridder took a left, then a quick right onto a road that looked like it ran behind the supermarket. He drove slowly to be able to peer down the few long driveways since large shrubs and thick, overgrown brush provided the homes with privacy. Within a minute, they had reached the town landing at the end of the road and the Oldsmobile's headlights illuminated a group of boats moored in the water.

"These driveways are too fuckin' long to see anything. Buster, get out and go down each one." Ridder pushed Sykes in the shoulder.

Sykes looked at Ridder, his lazy eye looking at his nose. "What am I looking for?"

Ridder shook his head. "A black Volkswagen, you stupid shit. Remember? The one the kid had at the airport?"

Sykes jumped out of the Oldsmobile and ran back up the road. Before he reached the first driveway, Ridder lost sight of him. A cloud cover had moved in and made the night dark and still; the air was heavy. A perfect night to rob a house, Ridder thought.

Within a few minutes, Sykes returned to the car. "Bingo. First one on the left there. The Volkswagen's in the garage."

Ridder reached under the front seat and pulled out the Glock .9mm, which he stashed in the waistline of his jeans. They put on latex gloves then left the car at the landing and walked up to the driveway.

At the end of the driveway, they saw two houses, a big one on the left, and a small cottage to the right, which had a Jeep Cherokee parked in front of it. No lights were on in either house. Ridder looked at Sykes and nodded once at the cottage. They walked around the side of the house and stopped at the door that opened into the kitchen. Ridder examined the door, then took a step back and kicked it with the bottom of his big boot. The molding on the inside of the door cracked as the deadbolt ripped through it and the door sprang open.

Once inside, he turned on the kitchen light, which shed light on the rooms downstairs. "Buster, you take down here. I got upstairs."

Upstairs, Ridder found two small bedrooms with a bathroom between them. Ridder turned on the bathroom light. The first room was a mess—clothes were piled on the floor, the beds were not made. Ridder quickly rifled through the clothes on the beds, kicked those on the floor, and checked under each mattress. He checked the small closet, but only found lacrosse equipment and more clothes. Under a stack of sports magazines in the bottom drawer of the small, white dresser that sat facing the two beds was a roll of money stuffed in a sock. Ridder grinned; stupid rich kids, he thought, as he tucked the roll into his pocket.

The other room was kept very neat, almost to the point where Ridder thought no one was using it. But when he opened the top drawer of the dresser, he immediately knew it was a female who slept there. With a cocky grin on his face, he pulled out a pair of lacy black underwear and studied them in the dim light. Nice, he thought, nodding his head knowingly.

He put the underwear back in the drawer and searched the rest of the drawers, then the closet. As he lifted the mattress he heard Sykes call him from downstairs. Quickly, he dropped the mattress and bounded down the stairs.

"You find the journal?"

Sykes sat at the couch in front of a laptop computer. "Check this out, Carson," he said with a smile, his left eye looking at the computer while his right eye looked at Ridder.

"Christ, Buster, we ain't got time to be playin' fuckin' computer games. Did you find the journal or not?" Ridder's teeth clenched.

"It ain't here, Carson. Says so right here. Look for yourself." He turned the computer toward Ridder who began to read. "This is an email to some guy at Harvard. Says they sent the journal to him so his colleague can figure it out. Guy's name is Nylan. Probably a professor would be my guess." Sykes looked up at Ridder.

Ridder grinned. "You know, Buster, for a dumb shit, you amaze me. How'd you learn this crap? Email? What the fuck?"

Sykes stood up and smiled. "I took a computer course, complements of the great Commonwealth of Virginia's penal system."

They left the cottage through the kitchen door and walked backed to the Oldsmobile at the landing. Sykes had wanted to take the laptop, but Ridder had convinced him he could buy as many computers as he wanted once they found the gold.

When Ridder connected the wires underneath the steering column, the car made no noise. "Fuck." He slammed the steering wheel then tried again with the same result. "Piece of shit car."

"What are we gonna do, Carson?" Sykes asked, a vacuous look on his face. Ridder froze for a second and looked at Sykes. Don't seem so smart now, do ya Buster? he thought.

"Wipe this one down, Buster, and keep your gloves on. I'll be right back." Ridder got out of the car and ran back up the street. Within a minute, headlights lit up the isolated parking lot.

Sykes got in the car, a look of confusion covering his face. "Jesus, Carson, this's Gallagher's car!"

Ridder grinned and floored the accelerator on the Volkswagen.

Traffic on the mid-Cape highway was light since it was past ten o'clock at night. Ridder pushed the '86 Volkswagen GTI to its top speed of seventy-five miles per hour. The car shook and vibrated under the strain, but nonetheless kept a steady pace as it passed the sign for exit three, Sandwich.

Ridder dragged on a half-spent Marlboro while Buster Sykes sat in the passenger seat studying a map of Boston he had bought at a convenience store. He had circled the area of Harvard Yard with a blue pen.

Suddenly, blue and white lights illuminated the inside of the car. Ridder braked quickly, but too late.

"Shit. It's a fuckin' cop. Be cool and take your gloves off, but don't touch nothin'."

He slowed the Volkswagen down then stopped in the breakdown lane.

Sykes turned his head to look at the police car, but could see nothing except the blinding blue and white lights. He turned back and looked at Ridder who he could tell even in the difficult light was tense as a board. "Hey, be cool now Carson. He's just got you for speeding."

"Shut up, Buster, just shut up. I'll handle this my own way. Find the registration in the glove compartment."

Sykes quickly rifled through some papers. The flashing lights on top of the police car provided him with just enough light to make out what each paper was. He threw the contents to the floor, mainly old tune-up records, until he found an envelope that had the word "registration" written on it. He handed it to Ridder who opened the envelope.

A knock on the driver's side window sounded and Ridder slowly rolled the window down. A large state trooper in a crisp blue uniform, knee high black boots, and a round brim hat cocked to the front, stood at the door. He held a large, silver flashlight in his left hand.

"License and registration, please." His square jaw barely moved as he spoke while his eyes never moved from the inside of the car.

Ridder reached into his back pocket and pulled out his wallet. He quickly reminded himself to give the cop the right license. He handed it and the registration to the officer who looked at each.

"This is my friend Matt Gallagher's car. He let me borrow it so I could go visit my mother in the hospital in Boston. She was just in a car accident and my car won't start. I know I was speedin', sir, but I sure want to get to my mother's side real soon," Ridder said in his most sincere voice while trying to keep his eyes as large as possible to convince the cop of his worry.

The trooper looked at the license and registration. "Wait here, Mr. Drogin."

Ridder watched him in the rearview mirror as he walked back to his cruiser and sat in the driver's seat.

"Wow, Carson, you handled that real good," Sykes said in a somewhat shaky voice.

"We ain't golden yet. That registration was outdated by a year." Ridder kept his eyes on the mirror.

They sat in the car for five minutes that felt like ten. Ridder could feel the perspiration running from his armpits down to his sides. He tried to remain cool but he had a bad feeling.

After each minute, Sykes increased the tension by worrying out loud. After the fifth minute he said, "Man, this is bad. What's taking this guy so long? A routine stop don't take this long, does it, Carson?"

Ridder didn't answer as he looked into the mirror and saw the large trooper step out of his cruiser and walk deliberately toward the Volkswagen. As Ridder watched the trooper, he reached under the driver's seat with his right hand, then drew it away.

The trooper's flashlight once again illuminated the front of the Volkswagen. In a commanding voice he said, "Mr. Drogin, I need you to step out of the vehicle."

Ridder thought to himself quickly. There's no way an expired registration demands this much attention. And the fake license is definitely clean. Shit, maybe the kid came home and reported his car stolen.

"Sir, step out of the vehicle," the trooper said in louder, more forceful tone.

Ridder glanced in the rearview mirror and found the break in the traffic he was looking for. He quickly reached under the seat with his right hand as he opened the door with his left. As he stood up, in a calm, uniform motion, he pulled the Glock out, pointed it through the open window, and pulled the trigger. Catching the bullet square in the chest, the trooper's legs buckled and he collapsed to the pavement like a rag doll.

"Jesus, Carson! Why the hell did you do that?" Sykes screamed.

"Shut up and put your gloves back on." Ridder shot an angry glare back at Sykes. "Help me put him in backseat before any cars come by."

"But, we…"

"Just do it, Buster!" Ridder yelled, the veins in his neck bulging.

Sykes ran around the car and picked up the limp trooper's legs and guided him into the backseat of the Volkswagen as Ridder pulled from inside the car. With a bit of struggling, they finally managed to stuff the trooper's limp body into the area behind the front seats.

"Follow me in the cop car, and don't you screw this up."

Sykes made it to the police cruiser just before the first car drove by and ducked as it passed. After fumbling with a few switches, he finally turned off the cruiser's flashing lights.

Ridder quickly pulled back onto the highway and drove the speed limit, checking his rearview mirror constantly to make sure Sykes still followed him. He turned off at the next exit onto a quiet road unoccupied by any houses, and only a few business establishments, which looked closed. Ridder drove for five more minutes until he found the perfect spot—the parking lot of a twenty-four hour supermarket. With quite a few cars in the lot for that time of night, Ridder figured the car would be less conspicuous, and, with a little luck, never noticed.

He parked the Volkswagen between a minivan and a SUV at the far end of the lot, reached back and pulled the tapestry that had covered the torn back rest of the rear seat over the dead cop, wiped down the Volkswagen, then replaced Sykes behind the wheel of the police cruiser. Within minutes, they were back on the highway.

They drove for a few miles before either said a word. Finally, Sykes broke the silence. Shaking his head, he asked, "You going tell me now why we're riding in a stolen cop car after killing a cop?"

"Listen, I know what I'm doin'," Ridder said with more than a touch of defensiveness. "I figured the cop was in his car for so long because Gallagher musta reported his car stolen. And if you don't remember, we got two murders on our heads now, you dumb shit!" He paused to let his anger subside, then grinned. "And this is my way at gettin' back at that little shit. Think about it. They'll find his car with the dead cop. He'll be up shit's creek tryin' to buy his ass out of that one. And while he's got the law stuck up his ass, we'll be countin' our millions." Ridder pounded the steering wheel, the adrenaline still pumping through his body.

Annie broke the embrace of the kiss so she could look at Tucker above her. For a minute they just stared into each other's eyes. When she felt him begin to move inside her again, she quickly moved her hands from his back to the front of his hips.

Tucker immediately stopped. "Are you okay?" he asked, then rolled off of her.

Annie reached over and grabbed her shirt and shorts and quickly put them on. She suddenly felt embarrassed. But she had wanted it. It had been so long and though she felt a bit ashamed of herself, it felt good to just let go and follow her desires. She suddenly felt more alive.

"Yeah. We should head back to the boat. The others are probably wondering where we are."

"Sure, that's probably a good idea," Tucker said, then put on his shirt, pulled up his shorts and stood up. "Annie, you sure you're okay?"

Annie stood up and kissed him on the cheek. "I'm better than I have been in a long time, and I want it to stay that way."

Clouds now obscured the moon, making the beach much darker. Annie gently squeezed Tucker's hand and smiled.

# CHAPTER 12

▼

O'Donahue, Ditchman and Hammond were waiting in the reception area when Gloria Maherski entered the room, a large, four hundred square-foot, mahogany and brass decorated room whose walls were adorned with original oil paintings from nineteenth century American artists. The look on her face immediately showed she knew these three visitors were not at all like the usual visitors to Ridley Johnson Gallagher III's plush corporate office. The regulars always sported expensive, Italian suits and carried leather briefcases. The combination of wrinkled casual wear and Dunkin' Donut large coffees made them look more like they were ready to take in a ball game on the weekend than to meet with one of the richest men in America.

O'Donahue stood as Maherski entered the room. Maherski smiled quizzically and proceeded right past the visitors to behind her large, dark oak desk that must have taken a crew of ten movers to carry into the room. She placed a mid-sized, over-the-shoulder bag behind the desk.

"Are you Gloria Maherski?" O'Donahue asked as she approached the desk.

"Yes, may I help you?"

O'Donahue quickly introduced herself and explained how they wanted to contact Gallagher. She made sure to include that they had a patrol car spend the night waiting for her at her apartment, but she never showed.

Maherski's face flushed and her eyes looked away when she said, "Oh, I was out with my girlfriends last night and I stayed over at one of their apartments so I wouldn't have to walk home."

O'Donahue looked at the bag Maherski had placed on the floor against the wall behind the desk, but said nothing. "Listen, we really need to get in touch with Mr. Gallagher."

Maherski suddenly stiffened and looked O'Donahue directly in the eye. "I've been directed by Mr. Gallagher not to divulge any information as to his whereabouts. I'm sorry, Detective."

Ditchman approached her desk and calmly said, "We believe his son could be in serious trouble so we need to find him as soon as possible."

Maherski's face lost any signs of resolution. She ran her hands through her thick, red hair. "I would like to help you, but I really can't get in touch with him."

"Can't or won't?" O'Donahue challenged.

Maherski shot her a look, then turned back to Ditchman. "He's not at a conference or on some business trip. He and Mrs. Gallagher are at a marital spa out west. She set it up. They're having troubles. God, I could get fired for telling you this."

Ditchman smiled warmly as he approached the desk. "How can we reach him?"

"That's just it. You can't. Mrs. Gallagher specifically picked a resort that didn't allow cell phones and pagers or any kind of contact with the outside world. She always complained that he was too consumed with running the company. I don't even know the name of the place."

Ditchman looked at O'Donahue, who raised her eyebrows, then at Hammond as an invitation for any interjection. None came, so Ditchman continued. "Do you know anyone who could help us locate Matt Gallagher?"

Maherski shot straight up in her chair. "Matt? Oh, I assumed you were talking about Michael, the older brother."

"Why did you assume that?" Ditchman asked.

"Michael can be, how shall I say it, pretty wild behind his father's back. And Matt, what's he about fifteen? How much trouble can he get in?"

"I think he's a bit older than that. Regardless, how can we contact Matt?"

She shrugged her shoulders. "I really don't know."

"What about the brother, Michael?"

"Hold on a second." She picked up her phone and dialed a number from memory. While she waited she said, "He runs our office in D.C." She paused, then said, "Hi, Alice, it's Gloria, is Michael in?" She shook her head to her audience. "When do you expect him?" She paused. "Alice, this is really important. Can I get his home number?" She wrote it down and thanked Alice, then dialed

Michael Gallagher's home number. "Alice will call me when he gets to the office. She expects him in the afternoon, but she said you can never tell with him." She paused. "No answer at his house." She wrote both numbers on a piece of paper and handed it to Ditchman.

O'Donahue handed Maherski her card and instructed her to call if she heard from any of the Gallaghers.

As they were leaving the reception area, O'Donahue's cell phone rang. She quickly answered it, smiled, and hung up. "The state examiner's autopsy report just came in."

Ridder looked at his face in the dirty bathroom mirror. The bruise below his left eye had turned the yellow hue of urine. Fuckin' kid's gonna pay, he thought. He tried to remember the last person to get the better of him, but could think of none. Not even that piece-of-shit Kellerman had gotten the best of Carson Ridder.

He doused his face with cold water and slowly dried it with a rough hotel towel that smelled of mildew. He could still feel the cheap booze in his veins. The stale taste of whisky lingered in his mouth. The feeling was familiar, almost comforting.

They had arrived in Boston the night before without detection. Ridder had figured every cop in the state would have been out in force looking for the stolen cop car and the person who had slain the state trooper. But the city was quiet, almost dormant, which worried Ridder.

As soon as they had reached Cambridge, Ridder dumped the stolen cop car in an empty lot behind an old, deserted warehouse near the Charles River. A loquacious Haitian cabbie took them to the Luck of the Irish Motel, just over the Cambridge line, in Somerville. After checking in, they sat in the dark, musty motel bar drinking three dollar shots of whiskey until closing time at one o'clock.

Ridder walked out of the bathroom and kicked the bed. "Get your dumb ass outta bed, Buster."

Sykes raised his eyebrows to placate Ridder, then groaned.

"Come on, Buster, don't be fuckin' around with me now, its past noon and we've gotta make a stop before we find this douchebag professor."

Sykes rolled away from Ridder and wrapped himself more deeply in the stained blankets. "Give me another hour, will ya? I feel like shit," Sykes said in a strained voice.

Ridder leaned over the bed, grabbed a large handful of blanket near Sykes' chest, and pulled. In an instant, Sykes' face was inches from Ridder who leaned over the bed while maintaining his firm grip on the sheets. His lips clenched together. His black eyes grew large as they pierced through Sykes' astonishment.

"Maybe I'm not makin' myself clear, Buster. Get the fuck outta bed, now!" He screamed the "now" causing Sykes to jump out of the bed and run into the bathroom.

After leaving the Luck of the Irish Motel they hailed a cab on the street.

"Where to, capt'n?" asked the middle-aged driver with an unshaven face and unlit cigar in the corner of his mouth.

"Nearest pawn shop," Ridder responded coldly.

Within ten minutes, they arrived in front of Thin Willie's Tried and True Pawn Shop. Dull metal grating covered the windows of the front of the small, lone standing building; the glass door in the middle had bars in front of it. Graffiti was spray painted across the concrete below each window. With so many layers of words, symbols, and pictures in the full spectrum of colors, the walls almost looked like a cheap rendition of modern art. Above the doorway, a sign read, "Experienced Goods Bought and Sold: Appliances, Computers, Jewelry, ETC."

Ridder looked at the sign; he hoped the goods he was looking for would fall under the category of etcetera. It was a shame he had had to toss the Glock off the Sagamore bridge into the Cape Cod Canal, but there was no way he was going risk being caught with the weapon that had been used to drop a cop, especially a statie.

Musical instruments, out of fashion women's clothing, and shelves littered with televisions, fans, toasters and air conditioners hung on the three walls. Glass cabinets filed with high priced junk, from radios to cubic zirconium rings labeled as real diamond rings, created a wide aisle that led to the back of the store and another glass case. Behind the back case sat an obese man on a stool, which looked like a toy under the large man. He said nothing to Ridder and Sykes as they approached him, just sat with his arms crossed on top of his corpulent belly, a frown of discomfort on his acne-scarred face.

Ridder had to bite his tongue to keep from laughing as he looked at the man on the tiny stool. Once composed, he growled in his gravelly voice, "I need to talk to the owner."

"You're looking at him, pal," the man said.

Thin Willie? Ridder thought. They ought to call you fat shit Willie, you fuckin' pig. But when he spoke, he was much more cordial.

"Willie, I was wonderin' if you could help me out here. I'm lookin' for a piece, no questions asked, top dollar paid. Know what I mean?" He pulled out his wallet and laid two one hundred dollar bills on the counter.

Thin Willie didn't move off the stool. He stared right at Ridder. "Don't sell that stuff."

"Maybe I didn't make myself clear," Ridder said as he put another hundred dollar bill on the counter.

"You a cop, mister?" Thin Willie asked.

"No, Willie, and I ain't gonna ask again." Ridder laughed and placed a fifty on the counter.

Thin Willie looked at the bills on the counter, then back at Ridder. He raised his eyebrows.

Ridder put another fifty on the counter.

Thin Willie smiled for the first time, revealing a set of crooked, nicotine-stained teeth, then struggled to transfer his weight from the stool to his feet. He wobbled back and forth as he moved. "Wait here," he said and disappeared behind a black curtain.

In a moment he was back, wobbling to the counter with a brown cloth bag in his large left hand. "Smith & Wesson .357. Serial number's rubbed. There's extra candy in the bag."

Ridder loosened the drawstring on the bag and pulled out the gun. He looked at it for a moment, checked its action, then put it back in the bag with the bullets. He looked up at Thin Willie and grinned. "Deal."

Back out on the street, they hailed another cab.

"Harvard University," Ridder said without looking at the driver in his rear-view window.

After a few minutes of rendering an unsolicited social commentary on the state of the economy in the "blessed Commonwealth of Massachusetts," the cabbie dropped his passengers off on Massachusetts Avenue across from one of the university's stately brick and iron gates.

Harvard Square bustled with activity. Summer students with bookbags, tourists with cameras, teenagers with skateboards, and street performers with guitars crowded the sidewalks. Behind them people sat at an outdoor cafe having a leisurely lunch with friends or business associates. To their left were a magazine kiosk and the stairway to the Harvard Stop on the T, the subway system of Boston. Recalcitrant teenagers, sporting hair of all colors but simple brown, black, or blond, repeatedly jumped their skateboards off a low brick wall onto a black railing. Each attempt ended with the board slipping out from underneath the zealous rider's feet while he tried to make it to the end of the five-foot long, slopping railing. After each rider landed in a splash on the brick sidewalk, to the exuberance of his fellow boarders, as if wiping out was the objective of the exercise, he would tenaciously take his position at the end of an informal line and encourage the others in their feeble attempts to conquer the railing. Ridder looked at the teenagers and grimaced as a man in a green army coat, with a stack of newspapers under his left arm, approached him.

"My good, man, care to buy a newspaper to help the homeless?" the man asked in a good-natured voice with a strong element of salesmanship.

"Get lost, asshole," Ridder replied, not trying to hide his hatred for the homeless.

Ridder turned to Sykes who stood looking around at the many people. "Come on, Buster, let's go. This place is filled with too many fuckin' weirdoes."

Once they were inside the gates of Harvard Yard, the hustle of the street crowds dwindled. They walked for a while along a sidewalk flanked by two plush greens, then stopped at a young man who sat beneath a large oak tree reading a book. He looked up when Ridder spat loudly on the sidewalk.

"You tell me where I can find a Professor Nylan?" Ridder asked.

"No, but you can ask in that building over there." The young man pointed to a large, boxy, gray building with a statue of a seated man in front of it.

While Ridder was in the building, Sykes waited outside, admiring the statue of John Harvard, the founder of the oldest university in America. Within minutes, Ridder reemerged.

"You find him?"

Ridder pulled a pack of cigarette's from his jean's pocket and extracted one. He bit off the filter and spat it on the ground. "Yeah," Ridder finally responded as he lit the cigarette. "He's in his office. I told the dumb bitch at the desk that I was an old student of the good professor. Fuckin' people will believe anythin'. She called to see if he was in. So now we've got ourselves an appointment."

They walked around the building to another large, open green. At one end of the green was Widner Library, a huge brick building with a set of twenty or so stone steps leading to its entrance beneath a portico enshrined by tall, Corinthian columns. A large brick and white trim chapel, with a steeple reaching high into the sky, enclosed the other side of the green. In front of them was another large, red brick building, Sever Hall.

A group of five students smoking cigarettes sat on the cement steps of the hall. As Ridder and Sykes climbed the steps, Ridder smashed his filterless butt with his boot on the steps before opening the door.

No one was in the building's corridors or stairways; the summer session was always much slower than the regular school year. A silence hung in the building, save for the sound of their steps on the wooden staircase as they ascended to the fifth and top floor of Sever Hall.

Upon reaching the fifth floor, Ridder checked the numbers on each door as they walked to the left. At the end of the corridor, a door with a window of frosted glass and writing on it opened. A young woman held the door partially open with her back to Ridder and Sykes.

"Okay, thanks again, Professor Nylan. I'll check in with you when I finish the rough draft."

She closed the door and walked quickly down the corridor without taking note of Ridder and Sykes, who had turned their backs to her and pretended to read the messages and advertisements on a bulletin board.

Once the girl had walked down a portion of the stairs, Ridder opened the office door. Professor Nylan sat behind a large wooden desk with neat stacks of papers and books at each end. His gray hair and wrinkled skin made him look older than seventy. He squinted through thick glasses as he looked up at them.

"Did you forget some...oh, hello, may I help you?" he asked in clear surprise that it was not the student with whom he had just spoken.

Ridder closed the door behind Sykes and flicked the deadbolt to the locked position. The unmistakable sound made the professor flinch. Sykes stood with his arms across his chest as Ridder walked closer to the desk. He put his large hands on the edge of the desk and leaned closer to the professor, whose face did not hide his astonishment.

"I believe you have something of mine, professor," Ridder said in a calm, deep voice.

The professor's eyes widened as his head jerked up. "I beg your pardon?"

Ridder grimaced. "Come on old man, stop wastin' my fuckin' time. I know my old journal was sent to you by Annie, I think you know her." Ridder grinned. "Now I want it back." He leaned closer to Nylan, causing the professor to instinctively shift back in his chair.

"I don't know what you're talking about, and if you don't kindly leave this instant, I will have to call campus security." As he reached for the phone on the desk, Ridder lunged to his right and grabbed the receiver out of his hand and slammed it against the professor's temple.

"Where's my journal, old man?" Ridder demanded loudly.

As he winced in pain, the professor gasped, "I received an email from my god-daughter that she was sending me a journal, but, I swear to you, I never received it."

Gripping the phone with increased anger, Ridder struck the professor repeatedly over the head until he fell to floor in a heap.

"Where is it, goddamnit!"

"I don't know," the professor replied in a whisper before he passed out from the trauma his frail body had endured.

Ridder turned to Sykes. "Those bastards must still have the fuckin' thing!"

"What the hell we gonna do now, Carson?" Sykes asked.

Ridder glared at him, then grinned at the professor. "Do? What are we going to do? I'll tell you exactly what we're going to do."

When O'Donahue entered her office, she immediately found the yellow, legal-size envelope on her desk. She quickly opened it and pulled out its contents, a letter on official state letterhead, and a collection of photos of Kellerman, some on the airport sidewalk, some on the examination table. O'Donahue glanced at the photos, then handed them to Ditchman. She quickly read the letter then handed that to him. "You were right, Ditch. Kellerman didn't jump. The bruises on his neck indicate he was probably held by a person with rather large hands, and the fact that he landed on his back implies he was not facing forward when he fell from the garage."

Hammond quickly looked at the photos and the letter. "No one ever takes a dive without looking. You were right, Ditch."

"We can rule out accidental cause of death, so now it's officially a homicide case," O'Donahue said as her phone rang.

In thirty seconds she was off the phone and smiling. "The latest recovered stolen car report's in. Neither is ours, which leaves us with the Buick Regal and the Beemer as possible leads."

# CHAPTER 13

▼

The ride back to Chatham across Nantucket Sound, which reflected the battle-ship gray of the overcast sky, was slow, wet and raw. It had begun raining on and off early in the morning and the pattern showed no signs of breaking by the late afternoon. Despite the Gerty's size, the Lockwoods and their guests felt the motion of every swell. Though she easily plowed through the whitecaps caused by the blowing wind, the *Gerty* climbed and descended every swell in a rolling, repetitious motion. In contrast to the day before when they had cruised to Nantucket on a gorgeous, calm, sunny day, the conditions on the voyage home forced them to bundle up in foul weather gear and huddle together in the main cabin to seek refuge from the wind-swept sea.

Mr. Lockwood stood at the helm, gripping the wheel with both hands; his eyes never diverted from their sweeping motion of the seas in front of the boat. He told no old navy stories on this trip for the unanticipated change in Mother Nature called for his full attention. Tucker stood next to him and held onto a polished brass railing. Below deck, in the head, Matt paid the price of drinking too many beers at the Hog. He had not heeded the warnings from Mrs. Lockwood that staying below deck made seasickness worse. Annie stood next to Mrs. Lockwood and gazed out the window on the port side of the cabin as sheets of wind-driven rain slapped against the window.

"Oh, what dreadful weather. Where in God's name did this storm come from? I do hope you had a good time, though." She put her arm around Annie's waist.

Annie smiled. "We had a great time, Mrs. Lockwood. Thanks again, this has been wonderful." She looked over at Tucker who stared intently out the front window. Thoughts of last night on the beach caused an arousing tingle on the back of her neck. She wanted to go over and stand with Tucker, or, better, have him come to her and put his arm around her and keep her warm.

Suddenly, she realized why men leave after spending a night with a woman. It was the awkwardness of the omnipotent question, "what now?" Part of her wanted to find out the answer immediately.

By the time they had sailed up the Oyster River to the mooring, Matt's stomach was empty and he joined the others on deck. While they unloaded their things into the Whaler, they all teased Matt, except for Mrs. Lockwood who tried to comfort him with a warm rub on the back.

When they reached their cottage, Matt's face was once again green, so he went straight up the stairs and lay down on his bed. Standing behind the couch, Annie suddenly found herself alone with Tucker for the first time since they had strolled back from the beach. She felt engulfed in that awkwardness she had wished to avoid and so tried to resist looking at him, but couldn't.

Once their eyes met, Tucker said, "Hey, Annie, I wanted to…I mean, I was going to…"

"I had a good time last night, too."

Tucker smiled back. "Good." He stepped closer to her and kissed her gently on the lips. "Hey, I'm going to walk to that supermarket to get the paper to see how the Orioles did against the Sox last night. Want to go?"

Annie laughed with relief. "Sure, I'd like that."

After about twenty minutes, Tucker and Annie returned to the cottage with the Boston Globe. His face showed no happiness; the Red Sox had swept the Orioles in a twilight double-header. Before Annie got a chance to gloat again, Matt walked down the stairs and into the living room. He slumped into the couch and moaned. Tucker sat in the wicker rocking chair and stared at him.

"Hey, governor, feeling much better?"

"A little." Matt rubbed his face with his hands. "Man, that ride sucked."

Annie called from kitchen, "Hey guys, come in here and look at this. The door frame on the back door's been broken."

Tucker jumped out of the rocker and walked into the kitchen just as the phone rang. He answered it. "Matt, it's for you."

Matt took a deep breath and lifted himself from the couch and sauntered into the kitchen. "Who is it?"

Tucker shrugged his shoulders and handed him the phone.

"Hello?" Matt said in a scratchy voice.

"Listen good, punk. I'm only gonna tell you this once. We've got old man Nylan here, and he's gonna take a real good hurtin' if you don't hand over that journal you told him you were sendin' him, which mysteriously didn't show up."

Matt's eyes narrowed as he took in what was happening. "Who the hell is this?" he asked, though he already recognized the deep voice.

"As I see it you've got two choices. Either we just waste the old man and be done with this, and then I come after you, or you can get your ass to his office in three hours from right now and hand over the journal. So what's it gonna be?"

Matt quickly thought to himself as he paused, then said, "Okay, okay, three hours."

"And no cops. If I see one badge or anyone lookin' at me funny, the old man's dead."

The line went dead. Annie and Tucker stood next to Matt, his face white from fear, his hands shaking.

"Matt, what's going on? Who was that?" Annie asked, her forehead wrinkled with concern.

Matt turned and looked her in the eye. "Those guys from the airport, they've got Albert. They think I still have the journal and they want it."

Annie's eyes instantly grew large; her mouth hung open. Tucker touched her shoulder. "We're going to call the police, right?" he asked.

"He said no cops or the professor will get hurt," Matt said softly.

"But we don't have the journal anymore," Tucker said.

Matt puckered his lips and nodded his head. "I know. It must have gotten lost or delayed in the mail. I swear I mailed it."

"So what do we do then?" Annie shook her hands. A look of panic began to form on her face.

"We have to call the police, Matt. What choice do we have?" Tucker said.

Matt looked at his watch. Seven o'clock. They would have just enough time. "There's got to be another way. If we call the police, he said they'd hurt Albert." He looked at Annie who began to cry.

"What about making a fake journal. They'll never know the difference," Tucker said.

"We don't know if they've read it or not. But seeing how that guy's bent on getting it, we can only assume they've read it and think it will lead them to the lost gold. I mean why else would they want it so bad?"

Annie took a deep breath and wiped the tears from her cheeks. "They may know about the gold, but not where it's buried. Why else would they take Albert?" She stopped for a second and thought, then said, "How did they know about…Jesus, the e-mail. They must have broken in. That's why the back door's broken." She looked at her laptop on the coffee table. "I never leave it open when I'm done using it. Oh, God, I must have left my email open."

"How did they know where we lived?" Tucker asked.

Matt shook his head and took a deep breath. "I'm sorry, Annie. God, I'm so sorry. I didn't want to tell you guys and get you all alarmed, but the same guys jumped me the other night at the Squire. I got away, but they must have found out where we live."

Annie bit on her lip. "And you didn't you call the police? What's going on with you, Matt? This is the second time they've gone after you and again you just act like it's no big deal? Now they've got Albert!" She began to cry again.

Matt reached out to Annie and pulled her to his chest, a pained expression covering his face. "God, I'm so sorry, Annie. I didn't mean for this to happen. I thought they would just let it go."

Annie pulled away from him. "So what are we going to do then? What if we call the police now and Albert ends up…"

Tucker had remained quiet for a while, deep in thought. Suddenly, he broke his silence. "If not a fake journal, what about fake gold. They don't know we haven't found it yet. They'll never know what it looks like." He raised his eyebrows in anticipation of their response.

"That's it," Matt said with excitement in his voice, "and I know exactly how we can pull it off. We'll get Albert and then call the cops." He looked at his watch. "Come on, Tuck, we've got to go now. We've got less than three hours."

"Wait a minute! What about me?" Annie said.

Matt grabbed her by her two shoulders, looked her straight in her eyes and shook his head. "Sorry, Annie. I can't let you come. I could never forgive myself if anything ever happened to you. I already feel bad enough about getting Albert involved in all this."

"But he's all I have left." She pushed away from Matt and stood for a second with her right hand to her mouth, trying to fight back the tears.

Tucker moved to Annie and hugged her, then firmly whispered into her ear. "Don't worry, Annie. We'll get him. Everything'll be okay."

After a few seconds in his arms, Annie stepped back, took a deep breath, and fingered her hair out of her face. She walked over to her purse, which sat on the coffee table, and pulled out a small, black can and threw it to Matt. "You may need this."

Annie walked with them to the front door and watched as they opened the garage doors.

"What the…where the hell's my car? Those bastards!" Matt slammed the garage door.

Before he had a chance to even ask, Annie was next to him with her keys in hand. They quickly jumped into the Cherokee and Annie leaned through the open passenger side window where Tucker sat. "At least tell me what you're going to do."

"We're going to see Wilkey to get some help," Matt said, then took the keys from Annie's hand. "Where's Albert's office?"

Annie wiped the tears from her cheeks. "On the top floor to the left in Sever Hall, an old brick building adjacent to Widner Library which has huge stone steps, you can't miss it once you're in the yard." She paused and took a deep breath, then kissed Tucker on the cheek. "Be careful," she whispered.

Matt turned the corner onto Main Street with such speed the Cherokee's right wheels momentarily left the ground. The tires squealed as the car regained its traction on the road.

Because he focused on keeping the Cherokee out of the left lane of on-coming traffic, he failed to notice the Chatham police car in the cemetery across the street. His stomach sank when blue lights burst into the Cherokee.

Matt looked in his rearview mirror and braked hard. "Damn it! We don't have time for this crap. God, I hate these cops! Always being a pain in the ass."

The officer took his time walking the short distance between the vehicles and by the time he reached the window, Matt's temper was raging. He rolled down his window and looked at the heavy-set officer, who looked like he was enjoying the moment.

"Son, I don't known where you're from, but we don't take kindly to smart asses driving like maniacs around our town. Now let me see your license and registration."

Tucker found the registration in the glove compartment and Matt handed the officer both items.

"Wait here." The officer strutted back to his cruiser and sat with the door open as he typed on the cruiser's computer.

"Come on, what the hell's taking this guy so long. Just give me the stupid ticket and let us go," Matt said and looked at his watch. It was seven-twenty.

"Here he comes," Tucker said. "Just apologize. Don't piss him off."

"No shit." Matt looked in his rearview mirror and saw the officer had his hand on his service revolver at his hip.

"What the hell? Tuck, check this out. He's getting his gun out," Matt said as he felt tightness in his chest.

Tucker looked back at the officer cautiously approaching the backside of the Cherokee.

Matt stuck his head out the window and said in a panicked voice, "Hey, what's going on? All I…"

"Put your hands were I can see them, both of you, and step out of the vehicle," the cop said in an incisive, deep voice.

"What?"

"*Now*, son! Don't make me repeat myself."

Matt froze for a second then jammed the Cherokee into drive and punched the accelerator. He looked in the mirror and saw the officer running back to his car.

"What the hell's going on, Matt?"

"He was going to arrest us. For what, I have no clue. But we have to get to Cambridge by ten or Albert's dead, so we don't have time to work this mess out, whatever it is."

The Cherokee's speedometer reached fifty as they raced down Main Street toward the village. At the rotary, Matt slammed the wheel hard to the left and the Cherokee jumped over the small island in the road, cutting off a Ford Escort in front off him. The Ford swerved and crashed into a truck coming from the opposite direction.

"Holy shit, Matt! Take it easy!" Tucker pleaded.

Matt increased the Cherokee's speed as he drove down Route 28. He looked in his mirror and saw the cop car slow down to avoid the accident at the rotary. Quickly, he turned onto a narrow, private road.

"Let me know if you see him." Matt gripped the steering wheel with so much force and tension his knuckles turned white.

At the end of the road, Matt took a hard right onto a busier road. After a few seconds, he turned left onto a dirt road that looked like a driveway.

"You see him?"

Tucker shook his head. "No, but I can hear his siren. He must be right behind us. Where the hell are we going?"

"Right up here."

The Cherokee skidded into the driveway of a small, dilapidated cottage with a rusty ship's anchor in the front yard. The height of the weeds around the anchor made it appear no one was living in the house, though an old black pickup truck sat at the end of the driveway. Matt drove the Cherokee up the driveway and then across the lawn to behind the house.

They sat in the Cherokee for a minute, securely blocked from the road by the cottage, as they listened to the siren of the police car. Matt finally recognized that his heart was racing uncontrollably; his mouth was bone dry, but his hands were wet with sweat. Finally, as the sound faded, Matt took a deep breath.

"What are we doing here?" Tucker said as he looked around.

"Just come on and pray he's in his workshop because it doesn't look like anyone's in the house."

Tucker followed Matt to a large, weathered, one-story building that looked like a utility shed. The lone window in the building tossed a faint light.

After Matt knocked twice on the rickety door, an old man opened it quickly and stood in the doorway. He wore a tattered red and black plaid shirt and grease-stained dungaree overalls. His white hair was wavy and unkempt. A white beard hung below his neckline. Deep, weathered wrinkles lined his forehead; crowsfeet decorated his eyes. Years on the water had wizened the old man's face, yet his smile was still large and warm.

"Well, well, if it ain't young Matty Gallagher," he said and stuck his hand out to Matt, who forcefully shook it.

"Hey, Wilkey, how've ya been? How's the leg? Heard you broke it."

"Took a nasty fall from my boat while in dry dock." He patted his left leg. "Be good as new. God, I haven't seen your sorry ass 'round here in years. What gives me the pleasure now?"

"This is my friend, Tucker." He turned to Tucker. "Tuck, this is the captain of the fishing boat I used to work on, Gerald Wilkinson."

He shook Tucker's hand with the same strength. "Well, nice to meet you, Tucker."

Though he looked more like a homeless person, no one knew the waters of Cape Cod better than Gerald Wilkinson did. He was a legend in Chatham, and for good reason. He followed in the footsteps of all the males in his family; there was but one true calling for a Wilkinson, and that came from the sea. Having spent the majority of his fifty-four years on a boat, he had few social skills and felt more comfortable keeping to himself while living a simple life, as his residence attested to.

"I've got something important I want to ask you about," Matt said in a serious tone. "And we're in a big hurry."

The inside of Wilkinson's two room workshop—one room being a closet-size bathroom—was dark, the air heavy. An old, torn, brown and tan easy chair sat in a corner in front of an even older television. A lamp on a table next to the chair suffused a dim light. In the opposite corner of the room, five large, plastic fish crates sat stacked one on top of the others next to a small, cluttered workbench. No pictures hung on the combination plasterboard and plywood board walls. A nine-foot harpoon and a coil of rope were the room's only decorations.

"Well, had I known you'd be stoppin' by and all, I'd had the maid clean up," Wilkey said with a deep laugh. "So, boys, what gives? What can I do for ya?"

Matt wrung his hands. He felt uncomfortable standing in the room, yet he realized there was but one chair. "We've got a problem I was hoping you could help us with."

Wilkey stopped smiling. "I figured so. The last time you paid me a visit here was when you got your daddy's boat stuck broadside out on the outer beach and the tide was poundin' her to pieces. Boy, that was a fun time righting that boat in that kinda surf. So what's the trouble now, Matty?"

Matt looked at Tucker, who looked anxious, then back at Wilkey. "Have you ever heard of the legend of the *Argo*?"

Wilkey scratched his beard with his blunt fingers and then said, "I assume you don't want a lesson in Greek mythology. Yeah, we grew up hearing from the old people all 'bout the legends and myths of the Cape and the ocean. Now what's this about? You fixing to be another one of them fools hunting for some lost Confederate gold?"

Matt looked down at his sneakers for a few seconds then proceeded to tell Wilkey how they had come into possession of the journal and now Annie's godfather was being held for ransom for the journal, which they no longer had, and the Chatham police were trying to arrest him for what he didn't know, and they had to be in Cambridge in less than three hours.

When Matt finished talking, Wilkey scratched his beard, nodded his head, then walked over and retrieved three Budweiser cans of beer from a small refrigerator next to the chair. He handed one each to Matt and Tucker.

"So what can I do for you?" Wilkey asked.

"Do you have any sinker jigs here and some gold spray paint?"

"Plan on making some gold, eh?" Wilkey smiled. "Sounds like your only option." He walked over to the lone closet next to the bathroom door and began pulling out various forms of fishing equipment. After littering the floor behind him, he said, "Bingo, we're in luck." He held up a wooden box. "You'll find every thing you need in this box. Set up the jig molds first. Use the iron slats to create the sides. The propane burner needs to be set up under the cast iron bowl. There should be enough lead there to make a few bars. I don't have any gold paint, but

I know were I can find some. So get to work. We ain't got much time. I'll be back soon."

While Matt worked on constructing the molds and heating the lead, Tucker went outside. When he returned, he held the dealer's nameplate, COSWAY JEEPS, he had torn from the Cherokee's tailgate. With a pair of tin snips he cut up the nameplate.

Once Matt poured the molten lead into the molds, they stood over the table to watch the lead solidify. After a few minutes, Tucker handed Matt the letters. Matt looked at the letters, C, S, and A.

"Good idea, Tuck," he said without taking his eyes of his work.

After waiting one more minute to make sure the lead was almost completely solidified, Matt carefully held the C with a pair of needle-nose pliers with a steady hand and pressed the letter into the lead. He repeated the process with the letters S and A. When he finished, he bent over and looked at the bar. Beads of sweat had developed on his forehead, but he didn't notice. He looked at Tucker. "Man, I hope this works."

"We'll make it work, don't worry," Tucker said calmly.

After Matt and Tucker spent a few minutes of silence staring at their creation to make sure the lead had hardened, Wilkey burst through the door.

"Got the final touch, and it's the fast drying kind, too." He held up a can of gold spray paint as he looked at the lead bars. "They look dry. Let's pop 'em out of the molds."

With dexterity only developed by years of working with his hands, Wilkey had the molds broken down and the two lead bars painted. When he finished, he took a step back from the table and stared at the bars.

"Well, whatta ya think? If I didn't know any better, I sure as hell say they was gold."

Matt looked at his watch. Quarter after eight. Jesus, he thought, we'll never make it in time. "Wilkey, we need to go," he said in a panicked voice. "But I need to ask you for another favor."

"Name it, Matty."

"The cops will be looking for our Cherokee, so there's no way we can drive it. Can we take your truck?"

Wilkey reached into his pocket and threw the keys to Matt. "Tank's full, captain."

# CHAPTER 14

▼

The 1982 Ford F-150 shook under the strain of the speed. With little traffic on the mid-Cape highway, Matt kept the truck traveling at an average of eighty miles per hour. The headlights illuminated the green sign for exit two. Matt looked at his watch. Eight-fifty. He felt himself relax a bit. Having traveled to and from the Cape so many times, he had memorized the arrival time from any place on the highway. He knew that once they reached the Sagamore Bridge, just two exits and five minutes away, they could be in Boston in only fifty minutes after that. Without traffic, they should just make it, he thought.

He looked over at Tucker who had been silent since they left Chatham. "How you doing, man?"

"I'm worried about…Jesus, Matt, slow down!" Tucker screamed.

Matt snapped his head forward and saw what commanded Tucker's sudden attention as they reached the peak of a rise in the highway. The truck's brakes locked as it skidded toward the car in front of it. Inches from the car's bumper, the truck shot to a stop as Matt and Tucker's heads snapped forward then back.

"Shit!" Matt cried. Ahead of them, a long string of red taillights lined the highway. At the end of the line, four police cars, with flashing blue strobe lights illuminating the highway, ushered cars through a roadblock.

For a few seconds they stared at the lights awaiting them as the cars slowly inched their way forward. Tucker finally broke the trance. "Oh, man, they must be checking cars. What are we going to do?"

"I don't know, but we can't risk driving past them; they could be looking for me now that they have my license." Matt paused. "Shit! What the hell's going on here. All I did was ditch that cop back in Chatham. There's no way they'd set up a roadblock for that."

Tucker was unconsciously wringing his hands. "Yeah, but do we want to take that chance? What if they are looking for us? If we get stopped, there's no way we'll make it to Harvard on time."

Matt paused for a few seconds as he stared forward at the blue lights. "This is what we're going to do." He proceeded to tell Tucker his plan.

"Okay, I'll try it. We're screwed if I get stopped," Tucker said in a skeptical voice.

When the line of cars paused for a second, and before another car pulled behind them, Tucker slid across the seat behind the wheel as Matt jumped out of the truck. Matt hugged the truck's side as he raced behind it, took a deep breath and then sprinted across the right lane behind an old recreational vehicle. He jumped the guardrail, caught his right foot on it, and tumbled down the small embankment. He quickly jumped to his feet and pushed his way into the thick brush, deeper into the darkness of the woods. Branches grabbed at his bare legs and tore at his face. Within seconds, he reached a clearing and relief. He paused, felt the blood on his face and then looked in the direction of the flashing lights a hundred yards away. The thickness of the brush broke the rays' piercing illumination. He realized if he couldn't see them clearly, they probably couldn't see him. Fighting the urge to run, Matt pushed on carefully trying not to disturb the small trees and brush which would reveal his presence.

When the blue lights were within twenty yards of him, Matt stopped to find the truck, but was too far below the level of the highway to see anything but the top of the cars in the near lane.

He slowed to a stop when he was finally parallel to the police cars and could hear the cops loudly instructing drivers to come to a stop. His heart raced when he saw the truck pull up to an awaiting cop. Come on, come on, let him through, Matt silently pleaded. The truck stayed stationary for what seemed an eternity, then slowly pulled forward away from the roadblock.

"Yes, go, go," Matt said in an excited, hushed voice.

While Tucker drove away from the roadblock, Matt turned to continue through the woods. His first step landed on a fallen, dead branch and the limb made a loud crack. He froze. Immediately, a white light panned the woods. Matt's heart stopped. Without moving his feet, he crouched, put his head down, and closed his eyes. He waited ten seconds and then forced his eyes to open. The light had disappeared. He waited for another moment before he carefully began to walk purposefully and silently.

When he had placed thirty yards between himself and the roadblock, he ran as fast as he could. Another twenty yards ahead, he found a clearing in the thickets to the highway. Stopping at the edge of the road behind the guardrail, Matt looked back at the flashing lights, but could not make out much because of the blinding effect of the oncoming headlights. He quickly looked to his right and saw the taillights of the truck two hundred yards away in the breakdown lane. Staying behind the rail, he sprinted along the embankment.

When he reached the truck, Matt yanked open the passenger side door and leapt into the truck. He looked up at Tucker.

"What took you so long?" Tucker said with a smile. "Man, Matt, you look awful."

Matt sat back in the seat and took a deep breath as Tucker pulled back onto the highway. He rubbed his hand over his face and felt the blood oozing from the cut on his cheek.

"God, that was close." He looked at his watch. "We've got forty minutes to make it. Step on it."

Tucker increased the truck's speed and turned on the windshield wipers; it had begun to rain.

Hammond rubbed his aching temples. His back was sore from sitting in virtually the same position for the past two hours hitting the redial button on O'Donahue's phone. He stretched his arms toward the ceiling and decided to try one last time to contact Michael Gallagher. He hit the redial button, listened and then hung up the phone in disgust.

"Any luck?" Ditchman asked as he walked through the doorway holding two pizzas.

"Nothing. He's a no show at work and at home."

Ditchman placed the pizzas on the table and opened up the top box. A waft of pepperoni pizza filled the room. He grabbed two slices, folded them together and just when he was about to take a bite, asked Hammond, "Speaking of home, when's the last time you called?"

Hammond looked at his watch. "Crap! Jeannie's going to kill me."

He picked up the phone and dialed his home number and waited for his wife to say hello. "What the heck?" He tried the number again, but met the same result. "What's going on? I can't get through."

"There's a huge storm coming up the coast," O'Donahue said as she walked into her office, a manila folder in her right hand. She grabbed a slice of pizza with her left hand and walked over to her desk. "Hurricane *Agatha* has decided to prove all the meteorologists wrong and come ashore. The latest report is she's heading straight up the seaboard and should run right over us sometime after midnight. The whole region's in a real panic because no one expected it."

"When the heck did this all happen? I don't remember hearing anything about a hurricane."

"That's because we've had our heads buried in the case," Ditchman said. "Where'd she come ashore?"

"Mid-Atlantic. It's the first of the year and wasn't supposed to be much. The weather report I heard this morning when driving in didn't even mention it. It's hitting New York City right now."

"That would explain why I can't get a hold off my wife."

"And Michael Gallagher," Ditchman said.

O'Donahue sat down in her chair and opened the folder. "Well, I've got some good news. The last two stolen cars we were looking for were found. The first one, the BMW, was never stolen. The owner suffers from senility and forgot he lent it to his nephew. But the last one, the Buick, was found behind an industrial park in Harwich, on Cape Cod. That could be the car we're looking for. A lot of college kids spend the summer at the Cape."

O'Donahue walked over to her desk and answered her phone on the second ring. She listened for a minute, asked one question and then hung up the receiver.

"That was Gloria Maherski. Michael Gallagher contacted his secretary and she called Maherski. Matt Gallagher is renting a house with some friends at, you guessed it, the Cape." She smiled, sat on the edge of the desk, and crossed her arms.

Ditchman stood up and approached her desk. "Did you get a town, an address, number, anything?"

She shook her head. "He didn't know any of that. But he did say he would suspect his brother would be in Chatham because that's where the family used to spend their summers." She smiled again. "And guess what town is next to Chatham?"

"Harwich, home of stolen Pontiac Regals," Hammond said. "So when do we hit the road?" He stood. "Let's go, we need to wrap this up while I still have a wife, and a job. Did I tell you, Ditch, Conrad called and told me that soon we'd be paying our own way on this goose chase, I think he called it, and out of our vacation time?"

"Hold on a second, Rusty." O'Donahue picked up the phone and in thirty seconds had an update on the weather from the state police barracks in Bourne.

The hurricane's outer bands of thirty mile per hour winds and torrential rain had reached the Cape. Already thousands were without power and the true muscle of the storm had yet to arrive.

O'Donahue rubbed her temples as she looked at Hammond. "Even if we could get there, Rusty, what could we do? There's no way we'd find Gallagher during the storm, not to mention, we still don't know for sure he's there."

# CHAPTER 15

▼

By the time they reached the outskirts of Boston, the rain was coming down in sheets. Though the truck's wipers worked at top speed, they simply couldn't keep up with the volume of water pouring out of the sky. Visibility was less than a car length and growing worse. The sound of water being thrown from under the truck made a deafening noise.

Tucker gripped the steering wheel with both hands while intently focusing on the road ahead of him. Occasionally, red lights would suddenly appear in front of them, forcing him to quickly swerve around the car to keep from smashing into it.

"How's the time?" Tucker asked without taking his eyes off the road.

"We've got fifteen minutes. Don't slow down. Keep pushing it," Matt replied loudly.

"Christ, Matt, I'm doing the best I can. I can't see shit in this weather," Tucker lashed back.

"Hey, come on, Tuck, you're doing a great job. I was just trying to tell you how it is. Let's stay calm here, okay. It'll be close, but we'll make it."

Tucker shook his head. "Sorry. I just got a bad feeling about this. Shit, I wish it wasn't raining so hard. I can barely keep this tank on the road at this speed."

Matt agreed but said nothing.

"So, what the hell do we do when we get there?" Tucker asked as he quickly swerved around a slower car, causing the truck to fishtail for a tense second.

Matt reached down between his legs to feel the duffel bag containing the lead bars. "I don't know. We're just going to have to play it cool and think on our feet. These guys are probably stupid white trash so they'll never know it's not real gold."

"Man, we better hope so."

Because of the storm, the Southeast Expressway into Boston was almost empty. Once into the Big Dig tunnel, a much-needed reprieve from the storm greeted them and so they increased their speed. When they turned onto Storrow Drive, and were again slammed by the driving wind and rain, Tucker had to slow the truck down to almost thirty miles per hour because of the lake-size puddles on the road.

Within a few minutes, they turned right on Massachusetts Avenue, took the Harvard Bridge across the Charles River, and were in Cambridge.

"Harvard will be on our right in a few minutes." Matt said.

Tucker pulled the truck to a stop in front of a Chinese restaurant.

Matt grabbed the bag and checked his watch. "We've got three minutes."

They jumped out of the truck and sprinted across Massachusetts Avenue. Within seconds they were soaked from the driving rain. The first iron gate they ran to was locked. Tucker followed Matt as he ran along the brick wall looking for an entrance into the Yard.

The next gate they checked was open. They sprinted into Harvard Yard and found themselves on a large green surrounded by formidable brick buildings. They stopped in their tracks and looked in circles.

"Look," Tucker screamed above the rain, "that's the library with the huge steps Annie told us about. So that must be Sever." He pointed at a large, boxy, brick building.

When they reached Sever Hall, Matt yanked at the wooden door, but it refused to open.

"Shit, it's locked," he said loudly. "Come on, let's try the back."

They raced around the building and found a back entrance. After repeated tries to force the door, it, too, remained locked. They stood there for a few seconds staring at each other in disbelief at having come all this way, dodging the cops and the weather, just to be locked out.

"Tuck, try that window down there." Matt pointed to a small window partly obscured by a large bush.

Tucker tried to open it, but the window remained closed. With his elbow, he smashed a pane, then reached in and unlocked the window.

They slipped through the open window and found themselves in a dark, smelly bathroom, the only light crawling from under the closed door. Without hesitating, they ran through the door and found the staircase.

After sprinting up the stairs to the fifth floor, their thighs screaming in pain from the exertion, Tucker and Matt slowed and tried to collect themselves. The hallway was dark except for light suffused from a window in the door at the end of the hall. Matt looked at Tucker, then at the end of the hall, and nodded his head. He felt a cold sweat break out on his forehead as panic raced through his body. His thoughts were abruptly ended as they reached the end of the hall. Matt stared at the name on the door's frosted window—Professor A. Nylan.

Matt knocked on the glass. "It's us." The door was unlocked and then opened.

Inside the office, Carson Ridder sat behind the large, brown, wooden desk, his big boots propped up on the top, a filterless cigarette precariously dangled from his lower lip. To the right, against the wall, Professor Nylan sat in a wooden chair. His hands lay in his lap in a submissive manner. A look of fright covered his old face, which was marked by a dark red welt on his left cheek. He didn't smile when he saw them. Across from the professor, against a large bookcase, stood Buster Sykes. He closed the door behind Tucker and stood there with his arms crossed.

"You're late, assholes," Ridder said sarcastically, then dropped his feet off the desk and stood up.

Matt and Tucker stood still, amazed at Ridder's size as he slowly walked around to the front of the desk and sat on the edge.

"Where's my journal, punk?" His eyes bore at Matt.

Matt began to speak, but his voice broke. He paused, took a gulp of air and then said in as confident tone as he could muster, "We did the work for you." He held up the bag. "The journal must have got lost in the mail, so to show you our good faith, we found the gold for you. I take it that's what you really wanted," Matt said in an attempt to mollify Ridder, then looked at him to gauge his reaction.

Ridder stepped forward toward Matt and ripped the bag from his hand. "Well, now, maybe you're not as fuckin' dumb as you look, pretty boy."

He laid the bag on the desk and unzipped it. Reaching his large hand into the bag, he pulled out one bar, then the other. He looked closely at each, then nodded at Sykes, who grinned, and then turned quickly to Matt.

"What the hell is this?" he demanded. "Two bars? Two bars? Bullshit, boys, bullshit! Where's the rest? There's no way there was only two bars." Ridder quickly reached into a pocket in his black, leather vest, and snapped open the five-inch blade of his butterfly knife with the dexterity of a sushi chef. The sound of the blade clicking open made the professor jump. Ridder held the knife up and allowed the silver blade to shimmer in the light from the desk lamp. "I want my journal. You holdin' out on me, boy? I'll cut your…"

"We'll give you the journal and tell you what we did with the rest of the gold once you let the professor go," Tucker interrupted.

Ridder jumped at Matt and held the knife inches from his throat. Matt swallowed, but remained as still as possible for fear that if he made a sudden move Ridder would be startled enough to use the knife.

Matt examined Ridder's face and saw nothing but anger and frustration. Ridder's black, greasy eyebrows pinched downward so hard his forehead turned red. The left side of his upper lip trembled erratically.

"I oughta just slit your puny throat." His scowl turned sadistically to a grin.

"Do that and you'll never get the rest of the gold."

"He's telling the truth," Tucker injected. "There's more gold, but too much for us to haul up here. It weighs a ton. Remember, you only gave us a couple of hours to get here."

Ridder's eyebrows rose a bit, easing the tension on his taunt face, but he kept the butterfly knife poised to strike. He turned to listen to Tucker.

"We don't care about the gold; you can have it. You let us go, and we'll tell you where an envelope is with the directions to the rest of the gold." He paused. "Come on, be reasonable. You let us go and you're a millionaire, possibly a billionaire. You can just walk away from this and go count your money. You'll never hear from us again, I swear."

Ridder stared at him for a few seconds, but Tucker didn't flinch. He kept his eyes locked on Ridder's eyes until Ridder withdrew the knife.

Matt let out an inaudible sigh and swallowed hard.

Ridder stepped back to the desk and picked up one of the gold bars with his left hand. He stared intently at the imprint of the letters C, S, and A. He bounced the bar in his hand as if he was weighing its value. A grin appeared on his face. Sykes stepped around Tucker to gaze at the bars.

"How do I know you ain't fuckin' with me again, and you ain't gonna send me on some wild goose chase while you retrieve all the gold? 'Cause, you know, if you did pull somethin' stupid like that, my friend and me," he nodded at Sykes who grinned and nodded back, "we'd hunt you down like an animal and…"

"I don't need the money," Matt said forcefully. "My father's got more money than the Pope. I already got my gold in the form of real nice inheritance that's not worth squat to me if I'm dead. Ever heard of a trust fund? So there, that's why I'm not fucking with you. So how about it?" Matt examined Ridder's face to judge his reaction.

Ridder looked at Matt, then at Tucker. He held the bar up in front of his barrel chest and caressed it with the blade of the knife. "I know where you live."

Matt nodded his head.

A painfully slow minute elapsed before Ridder said, "The journal and the rest of the gold for the old man." When he went to put the bar back into the bag, it slipped from his hand, hit the corner of the desk and fell hard to the floor.

"What the hell?"

He reached down and picked up the bar. A scowl formed on his face as he examined the corner of the bar where it had hit the floor. He took his knife and cut at the corner. Flakes of gold paint lifted off the bar. His eyes grew with fury. "This ain't..."

The office door opened and a man's head peeked around it.

"Professor Nylan? Are you still...what the?" The man in a brown work suit froze mid-sentence in fright as he saw the knife in Ridder's hand.

Sykes reached into his waistline and quickly pulled out the S&W .357 and aimed it at the janitor.

"Mind your own business, asshole."

Tucker lunged at Sykes and knocked him into the bookcase. The gun exploded, smashing the glass in the door. Without hesitating, Ridder went at Matt with his knife drawn, but screamed in pain as pepper spray hit his eyes. He fell to the floor, dropped the knife and ripped at his eyes while screaming from the agony of the burn. Matt quickly turned to Sykes, who was struggling with Tucker on the floor, both trying to gain control of the gun in Sykes' hand. Though Tucker had both his hands wrapped around Sykes' hand, he couldn't prevent Sykes from firing the gun. He got off two rounds, one into the ceiling, and the other into the wall just above the professor's head. Matt quickly looked to his right and saw the professor was not hit, and then squirted the pepper spray directly into Sykes' eyes. Sykes immediately let go of Tucker and screamed as he rolled on the floor like he had been electrocuted. Tucker quickly rolled away from Sykes, who began shooting into the air until Matt kicked the gun out of his grasp. Matt turned to the professor, who was also on his feet, his face whiter now.

"Come on, come on, let's get out of here." Matt grabbed the professor by the elbow and pulled him quickly toward the door. As he stepped past Ridder, who lay thrashing on the floor, screaming and clawing at his eyes, Matt stopped and kicked Ridder as hard as he could in the groin. Ridder let out an agonizing scream and clutched his privates.

Once in the hallway, they ran to the stairs. One flight down, Matt turned to the janitor. "Go call the cops. Tell them what happened." The janitor's face was paralyzed with fright. He said nothing, just nodded his head slightly a few times, and then ran down the hallway.

Matt, Tucker and Professor Nylan ran down the stairs as fast as the professor would go. Matt had to pull him along to make him go faster, but the professor could only go so fast. At the lobby, he stopped dead in his track.

"Come on, Professor, we can't stop now," Matt pleaded. "We have to get out of here."

The professor stood hunched over at the waist, holding onto Matt with one hand, the banister with the other. He took deep, wheezing breaths that sounded like his throat had something stuck in it. He struggled to speak.

"Emphysema—I can't run like this."

"Come on, we'll be fine once we're out of the building," Tucker said in a frantic voice.

"No." The professor shook his head and took in a labored breath. "I know a safer way out. Go to the basement level."

Suddenly, they heard Ridder yelling at the top of the staircase. "Grab the gun, Buster!" Then a pause. "Move it, Sykes!"

Matt's heart raced as he heard the booming voice. A rush of adrenaline pumping through his body returned his focus to reaching safety.

Within seconds they were at the basement level. Tucker turned to the professor.

"Where to now? It looks like a dead end." Tucker's usually bronze face was white now.

The professor pointed to a paneled wall at the base of the stairwell.

"Jesus, come on, there's no door there! We have to go back up before they get down here," Matt whined as he grabbed the professor by the arm and started to pull him to the steps. But the professor broke free and staggered to the far wall.

Mustering a stern voice, he said quietly, "There's a hidden door here that opens into a tunnel. We'll be safe there. Outside, we'll never get anywhere."

Matt looked at Tucker and realized they were thinking the same thing—the openness of the greens on both sides of Sever Hall and an old man that could hardly move, never mind breathe.

Tucker stepped to the wall and quickly examined it with his fingers. "Shit, there is a door here. The molding is actually a frame. Professor, do you have a key?"

"No."

Tucker looked at Matt and they nodded at each other before slamming their shoulders simultaneously against the hidden door. But the door remained closed.

The deep thumping sound made by their shoulders told them the door wasn't some flimsy barn door. They tried again, but with the same result.

"Shit! This is useless. It won't budge. Let's go back up," Tucker declared.

Suddenly, they heard running footsteps on the staircase and froze.

Oh, god, they're going to be down here in seconds, Matt thought. He quickly thought of the distance between each floor as he pictured Ridder and Sykes jumping down the staircase in barely controlled bounds.

The sounds abruptly stopped. Then they heard a scream ended by a single gunshot that echoed through the hallways and staircase.

Matt looked at Tucker and they turned to the obstinate wall and charged it with renewed vigor and determination. As they slammed into the wall, the door crashed in with a loud crack and Matt and Tucker landed on the concrete floor inside the tunnel.

They quickly jumped to their feet and Matt grabbed the professor by the arm and pulled him into the tunnel. As Tucker began to shut the large, wooden door, they froze.

"They gotta be in the basement," Sykes yelled.

Matt felt his heart race. "Close it quietly," he whispered to Tucker.

Footsteps pounded down the staircase.

Matt looked through the small opening between the door and frame and froze as Buster Sykes looked right at him.

Matt stood perfectly still and watched. When Sykes turned his head, Matt quietly pushed the door closed.

"I think they're down here," Sykes yelled.

Matt held his breath until something caught his eye.

In the dim light of the tunnel, the deadbolt glimmered just slightly.

Matt crouched down and inspected the door lock. Running his finger along the doorjamb, his fear was realized.

He leaned close to Tucker's ear. "The door won't lock. The deadbolt ripped through the wood. We need to move."

Through the door they heard Ridder's voice. "Well, keep lookin' you dumb sonofabitch. They's gotta be down here somewhere."

A frightening thought entered Matt's head. Could the wood on the outside of the doorjamb be broken as well? What if some pieces of the broken jamb fell on the floor outside of the door? If Ridder and Sykes saw any pieces of wood on the floor, they might just be smart enough to inspect the area. And with the door being unlocked…Matt stopped thinking.

"Professor, we need to move quickly. The door won't lock."

"No matter. There's a four way junction right ahead, if my memory serves me correctly. It has been many years since I've been in these tunnels, but I remember that. If we can make it there, we'll have better odds."

The air in the tunnel was stale and heavy. Matt thought the smell was familiar, like that in the old, underground subway stations in Boston. Low wattage, yellow utility lights on the ceiling every hundred feet threw off just enough light for them to see the edges of the concrete walls.

Within a few minutes, they reached a dimly lit, four-way junction and stopped.

"Which way, Professor?" Tucker asked.

The professor paused and ran his wrinkled hand through his gray hair.

"Give me a second, I have to get this right, you know."

Before the professor spoke again, the creaking of a door and muffled voices shattered the silence in the tunnel.

Matt and Tucker stared at the professor, but said nothing. Matt held a finger over his lips.

Finally, the professor led them down the tunnel to the left.

They walked close to the wall, trying to be as silent as possible. Every step was taken with deliberate care. It was like walking through an unfamiliar room in the dark and fearing that with every step you were going to smash your shin on some hard object, or worse, kick over a can and announce your presence.

After a minute of purposeful walking, they reached a right angle in the tunnel. Fearing that the professor's labored breathing would reveal their choice of tunnel if they were to press on, and realizing they would not find a better stopping spot, Matt motioned for the professor and Tucker to wait against the wall, around the corner, in the darkness.

Matt stood with his back pressed against the wall. He willed his breathing to slow down so that his hearing could be more acute.

The only sound in the tunnel was the rhythmic hissing of the professor's breathing. He took out his inhaler and blasted a jolt of medicinal mist into his mouth. Instantly his breathing quieted to a barely perceptible wheeze.

Tucker stood up and whispered in Matt's ear. "Shouldn't we keep going?"

Matt put his arm across Tucker's chest to keep him still.

"You fuckin' little pricks. You're dead! You hear me? Dead!" Ridder's voice echoed through the concrete tunnels.

They waited at the corner for another minute, then the professor said in a whisper, "Good. As I had hoped, they picked the wrong tunnel. It's probably safe to proceed now."

Tucker helped the professor up and they slowly resumed their way down the tunnel.

After walking silently for another few minutes, they again came to another intersection. Again, the professor chose the tunnel to the left. Most of the utility lights in this tunnel did not work, and so they walked in near total darkness at times. Matt led the way, with Tucker holding onto his belt, and the professor clinging to Tucker's right hand.

As they hugged the wall to find their way, Matt couldn't shake the dreaded feeling he was going to run into something, or someone.

"Hey, Professor, what exactly is this place?

The professor cleared his throat. "We're in secret evacuation tunnels built during the Second World War. With so many brilliant minds here working for the military, the government had these tunnels constructed in case of a Nazi invasion. They link Harvard Yard, the Business School across the river, and M.I.T. I suspect those men who abducted me are on their way towards the Charles River, or towards a dead end. With a little luck, I believe they'll get quite lost in this labyrinth."

He paused to catch his breath. "So are you going tell me what this is all about? I sure would like to know why a couple of thugs burst into my office and held me against my will."

While they walked, Matt proceeded to tell the professor about the journal, the fight at the airport, Ridder and Sykes chasing him in Chatham, making the fake gold, and their subsequent run from the law. Within thirty minutes, Matt had finished the story with the aid of Tucker's acute memory for details.

"Well, if I hadn't been involved, I'd never believe it," the professor said.

They reached the end of the tunnel and found the exit blocked by another thick, heavy wooden door. Matt and Tucker once again threw their bodies unmercifully against the door until it, too, broke open.

They found themselves not in a basement as before, but in an academic hall, right in the front where a professor would stand to lecture his class.

Matt looked around at all the empty seats seemingly staring at him and wondered if any students ever gave any thought to what was behind the person at the podium, or were they just too focused on the lecture on nanotechnology to let their minds daydream wild adventures.

His mind snapped back to focus. This wasn't any wild adventure. A single thought ended his euphoria at reaching the end of the tunnel.

"Jesus, Tuck, you know what I just realized? Shit!" he shook his fists in anger. "Ridder knows where we live. If they doubled back instead of getting lost in the tunnels, they're…"

"Annie!"

Tucker quickly turned to the professor.

"How do I get back to Massachusetts Avenue?"

The professor rubbed his lower back with his right hand and said in a tired voice, "I don't know."

In less than a minute they had made their way out of the lecture hall, gone down two dark, empty corridors, and found a street level exit. The professor looked out at the surrounding buildings and nodded his head.

"Take your second right up the street and Mass Ave. will be just a few blocks further."

"I'll run back and get the truck and meet you here. You guys find a phone and call the cops."

Pushing himself harder than he had ever run, Tucker reached Wilkey's truck within fifteen minutes. His lungs burned from the exertion, every muscle in his legs screamed in pain, and his face and eyes hurt from being stung by the rain. But by the time he reached M.I.T., the exertion-induced nausea had subsided, though his panic had not.

When Matt jumped into the truck, Tucker looked at him in surprise.

"Where's the professor?"

"Let's get going. Head across the river." Matt pointed down Memorial Drive toward the next bridge across the Charles River. "The one phone in there was busted. I told him to find one as soon as possible and call the cops in Chatham so they can get over to the house, and then to call Annie. God, I pray she's alright."

Tucker drove the truck in silence. Finally Matt broke the silence. "What?"

"*What* what?" Tucker returned.

"You're being silent. What's going on?"

Tucker tilted his head slightly to the side. "I don't know. I was just wondering if you should have brought the professor with you. I mean, I would have…"

Matt quickly interrupted him. "Hey, Tuck, I figured he would slow us down, okay? He said he wasn't feeling well. What the hell was I supposed to do about it? I mean, Christ, the poor guy's dragged into this mess because of us. Not to mention, someone had to call the cops and Annie. Okay? So back off!"

Tucker looked over at Matt and waited for him to cool off. "Hey, come on, man, I'm sorry. That's a good idea getting him to call the cops. I wasn't second-guessing you. In fact, I think you're right; he probably would have slowed us down." Tucker looked over again at Matt, but Matt just stared out the window.

After driving at break-neck speed for twenty minutes along the darkened and water-choked Southeast Expressway, dodging reservoirs of standing water and more cautious vehicles, Tucker pulled off the highway and into the parking lot of a deserted 7-Eleven store. Matt quickly jumped out of the cab and ran to the free-standing phone booth.

When he returned, his facial expression answered Tucker's lone question. Matt shook his head, and then slammed the dashboard with his fist. "Fucking storm." The phone lines were down. "Of all the nights to have a Nor'Easter!"

# CHAPTER 16

▼

Vesali Bulgakov felt a deep cramp developing in his left calf muscle. It felt like his leg below his knee was twisting slowly into rock and no matter how hard he tried to relax his leg, the tension continued to escalate. He wondered how much longer it would be until it was safe to leave the security of his hiding spot, the small opening under the wooden desk that provided barely enough room for his legs when he sat at the desk, never mind stuffing his entire six-foot-two frame into it. He estimated he had been under the desk for over forty-five minutes at least, though his body felt like it had been hours.

He strained to see the face of his watch, but with no light in the twelve by fifteen-foot classroom in Sever Hall, especially under the desk, Bulgakov's eyes played tricks on him. He wondered if they had seen the light before he had turned it off and partially shut the door. Did they know he was there? If they did, would they shoot him too? Jesus, he thought, what possessed me to come here? His father was right. America was no place to study. Nothing but crime and corrupt capitalists in America, he remembered were his father's words.

He tried to stretch his legs out a mere extra inch to gain some relief, but realized it was futile to believe any measure of comfort could be gained in such a tight space.

Finally, the pain in his legs reached the breaking point. He struggled out of the cramped space and stood up. The feeling was exhilarating, but only lasted for the few seconds it took for reality to set back in as he felt his heart begin to race again. He crept to the door and opened it slightly more to look, half expecting them to be waiting for him, ready to shoot him, but the hallway was dark and empty as far as he could tell. He took a deep breath and left the room in search of the quickest way out and a phone.

Flip Gustufson stared down at the drink in his right hand. He placed his left hand on the bar top to steady himself in preparation for bringing the shotglass successfully to his mouth. He could almost taste the whiskey already. With only enough money to buy one more shot of Jack Daniel's, and his Visa card long ago maxed out to the limit, Flip Gustufson wanted to savor ever last drop of the golden, warm liquid. Not enjoying every drop of the four ounces would simply be a tragedy.

As Gustufson concentrated on the tiny glass, his vision went in and out of focus. He blinked his eyes. Still, the glass moved. He shook his head, but the more he concentrated, the more he realized it was futile to try. He felt himself slightly swaying back and forth as if he and only he could hear a wonderful melody. He closed his eyes and enjoyed the motion of his body, then quickly opened them and in one well-practiced motion lifted the glass to his mouth and gulped the whiskey without even noticing the large dribble as it snaked its way down his chin to his throat and onto his brown-stained undershirt.

In his early forties, Flip Gustufson looked like a barfly; wearing blue uniform pants and a white, arm-pit-stained undershirt, he had unwashed, greasy, black hair and three days' worth of stubble on his round chin. He drank because he knew it was the one thing he was good at, and it made him feel good. Though he had tried a few times to stay sober, he never lasted very long, especially after being fired from another job.

Three hours earlier, the Poalston Security Corporation had employed him as a security guard at a technology firm in Cambridge, but his short tenure with the company came to an abrupt halt when his supervisor found him sleeping on the job for the second straight day. Within two weeks of getting his third job of the year, Flip Gustufson was once again unemployed. But now he was back where he felt in control, where no one was going to call him a good-for-nothing, stupid, lazy bum. He sucked a breath in and felt his chest enlarge as a surge of self-confidence swelled through his body.

"'Nother J.D.," he exclaimed as he smacked the shot glass on the bar.

The bartender, a man in his late fifties whose wrinkles made him look like a smile had never graced his face, stepped over to in front of Gustufson. "Last one, mac." He filled the shot glass, placed it back in front of Gustufson, who grabbed it and swallowed the liquor in one seemingly wild motion.

"Let me call ya a cab."

Gustufson pulled the last five-dollar bill from his pocket and slapped it on the bar. Without a word or even acknowledgement to the bartender, he got up and staggered out the door.

He was immediately glad he had parked his car right in front of the bar. If it weren't the first thing he saw when he opened the door, he probably wouldn't have found it. With the driving rain and wind ripping at his face, he couldn't tell if it was the weather or the booze causing him to have tremendous trouble crossing the ten-foot wide sidewalk.

Finally, he reached his car and after dropping the keys twice into the gutter, managed to open the door of his 1982 Oldsmobile Delta.

"Freakin' Noah's ark kinda weather," he said outloud to himself as he climbed behind the wheel.

Despite the alcohol freely flowing through his veins, he was able to start the car with relative ease just as he had done many times in such a condition. He pulled onto the road and began to drive.

Immediately, Gustufson's eyes began to hurt as he strained to see out through the rain-soaked windshield despite the overtime work of the wipers. Suddenly, he saw a red light appear in front of him and he slammed on the brakes. The Oldsmobile hydroplaned for a brief second then came to a stop in front of an intersection. When the light turned green, Gustufson took a left. But then he realized he didn't know where he was going. At the next light he took another left. Soon, after a series of turns, he was completely disoriented and lost. He decided he would stay on this road until he recognized a familiar landmark. Shit, he knew Cambridge so well, finding a familiar place would be as easy as finding his pecker in the dark.

After a few blocks, a car, the first one he had seen since leaving the bar, approached Gustufson in the opposite direction. As it neared him, he realized it was flashing its lights on and off at him.

"Crazy nut, keep ya lights on, ya fool."

Suddenly, he realized why the car was flashing him. He reached forward with his left hand to pull the light switch on the dashboard, but couldn't find it. He became frustrated and looked down. The car began to drift to the left. Gustufson found the lights, pulled the switch, and looked up just as the Oldsmobile jumped the curb. In a split second, Gustufson saw what he was heading for and pulled on the wheel to avoid the collision. The last thing Flip Gustufson saw before his car crashed into the brick wall was the face of a terrified, old man as the corner of the car's bumper struck him.

*          *          *          *

While they drove through the night, neither talked. Each just listened to the rhythm of the windshield wipers, the drumming of the rain and the constant whoosh of water being swept aside by the tires. The unpredictable wind gusts made keeping the truck in its lane an adventure. Finally, Matt spoke.

"I think I figured out how I ended up with the journal."

"How's that?"

"Remember that guy who bumped into me when we were going into the bar at the airport? I always thought it was strange how he bumped into me. Now that I think about it, I know he did it on purpose. I bet he dropped it into my bag because Ridder and Sykes were after him. Now there after us."

"Matt, do you mind if we talk about something else?"

"Yeah, sorry. So how's things going with you and Annie?"

Tucker shook his head. "I don't know. I mean, I can feel something there. It's weird. I've never felt an attraction like this before. I mean, I can't stop thinking about her. Christ, I even keep smelling her. Ever had that happen to you? You know, when you never stop thinking of someone because it makes you feel so good. And, yet, I'm miserable."

Matt nodded his head. "I'd be lying to you if I said I ever had feelings like that. Hell, my middle name's lascivious, not love. I've been so far away from love in every relationship, it makes me sick when I stop and think about what I'm doing. But, you know, Tuck, with Annie, I know what you're talking about. I mean, I could see that happening with her. You're pretty lucky. Seems like all the girls I ever get close to are naked one minute, then gone the next, like that redhead on Nantucket. The only thing I ever think about is whether I'm going to remember her name when I see her again. Remember that time when we ran into that girl Rachel at the campus bar and I couldn't remember her name."

"You remember her name now."

"Hard to forget a girl who dumps a pitcher of beer on your head." He paused. "But don't tell me you're miserable. I'd take that misery any day. At least you have the potential for something whole, something meaningful, not some shallow, make-yourself-feel-like-a-playboy feeling that leaves you having a hard time looking yourself in the mirror and wondering why you're at it again the next night."

"Jesus, I didn't mean it like that, man. Sorry, I didn't know you felt like that. To tell you the truth, I always thought you liked playing the role of the stud and all. I mean, you always had girls after you at school."

"That's just it, Tuck. Where did it get me, huh? Worrying about S.T.D.'s and whether I should buy an engagement ring, or whether there's a little Matty running around crying because he doesn't know his daddy, that's where. Shit, I would trade places with you in a second. So let me at least live vicariously through you, okay? Seriously, what's the deal with you and Annie?"

"I definitely feel something there, both ways. But she seems preoccupied most of the time. I get these vibes from her, you know, and then she becomes distant, like she's thinking of something other than the moment. On the ride over to Nantucket, she kept giving me these looks while we were on the front deck. I wasn't born yesterday; I know what those looks mean. Then that night, we took a long walk on the beach and one thing led to another, and I felt it, Matt, I'm telling you, it was real, not some bullshit you feed yourself to persuade your guilty conscience. It was unbelievable. I've never felt a rush of, I don't know, absolute desire come over me. But not some cheap feeling, you know, or like it's my first time ever and I'm completely stupid about it." He paused and shook his head. "No. This was big time real. Then as soon as things are over, she becomes totally introverted. I'm thinking maybe I pushed it a little too fast and I've blown it. But then she held my hand all the way back to the boat. If your head weren't stuck in a toilet all the way back from Nantucket you'd have seen how she was acting. She couldn't get far enough away from me on the boat. But every once in a while I'd catch that look again. It's almost like she wants to move forward, but something's holding her back. Know what I mean?" Tucker shook his head in bewilderment.

Matt let out a chuckle. "I know exactly what you mean. Annie can be, well, complicated. But you have to remember what she's been through."

"You mean losing her parents?"

"Yeah, she's come a long way since then, but she's still fragile. That's a pretty heavy duty load to bear, especially without having anybody close to turn to who knows what she's feeling."

"But I always thought you guys were really close. You used to call to her all the time. And she told me you used to date, right? What happened?"

Matt ran his hands through his hair and let out a puff of breath. "Yeah, we dated for a while during the summers." He looked at his friend. "I know I can tell you this because we're best friends. But, Annie's the only girl I ever fell in love with. She was so different than all the others I used to chase. You can see that. She's one of a kind."

"So what happened?"

"Well, it was when we were in high school so it never got too serious. And then when her parents died, I realized that she needed me more like a brother than a boyfriend and we grew closer in a much different way. My feelings of romantic love had to give way to providing her moral support. I guess I would say I think of her now like a sister because the love is deep, not romantic. It couldn't be anything else after her parents died. But don't worry. I am fully behind the idea of you and Annie. My two best friends hooking up? What could be better?"

"You sure you're okay with it?"

"Hell, I'd be lying if I didn't tell you I was a bit jealous. But what Annie and I had was teenage puppy love. I can see it in her eyes that she feels something much different for you. So, it's totally cool, Tuck. Just remember that I'll kick your ass if you hurt her."

Tucker unconsciously gripped the steering wheel tighter and flexed his arm muscles. "Thanks, man. God, I hope she's alright."

They sat in silence for a few minutes, until Tucker broke the tension. "See if you can get any news about the storm on the radio."

Matt fiddled with the dials on the old radio until he locked onto his father's favorite news station.

As Tucker concentrated on keeping the road, they listened intently to the static-filled sound of a man's voice, confident, strong, coming from the lone speaker on the dashboard.

"…in the upcoming congressional race. And now back to our top story—the weather. The National Weather Bureau has just upgraded tropical storm *Agatha* to hurricane status. Since tracking back over water, after meteorologists had expected the storm to stay inland, she has picked up speed and intensity. Flooding has been reported up and down the New England coastline, with the greatest concern coming to those regions on the Cape which will be experiencing high tide in about an hour. Power and phone lines are reported down throughout southeastern Massachusetts. Here with a live report from Falmouth is reporter Dan Hicks. Dan, what's the storm's status on the Cape?"

Matt felt himself tense as he anticipated the news of what they could expect.

"Well, Peter, I don't know what's worse," the reporter yelled, "the wind or the rain. It is unbelievable here. Power outages have been reported throughout the Cape and Islands, and the utility companies don't expect to have the electricity and phone lines back to these poor people for quite some time as this storm is expected to rage on through the good part of the night. All we can do here is hunker down and ride her out. Updating you on the storm live from Falmouth, this is Dan…"

Matt flicked the radio off. "This is bad."

"Turn it back on; I want to hear anything about the road conditions."

Matt quickly complied.

"…update on our other lead story tonight, the shooting of a state police office, here's reporter Ruth Garcia."

"Peter, I just spoke with State Police Sergeant Earl Flemmings concerning the fatal shooting of State Trooper Jackson Gargulio. The police are still trying to recreate the crime scene, but weather conditions have made progress quite difficult. What we know at this point is that Trooper Gargulio was found in back seat of a black Volkswagen in Sandwich, with a gunshot wound to the chest. The police believe Gargulio has been dead for more than twelve hours, but forensic and autopsy tests will give them a more definitive answer on the time of death. The police speculate at least two people were involved in the shooting because Gargulio's cruiser was commandeered and according to the radio dispatcher's log, Gargulio called in a stop for speeding on the mid Cape highway just before four o'clock yesterday afternoon."

"Ruth, do the police have any leads in the case as of yet?"

"The state police have just released the name of the owner of the Volkswagen—who they are seeking to question—a Matthew Gallagher, age twenty-two, from Brookline. He is the owner of the car Trooper Gargulio pulled over and then was later found in."

The blood drained from Matt's face and his stomach sank as he heard his name over the radio. Tucker let out a gasp.

"Holy shit. Those assholes must have killed that cop!" Matt yelled.

"That's probably…"

Matt cut Tucker off. "Hold on, there's more."

The reporter continued. "The latest report is Gallagher was stopped by the Chatham police earlier today for a traffic violation. However, when the officer tried to remove Gallagher from the car he was driving, a green Jeep Cherokee, Gallagher sped away and led the officer on a wild ride through Chatham, causing two accidents before eluding the police. We'll know more in a few hours when the State Police update us again. This is Ruth Garcia, reporting live from the Cape."

"Thanks, Ruth, and keep it here for continuing reports from…"

Matt turned off the radio.

"That's why that cop was acting so skittish. They think you're the one who shot that state cop."

Matt buried his face in his hands. "What the hell's going on? I feel like the world is just spinning out of control." He suddenly jerked up. "Tuck, we have to tell the cops what's happened. We have to do it now." There was a sense of panic in his voice that made him even more nervous.

"Yeah, but what if Ridder and Sykes do go to Chatham? Huh? What then? Do you think the cops are going to believe a cockamamie story like this?"

Matt shook his head. "Who cares if they don't. At least we can get them to send somebody over to the cottage to check on Annie."

"What if you're wrong? What if they don't send somebody out, they just say they did? Then what? We'll have no way of knowing. And in the meantime, Annie could be in serious trouble. Come on, man, this isn't about you. We gotta think of Annie."

"Oh, and I bet you think I never sent the journal to the professor right?" Matt glared. "Fuck you, Tuck!"

They sat in silence for a minute after Matt's outburst. They were cold, scared and confused. And the more the night drew on, the harder it was for them to keep their cool, especially with each other.

"I'm sorry, Tuck," Matt broke the tension in a calm voice. "You're absolutely right. It's just that I want this nightmare to be over so badly. This is all my fault. I thought this was going to be some great fucking adventure, you know. We'd go dig up some lost Confederate gold and be famous and all. Bullshit. I hope I never see that stupid journal or those guys ever again. I just want it all to be over."

Tucker reached over with his right hand and patted Matt's knee. "So do I, man, believe me, so do I. But we're not there yet. So let's just stay together on this and try not to kill each other, all right? And just for the record, I never doubted that you mailed the journal. The thing will probably show up at Harvard tomorrow, you know, just a case of bad timing." He paused, then continued. "But I'll tell you, Matt, I still got a bad feeling about tonight. I don't want to add to the tension, but there's just…"

"I know. Let's not talk about it. I just want to think good thoughts now. We'll find Annie first and then call the cops."

They traveled through the South Shore without but a few cars to slow their speed of seventy miles per hour, the maximum speed the truck would go before it began to hydroplane on the standing water on the highway. The rain continued to hammer the truck, while the wind gusts forced Tucker to constantly compensate his steering to keep the truck from darting off the highway into a guardrail or tree.

When they drove over a precipice, just after Plymouth, Matt noted that the lights atop the Sagamore Bridge were not visible through the storm. As they drove closer to the canal, the dim yellow lights became fuzzy pinpricks that appeared to flickered on and off.

The rotary at the entrance of the bridge was deserted and no lights were on in the few stores on the north side of the rotary.

"Careful going over the bridge, Tuck. The wind gust could make it pretty hairy," Matt advised in a solemn tone.

Matt suddenly thought of the game his family used to play when he was young. Before driving onto the bridge, each family member guessed how many boats were in the canal. The one who guessed correctly didn't have to help with the dishes that night.

Zero, Matt thought to himself. We're the only idiots dumb enough to be out on a night like this.

He glanced out the side window as the truck pulled off the rotary onto the bridge, saw the sign advertising the help of the Samaritans and scoffed at the irony.

While Tucker concentrated on navigating the turn off the rotary, neither he nor Matt noticed the police car pull from behind the fire station on the rotary and follow them from a safe distance onto the bridge.

Matt found himself tensing for the first blast of wind thundering down the canal, but the first hundred yards of the bridge proved to be no rougher than the rest of their trip had been. As the truck passed the point of protection from the five-foot concrete and brick side walls, about a quarter of the way across the bridge, a violent wind gust drove into the side of the truck causing Tucker to struggle to keep control of the wheel.

"Holy shit, that wind is nasty," he cursed.

"Just keep it slow and watch that car coming!" Matt advised, feeling a sense of powerlessness.

When they reached the crest of the four-lane, arched bridge, directly in the center, three hundred feet above the black, turbulent waters of the canal, a vicious gale wind struck the right side of the truck. The truck swerved to the left across the double solid line despite Tucker's attempts to control the vehicle. He looked up at the oncoming headlights of the car in the other lane. Quickly reacting to the loss of control, Tucker overcompensated in trying to bring the truck out of the oncoming traffic. The truck fishtailed on the wet pavement for a few tense seconds. A car horn blared past them, just as the truck shot across the yellow lines into the foot-high granite curb at the edge of the right lane. Matt unconsciously held his breath as he stared at the blackness over the guardrail. We're going over, he thought. But the truck bounced off the curb. Suddenly, the wind stopped toying with the truck as they reached the safety of the other side of the bridge.

Tucker let out a sigh of relief while he forced his hands to release the death grip he had unknowing placed on the steering wheel. Matt ran his fingers through his hair as he melted into the back of the seat.

"Nice, driving…"

Before Matt finished his congratulations, their sense of relief turned to panic as flashing blue lights lit up the highway.

"Shit! Where'd he come from?" Tucker couldn't hide his surprise or panic. "Should I try to out run him?" He instinctively pressed on the accelerator.

"No, no, slow down and pull over!" Matt yelled. "We'd never outrun him." Matt looked back at the police car. "He must have seen us lose control on the bridge. Just be cool."

"Yeah, but what if he's stopping us for another reason?"

"Tuck, there's no way we could ditch him in this tank. Our best bet is to pray he just gives us a ticket."

Tucker shook his head as he pulled the truck to a stop on the shoulder. For what seemed like an eternity, they waited in silence for the cop to approach the truck.

Having stopped for the first time in over an hour, they began to get a real sense of the violence of the storm. The howling wind and pounding rain rocked the truck and increased their anxiety.

The raingear-clad officer methodically approached the truck as if was just another routine night on Cape Cod. His air of indifference to the weather made Matt even more nervous. Guy's a hard ass, he thought.

Tucker rolled down the window as the officer reached the cab. But the officer didn't say anything; he just meticulously surveyed the truck and its occupants.

"Evening, boys. Everything okay?" he asked in a skeptical tone.

"Yes, sir," Tucker responded quickly. A little too quickly, Matt thought. "The wind just caught me on the bridge. I wasn't expecting it to be that bad."

Tucker looked at the cop, anxiously awaiting his next statement or question. But the cop said nothing, just eyed them.

"We're trying to make it to Chatham," Tucker said, trying to break the cop's silence.

Jesus, we've blown it now, Matt thought. Why the hell did ya have to tell him we're going to Chatham?

The cop remained silent for a few more seconds, then said, "Take it slow. The roads are real wet and there was a two-car accident about ten miles ahead of here, but that should be cleared by now, but still take it easy."

Tucker quickly thanked the officer and rolled up the window to end the conversation before the officer became suspicious.

"Jesus!" Matt slumped back in the seat. "I thought for sure he was going to bust us. Maybe our luck's changing."

After waiting for the police car to get back on the highway first, Tucker carefully pulled the truck back onto the road. "Don't get too comfortable. We've got a ways to go, right? And for some reason, I can't shake off the feeling that that was just too easy."

"Why?" Matt asked, his sense of caution returned after its brief hiatus.

"Think about it. According to the radio, every cop in the state is looking for you. You'd think they'd all have your face etched in their memory, especially the cops working on Cape Cod. Which is why I can't believe that guy didn't recognize us."

"Come on Tuck, don't go flipping out on me now. That cop probably just didn't get a good look at me." Matt looked right at Tucker. "What else would explain it?"

A replay of Game Six of the 1975 World Series Game between the Boston Red Sox and Cincinnati Reds failed to distract Ditchman as he poured over his notes. Hammond, however, lay on the airport hotel bed fully engrossed in the extra-innings game of historical proportion. Just as Carlton Fisk came to bat in the twelfth inning, the phone rang. Ditchman reached over and grabbed it. In a minute he was off.

"Ice just broke, Rusty. That was O'Donahue. She just got two calls. The state police just found Matt Gallagher's car on Cape Cod with a murdered trooper stuffed in the back seat. They also found a map of Cambridge under the seat. Harvard Yard was circled. And they found the cop's stolen cruiser in Somerville, which is next to Cambridge."

"Why Harvard Yard?" Hammond raised his eyebrows.

"That brings me to the second call." Ditchman grinned. "O'Donahue knows a cop on the Cambridge force. A janitor was shot at Harvard, in one of the academic buildings."

"I don't get it."

"A student called it in. He didn't see anything but claims he heard a bunch of shots and, get this, he heard the name Sykes used."

"Which is how Gallagher's car is connected to Harvard?"

"That's what were going to find out when we get there."

# CHAPTER 17

▼

Tucker deliberately drove the truck slowly the rest of the way to Chatham as the driving conditions continued to worsen because of the amount of standing water on the highway. Every thirty seconds or so, he checked his rearview mirror, but the highway was distinctively empty of any other cars.

It was almost three o'clock in the morning when they drove through Chatham. The roads were littered with wet, green leaves and tree limbs. No streetlights were on, and every house was dark. Even the parking lot of the twenty-four hour supermarket was deserted.

As they drew closer to the cottage, Matt felt his anxiety and fear surge. He wondered if they would find Annie peacefully in bed, sleeping through the storm. Or had Ridder…he forced the thought out of his head but couldn't shake the feeling that they had made a grave error by not going to the police in the first place.

When they pulled into the Lockwood's driveway, they saw no lights were on in the cottage, and only a faint light emanated from the Lockwood's kitchen. The Lockwood's Chrysler LeBaron sat parked in front of the garage. Nothing looked out of the ordinary except the large amount of leaves and tree limbs spewed across the driveway and yard. The wind and driving rain was much worse here then it had been along the highway, but that was to be expected since Chatham was the eastern most part of the Cape.

"Looks pretty quiet," Matt commented

"Yeah, and no cops," Tucker responded as he parked the truck.

As they dashed from the truck to the cottage, each turned his head away from the driving wind and pelting raindrops that stung their faces.

Matt burst through the door first.

"Annie? Annie? You here?" he yelled.

No response.

He sprinted up the narrow staircase.

She was not in her bed.

Matt's heart pounded harder and he felt a sickness rising to his throat.

"Let's try the Lockwood's," Tucker suggested from the bottom of the stairs.

In seconds they were across the lawn and in the small screened-in porch between the garage and kitchen. Matt turned the doorknob on the wooden door leading to the kitchen. He hesitated slightly when the knob turned freely. The Lockwoods were not the types to leave their doors unlocked in the middle of the night. But then again, maybe they just had forgot to lock it, being distracted by the storm and all, Matt consoled himself.

The kitchen was dark except for the glow from the four pilot lights in the stove and a small, battery-operated lantern that spread just enough light throughout the kitchen so Matt could see that everything seemed to look in tidy order just the way Mrs. Lockwood liked to keep her kitchen. Pots and pans hung in a neat, orderly fashion from a cast iron pot rack suspended from the ceiling above the island counter in the middle of the room. Pictures of friends and family and Mr. Lockwood holding his various catches, his smile eclipsing his face, decorated the double-door refrigerator. Matt felt a sense of ease just being in the room, like nothing could ever be wrong in a room so wholesome.

"Hello? Hello?" Tucker called out in a hesitant voice. "Anybody home? It's Tucker and Matt. Mr. and Mrs. Lockwood? Annie?"

Tucker turned to Matt and shrugged his shoulders. They were about to turn to leave when they heard a soft voice.

"We're in the living room."

Annie's voice. She sounded calm. Matt felt his body relax. Finally it was over; she was safe.

They walked out of the kitchen into a short hallway next to the staircase to the second floor and into the living room.

"God, Annie, we thought you might be..." Matt began to say as they turned the corner into the living room.

Their fears stopped them dead in their tracks. Light from a kerosene lantern hypnotically illuminated the room. Mrs. Lockwood rigidly sat next to her husband on the couch. Their faces bore the expression of pure fear. Behind them stood Buster Sykes with an eight-inch field-dressing knife in his hand. To their right, Annie sat paralyzed in an easy chair, Fenway obediently at her feet. Carson Ridder held the .357 to her right temple. He smirked as they looked at him.

"Welcome home, boys. We've been expectin' you. What took you so long?" He laughed sadistically.

A cold shiver ran up Matt's back. How could this have happened? How had they beaten them back to Chatham? Weren't they supposed to get lost for hours in the tunnels under Cambridge? Why hadn't the professor called the cops? He suddenly felt nauseous and fought the urge to throw up.

They stood just inside the doorway to the living room. To their left were the sliding glass doors that opened to the deck overlooking Oyster Pond. In the corner to their right was a baby grand piano with framed photos displayed on its top. Next to it was the entrance to the dining room. In front of them now stood Carson Ridder, all six-foot-four inches of him. He stared at them as if he were beckoning them to make a move against him, but they just stood there dripping wet, in complete disbelief.

Ridder shifted his stare from Matt to Tucker, never losing the same intense combination of looking completely pissed off, yet somehow enjoying it.

"Sit down!" he ordered Tucker, who quickly found room next to Mrs. Lockwood on the couch. She put her arm around him and pulled him close to her.

Ridder took a step closer to Matt so that he was a few inches from him. Though Matt was not short on size compared to the average guy, he appeared almost frail toe to toe with Ridder. Ridder shook his head back and forth, all the while grinning like he was sizing up his prey. Then his grin turned to a scowl of rage and he lifted his hand that held the gun and struck Matt across the face. Matt fell to one knee and grabbed at his bloodied face, wincing from the deep pain.

"Tough guy, huh?" Ridder's knee shot up and hit Matt square in the nose. Blood burst from his nostrils and he fell to the floor. The fight gone from him, he slowly rocked back and forth in the fetal position, his knees close to his chest, his hands holding his face.

"Stop it! You're hurting him," Annie yelled as she stood up.

Her sudden outburst startled Fenway, who began to bark.

Ridder whipped around and pointed the gun straight at Annie.

"Shut up, bitch, and shut that mutt's trap or I'll do it myself." He pointed the gun at Fenway.

"Hey, asshole," Tucker rose out of the couch, "let's see how tough you are without the gun. I'll go a few…"

Before Tucker could finish his challenge to Ridder, Sykes brought the butt of his knife down hard on the back of Tucker's head. He collapsed onto the couch in a daze.

Ridder stared at Annie, who immediately sat back down in the chair and cradled Fenway in her arms to stop her from barking. Then he turned back to Matt, who still lay on the floor. With his huge hand, he grabbed Matt's arm and effortlessly yanked him to his feet. Crimson blood covered the lower half of Matt's face and the top part of his shirt. Although Matt held his hand tightly against it, his nose continued to drip blood onto his upper lip at a steady pace. Ridder threw him into the vacant rocking chair.

"Now listen up folks, we can make this real easy for ya, or we can do things the hard way. And I gotta tell ya," he laughed, "with how pissed off I am, I could really go for some more head bashin', know what I mean?" He stared right at Tucker, who was beginning to regain his senses.

As Ridder walked around the room glaring at his captives and ranting about the bad mood he was in and how when he was in a bad mood the only thing he liked to do was "bust heads," suddenly, the electricity came back on in the house and three lamps illuminated the living room. Matt looked at Ridder, barely able to focus his vision, his face still throbbing from the blow from Ridder's knee. Ridder looked different than he had at Professor Nylan's office. Matt couldn't make out what was different about him. Maybe it was his unclear vision, but Ridder looked like he was flexing his muscles without trying. The man in Professor Nylan's office was someone you could hope to reason with, but the man in front of him now was beyond approach, beyond reason. He looked tired and ready to explode. Matt decided in an instant not to intentionally try to challenge Ridder; he would have to play things out and pray the police would show up.

Ridder picked up a white ceramic lamp from the end table and hurled it against the wall. The lamp shattered in an explosion causing Mrs. Lockwood to jump and scream. Mr. Lockwood hugged his wife tighter.

Ridder strutted toward the baby grand in the corner, turned to the wall and grabbed a brass floor lamp and said, "I'm gonna say it one last time, and then it gets ugly." In one motion he picked up the lamp and hurled it like a javelin at the large mirror behind the piano bench. With a loud smash, which jolted everyone although they saw it coming, the mirror shattered into hundreds of pieces behind the piano. The room was instantly darker. Ridder turned back to them and squinted his eyes, looking no more composed after having vented some of his frustration, his eyes still on the edge of madness. "Where's my journal?"

When no one responded immediately, Ridder began to quicken his pace back and forth between the chairs and the couch. He ranted about respect and threatened to start experimenting with kitchen utensils if someone didn't answer him real soon.

Each time Ridder turned at the end of the couch, Mr. Lockwood looked at the phone on the table next to him. After Ridder made another turn away from him, Mr. Lockwood casually lifted his left hand off the armrest and slowly put it on the edge of the table. He looked at Sykes who stood with his arms crossed at the other end of the couch. Sykes' eyes fixed on Ridder and he nodded as if in agreement each time Ridder promised to "carve somebody up if he didn't get some cooperation real fast."

As his dizziness began to subside, Matt looked around the room to take in the situation. He looked to his immediate left at Ridder, who paced back and forth, angrily pointing the gun into the air to reinforce his threats. Sykes stood on the other side of Ridder with the knife in his hand. Below Sykes, and slightly to his left, sat Tucker, then Mrs. and Mr. Lockwood. Tucker looked pissed. Matt had seen the look during every lacrosse game, and at every party where some drunken idiot started shoving people around. The look worried Matt. He looked at Annie. She clutched Fenway tightly against her legs. Even in the dim light, Matt could see the blood had drained from her face. She looked absolutely terrified. Her mouth hung slightly open; a glaze of tears canvassed her eyes. She tilted her head ever so slightly to the left, as she always did when she felt vulnerable.

Everyone sat completely still as Ridder commanded their attention with the gun, but a slight movement by Mr. Lockwood caught Matt's eye. He was slowly reaching for the phone next to him. Matt quickly turned his head back to Ridder, who was about to turn around again and would be staring right at Mr. Lockwood.

"Listen, I told you before, I sent the damn thing a couple days ago," Matt said loudly, trying to prevent Ridder from making the turn toward Mr. Lockwood. "I personally stuck it in the mailbox. So maybe you ought to just go back to Cambridge and wait for it a little longer. Come on, man, I'm telling you the truth. We don't have the journal. If we did, why wouldn't we just give it to you?"

While Matt talked, Mr. Lockwood picked up the phone's receiver and delicately placed it next to the base on the table. He slowly withdrew his hand. Matt strained his peripheral vision to watch Mr. Lockwood remove his hand from the receiver. He quickly realized what Mr. Lockwood was going to try to do. If he could keep Ridder distracted long enough, Mr. Lockwood could dial 911. Jesus,

Matt thought, but what if they hear the operator on the other end? He quickly surmised that by talking, Ridder would never be able to hear the operator's voice.

"Come on, man, be reasonable, there's no need..."

Ridder suddenly turned to his left and seeing the phone off the hook lunged in the direction of Mr. Lockwood. He grabbed the receiver out of his hand, then slapped Mr. Lockwood across the face with the back of his huge hand, snapping the older man's head to the side as if Ridder had used his fist.

"You stupid, old man!" Ridder slammed his right fist into the phone; its face shattered as if it were a glass hit by a hammer.

Mrs. Lockwood cradled her husband in her arms and began to cry again, as she gently touched her husband's bruised face. Stoically, Mr. Lockwood stared at Ridder.

Ridder paced around the room, ire boiling throughout his body. His lips pursed into slits of rage while his mammoth arms pumped up and down from the blood and adrenaline rushing through him.

Matt held his breath and looked at Tucker, then Annie. Both had their mouths open, too scared to move or say anything for fear of bringing attention to themselves.

"Maybe you people are just too fuckin' stupid to understand the situation." Ridder walked over to Annie, bent over and malevolently yanked Fenway by the collar. The dog let out a yelp as Annie clutched at empty air. Ridder drove the gun into Fenway's head.

"No, please, don't hurt her," Annie cried as she desperately held out her hands for her beloved dog.

Ridder's face turned from a scowl to a sadistic grin. "You give me my journal right now, or I waste the mutt," he said in a calm voice. "Then I'm gonna waste one of you." He looked around the room and stopped at Mrs. Lockwood. "Startin' with the old broad."

"I'll tell you were the gold is. We don't have the journal, that's the truth, but I know were the gold is," Annie quickly said.

Ridder slowly turned to her.

"Bullshit. If you fuck with me..."

"No, no, I won't. Please don't hurt anyone. I'll tell you."

"And how the hell do you know where the gold's at?" Sykes said in a challenging tone.

"Because I read the journal," Annie challenged him back.

"She's got a photographic memory," Matt offered.

"Bullshit, no such thing." Sykes looked at the Lockwoods.

"It's true. She's had it since she was a child," Mr. Lockwood said, nodding his head.

Sykes walked over to the coffee table in front of the Lockwoods and picked up the recent edition of *Time* magazine. "You were looking at this before, weren't ya? Okay, miss smarty-pants," he said sardonically, "what's the lead article say?" He flipped open the magazine to the cover story on the Middle East.

They all looked at Annie in anticipation. She paused for a few seconds, looked at Ridder who still gripped Fenway by the collar, the gun stilled pressed against her head.

"The title of the article is 'Middle East Terrorism Threatens Peace Accord,' written by Robert A. Steinley." She closed her eyes. "The first paragraph says the delicate Rose Garden Peace Accord, signed by the United States and Union of Islamic Nations in May, is threatened by recent terrorist violence against United States citizens abroad, most recently the bombing of a tourist bus in Paris, which claimed the lives of six Americans. According to the Central Intelligence Agency, the mastermind believed to be behind the recent string of unknowing attacks is the Islamic fundamentalist, Rasheem Bin Remeen, the self-proclaimed 'Defender of the Word of Allah,' the man wanted by the FBI for the bombing of U.S. Embassy in Saudi Arabia."

Annie stopped and opened her eyes. She stared coldly at Ridder and did not blink.

Ridder turned away from Annie and looked at Sykes.

Sykes' mouth hung open in disbelief. Without looking up from the magazine, he said, "Holy shit, I don't believe it. That's almost word for word."

Annie released the breath that she had been holding, thankful that she had read the article days before as well.

Ridder threw Fenway into Annie's arms. "You've proven your point. Now tell me where the gold is."

"I'll tell you only if you swear that you'll let us go."

Ridder laughed. "You're in no position to be makin' demands here. As far as I see it, you tell me or I'll kill you, that simple. If, and when, we find my gold, then I'll consider your future. But for right now, you ain't in any position to be dictatin' no demands to me. So what's it gonna be?"

Annie looked at Matt who nodded his head.

"It's buried near a deserted, old lighthouse at the southern end of Monomoy Island. The spot's marked by a pile of rocks."

Ridder laughed sardonically. "Bullshit. How the hell do you expect us to find the right pile of rock? You're full of it."

"Monomoy is nothing more than a huge pile of sand. There's probably only a handful of rocks on the island, never mind in a pile near the lighthouse." Annie held her breath as she hoped to God Ridder believed her about the pile of rocks. There was no way he was going to believe the poem in the journal. She watched him closely to judge his reaction, but he just stood frozen with his right hand gripping the gun rigidly in front of him.

"You know where it is now, so *please*, just let us go," Mrs. Lockwood pleaded in a shaking tone.

Ridder ignored her and began to pace.

When he turned back toward Annie, his eyes focused on an object behind her. He quickly walked behind her chair to a table against the wall. He stared at the collection of picture frames on the table, then picked up a picture of Mr. Lockwood poised on the bow of his Boston Whaler, a large striped bass trophy in his hands. He put the frame down, then snatched up a picture of the Lockwoods standing proudly on the stern deck of the *Gerty*. He threw the picture down on the table, not caring that the glass broke, and turned back to his audience.

Ridder shook his head. "No, I ain't done with you yet." He looked at Mr. Lockwood. "Where's your boats?" he demanded.

"Moored in the pond behind the house."

Ridder grinned. "Perfect. First thing in the mornin', we're gonna take a little boat ride." He looked at Annie. "And you better pray you find my gold, or," he pointed the gun at Annie and mouthed the word, "pow."

Ridder turned and looked at Matt, then at Tucker. "And if you two assholes try any more of your bullshit heroics, first I'm gonna have my way with the ladies," he thrust out his hips, "then I'm gonna kill them and you." He stared at Matt and grinned.

Though pain shot through his entire face each time his heart pumped, Matt's senses were slowly returning. He defiantly looked back at Ridder, his hands steadier, his vision clearer. He prayed the professor had called the police. But he knew that if he had, the police would have already arrived.

Matt looked at his hands and clutched them into fists. Despite being used as Ridder's personal stress reliever, he still felt strength in his hands. He looked up at Annie. Fenway's shoulder cradled her face, her eyes tightly closed. Sudden thoughts of losing Annie seemed to pump more resilience into his body. Somehow he felt responsible for all this. Suddenly, he had an overwhelming desire to lunge at Ridder's throat, catch him off guard, knock him to the floor and pummel the life out of him and end this nightmare once and for all. But then Annie looked him right in the eye. Her intense, brown eyes spoke volumes of her sadness; where once a sparkle had been, only fear and apprehension showed. In painful silence, her eyes seemed to scream for sanity and peace. The adrenaline stopped pumping through Matt's arms; he dared not do anything that would endanger Annie's life.

Ridder's raspy voice broke Matt's thoughts. "Now I suggest we get a little shut eye before we do a little treasure huntin' in the morning." The corners of his lips turned up as he said the word "treasure." "And if one of you dumbasses even stir an inch, you ain't gonna live to have your next breakfast." He waved the gun in the air for effect.

"Buster, turn off all the lights, except for that one." Ridder pointed to the ceiling light in the hallway by the backdoor.

When Sykes had done as he was told, he went over to Ridder, who stood by the doorway to the living room. They stood in silence for a while, looking to see if anyone stirred. Ridder then grabbed Sykes' elbow and led him into the adjoining dining room.

"Buster, you got first shift," Ridder whispered firmly into Sykes' ear. He handed Sykes the gun and took the knife. "In a couple of hours wake me up and then you can get some sleep. And, Buster, so help you if you fuck this up. You got me? Those punks ain't gonna screw with me again."

Sykes nodded his head in obedience. "Carson, what about the journal? And do you really think they know where the gold is?"

Ridder looked him straight in the eyes. "Put it this way, Einstein, I'm sick of chasing that fuckin' journal and if these assholes had it, they'd handed it over by now. And since we're at it, we might as well finish this fuckin' wild goose chase after comin' this far. Maybe you were right for the first time in your life and some lost fuckin' gold does exist. Either way, we take all their bank cards and credit cards, then waste 'em because they're the only ones connectin' us to the journal at this point."

Sykes raised his black, bushy eyebrows. "How we supposed to do that and get...I mean, there's no..."

Ridder grabbed Sykes' arm and bent his head down to the smaller man's level. "Did you see the picture I was looking at? The old man's got a real nice cabin cruiser. We'll take 'em out to sea and dump the bodies. We'll just tie 'em up with rocks. Ain't nobody gonna find five bodies in a couple hundred feet of water, 'specially after the sharks get through with 'em."

# CHAPTER 18

▼

O'Donahue rolled down the cruiser's window and flashed her badge at the orange raincoat-clad officer who had been assigned the miserable duty of regulating the east gate at Harvard Yard. Without fanfare, he waved her past his post.

The scene outside the five-story Sever Hall was unlike any typical crime scene. Ten police cars, a combination of Harvard University, Cambridge, and state cruisers, created a full parking lot on the small green between the building and the iron gates. A kaleidoscope of blue and white flashing and circulating lights illuminated and bounced off Sever Hall and the two buildings which stood to the left and right, as well as the dormitories and houses across the street. Despite the amount of lights and cars, which usually drew large crowds regardless of the time of night, the severity of the storm discouraged even the most curious. Only the waterlogged, lone cop guarding the gate to the green was outside. Inside Sever Hall was quite a different scene.

More like a typical day on the floor of the New York Stock Exchange during a bull run than a crime scene being methodically investigated, Sever Hall was a sea of confusion and rising tempers as cops yelled at each other over jurisdiction and crime scene etiquette. O'Donahue turned to the first cop she saw who was not engaged in an argument.

"Where can I find Detective Hillendyke?"

"Third floor."

As they reached the landing of the third floor, Hillendyke and another officer burst through the double wooden doors.

"And I say we gotta cooperate on this one, so get on board." Hillendyke slapped the younger officer on the back and then stopped just before walking into

Ditchman. He looked up at Ditchman and didn't try to hide his annoyance. Then he looked at O'Donahue and a smile replaced his scowl.

"Now there's a ray of sunshine in a rainbow of shit kind of night. How are ya, Marty?"

"Thanks for calling, Rob." She forced a half smile. She hated how Hillendyke always acted overly sweet to her. And despite her ambivalence toward him, he repeatedly asked her out. She knew it was for only one reason—to prove he was not the male chauvinist she thought he was so he could get her into bed. O'Donahue had long ago learned that she would have to endure jerks like Hillendyke if she ever wanted to advance her career.

"These are Detectives Ditchman and Hammond from Richmond. They've been assisting me on the case I told you about."

He smirked, quickly shook their hands and turned back to O'Donahue. "I told you going out with me would be worth your while."

"Get off it, Hillendyke, it wasn't a date. Now cut the crap and stop wasting my time. What's the story here?"

Hillendyke caught Ditchman's eye and a shade of crimson suffused his face. He immediately retreated to the safety of his profession. He nodded to the staircase to the upper floor. "Next floor to the right, we got a janitor with a single shot to the head, close range. Real mess. Top floor, a professor's office was shot up. Guy's name is Albert Nylan, older guy based on university records. We haven't been able to find him yet. Can't imagine he's caught up with all this. Guy's been here something like since Roosevelt was in office."

"Which one?" Ditchman jested.

"Which one what?"

"Never mind."

Hillendyke rolled his eyes at Ditchman then looked down the stairs. "And in the basement, we found a panel doorway that leads to some crazy mess of underground tunnels. The university cops are checking into it, but they're gonna need a friggin' map to get around in there."

"Or maybe a minotaur?" Ditchman jested, but Hillendyke gave no reaction.

"What about the witness you mentioned when you called?"

"Russian kid, here studying for the summer. Micro-something or other. Yeah, welcome to America. Anyway, he didn't see anything, just heard a couple of shots and some yelling. Apparently he heard a name." Hillendyke glanced at his notebook in his left hand. "Says he heard the names 'Buster' and 'Sykes.' I remembered you mentioned the name Sykes when you told me about that airport shooting, so I called you."

As they made their way to the fourth floor, Hillendyke pumped O'Donahue for information on Sykes, but she offered little because she didn't want to have to work "in cooperation" with Hillendyke's Cambridge detectives, which meant spending more time than she could tolerate with Rob Hillendyke.

Hillendyke led them down the corridor to where the janitor's body had been found. They ducked under a yellow police line tape stretched across the ten-foot wide hallway to reach the office. A plain clothes detective pulling white rubber gloves off his hands stood outside the office. He looked up when they approached.

"Just finished Rob. Best I can tell nobody put him in the closet. Based on the mess in the guy's pants, he knew what was coming and was trying to hide. Place reeks."

"Which means he ran into the shooter somewhere else," O'Donahue offered.

The plain clothes detective looked at her and raised an eyebrow.

"Detective O'Donahue, State Police, and her guests," Hillendyke said tersely as he nodded in the direction of Ditchman and Hammond.

"Maybe," the detective answered.

"Would explain why he was hiding in the closet. How else would he have known the shooter would be looking for him?" Ditchman said.

"Anyway, Rob, forensics will do a complete job on the clothing and the contents of the vacuum bags. If there's anything, we'll find it. Doesn't look like they were here for any other reason but to waste the guy, unless Harvard janitors are in the habit of storing cash along with their cleaning supplies."

The room was no larger than the average home's full bathroom. A four-foot long incandescent light hung from two thin chains in the middle of the room. The lone window at the end of the room covered the entire back wall. On the right wall, six shelves, evenly spaced, held rolls of toilet paper, paper towels, and an assortment of liquid cleaners in worn bottles with no labels. On the opposite wall hung an arsenal of mops and brooms. The lone closet was built into the corner, next to the door.

Ditchman, then Hammond, followed O'Donahue into the office to look into the closet. The limp and slightly blue body of Felix Lillioso lay awkwardly slumped against the back corner of the closet. A half-full mop bucket of dirty water propped up his body so that it looked as if he were about to fully stand up if it weren't for the black hole in his forehead and the frozen look of unambiguous fear on his face. His open eyes screamed for the help that never came.

Ditchman looked at the body then tilted his head to get a better look behind it. Red and gray brain matter stained the back of the closet. He felt a twinge in the back of his throat, the feeling you get when your heart drops and you can't swallow. He only had the feeling when he saw a victim, not a perp. It was a familiar feeling to Ditchman, but one that he never became used to, nor wanted to.

In the corridor, Ditchman took a deep breath of what he believed had to be cleaner air. He made eye contact with Hammond and stepped over to talk to him while O'Donahue was occupied with dealing with Hillendyke.

"I know what you're thinking, Ditch."

"What's that?"

"If this is our guys, they just upped the ante."

Ditchman nodded his head. "And they're playing for keeps. Whatever this is about could be a lot bigger than we thought, Rusty."

"Three bodies and counting," Hammond said matter-of-factly.

A uniformed cop approached from the other end of the corridor and stopped in front of the janitor's office door. "Detective?" He waited until he had Hillendyke's attention. "They're finished upstairs."

When they reached the professor's office, they waited at the door to allow two forensic technicians to leave. When they stepped through the doorway, Hillendyke introduced them to his lead forensic specialist, Vincent Lacey, a frail man with oversized round glasses which made his face look even more boyish than it already did.

"Anything new, Vinnie?"

"I think we've got plenty to go over back at the lab. We'll know a lot more then. There were fingerprints everywhere, especially on the doorknobs, mostly partials, and the front and back of the desk. But seeing that it's a professor's office and all, who knows, could have half the student body's prints. We'll find out soon. Anyway, we got four bullets, one through the door, lodged in the ceiling tile, two in the ceiling five feet inside the door, and one in the right wall at the top." As he spoke, he pointed at each spot where a thirty-six inch square block had been removed from the wall so the bullets' trajectory could be determined and then the bullets carefully removed and examined. Lacey pointed to the pile of books on the floor. "Found what appears to be pepper spray on the books, know better once we test it, you know. But I'm pretty sure." He became suddenly erect as if excited. "Oh, and I didn't tell you this yet, Detective." He looked at Hillendyke. "I found some small flakes of gold paint on the corner of the desk there and on the floor." He pointed. "Again, we'll know more back at the lab."

"Mind if we take a look around?" Ditchman asked.

"Be my guest; everything's been dusted and photographed already."

Ditchman, Hammond and O'Donahue slowly walked around the office in silence. They looked with a questioning eye at everything from the door's shattered glass on the floor and the remains left in the door frame to the books fallen from the bookshelf just inside the doorway. Ditchman paid special attention to the views from various standing points in the room. He even sat in the two chairs and looked around.

After a few minutes, Hillendyke asked, "So what do you think?"

O'Donahue looked at Ditchman.

"Shooter was standing here." He positioned himself five feet in front of the door. "Bullet was found in the ceiling in the hallway, right?" he said, though it wasn't a question. "For a projection like that to the ceiling, the shooter would have to have been sitting in a chair, or on the floor." He looked at both chairs. "The floor's doubtful and the chairs don't line up with the angle of entry in the ceiling. So that leaves what? The shooter was aiming up?"

"What if the shooter didn't intent to shoot upward at that angle?" Hammond asked.

"Maybe someone hit him right before he shot and knocked his hand and the gun upward," O'Donahue said.

"Which gives us at least two people—the shooter, a person there," Ditchman pointed to where Hillendyke stood.

"That's my guess, two people here, plus the janitor."

Hammond stood up and reenacted the shooter. "The shooter has his gun out, maybe trained on the second person and maybe the janitor comes through the door." He turned quickly to the door. "The guy's freaked and he brings up the gun to shoot, but the second guy tackles him."

"Which may also explain the books on the floor," Ditchman said. He turned and looked at the two partially empty shelves in the middle of the wall bookcase, and then at the pile of a dozen hardback books strewn about the floor at the bottom of the bookcase.

O'Donahue stepped closer to Ditchman and nodded her head. "That could explain why just a section of books came off the shelves."

Ditchman looked around the room, still deep in thought; his forehead crinkled from being in what Hammond called "the zone." He knelt down next to the pile of books and examined them.

"Two guys on the floor, one uses the pepper spray. Would explain the traces on the books," he looked up at the ceiling and then the far wall, "and the other three shots."

A uniformed cop appeared in the doorway holding two clear, plastic evidence bags. "Detective Hillendyke, I was told to show you this. We just found it in the tunnels in the basement, about three hundred yards from the entrance."

They all looked at the objects in the bags as Hillendyke held one, Lacey the other. Lacey stuck his face inches from his bag as if his quarter inch thick glasses didn't work.

"Looks consistent with the gold flake on the floor." Lacey rotated the bag and tilted his head. "I'll know better after I check it for prints and put it under the scope, but based on the broken corners I'm pretty sure these are a couple of pieces of lead painted to look like bullion. Very interesting markings—CSA. I'm willing to bet the paint chips match up, which means you can put these in the office. I'll let you know."

Lacey took the other bag from Hillendyke, nodded to Ditchman and left the office.

"What do you think, Ditch? Another piece of the puzzle?" Hammond said. "Wasn't Hutchinson's research on some lost Confederate gold? Maybe this is a connection?"

"Maybe, but let's consider all the evidence before we start hypothesizing, Rusty." Ditchman paused. "Let's get back to the number of people. The Russian kid says he heard someone yell 'Buster' and 'Sykes,' right?"

Hillendyke nodded. "Yeah, that give us two more people."

"Wrong. It's the same guy. 'Buster' is Sykes' nickname," O'Donahue said.

"Maybe it was his big friend from the airport who yelled his name. They came this far from Virginia together, why split up?" Hammond said.

Ditchman walked over to the bookcase behind the desk and examined the framed photos. "The one guy in most of these pictures must be Nylan." He took down a picture of two white haired men smiling cheerily in front of Mt. Rushmore. "If we assume Nylan was in his office, based on the looks of him in this picture, he's pretty old. I doubt he took on both Sykes and his friend, which means there was one, probably two other people in this office."

"Gallagher and his friend?" Hammond said.

Ditchman raised his eyebrows.

"Did you find Nylan's appointment book?" O'Donahue asked Hillendyke.

"Yeah, found it in his top drawer, along with his wallet, forty-five bucks in it. So we can rule out simply burglary. I had my men talk to the last two students he had appointments with, couple of coeds, neither saw or heard anything. Both claimed Nylan seemed completely himself."

They all looked at the doorway when a uniformed cop appeared. Hillendyke nodded his head at the cop.

"Harvard boys just got a call from Mt. Auburn Hospital. They got an old guy. Drunk ran him over on Mass. Ave. Messed up pretty bad. He's in ICU. Can you believe that crap? Guy was on the sidewalk and the bastard still hit 'em."

"No I.D.?"

"Guy was wearing a tie with all the Harvard shields on it. You know, all that Veritas crap or whatever. Anyway, they figured they'd call over here, maybe make an I.D."

Hillendyke looked at O'Donahue then at the cop. "Get on over there and call me if it's him."

Without having to be told, Ditchman grabbed the Mt. Rushmore picture and they headed out the door.

They arrived at the Mount Auburn Hospital, located less than a mile west of Harvard Square, in less than three minutes because they only had to fight the raging storm and not the ubiquitous Harvard Square pedestrian. The emergency room lobby was no different. People evidently found their need to visit the emergency room quelled by the violence of Mother Nature.

The immediately present smell of the hospital triggered memories in Ditchman that the commotion of the past four days had suppressed. He suddenly was cognizant of his chest and the hole the bullet had left there. He felt the ten-inch scar, still red with infancy, come to life as if smelling salts had been placed under its nose. Despite being soaking wet from briefly being outside, Ditchman could feel tiny beads of sweat beginning to develop on his forehead.

Hammond looked at his partner, then touched his elbow. "You all right?" he said in a low voice.

"Yeah, just some ghosts stopping by to say boo." He forced a smile. "Let's get to work."

The receptionist directed them to the third floor and the ICU. They checked in with the nurse behind the desk at the unit, and found the Cambridge cop in the waiting room. A television in the upper corner of the waiting room immediately captured their attention despite the volume being barely audible. A news reporter in a yellow raincoat, standing on what looked like the remains of a beach, tried in vain to deliver a report on the storm while wind gusts knocked him off balance like he was thoroughly drunk. His face cringed as the wind whipped the rain into his bare face.

Ditchman stood and turned up the volume, happy to have the distraction while they waited for the doctor.

An anchorwoman appeared on the screen and reviewed in theatrical fashion the statistics of the storm as if nothing like its sort had ever been experienced by New Englanders. Eighty mile per hour winds, with gusts over one hundred, major coastal flooding in the low-lying areas, beach erosion at those coastlines facing the north and east, tens of thousands without electricity, storm to blow out to sea by dawn. As she cut out to another reporter covering the storm, a doctor walked into the waiting room and introduced himself as Dr. Pardue.

In his late thirties, with the stubble of a beard three days old, he wore his sandy-blond hair in a long ponytail that he released from his sanitary cap with a sigh of relief. Though he looked more like he belonged at a 1970s rock concert, the focus in his eyes spoke volumes of his confidence in his medical abilities.

They stood and introduced themselves and O'Donahue explained how they might know the identification of the "John Doe" patient, as he may be involved with an investigation. Ditchman produced the photograph, which the doctor examined for a few seconds.

"That's him. But he's still unconscious."

The Cambridge cop excused himself to make a phone call.

"His name is Albert Nylan. He's a professor over at Harvard. Can we see him?" O'Donahue said.

"I don't know what good it will do you. He's in pretty bad shape and may not make it. Come on, I'll explain on the way."

He turned and led them down the corridor just as a photo of Matt Gallagher and Trooper Jackson Gargulio appeared on the screen and the anchorwoman announced: "Despite the storm, the manhunt for the chief suspect in the shooting of a state trooper intensifies…"

Halfway down the hallway Dr. Pardue explained the professor's condition in a somber, matter-of-fact way. "He was hit by a car tonight. Drunk driver plowed into him before burying himself into the dashboard of his car when he hit a brick wall. EMT's don't know how long it was before they got to the scene. Not many people out to call it in. They needed the Jaws of Life to peel the drunk's sorry ass off the engine block." He stopped and looked at them. "Sorry, it's hard to remain objective with these murderers."

"How's Nylan?" Ditchman asked.

They began walking again.

"He had lost a lot of blood by the time they found him. Left femur's broken; the hip's shattered and he's got a large subdural hematoma. The impact threw him twenty feet into a brick wall. It's amazing he made it past that. En route here, he went into arrest. He just came out of surgery and hasn't regained consciousness." He stopped outside the door to the intensive care unit. "With all that trauma to his old body, he developed ARDS."

"What's that?" Ditchman asked.

"Adult respiratory distress syndrome. It's usually caused by shock and trauma. We've got him on a ventilator now."

"What's his chances?"

Dr. Pardue looked at Ditchman and shook his head. "Less than fifty percent with the ARDS. And with the amount he bled out," he paused, "let's just hope the professor is tougher than he looks."

They stopped at the window to room 343 and peered through the partially open blinds. The left side of the room was filled with a series of machines each about the size of a dresser. A nurse stood with her back to the window as she monitored the multitude of colored lights, LCD screens, and paper tapes on the machines that remained the only signs that the professor was alive. He lay corpse-like in the bed, connected to the machines and intravenous bags by tubes and wires. A blue, ribbed tube ran from his mouth to a ventilator.

Dr. Pardue tapped the window and the nurse entered the hallway and introduced herself. Dr. Pardue explained how she had been with the professor since he arrived in the ambulance.

"Has he been unconscious the entire time?" O'Donahue asked.

"No. He came to twice. Barely for a second if you'd even call it being conscious."

"Did he say anything?" Ditchman asked.

"The first time he mumbled the name Andy or Annie, or something. I couldn't really tell. I had to do a double take, you know, because I couldn't believe he came to, never mind said something. But I'm pretty sure."

"What about the next time?"

"Right before the surgery, right before I put the mask over his mouth, I saw his mouth moving slightly so I put my ear to it and I could have sworn he said 'Chatham.'"

Ditchman and O'Donahue looked at each other in shock.

"That's where Gallagher's brother said he was renting," Ditchman said.

"Of all the things to say, Nylan chose to say that. It can only mean one thing."

"True. We need to get to Chatham as soon as possible," Ditchman said then turned to Hammond and raised his eyebrows.

"But we have no clue where to go," O'Donahue said.

Hammond looked at his watch. "It's almost four in the morning. It's not like there'll be tons of people up and about to ask. How do you expect to find them?"

Ditchman looked at his partner. "That's why I want you to stay here. Rusty, we can't rely on these locals to keep us informed. I need you to stay here in case Nylan regains consciousness."

Hammond gave him a puzzled look.

"All we have is Chatham and a couple of names. If we get down there with just that, it'll be impossible to find them before they kill someone else. Think about it. Of all the things to say, Nylan says that? But if he comes to, maybe you can question him. And in the meantime, we can save some time by getting down there."

"But it's not like he's going to sit up and have a conversation with me."

"No, but he may give you a little more than what we're going on now. And he may be able to connect this Andy or Annie to Gallagher and thus to Sykes and his buddy."

"Ditch, that's if they're connected. A big *if*."

# CHAPTER 19

▼

The lone hall light cast a dim illumination on the living room so that the room bordered on that fine line between just enough light to see and not enough, an amount that tends to play games with your eyes and mind. In such dim light, objects could be better perceived if not stared at for too long a period.

On the right end of the couch, the Lockwoods slept cradled in each other's arms. Though they had feared falling asleep, the exhaustion of the ordeal had finally overcome them, and their aged bodies shut down.

At the other end the couch, Tucker slept with his head precariously positioned on the armrest, his neck strained from the sharp angle of his body. His eyes twitched violently under their eyelids as if he were dreaming that he was fighting for his life. Dried blood from the wound on the back of his head, courtesy of the butt of Sykes' knife, stained the blue and white striped fabric.

In the high back, wicker rocking chair adjacent to Tucker, Matt slept awkwardly, his head tilted down, his chin resting against his blood strained chest. Completely exhausted, he had had no trouble falling asleep despite the throbbing pain in his face. Because his nose was broken, he breathed heavily out his mouth. A line of continuous drool snaked from the left corner of his bloodied lower lip, making a softball size wet spot on his shirt to match the blood stain above it. Even asleep, he looked in agony.

Annie slept curled up sideways in the easy chair across the coffee table from Matt, her hands neatly tucked under the left side of her resting head, her left knee tightly pulled up against her chest, her right leg hanging over the front of the chair. Fenway lay on the floor in front of the chair, leaning against her dangling leg.

When Fenway shifted, as dogs always do when sleeping, the movement against Annie's legs startled her awake. For a brief second she forgot what had happened and where she was. But as her eyes adjusted to the darkness, she slowly looked around the room by moving her head ever so slightly and the fear returned to her immediately, gripping her so tightly she almost gasped for a breath.

It was not a bad dream, it was reality, and the proof was sleeping with his head down on the dining room table fifteen feet behind the couch on which the Lockwoods and Tucker slept. Ridder rested his head on his crossed arms on the table, his back rounded from the position, his head turned toward the living room. Though the distance and poor lighting made it difficult to be positive, Annie figured he was fast asleep by the limp posture of his huge body.

Annie slowly, imperceptibly, she hoped, turned her head back to its original position, her left ear tucked against the back of the chair, the back of her head facing the dining room. As she continued to allow her eyes to adjust to the darkness, she began to notice something strange about Sykes.

Sykes had begun the gun-imposed sleep time in a chair he had brought in from the dining room. He was still in the same chair, in the same position, a few feet to Matt's right, in front of the television console, a position that completed a human circle around the coffee table.

Annie strained her peripheral vision to study him and noticed something strange. He sat completely still, his head upright, but slightly tilted to the left. At first, Annie thought he was awake, but the more she examined him, the more she became convinced that he, too, was asleep. The pull of gravity slightly distorted his open mouth. His arms were limply folded across his potbelly, which rhythmically moved with his steady breathing. Then she spotted the gun limply resting in his right hand, his grip barely tight enough to keep it from falling to the floor.

She watched him for three more minutes, noting the rhythmic movement of his chest as he breathed, hoping her eyes were not playing games with her mind. Finally, Annie concluded he definitely was asleep. Slowly, and methodically, as if she were repositioning herself in her sleep, she shifted her back in the other direction. She counted to sixty, then slightly opened her eyes and peered through her long eyelashes.

The Lockwoods and Tucker were still asleep, but Ridder's head was now turned away from her, toward the large picture window that looked out toward Oyster Pond. She strained to detect a reflection of his face in the window, but the light was too dim to cast any image. But other than his head, he hadn't moved.

Annie sat perfectly still and watched Ridder. Her heart began to race so much she worried that she would have to take a deep, audible breath. She calmed herself by thinking about the soothing motion of a boat on calm waters.

Annie carefully studied Ridder for two more minutes, and when he didn't stir, she methodically turned her head back to look at Sykes. He hadn't moved either. She stared at the gun in his hand only ten feet away from her. A chill ran down her back as she reluctantly concluded what she must do.

As Annie slowly stood up, careful not to nudge Fenway, she glanced at Ridder, then back at Sykes. She held her breath as she stepped over Fenway, then took two steps. Suddenly, she froze.

Oh, God, what am I doing, she thought. Then she looked at Matt, his face bruised and bloody from Ridder's attack. They'll never let us go, even if we do find the gold, she concluded. We know their names. And what are the chances even of finding any gold? She bravely took two more steps and found herself an arm's length from the gun.

Closer now, she saw drool had run from Sykes' open mouth into a pool on his shirt. She paused again. A quiet snort gargled from Sykes' nose every time he took in a breath. Just grab the gun, she yelled at herself.

She took a deep breath and reached for the gun. Sykes suddenly stirred. Annie froze, her arm still stretched out. She contemplated jumping back into the safety of her chair, but her body refused to move.

After a few snorts, Sykes settled into a new position but his eyes remained shut, the gun still resting loosely in his slightly open hand. Annie slowly extended her hand toward the gun, her eyes riveted on the black metal. A few inches from the gun, her body froze stiff as the paralyzing cold steel of Ridder's knife pushed into her throat. Her head snapped back as he violently yanked her hair.

"You dumb, fuckin' bitch!" Ridder bellowed.

Ridder's loud voice immediately awakened everyone in the room, including Sykes, who jumped to his feet and nervously pointed the gun with a shaking arm straight at Annie.

Fenway jumped to her feet and began barking. Mrs. Lockwood cried out and clutched her husband's arm.

Annie felt the blood drain from her head. A woozy feeling enveloped her body. Her legs felt weak as if she was about to collapse, but she held her ground for fear of having her throat slit if she fell.

When Matt and Tucker realized what was happening, it only took a split second for both of them to get to their feet. Tucker immediately rushed toward

Annie, but Ridder froze him within a step by yanking Annie around in front of Tucker, the knife firmly held against Annie's bare neck.

"Take one more step and she's dead!"

Tucker brought his hands up in front of his chest and held out his palms. "Take it easy, man. Be cool. Nobody wants to get hurt, okay?"

Ridder's face scrunched up and shook uncontrollably. Through clenched teeth he said, "You people don't understand who you're screwin' with. Obviously, I need a more convincin' way to show you assholes that I mean business here!"

He pressed the blade harder against Annie's throat. The skin reddened from the pressure.

"You wanna keep fuckin' with me? Do ya?" Ridder screamed. "Then kiss this bitch goodbye!"

"No, wait!" Tucker yelled as he held out his hands. "You kill her and you'll never find the gold."

Ridder wheeled toward Tucker. "Bullshit! She already told me where it is."

"No, she gave you the area where it's buried, not the exact location and she's the only one who read the journal. You'll spend all day digging without the exact spot. And those waters out there are heavily fished. Someone will see you, call the cops, and your sorry ass will be hauled off to jail, all because you were too stupid to listen to reason." Tucker took a deep breath.

Ridder's eyebrows pinched down against his deep eye sockets as his eyes somehow became even darker. He pursed his lips, then threw Annie on the ground in front of him.

Annie let out a gasp as she landed hard on the floor. Matt and Tucker quickly rushed to her side and helped her up. She desperately grasped at Tucker as he cradled her in his arms.

Ridder gave Sykes a dirty look and grabbed the gun from him. "You assholes need to be taught a lesson. No one fucks with Carson Ridder!"

He held the gun out in front of his chest and pointed it at Mrs. Lockwood. Mr. Lockwood instinctively embraced his sobbing wife to protect her. Ridder eyed his target, then quickly turned to his right, lowered the gun and fired.

Fenway collapsed to the floor as blood from the wound in her belly pooled on the rug. Annie screamed, as did Mrs. Lockwood. Annie ran to her dog and cradled Fenway to her chest. Her sobbing quickly became uncontrollable as she rocked back and forth on her knees, her dog in her arms, her cheek resting against Fenway's head.

Ridder stood over Annie and laughed sardonically. Then he stopped abruptly and looked at Matt and Tucker, who stood still, their eyes wide in complete disbelief at what Ridder had done.

"Sit your sorry assess down or the old lady's gonna join the mutt in hell. I'm done screwin' around here."

Tucker and Matt quickly followed the direction.

Ridder then looked at Mr. Lockwood. "Get her on the couch, old man, now!" he barked and pointed at Annie with the gun.

Mr. Lockwood quickly stood up and gathered Annie in his arms. "Come now, Annie, she's gone. There's nothing we can do for her now. Come now, please."

Annie refused to release Fenway. Her arms were frozen to the last connection she had to her family. And now it was gone. She was completely alone.

Finally, Mr. Lockwood reluctantly pried Annie away from Fenway. Once she was on the couch, she erupted again in wild hysterics, while Mrs. Lockwood tried to comfort her.

Ridder turned to Sykes. "Throw the mutt outside."

When Sykes returned a minute later, Ridder looked at his watch. "Change of plans. I'm sick of waitin' to get rich. So we're gonna get my gold now."

Matt looked at the wall clock. Four-thirty. "It's still dark out. We can't go…"

Ridder shot a stern look at Matt. "Shut your fuckin' pie hole. I've had enough of your lip." He turned to the Lockwoods. "How far out is that island?"

"The far end is about seven miles from the coast. Closer to ten miles from here."

"Fine." He looked at Matt. "By the time you get out there, you'll have all the light you need." He turned back to Mr. Lockwood. "Where's your boat, the small one?"

Mr. Lockwood hesitated, then said, "It's right out front of the house at its mooring."

"Good. Now listen closely, pops. I want you to get all the shovels you have. Bring the boat in and load it up with the shovels. And, pops, you even think of screwin' with me on this and I'll just have to have my way with your pretty, little wife." He turned and grinned at Mrs. Lockwood. "Now, get goin', you got ten minutes. If you're late, consider yourself a widower, understand?"

When Mr. Lockwood returned, he was soaking wet, out of breath and panting furiously. His face was red from the exhaustion of running back and forth to the water and bringing in the Whaler. "It's all set," he gasped to Ridder, "boat's on shore, key's in the ignition."

Ridder nodded his head in reluctant satisfaction. "Good man, pops, now sit your wrinkled ass down. I'm not done with you yet." Ridder turned to Matt and Annie, who sat together on the couch next to the Lockwoods. "You two are going treasure huntin'."

Ridder then nodded to Sykes to follow him into the dining room. Ridder stood at the large, picture window and looked out towards the water. The soft light was beginning to emerge and bring the view to life. Ridder turned to Sykes and handed him the gun.

"Buster, I'm countin' on you to find my gold. If they give you any trouble, waste 'em." He took a step closer to Sykes so that he stood toe to toe with his partner. He leaned down to speak in Sykes' ear. "Do I make myself clear?"

Sykes swallowed hard and nodded. "You can count on me, Carson. We'll find the gold, or they ain't comin' back." He shook the gun in the air to reinforce his promise, then looked back toward the living room, then at Ridder.

"I gotta ask you, Carson. Why the big one?"

Ridder grabbed Sykes' shirt just below the neck and lifted him to his toes. "'Cause the little one can kick your ass, or don't you remember the airport? And I gotta keep someone here for insurance other than mom and pops 'cause I don't know how much they care about them old folk. But they won't mess with you knowin' I got their friend."

Sykes nodded in agreement as Ridder let go of his shirt. "Good idea, Carson. Good idea."

"And when you get back, meet me at the old man's big boat. You'll see it when you leave."

Sykes gave Ridder a confused look so Ridder again grabbed him by the shirt.

"Because after you find my gold, were gonna take a nice cruise out to the middle of the ocean and get rid of any evidence. Know what I mean?" He looked back at the others. "Then you and me will cruise in style down to Florida." A large grin formed on his face. "Now get goin', Buster, and don't screw it up."

# CHAPTER 20

▼

A stiff headwind blew across Oyster Pond with enough piercing force that Annie, Matt, and Sykes had to shield their faces by tucking their chins to a shoulder, leaving one eye to see, while pushing with every step to the shoreline. The wind blew so fiercely they had to lean into it while still bracing for the unpredictable gust which inevitably gave them little reaction time to resist its intention. By the time they heard the sudden increase in the wind's pitch and volume, the gust was knocking them off balance. Walking in the loose, rocky sand didn't make it easier.

The center of *Agatha* had passed over Cape Cod in the night on its way toward Georges Bank, a hundred miles off the coast of Nova Scotia. The southwestern side of it now blanketed all of New England and as evidenced by the swift movement of the cloud covering, the storm was once again garnering energy from the sea.

They found the Whaler on the beach, wind-driven surface waves pounding squarely into and mostly over the transom.

Annie scrambled into the boat at the bow and Matt handed her the shovels, which she positioned in the rod holders attached to the center console. Annie then opened the front hatch and extracted an L.L. Bean canvas bag that contained foul weather gear. She pulled out three jackets. Sykes impatiently jerked the first jacket, an orange one, from her hands. Annie threw a yellow jacket to Matt, who still stood on the beach, then put on a yellow one herself. When she fished out the only pair of rain pants, Sykes again impatiently grabbed it from her.

"Hurry up before I freeze to death," Sykes said.

Annie shook her head in disgust as she moved behind the center console. She quickly oriented herself with the boat she had fished on with her father so many times. She turned the key one notch and engaged the Yamaha's tilt mechanism. A faint whirring came through the wind, then abruptly halted.

"That's as low as it goes, let's give it a try," she yelled to Matt, who nodded his head instead of trying to throw his voice upwind.

As Annie gunned the engine in reverse, Matt pushed on the bow, his face immediately turning red from strain. Within a second the two stopped.

He shook his head and yelled, "No good."

Annie stepped back to the engine and looked over the transom. The lower unit of the engine was barely in a foot of water, which was not enough to allow the engine to pull the boat off the beach against such a stiff wind and crashing waves.

Matt nodded once at Sykes and yelled, "Hey, get out here and give me a hand."

Sykes pointed at himself in disbelief, then pointed to Annie. "You do it."

Annie stared at his empty, cowardly eyes. As she pushed past him she said, "Then get to the back of the boat, asshole."

Sykes grabbed her arm and pulled her close. "What you say?"

Annie didn't blink. "Get to the back of the boat."

Sykes's upper lip trembled and his head tilted slightly to the left. He stood for a second glaring at Annie, then moved to the stern.

Once Annie and Matt had pushed the Whaler into deeper water, Matt helped Annie climb over the bow rail and she lowered the engine and held the boat steady against the push of wind as Matt pulled himself on board.

Annie and Matt stood next to each other behind the center console, which granted them some relief from the biting wind, as Annie maneuvered the Whaler around the last few moored boats and into the cruising lane of Oyster River. Sykes held onto the rail behind the center bench.

"Hey," Sykes yelled just before Annie gunned the engine.

Annie and Matt looked behind them. Sykes held the gun close to his chest.

"No bullshit out here, get my point?" He shook the gun at them.

The mile-long Oyster River looked as it did during the winter. People had hauled most of the boats out of the water as a safety precaution and none of the usual activity of people digging for clams, floating on rafts, or children exploring occurred along either shoreline. Annie strained her eyes to find a light on in a house in hopes that maybe someone would be looking out at the water and see them. But she knew it wouldn't help if anyone did see them. People would just think they were another boat of diehard fishermen looking to wet their insatiable appetite for angling. The shovels would cause no alarm; people would just think they were three amateur clam diggers who'd never seen a clam rake.

The air felt as if it held millions of tiny daggers attacking any exposed skin. The combination of the driving rain and boat speed of twenty-five miles per hour made the tumultuous ride barely tolerable for Annie and Matt. For Sykes, who had never experienced such weather, and whose long, greasy, black hair was flung around in the wind as if it was electrified, being out on the water in such trying conditions made him look as if he was going to cry like a child.

Annie caught a glance of Sykes and immediately the first smile in ten hours graced her face. Then she thought of Fenway and quickly her face lost any sign of positive emotion. While the effect of shock wore off and the realization of what had happened sank in, Annie suddenly felt more alone than she ever had. She stared ahead like a robot, empty and without direction. Then she looked at Sykes and a sudden resolve erupted deep in her. She clenched her teeth. There was no way she was going to let them take away her will to live; she'd been there before and swore she would never return.

When they reached the end of Oyster River and entered Stage Harbor, Annie looked around for any boats, particularly a harbor patrol boat, or better yet, the ubiquitous orange Coast Guard boat. Maybe, she thought, she intentionally could get them to stop her. If they did, there was no way they wouldn't be suspicious about a boat being out in this weather. She pictured Sykes fumbling to answer the Coastie's questions. As she looked around, she saw Matt doing the same thing. When their eyes met, he leaned closer to her as she turned the Whaler into the channel at the cut in Harding's beach.

"I don't think we can expect to see anyone out on a day like this. Least not this early," Matt said just loudly enough so that Annie could hear him.

Annie leaned her shoulder into Matt's chest. The hardness and strength of his chest gave Annie a brief, but real feeling of comfort. She looked at him. "What do we do?"

Matt leaned his head lower. "No choice." He looked to his left and saw Sykes looking out at the passing beach. "If we don't get the gold, they'll kill Tuck and the Lockwoods."

"What if there's no gold? I mean, do you really think we're going to find it? Come on, Matt. We need to…"

Sykes suddenly stuck his unshaven face into their view, a few inches from Matt's face.

"Shut up and drive! And any lip out of you, pretty boy, and you're shark bait." He pointed over the side of the boat with his head, then forced a grin. "Now shut up and drive."

Matt winced from the intimate view of Sykes' rotten, brown teeth.

The waters outside the Harding's Beach cut were considerably rougher than inside the harbor. The Whaler's hull pounded on the whitecaps like a jackhammer to the point where the banging sound and jolting shock became rhythmic because of the constancy of the wind-driven waves and speed of the boat. Annie kept the Whaler slightly pointed into the wind to prevent being blown completely broadside as they traversed the maze-like series of orange and white channel and bar markers out to the west side of North Monomoy Island.

With the exception of three distant commercial fishing boats, which looked like toys in the distance, Annie did not see any boats. She had been out on the water in bad weather before and there had always been a few intrepid bass fishermen; but not on this tumultuous morning. They were alone, battered by an angry ocean and a merciless wind, going to find a lost treasure. Despite the sunlight that had just peeked over the eastern horizon, a dark gloom remained suspended over Chatham. Annie felt a shock of futility in her stomach. Buried treasure. The mere thought of searching for it was ridiculous.

With half of the seven-mile journey completed, it began to rain more heavily, enough to force Annie to slow the Whaler to half its previous speed to improve visibility and decrease the stinging blows of the rain drops on their faces. Annie's jeans were completely soaked, as were Matt's. Sykes had tucked his raincoat into his rain pants, a novice mistake, and so his pants were soaked as well, but he didn't realize why. He futilely kept checking the pants for holes.

Though protected by Monomoy from the full force of the Atlantic Ocean, the waters of Nantucket Sound five miles off Chatham's coast behaved much more like the open ocean. Five-foot swells rocked the twenty-four foot boat, while the surface whitecaps continued their pounding of the hull. The appearance of the swells, and their increasing size, made it more difficult for Annie to navigate the boat so she decided to use an old Navy trick Mr. Lockwood had taught her. She steered the boat toward the shore.

"Good idea," Matt said above the roar of the wind and rain.

Within two minutes, they had found calmer waters by cruising ten feet from the break of the waves on the beachhead. Now Annie had to keep an eye out for any swells that made it this close to the beach. If one did, and she didn't see it, the swell potentially could push the boat broadside onto the beach where it would be pounded by the surf. She had seen others use the tactic, but never had experienced driving a boat on the thin line herself. After a few random swells made their way to the beach, and more than a few tense moments of not knowing which side of the wave the boat would come down on, Annie developed a knack for navigating under such dangerous conditions.

After thirty minutes, they reached the southern end of Monomoy Island. Atop the crest of a very large swell, Annie spied in the distance the distinctive shape of the lone lighthouse. After finding the best possible wave break along the seemingly homogenous shoreline of wave-tumbled sand, Annie brought the Whaler to a notch above idle.

"Go up front and get out the bow anchor. I'll drop you off and then anchor the stern," she said loudly, looking back and forth between Matt and Sykes.

"Nice try. No way you're just leaving us here. You put this thing on the beach now. I'm freezing my ass off here, so stop screwing around," Sykes said, his hands shaking from the cold.

Annie shook her head. "Listen, if we leave the boat on the beach, by the time we get back it will be in two pieces, swamped, or so far pushed up the beach that we'll never get it back in the water." She smirked. "Now, the other option is for *you* to place the stern anchor, but then you have to swim ashore."

Sykes quickly moved to the bow.

"Annie, let me set the anchor," Matt said.

Annie shook her head. "I don't want to be stuck out here with that asshole if something happens to you. So you go ashore with him. I'll be fine. I've done this before, you know." She handed him her raincoat. "Tide looks like we've got some time before it starts going out. Just give it plenty of line."

Once Matt had set the bow anchor at the top of the beach head, Annie needed but two tries to firmly set the stern anchor with just the right amount of slack in the lines to allow for the change in sea level. Satisfied with her job, she took the key from the ignition and jumped off the bow while she prayed she wouldn't land in a hole.

She landed in water up to her chest and quickly scampered out of the water in five strong strides. Matt met her at the water's edge and handed her the raincoat. She looked over Matt's shoulder and caught Sykes grinning at her wet shirt. Sykes' maniacal gawk rattled Annie for a second until the picture of Fenway's lifeless body popped into her mind and filled her with anger-driven resolve. She would survive only if to see Buster Sykes and Carson Ridder burn in hell.

They began to trek across Monomoy's lunar landscape of rolling dunes and mud flats, Annie and Matt leading the way, carrying the shovels; Sykes, being completely unused to walking in sand, struggled behind to keep up. They walked most of the time straight into the biting wind. The sand was thick with moisture and the mud flats impossible to traverse because the rains had rejuvenated their sticking power. With little brush, and that being only waist-high, the northeast wind off the Atlantic Ocean had little to deter it from sweeping across the narrow island. They met relief only when they walked in a trough below a tall sand dune. The thunderous roar of the pounding surf on the east side of the narrow island made it seem like they were only a minute's walk from the far shore though a half mile lay between them and their destination. Annie looked up at the gray sky and prayed the drizzle wouldn't turn to total rain.

After zigzagging their way for ten minutes, Sykes fell to his knees exhausted.

"Stop!" he gasped in a wheeze. "You trying to kill me here? Why the hell are we walking all over this fucking island." He tried to catch his breath by taking gulps of air while futilely trying to wipe the sweat from his eyes. His round face bulged like a balloon ready to pop. "Ever heard of a straight line? Christ, I can see the lighthouse from here," he pointed to his right, "so why the hell we walking away from it?" Sykes pulled the gun from his waist and waved it at them.

Matt shook his head in defiance. "Because there's a series of mud flats and spring-fed ponds between here and the lighthouse." Matt's tone turned angry and Annie grabbed his arm at the elbow.

"We've been out here before; you're just going to have to trust us," Annie said firmly as she remembered the sunny day she, Matt and some friends had come here to fish for large mouth bass in the fresh water ponds. She had caught and released forty fish to Matt's thirty-nine, and had never let him forget it. "Believe me, we're going the quickest way because I want to get off this island a lot more than you do."

Annie pulled Matt around and began walking before Sykes had a chance to answer. She thought of Sykes futilely trying to find his own way back to boat. The picture of the demented, bald man lost in the dunes gave Annie a whiff of wishful, fleeting pleasure.

Over four more sand dunes and around an acre size pond and they looked at a direct path to the lighthouse. Annie could feel herself breathing more heavily, but she still felt resolved. She looked to her left at Matt. His face was bright red from the effect of the cold wind and rain. Despite the bruises under his eyes and his broken nose, which was swollen to twice its normal size, the look of determination in his bloodshot, blue eyes gave Annie comfort.

The lighthouse stood near the original shoreline of the three thousand-acre barrier beach, now more than a half mile from the Nantucket Sound and Atlantic Ocean shorelines, and three quarters of a mile from the island's southern tip.

Rolling dunes, some twenty feet high, and knee-high green and brown grass marked the wind-swept landscape. The forty-foot high light tower and two-story keeper's house stood atop a modest bluff. Originally built in 1828, it served as the warning to nearby ships of the danger of the treacherous Pollock Rip and shallow shoals just off the island's tip. Decommissioned in 1923, it eventually became part of the Monomoy National Wildlife Refuge under the government's domain. A black lantern sat atop the red cast iron tower, making it look like the Statue of Liberty's torch. The glass, which had once encapsulated the lantern, had been removed so the wind whipping through the structure made a lonely whistling sound. To the backside of the light tower stood the boarded up keeper's house, a two-story Cape Cod with weathered shingles and white trim and white boards across each window and door.

Annie had never seen the lighthouse this close up; she had seen it from afar on the way out to fish the rips and closer when she and Matt had fished for large mouth bass in the ponds. At a distance, it looked stronger, almost majestic, in the way it stood defiantly proud against the test of time out on the island with no protection from everything New England coastal weather threw at it. But now, after seeing the true condition of the old light, Annie felt a sense of loss, and a bit less brave. Suddenly, she felt more cold and wet, and the severity of their situation set it. She tried to recite the last line of the Confederate soldier's poem, but couldn't remember it. Without that last line, she knew, they wouldn't have a prayer of finding anything or making it off the island.

Sykes grabbed Annie's arm and shook her. "Enough already, earn your keep. Where's the gold?"

Annie looked at Matt without the determined look she had carried all morning.

"We just need the last line, Annie," he said.

"Matt, I can't think of it. Oh God, I can't remember." She began to cry.

Matt hugged her and walked her away from Sykes. "Try reciting it from the beginning. I remember it rhymes, right? Maybe that'll help."

Annie closed her eyes, then began. "At the elbow, an afternoon of sand. See no life until the guiding hand. Stand against it...stand against it..." She paused. "Stand against it, facing first morn', a year to uphold the duty sworn." She opened her eyes and let out a deep breath.

"So what's it mean?"

Annie repeated it again then walked over and stood against the foundation of the lighthouse. "Facing morn' I think means to face the morning, which I guess means to face the sunrise."

"What about the last line?"

"A year to protect the duty sworn? Well, the guy was a soldier, right? So he probably took an oath or something. A year to protect? If he was out here, looking east, why would he need a year to...I got it, Matt. His duty is to find whatever he buried, right? A year is a measurement. But I don't think he was talking about the measurement of time; he was talking about distance."

"Three hundred and sixty-five paces from the light house toward the sunrise. Annie you're a genius." Matt gave her a bear hug, then quickly let go. "But the sun isn't rising."

"I know. So we do out best." She pointed. "I'm pretty sure East is that way. If it were me, I would have put something out there to mark the spot. If the guy knew anything about beaches, he would have known how over even a brief period the sands can shift dramatically. Not knowing when I would be back, with the war going on, I would have used something a little bit more permanent that a couple of sticks placed in an X."

Matt smiled. "Out here, not much but sand, maybe a few rocks. Maybe the guy busted off some bricks from the lighthouse."

"Too obvious."

"Well, so is a pile of rocks on a beach."

"Not if he covered them with sand."

Sykes stepped over to them and waved the gun at them. "Get going, I'm freezing my ass off."

Annie and Matt stood ten feet from each other against the lighthouse, then began pacing off in the direction they each faced. Sykes walked slightly behind them. The further they went away from the lighthouse, the greater the distance increased between them until they were more than fifty yards away from each other.

When Matt finished pacing off the three hundred and sixty-five steps, he stopped and looked around. The island at that spot was relatively flat, with the exception of the rolling accents the wind inherently creates in sand. After poking around with the shovel for a few minutes then inspecting the area to make sure he had not overlooked a thing, he gave up and walked over to Annie.

"Nothing but flat sand over there. This looks more promising," he said, as he looked around at the three car-sized mounds of sand in a triangular formation twenty feet from each other.

Sykes stood with his arms folded above his belly, the gun tucked under his left arm. Every so often, he nervously looked around as if he expected someone to suddenly appear.

Matt dug with such anger that after fifteen minutes of digging, he declared defeat and rested against the shovel as he watched as Annie slowly, but steadily, moved over three square yards of sand. Matt then joined her and after five more minutes of digging they had not only leveled the mound, but had dug a hole the size of a couch.

Annie stepped out of the hole and threw her shovel to the ground, then sat down. Matt followed suit.

"Hey, nobody gave you permission to rest." Sykes waved the gun as his authority. "Now get up and get digging."

"Asshole," Annie said under her breath as she stood and wiped the matted hair from her red cheeks.

The last mound was the smallest of the three in height, about three feet, and much less symmetrical. It looked more like a large snake with its ends curving in opposite directions.

"I'll meet you in the middle," Annie said.

After continuously digging for twenty minutes they had moved the mound to a new position, dug a hole larger than the first two, but hadn't found anything. They kept digging until the hole was four feet deep and they had to throw the sand up to get it out of the way.

Finally, they stopped, exhausted and beyond caring. Sykes appeared above them and looked at the hole and shook his head.

"I think you just dug your own grave." He pointed the gun at Matt. "Turn around."

"No, wait! It's my fault. Of course, how could I have been so stupid?" Annie shouted.

Sykes pointed the gun at her.

"I paced off by my stride which is probably shorter than a man's."

Annie scrambled out of the hole and looked around. "There." She pointed at a small mound twenty feet away. "It could be there."

"You better hope it's there."

Matt and Annie shoveled the sand mound with renewed desperation as Sykes stood watch over them. After ten minutes, Matt abruptly stopped digging.

"Stop, Annie. It's not..."

Annie's shovel made a thud. She looked up at Matt, her face full of hope. "There's something here. Help me dig."

Matt began digging again until his shovel, too, hit something. "It's a pile of rocks."

Using the shovels to pry under the rocks and their hands to brush off the sand, they unearthed three basketball-sized rocks, which they removed from the hole.

Once the last rock was removed, Matt used his foot to scrape the sand to the side, then stomped his foot.

"There's a board under here!"

"Find the edge of it," Annie said.

For two minutes, Matt furiously pushed the sand away with his hands until he could see a large cross scored into the top of the board. "It's some kind of box. There's sides to it."

"Open it up, it's the gold!" Sykes yelled.

Matt pinched the shovel tip into the corner of the six-foot by three-foot box and pushed down. The box screeched as the rusty nails gave way. He did the same to another corner and the lid popped up three inches on the left side. Matt jammed the shovel into the opening, took a deep breath and then pried with a loud grunt. The cover sprang open. They stared at a gray blanket folded over in the middle. Cautiously, Matt used the tip of the shovel to move the blanket.

"Jesus Christ," Sykes cried.

The three stood there in disbelief at the sight. Lying in the box were the skeletal remains of a Confederate Soldier dressed in a decayed gray uniform. The skull, creamy and round, held no secret to the soldier's death. A hole the size of a quarter marked the left temple. A visible two-inch-long crack ran down the left side of the prominent mandible. The soldier's arms had been placed on his chest so now the hand bones lay exposed beyond the uniform sleeve. Surprisingly, it didn't smell.

"That's what this fucking goose chase has led to, a coffin of some old dead bastard?" Sykes pointed the gun at Matt. "Game's over pretty boy, you're joining the soldier."

"Wait, maybe it's in here. Matt, pull him out," Annie yelled.

"I'm not touching that thing." He pulled back.

Without hesitating, Annie searched the pockets of the dead soldier's uniform. When she found nothing, she grabbed the coat. As she pulled, the skeleton fell apart.

"Come on, Matt, give me a hand. Grab the pants."

Matt knelt and together they pulled the skeletal remains out of the coffin. The skull fell onto the sand and rolled to a stop by Annie's knee. With the shovel she banged the bottom board of the coffin.

"Sounds hollow. Help me open it."

Without much effort, they pried the bottom board up and made a collective gasp as they stared at the dusty gold bars. Annie reached down and slowly picked up a bar and held it as if weighing it, her eyes wide with astonishment.

On the top of the three-inch by six-inch bar were the letters "C.S.A." Annie quickly flipped it over. Imprinted on the bottom was the number "306.5" and the words, "Tredegar I.W. Richmond Wt. in oz."

"This is real," Annie said incredulously as if she hadn't been holding the gold, she'd never accept its authenticity.

"Look, there's a row underneath the top bars." Matt quickly counted. "There must be close to eighty bars here." He picked up a bar in each hand. "These things weigh at least ten pounds each. Jesus! This has got be worth over five million dollars!"

Sykes knelt next to the coffin like he was about to enter into prayer and picked up a gold bar with his left hand. He cradled it like it like he was touching a naked woman for the first time. A drunken gaze appeared in his eyes as he admired his prize. He quickly lay the gun down in the sand and picked up another bar with his right hand.

"Too bad you'll never get to spend it," a voice from behind Sykes said.

Startled, they all turned and found Gerald Wilkinson standing behind them dressed in fish-gut-stained, pale yellow foul weather gear, his gray hair flailing in the wind, a sawed-off shotgun poised in front of him.

Matt jumped to his feet. "Wilkey! Thank God you're here. How'd you…"

Wilkinson trained the shotgun on Matt, a look of unnerved coldness in his eyes. "Sit down, Matt," he commanded.

"What?"

"I ain't here to save nobody." He paused. "I want the gold."

"You can have it, Wilkey. Now let's get going. We'll call the police from the boat so they can get to the Lockwoods. This guy's partner has them and Tucker at their house and he's completely crazy."

Wilkinson shook his head, his eyes never flinching. "Sorry, Matt, I can't do that."

"What are you talking about?" Matt went to stand again.

Wilkinson cocked the shotgun. "Don't push me, Matt."

Matt knelt back in the sand. "What the hell's going on? If you want the gold, go ahead, take it. We'll say that you found it. Everything will be cool."

Wilkinson shook his head. "It ain't that easy."

"Why not? You found it; you keep it. Just let us go. We have to get the cops to save Tucker and the Lockwoods before it's too late."

"I can't keep it. I need it for something else."

"Come on, Wilkey, what are you talking about?"

Sykes swiveled on his knees to look at Wilkinson, and then glanced at his gun a foot away from his right knee in the sand.

"Don't even think about it fat man."

"Wilkey, what the hell's going on?"

"Ain't none of your business, Matt."

"Come on, Wilkey, this is crazy. What's going on? Talk to me. This is crazy."

Wilkinson looked at Matt with almost a hint of sadness in his eyes for what he had to do. "Last winter, I lost my boat in the storm. Had canceled my insurance a couple months before 'cause I couldn't pay the bill. Why the hell do you think I'm living in my tool shed? I'm trying to rent the house. Christ, close to losing that, too. Goddamn bankers."

"I thought you got a new boat."

"It ain't mine. You wouldn't understand and won't help ya none anyway."

"Try me," Matt pleaded as he groped for Annie's hand. "Come on, Wilkey, this is Matty here. I'm on your side."

Wilkinson paused for a few seconds, then the tension eased from his taught face. "I got a loan for the new boat from a guy in New Bedford who had some connections. But I had a hell of time meeting the payments 'cause of the god-damn government's moratoriums and catch limits. It was impossible to make it under those conditions. So I placed some bets with the same guy; won some quick, whole lot, so I played some more. Next thing I know, everything I touch is a squid and this guy's boss sends some thugs over. They busted me up real bad. I didn't break my leg jumping off the top deck. They did it. Broke my leg in two places with a goddamn sledge hammer!" He swallowed hard and wiped his mouth with his sleeve. "Can you believe that? A sledge hammer. Pure animals. Couldn't fish for six weeks. Said they'd kill me if I didn't pay them." A tear rolled down his cheek into his tangled beard as he struggled to keep a semblance of composure.

"How much?"

"More than I got." He paused then shook his head as if to regain his nerve. "Before you came by yesterday, I figured the only way out of it was to end it all." His eyes narrowed. "Then you start telling me about some journal and buried gold. I'd always thought it was just a ghost story; but hell, I was desperate. So I started keeping a watch out from atop the bluffs on Morris Island for any activity out here."

"But why not let us go?" Annie pleaded. "You can take enough to pay off your debt and just let us go."

"You don't understand!" His temper rose. "If I give them the gold and then word leaks out about it, who you think they're coming for first? No way!" He shook his head violently, then pointed the gun at Sykes. "And what about this guy and his partner? You think I can trust them? No way! The cops will get involved with your deal and then they'll start asking questions. I can't go through that. I won't go through that." His face went expressionless. "This is the only way."

"So what, you're going shoot us? Pretty big mess out here to clean up," Matt said in a challenging tone. "Or you going to deep six us a couple miles out? There's no way you'll get away with it. One way or the other, the trail will lead to you so you might as well help us and we'll get the cops to protect you."

"No! Either you come to my boat with me or we can do it here. Make it look like fat boy here did it." He raised the shotgun and pointed it at Matt then at Sykes.

"Okay, okay," Matt pleaded. "We'll go to the boat." As he stood up he grabbed a hand full of sand, stood and threw it in Wilkinson's eyes. Wilkinson screamed, stumbled backwards, and fired the gun. Sykes leapt to his feet and lunged at him, knocking him to the ground and the shotgun from his grasp. Matt grabbed Annie by the arm and pulled her to her feet.

They sprinted through the sand over the closest dune, took a sharp right towards the west around two mounds, and dove to the sand behind a dune covered in two-foot high beach grass. Neither breathed. Annie closed her eyes and buried her face into her hands. Matt touched her elbow and she turned her head slightly to look at him.

"I say we make a run for the boat," she whispered.

Matt shook his head and was about to respond when a gun blast rang out from the other side of the dune. They froze.

"Which one?" Matt whispered.

"I hope it was both of them. Let's get out of here, please, Matt!"

Matt slithered slowly on his belly up to the crest of the dune, waited there for thirty seconds, then slid back half way down to Annie.

"I can't see either of them from here, but I can see the gold bars we dropped."

Annie tugged on Matt's foot. "Come on, Matt. Forget about them. Let's get out of here. Please!"

Matt wiggled on the sand back to Annie. "We have to get the gold."

Annie's eyes grew even larger. "*What*? Are you crazy?"

"If we don't bring the gold back, Ridder will kill Tucker and the Lockwoods."

"Why can't we just call the police?"

Matt reached over and gripped Annie's shoulder. "It'll work out. Just stay here. I only need to grab a couple of bars." He quickly kissed her on the cheek and scrambled away.

Annie buried her face back in her hands. The sand felt cold against her body. The sound of the crashing breakers on the beach not far off filled her ears. It had always been a soothing sound for her, but now it left her deaf to what could be happening just fifty-feet away. She wanted to crawl to the top of the dune to watch Matt, but she couldn't command her body to move. She closed her eyes as tightly as possible and prayed.

The path to the hole containing the coffin and the gold lay clear. On his belly, Matt pushed his head up to just below the height of the swaying dune grass. Though it wasn't very thick, he hoped it gave him enough cover. He strained his eyes to find either Sykes or Wilkinson until the burn of the wind made his eyes tear up so he closed his eyes to concentrate his hearing, but heard only the whistling of the wind in his ears and the rhythmic pounding of the surf. Maybe they shot each other, he thought as he pictured the two dead bodies lying on the other side of a dune thirty feet away. He took a deep breath and rose to his knees, exposing his torso, to get a better look, but he saw nothing.

Like a steroid-pumping linebacker after a wounded quarterback, Matt came out of his stance into a full sprint. He reached the bottom of the dune in two bounds, dodged the next mound, and threw himself behind a thick clump of grass. His heart raced, but he hesitated only a second behind the security of the grass. He knew he would have only one chance and so rolled to his feet, ran to the backside of the dune to his right, and crawled to the top of it. When he peered through the grass, he took in a full view of the coffin with the dune he had come from directly in line one hundred feet behind it. He had done a one-eighty around the coffin and yet still couldn't see either Sykes or Wilkinson. He pictured Wilkinson dead and Sykes wildly running, lost in the myriad of dunes. Suddenly, he realized his yellow raincoat made him stand out like a red wine stain on a wedding dress and quickly shed the coat.

The dash to the coffin had made him feel like he was running a mile long gauntlet in a shooting range, and he was the target. But in two seconds, he was back at the coffin. He fell to his knees in front of the skeletal Confederate and looked around in a panic, half expecting to see one of them sitting near by, a grin on his face as he pointed a gun at him. But no one was around. It was as if he was on Monomoy by himself, a shipwrecked pirate and his buried treasure on a deserted island. He quickly regained his focus when he looked at the skull of the soldier. He picked up a bar of gold then froze. How was he supposed to transport the gold to the boat? They had never thought of that. He looked around himself in a near panic. There were two shovels, the wooden coffin, which he could never carry himself, and the dead Confederate. He stared for a second at the soldier. Suddenly, he realized he had to retreat to the dune and retrieve his raincoat to use it to carry more than a few bars.

He looked back at the skeleton, reached down and felt the soldier's wool uniform. Maybe he wouldn't have to run back to the dune. The wool felt thick in his hands, but crumbled like sand in his fingers once he pulled on it. Without hesitating, he sprinted back to the dune and retrieved his raincoat. As he ran back to the coffin, he looked around the area, but still didn't see either man.

He laid it open in the sand and quickly piled six gold bars on it. As he grabbed a seventh, he paused, then dropped it when his judgement got the better of him.

"Damn it," he blurted as he looked at the remaining bars and the skeleton. He looked around quickly, and seeing no one, pulled the skeleton by the backbone into the coffin and onto the gold. He put the coffin top back in place and then hastily raked the sand with both his arms into the hole. Within thirty seconds, the coffin was covered and the hole was not much more than a slight depression. Matt quickly looked around to get a visual mark of where he stood so he could return later to find the rest of the gold. He tied the arms of the coat together so that the middle of it formed a pocket around the stacked bars, then with both his hands reached under the jacket and lifted the gold as if it were a set of fireplace logs. His legs and back strained as he straightened up. It was much heavier than he had anticipated, but not so heavy that he couldn't move quickly.

Matt looked around as he stumbled as fast as his legs could move him with the added hundred pounds. The dunes were empty, but he kept looking, half-incredulous at not seeing anyone. Rounding a dune, he felt a surge of adrenaline shoot through his body for having retrieved the gold. But as he turned to his left and took two steps behind a dune, he froze.

"You are a dumbass, ain't ya, boy?" Sykes grinned at Matt as he held the handgun to Annie's head with his right hand while forcefully gripping her left arm with his other hand. The sawed-off shotgun dangled in his belt.

Annie's face bore a picture of pure hopelessness. Her eyes drooped slightly as if they were difficult to keep open. She looked limp in Sykes' control; the elan she had somehow previously maintained no longer carried her.

Sykes stood up with Annie, keeping her between himself and Matt.

"Where's Wilkinson?" Matt asked, incredulous at seeing Sykes, as he dropped the gold.

Sykes' smile turned to a grin as he nodded once to his left. "That crazy bastard won't be trying to steal my gold no more."

"He's dead?"

"I grabbed his shotgun. He ran, not too far with that lame leg and all." He laughed. "Like hunting wild hog; they can't run so fast. But this sand sure makes it easy to bury a body, don't ya think?" He laughed even harder.

Matt's stomach dropped as the adrenaline drained from his body. He realized how drastically things had changed. With the knowledge to locate Wilkinson's body, there would be no way they ever would get to walk away from all this, gold or no gold. The realization of his fate shot through him as if Sykes had gunned him down, too. Matt looked at Annie's eyes and realized she understood their hope had been snuffed out the moment Sykes had pulled the trigger.

His mind raced though his options. He wondered what kind of swimmer Sykes was. Could he and Annie survive if he capsized the boat? Certainly their chances would be better in the water. Maybe Sykes would drop both guns. Maybe he couldn't swim at all. But what if something happened to Annie? He realized Sykes only needed him to get the gold back to Ridder. If they accomplished that, they were dead. What if they arrived without the gold? Would Ridder erupt into such a tirade that he'd kill them? As long as Sykes held them captive, with or without the gold, he would force them to return to face Ridder. With sudden clarity he realized he had to figure out how to escape from Sykes and contact the police. Reality left no other option.

Sykes shoved Annie toward Matt. "You stealing my gold, boy?" He raised the gun.

"I thought it was Ridder's," Matt said defiantly.

Sykes took two steps forward, raised the gun and cocked the hammer. "We can do this real easy, see. Either you cooperate or you join your buddy as a permanent resident of this here island." A scornful twitch replaced his grin. "I plan on getting the hell off this island. So it's your choice, boy."

Matt stared at him.

"Good." The grin returned, but he didn't lower the gun. "Let's go get the rest of it."

After uncovering the coffin again, and removing the skeleton, Annie and Matt attempted to lift the gold-filled coffin out of the hole but merely strained their already sore backs.

"We'll have to make a few trips," Matt said as he looked at Annie, who just nodded silently.

They placed twenty bars on the coffin lid, which surprisingly remained in decent shape despite its age and habitat, and strained to lift it from each end. The aged boards sagged in the middle, but held together. With Sykes walking behind them cradling two bars in his left arm, the handgun in his right hand, and the shotgun in his belt, they began their first trek back across Monomoy.

# CHAPTER 21

▼

With the blue lights serving as protection from being stopped by a fellow cop, and the car's siren to push aside the few cars out on the road despite its being the early morning and horrible weather conditions, O'Donahue drove the Crown Victoria hard and made it across the Cape Cod Canal in less than forty minutes. They had spent most of the ride in silence. There was no need for small talk and they already knew all the particulars of the case. Speculation and playing the "what if" game beyond the facts was not in either detective's dossier. The silence stood as a reminder that they were running close to empty on leads and Hammond had yet to call.

"We'll be there in about twenty-five minutes," O'Donahue said.

"What's your plan if we don't hear from Rusty?"

"Other than praying? We'll check in with the local brass. According to his brother, Gallagher's renting a place, so we should talk with real estate agents, too. Of course, the house could be in another name. Any other ideas?"

"Find out were the college crowd hangs out."

O'Donahue's cell phone rang. "O'Donahue." She looked at Ditchman. "It's Hammond." She listened, then said. "Good job, Rusty. We'll meet you down there." She hung up the phone. "Nylan died, but not before he came to long enough for Rusty to questioned him. He kept saying over and over 'Orr, Williams, Cousy, Russell, Orr, Yaz, Yaz.'"

"What's that mean?"

"Boston sports legends."

"What?"

"It's a phone number." She picked up her cell phone. "Rusty found some die-hard Boston fan at the hospital who knew all their uniform numbers. 495-6488."

Within a minute, O'Donahue contacted the State Police office and had a search of the phone number and a matching address conducted. The phone number was for Chatham. She quickly called the Chatham police and explained the gravity of the situation to the officer on duty, who agreed to her plea to check out the address.

"Maybe our luck's changing," she said.

Within fifteen minutes they were in Chatham and thanks to the directions she had received from the local police, found the road with ease. She pulled into the driveway and parked behind the lone Chatham police car. A young cop with a peach fuss mustache immediately stepped out of the cruiser.

"You O'Donahue?" he asked, his head tilted away from the biting wind.

She nodded her head, "Find anyone?"

"Nope. I don't know what the big fuss was about. We had half the force here." He looked at her crossly.

"Did you search the house?"

"Like I said, nobody home. No sign of forced entry. In fact, the front door was left unlocked. See for yourself. I gotta get back to work."

O'Donahue shot the cop a look of anger. "That's it?"

He returned her look. "Yeah, lady, that's it. Listen, I don't know how they do it up in Boston and all, but our chief is pretty pissed that you got us all riled up for nothing. So he said he's not wasting any more of the force's time. So they left. I was told to wait for you and then leave. So that's what I'm doing."

O'Donahue shook her head and stared at the young officer as he drove his car around the clamshell circular driveway and past them.

"Nice guy," Ditchman said, shaking his head.

"Probably a summer rental. Let's have a look."

They entered the cottage through the unlocked front door, each of them silent in their observatory mode on concentration. O'Donahue quickly looked upstairs while Ditchman looked through the rooms on the ground floor. Within a few minutes, they met back outside.

"There's two rooms upstairs and by the looks of them, there's two guys staying in one and a female in the other."

"Back door was broken. Lock ripped right through the molding. But it doesn't look completely fresh because there's no wood pieces on the floor. Maybe that's why these locals didn't call it a forced entry."

Back at the car, Ditchman looked around the grounds before getting in. "Now what?"

"Plan B. We wait until the local hangouts open up."

O'Donahue backed the car onto the street and drove halfway up the street when Ditchman said, "Wait. Go back."

"What?" She backed down the street and pulled into the driveway.

"The other house. Look, the way the two sit together on the same circular driveway. That one looks like the main house and the other the cottage." He got out of the car and walked over to the house. He examined the LeBaron, then knocked on the front door. He paused ten seconds at the door, then walked around to the back of the house where O'Donahue joined him. Both cupped their hands against their eyes to look through the sliding glass windows on the back porch.

"I can't see much," O'Donahue said.

"Look to the right. See that chair tipped over?" He pulled at the door but it remained closed, then stepped off the porch.

"Where you going?"

"Hate to have to break a window when a door might be open. Wait there."

In thirty seconds Ditchman appeared at the glass door and opened it.

"I had to take liberties with a window on the door off the side porch." Ditchman wiped his left hand on his pants.

O'Donahue nodded and stepped into the dining room and looked around until she found a light switch.

Immediately, they saw their entrance to the house justified.

"Check this out." O'Donahue held up a smashed phone.

Ditchman stood in the center of room and slowly looked around. "Large amount of blood on the rug in two places and on the chairs next to the spots."

"Check out the broken lamps and the smashed mirror. Looks like there was quite a fight here. Keep looking around. I'll check the upstairs."

While O'Donahue was upstairs, Ditchman slowly walked around the room, back in the zone. He stopped at the television and looked at the arrangements of framed photographs on top of the console, then at the photographs on the small table.

"The rooms upstairs are undisturbed. The bills on the desk are all to this address. Name's Lockwood. Find anything down here?" O'Donahue said as she walked into the living room.

Ditchman nodded toward the small table. "The common people in these photos are a couple of seniors. Was everything in meticulous order upstairs?"

"You could bounce a quarter off the bedspreads. Not very compatible with smashed phones and blood-stained carpets."

"My thoughts exactly."

As they stepped out onto the deck off the dining room, Ditchman stopped and stared out at the water.

"What's the matter?"

Ditchman didn't answer. He quickly stepped back into the house before O'Donahue closed the glass doors. In a few seconds he appeared with two photographs in his hands.

"Look at this." He handed O'Donahue the frames.

"What? So the guy owns a fishing boat and a cabin cruiser, so what?"

Ditchman pointed to the photograph in O'Donahue's right hand. "Look closely at that one."

She examined the photograph of a man aboard a Boston Whaler holding a string of striped bass. "I see it. In the background. The big boat's anchored to the left and behind it is this house." She quickly looked out at the water. "And neither boat is out there now."

"Exactly. Come on."

As they reached the edge of the lawn, Ditchman stopped and pointed to a matted spot in the hip-high dune grass five feet away. He cautiously took two large strides through the tall grass then froze.

"What is it, Ditch?"

Ditch bent down, paused a few seconds, then stepped out of the grass. "Dead dog. Gunshot to the chest looks fresh."

"We'll recover the slug later. Two to one says it matches the one taken from the Harvard janitor."

They walked down a path through dune grass until they reached the shore of Oyster Pond. Though the wind had died down considerably during the previous three hours, it still brought a sting to bare skin. They stood at the water's edge surveying the water, each with their hands protected under their arms.

"See the guy getting out of the white boat with the little cabin over to the right?" O'Donahue asked.

"Good idea."

They walked over and waited until the fisherman rowed his pram ashore. He wore yellow, rubber overalls that were covered in fish blood. A black wool-knit cap covered his head and part of his weather-beaten face. He smiled when he saw them.

"Howdy."

"Excuse me," O'Donahue said, "by any chance did you see either of these boats while you were out?"

The fisherman wiped his hands on a rag hanging from his belt and took each frame, quickly looked, then handed them back.

"Sure. Both were at their moorings this morning when I went out. God awful day to making a living if you know what I mean." He looked out at the two moorings. "Didn't see the Whaler, but the wooden boat was in Stage Harbor when I was coming in."

"Are you sure it was this boat?" Ditchman held up the photo of the cabin cruiser.

The fisherman smiled. "Every day I go out and I come in. Same spot. You get to know all the boats. Why?"

"Where's the nearest Coast Guard station?" O'Donahue asked.

The fisherman scrunched his eyebrows. "Station's up next to the lighthouse, but there's usually a boat at the Bridge Street marina which is on the way."

After thanking the fisherman for his help and directions, a few minutes later they parked on Bridge Street across from the marina. Comprised of a saltbox, a deeply weathered-shingle building, a few outhouse-sized fisherman's shacks, and a small arrangements of floating docks which created the slips, the marina looked as unpretentiously New England as a marina could. Stacks of weathered lobster traps cluttered the narrow patch of dead grass between the building and the edge of the water. A lone gas pump from the 1950s stood as reminder of how little life on the ocean had changed.

Fifteen boats of all types were at a slip or tied to a mooring near the docks, proof that the owners had been caught off guard by the hurricane and hadn't had time to pull their boats from the water. A logjam of dinghies crowded the slip closest to the breakwall. Ditchman and O'Donahue stood on the concrete wall and surveyed the boats. Just as the fisherman had said, they spotted a twenty-five foot orange and black inflatable boat, with the distinctive markings of the Coast Guard—a thin blue slash to the left of a thicker red slash on the bow.

"Found the boat, but no Coast Guard. Fifty percent still fails," Ditchman said.

They heard a creaking sound to their left and looked to see a Coast Guardsman step out of the out-house still in the act of zipping up his fly. His face showed no embarrassment when he looked up and saw O'Donahue and Ditchman.

O'Donahue introduced herself and Ditchman and told him about the missing boats and how they were looking for a group of people they believed to be connected to them. When she explained how they had found the condition of the owner of the boats' house, particularly the bloodstains on the carpet, and that a fisherman recently had seen the cabin cruiser in Stage Harbor, Boatswain's Mate Phil Burner needed no more cajoling. As they left the dock, Burner made a call on his radio.

# CHAPTER 22

▼ ─────────────

An hour after they had begun lugging the gold to the other side of the island, they reached the shore a fourth and final time. Annie and Matt dropped the board in the sand and collapsed to their knees in exhaustion. Sykes didn't bother to kneel, but just sat down, wheezing for air.

Matt took a deep breath and felt his head get lighter. His hands, cramped from carrying such weight for so long, refused to open. His back screamed in pain worse than when he had fractured a vertebra in a skiing accident. He closed his eyes and concentrated on the throbbing pain from his broken nose. The nightmare would be over soon, he told himself. He opened his tired eyes and looked at Annie. She looked worse than he had ever seen her. Her lifeless face looked as if it were about to slide off her drooped head. Her mouth opened and closed as if she were gasping for water to sooth her burning dryness.

"You okay?" he asked, incredulous that she had had the strength to carry the gold.

She looked up and shook her head. "No, but let's just get going."

They retrieved the boat and loaded the gold in the stern and within five minutes were back on the water heading for Stage Harbor. Matt drove the boat and Sykes stood behind him. Annie, barely strong enough to stand, leaned against Matt and the bench. Matt put his right arm around her and squeezed her tight. She looked up at him and forced a "thank you" smile with her mouth closed.

As he drove, clutching the wheel with one hand and wrapping the other arm around Annie, Matt's mind raced as if he had been given a shot of adrenaline. There was no way they would be allowed to just walk away. That fear was reality. If it were up to him, he wouldn't let them walk away. The perfect crime has no witnesses. Every way he imagined the scene of handing over the gold, it ended in the same manner. There had to be a way to use the gold as a bargaining chip to get Ridder to release the Lockwoods and Tucker. He glanced back at Sykes and realized he had no power to bargain because in essence they already had the gold. He was just the deliveryman. But that could change drastically if they alone controlled the gold. There had to be a way to get rid of Sykes. The picture of the boat capsized flashed again in his mind. Was it the only way? How could he warn Annie about it first? And what good would it do if they lost the gold? If it were done in shallow water, they could retrieve the gold. The tide was going out so it could be done. Then they'd have to carry it back because the boat would be useless. But why would they have to get all the gold? He could take a few bars back, exchange them and the location of the rest for the release of the Lockwoods and Tucker. Ridder was going to buy that deal before, why not again? He could even stash some away. No, he wouldn't risk his friends' lives. But could he capsize the boat?

They reached the cut between North and South Monomoy and in a few minutes, Matt knew, they would be in Stage Harbor where the water would be calmer. If he were to try to flip the boat, it would have to be outside the harbor. He looked over at North Monomoy as he sped by the beach. No way he could veer off and run the Whaler over the breakers at the edge of the beach. In chop that big, he might not be able to control the boat enough to survive the roll. He looked off the bow. In a less than a minute, they would enter the maze of sandbars and the orange buoys that marked a boat's safe route. If he took one of the turns too quickly, the boat would surely flip. But what about Annie?

He tried to get her attention, but she had a glazed look on her face, and kept turning slightly in the opposite direction to garner some relief from the wind. Matt nudged her with his elbow, but she still didn't look at him. Without moving his head too much, he strained his eyes to the left to catch Sykes' position, but couldn't see him. He had to be directly behind the seat. Would he see if they spoke? Matt maneuvered the Whaler around the first buoy. Not much time. He couldn't try it without warning her first. He turned past the second buoy. He nudged her harder with his elbow. She looked up at him with a confused expression. He mouthed the words: "Get ready to jump." But she didn't understand. She leaned closer to him. He spoke.

"Get ready to…"

Sykes jabbed the gun into Matt's ribs. "Shut your yap and drive, pretty boy." He drove the gun deeper and Matt winced from the sharp pain. "I'm watching you."

Matt turned his attention back to buoys ahead. His mind raced. They couldn't go back. They'd be dead. He looked at the next buoy and then, as he had learned from experience, he used the time before reaching the next buoy to track his course through as many buoys as he could see. He found the next two. An easy turn. They wouldn't have to slow down. Maybe Sykes wouldn't remember the way back. If Sykes wasn't watching, he could drive past the mouth of Oyster River and head into the harbor. There was usually a Coast Guard boat somewhere in the harbor. As he headed for the next buoy, in the direction of the breakwater beach that protected Stage Harbor, he looked to his left to plot his course through the remaining buoys. Then he saw it. He stared in disbelief for a few seconds. Then it turned. He drew a breath of relief. He steered the Whaler around the buoy and looked off the bow. Heading straight toward them it looked just like any other boat, but he had seen the distinctive orange stripe on the bow and prayed Sykes had not. He quickly evaluated the distance each boat was from the Stage Harbor cut. If the Coast Guard cutter could get to the narrow channel first, there was hope they'd be saved. He slowed the boat slightly as he maneuvered into a tough turn. He looked at the cutter; it was much farther away from the cut then the Whaler. He pulled back on the throttle. The Yamaha's pitch changed. Still too fast. He eased back on the throttle again and Sykes punched his left shoulder.

"Faster, asshole," Sykes yelled above the sound of the engine.

Matt felt the gun in his back and obeyed. He glanced slightly to his left to find the Coast Guard cutter. It was still more than a mile away from the cut. He navigated around the last buoy and into the channel leading to the cut while Sykes kept the gun stuck firmly in his back.

The wind slapped their bare faces as they cruised at four knots through the lower part of Stage Harbor in front of the yacht club. Ditchman and O'Donahue stood holding on to the gunwale rail on either side of First Mate Burner. As they passed a fishing boat trudging its way out to the Sound, Ditchman spotted the *Gerty* anchored just northwest of the mouth of Oyster River, two hundred yards from the cut to Nantucket Sound.

"At one o'clock off the bow."

Burner held his binoculars to his eyes, then picked up the handset of the radio and quickly spoke into it.

"Vessel in sight. Four subjects visible at stern. Smaller vessel approaching. Please advise."

\*　　\*　　\*　　\*

When Matt saw the *Gerty*, his throat tightened. He quickly looked to his flanks at the pitched sandbanks of the channel and contemplated beaching the boat as the Whaler shot through the cut. Suddenly, he didn't feel the gun in his back. He looked to his right and saw Sykes holding Annie by the shoulder with his left hand, his right hand pushing the gun into her back. There were no options now but to hand over the gold. Matt cursed under his breath for his inaction.

"Pull up to the big boat over there." Sykes pointed with a nod. "Keep it pointing out."

As Matt swung the Whaler around, he saw the Lockwoods sitting in two deck chairs, holding each other's hands. Mrs. Lockwood's gray hair was a tangled mess from the wind. Mr. Lockwood's face was a study of tension. The look of white terror hadn't left their aged faces. Ridder stood behind them, the six-inch buck knife poised to strike in his hand.

Tucker helped guide the Whaler to a rest along the port side the *Gerty*; each boat's bow pointing toward the cut. As Matt locked arms with Tucker to steady the Whaler, they looked into each other's eyes, but did not say a word. Tucker looked tired and worn, his eyes glazed. He looked at Annie and didn't break the visual embrace until Ridder shoved him to the side. He regained eye contact with her and mouthed, "You okay?" She forced a small smile, nodded and stared into his eyes with a passion only a person in love could instill.

Ridder looked into the Whaler and saw the pile of gold bars. His scowl turned to a grin.

"Almost eighty bars, Carson. At least five million dollars. We did it." He raised both arms, and the shotgun, in triumph.

"Give me the piece in your belt, and stop celebratin', dipshit. We gotta finish the job."

Sykes tossed Ridder the handgun.

As Ridder caught the gun, his attention was drawn to the middle of Stage Harbor. His face immediately changed back to a scowl as he carefully watched an orange boat with three people in it cruise in the harbor's main channel. Ridder studied the boat for a few seconds. When it picked up speed and turned straight toward them, Ridder swore. He looked to his right to the cut. Three twenty-five foot boats, two with red slashes on its bows and one with a blue slash sat motionless in the cut. A fourth boat raced toward them. Flashing red lights danced atop each boat's center console rigging. Ridder looked back at the other boat. Red lights flashed from it as well.

"Grab her, Buster," he commanded, then pointed the gun at Matt. "Into the water, asshole. Now!"

Matt froze as he took in what was happening. He looked behind him and saw the Coast Guard boat speeding toward them. He looked back at Ridder.

Ridder pulled back the gun's hammer and shook the gun violently at Matt. "You got three seconds. One, two…"

"Please, Matt, do it," Annie screamed.

Ridder jumped into the boat and held the gun to Matt's forehead. Matt didn't move.

"Matt!"

Ridder's hand shook as he held the gun to Matt's head, then he abruptly lowered the gun and shoved Matt over the side. He looked up to find the approaching boats, then quickly got behind the wheel and gunned the throttle. The Whaler's engine dug into the water.

Without hesitating, Tucker sprinted down the starboard side of the deck to the bow and launched himself toward the Whaler as it passed. He reached for Annie as he flew across the stern of the Whaler, but his hand only grazed her shoulder before clasping onto Sykes' shirt, propelling him over the side of the boat.

It took the Whaler ten seconds before it was out of its initial plow and fully accelerating. Ridder cursed the boat's sluggishness. He held Annie tightly by the wrist with his right hand so that any movement on her part caused excruciating pain to erupt on her face. She struggled to hold the gunwale railing with her free hand.

Ridder looked back at the Coast Guard boat and swore as it closed in on him. He quickly looked off the bow and cursed again as he saw the other Coast Guard boat had returned to the middle of the cut and was forming a blockade with the other three boats. Ridder slammed the throttle to make sure it was down all the way and the boat hurtled across the water straight at the blockade a hundred yards away. He looked back; the Coast Guard boat chasing him had decreased the gap to twenty yards and wasn't showing any sign of heeding the blockade either. Within twenty yards of the blockade, Ridder threw the wheel to the right and the Whaler bit into the water as it tilted on its side and headed straight for the sloped beachhead. The Coast Guardsman in the nearest boat saw what he was doing and quickly moved within ten feet of the shore.

Just before hitting the beach, Ridder threw the wheel back to the left and the Whaler shot past the Coast Guard boat at the beach's waterline, the slope acting like a ramp. The engine screamed as the sand slammed the propeller out of the water, but the Whaler's momentum carried it back to deeper water where the engine regained its torque.

Ridder looked behind him. The grin on his face lasted less then a second as he saw the orange and black Coast Guard boat also jump across the beach and through the blockade without losing any speed.

Ridder yanked Annie toward him. "Drive!"

While Annie held the wheel with her right hand, Ridder gripped her left wrist. He stood facing the stern and pulled out his gun.

Despite holding onto the starboard-side rail with all his strength, when the inflatable went up then down the beach's slope at the edge of the water, Ditchman felt the boat go out from under his feet. The jolt back into the water snapped his head back. By the time he regained his senses and found the Whaler again, less than fifteen yards in front of them off the starboard side, it was too late. The instant he saw the gun, he felt the bullet rip into his right shoulder, tearing muscle to shreds. The might of the blow forced him to let go of the rail and fall backward. Burner instinctively reached out and grabbed him before he fell out the stern.

As Ditchman struggled to his feet, Burner swerved the inflatable back and forth behind the Whaler as bullets slammed into the inflatible's body and whistled past them. O'Donahue held her gun out in front of her body then lowered her arm.

"Get closer. I don't want to hit the girl," she screamed to Burner.

Traveling at forty miles per hour, the Whaler headed straight at the Widower sandbar. Being low tide, the sandbar rose fifteen feet out of the water, its face a ten-foot wall almost perpendicular to the water.

"Jesus," Burner yelled. "Look out!"

Annie glanced at Ridder, noted he remained facing the stern, counted to three then bit his hand until she felt her teeth hit bone.

"Arrr!" Ridder screamed and let go of her wrist.

With blood running down her lips, Annie yanked her head back. She quickly looked off the bow at the wall of sand screaming toward the speeding boat. Without hesitating, she mustered all her strength and threw her body over the side of the Whaler.

When Ridder regained his senses, he had just enough time to look forward as the Whaler slammed into the sandbar.

A thunderous boom erupted as the twenty-four-foot fiberglass boat splintered into thousands of gagged pieces. A micro-second later, the momentum of the stern hurled the two twenty-gallon gas tanks into the sandbar sparking a forty-foot fireball that in an instant engulfed the wreckage and Ridder.

Burner had seen the collision coming just in time to slow the inflatable so that the explosion did not engulf his boat. They covered their heads as smoldering debris showered the inflatable. He quickly pulled the inflatable over to within fifteen yards of the flaming wreckage, and spoke into the radio handset.

"Search and rescue! Search and rescue! Female in the water! Repeat, female in the water. Request backup!"

Burner cut the engine, grabbed a diving mask from the center console and jumped into the murky water. In an instant he could not be seen because of the sand, oil, and debris in the shallow water.

As soon as Ridder had raced away in the Whaler with Annie, Tucker had pulled Sykes on board the *Gerty* through the transom gate and tied him up with the stern line. Mr. Lockwood fired up the boat's engine and they proceeded to the cut as quickly as the old cruiser would take them. Matt kept them informed as he watched the chase with the use of binoculars. When they were just inside the cut, they saw Annie jump out of the Whaler just before it hit the sandbank and exploded.

They watched the Coast Guard and Harbor Patrol boats race to the wreckage while they painfully waited to reach the scene. No one spoke for the minute it took to get there; each just prayed Annie would be pulled from the water.

Just as they reached the sandbar, Burner erupted through the surface with Annie limp in his arms. He struggled ten feet through chest-high water to the bar and laid her motionless body on the sand. Three other CoastGuardsmen reached them in seconds and encircled Annie.

Matt, Tucker and the Lockwoods stared in silence, their faces white with fear. Matt held the top of his head with his hands. Mr. Lockwood embraced his wife. Tucker made the sign of the cross and said a silent prayer.

Suddenly, the men reared up and Burner turned Annie on her side as she threw up seawater. Burner looked at the *Gerty* and thrust his hand in the air and gave them the thumbs up sign.

# CHAPTER 23

▼

Ditchman stood patiently in line to check his lone bag through the security gate at Logan Airport. Hammond had gone back to Virginia ten days earlier after being reassured by Ditchman's doctors that the gunshot wound, though complicated because of the previous wound, required just rest and supervision.

"Hey, I caught you just in time."

Ditchman looked to his left and saw O'Donahue approaching him. She wore a black pantsuit that made her look like a business executive rather than a cop. Ditchman smiled and stepped out of line.

"I was hoping I'd get a chance to see you before I left."

She smiled. "How's the shoulder?"

"Months of PT, but should be good as new."

They stood looking at each other for a few awkward seconds. Ditchman stroked his mustache then broke eye contact.

"Rusty called me before I left the hospital to tell me the Virginia and Massachusetts DA's have worked out a deal so Sykes will stand trial in Virginia for the murder of the UVA professor, then up here for the murder of Kellerman, the Harvard janitor, Wilkerson *and* the State Trooper. It's too bad the two states can't agree on who has rightful claim to the gold the Coast Guard recovered from the accident scene. He said they're even fighting over the soldier's journal."

"Actually, both states, Harvard and the Federal government are laying claim to the journal. Harvard claims it belongs to the university because if was sent to Professor Nylan's office. And the Feds claim that since the journal was still lost in the U.S. Postal Service system when Nylan died, it falls under their jurisdiction as unclaimed property, if you can believe that."

"Typical bureaucrats. I heard Sykes squealed like a baby under examination so they'll be adding a slew of other charges in connection with what went on at the Lockwood's house."

Ditchman nodded his head and stroked his mustache. "Rusty said the Charlottesville DA will probably ask for the death penalty for Professor Hutchinson's murder." He shook his head. "It's a shame the guy never got to see the result of all his searching. His colleague, Triste, told Rusty that he figured out the big news Hutchinson wanted to tell him the night he was killed. I guess he was a better detective then us because he found out that Hutchinson had spent the last few days of his life in the UVA library's archives, which is were Triste believes he found the old journal. Imagine that. The poor old guy spends years trying to find the final clue and all that time it was sitting on some dusty shelf right under his nose and when he finds it some low life dirt bags take it all away from him in a flash."

They stood in silence for a few seconds, then Ditchman turned to her and smiled. "Thanks for all the cooperation, Marty."

"No problem, Ditch. Listen, if you're ever back in Boston and don't have bad guys to chase, give me a call. I'm sorry we never got a chance to catch our breath with all that went on."

Ditchman smiled. "Quid pro quo, Detective. I've been to Boston. Now it's your turn."

O'Donahue lightly touched the sleeve of his good arm. "Take care of yourself, Ditch."

Annie lay a single red rose on top of the gray headstone, then knelt in front of it and traced her finger through the name of Albert Nylan. A tear ran off her cheek onto the newly planted sod in front of the headstone.

"I'm sorry, Uncle Albert," she whispered, then stood up and stepped back.

Tucker and Matt each placed a hand on her shoulders. She had missed Professor Nylan's funeral while she recovered in the hospital from the boating accident. After two weeks, she was able to take off the neck brace and her headaches and severe dizziness had subsided so her doctor finally released her.

The physical pain, she knew, would eventually go away. It was dealing with the emotional pain of losing another loved one that worried her. Yet, it didn't hurt as much this time and that troubled her. Maybe it was because her parents' death had hardened her. Maybe it was because she had better coping skills and more easily accepted heartache. Regardless of why, she felt guilty for not feeling worse.

Tucker slid his hand into Annie's. "So you're still going to go through with your trip?"

Annie looked at him and smiled. "A road trip cleanses the soul. Don't worry, I'll stop in Maryland on my way back. Probably in October. I need to go on this trip, for me. But I can't wait to be in Maryland." She kissed Tucker, then hugged him for a minute.

"So, you're going to work for your father after all?" She smiled at Matt. "That makes me happy to see you're trying with him."

"It beats having to look for a job, right?" Matt paused for a second and looked at Annie. "Actually, I've come to accept that I'm a lot more like my Dad than I like to admit. After all this has happened, we actually talked for the first time, I mean really talked. And we reached a compromise. I agreed to come to work at his firm and he agreed to pay for me to go to night classes at the culinary institute downtown. That way, I can make an 'informed decision,' as he put it, as to whether I want to follow the family footsteps and be a stock broker or become a chef."

Annie reached into her pocket and pulled something out and placed it in Matt's hand.

"What's this?"

"The Coastie who saved me stopped by the hospital before I left. He found pieces like this in his boat. I thought you should have it as a reminder that I don't blame you for any of this."

Matt opened his hand and gazed at the marble-size piece of gold. As he looked at the gold, a tear rolled down his cheek. He looked up at Annie then delicately took her hand and placed the gold in it, closing her fingers around it.

"I rather you keep it as a reminder that I will always love you, Annie." He hugged her tight to his chest. "I was dying to see what was out on Monomoy and almost got us killed." He put a hand on Tucker's and Annie's shoulders. "This whole thing has made me realize that I should do a much better job treasuring the gold I already have instead of searching for more."

978-0-595-34815-2
0-595-34815-7

Printed in the United States
41128LVS00004B/226-231

9 780595 348152